invasion

PENDYFFRYN: THE CONQUERORS

BOOK I

Lily Dewaruile

EresBooks.com

Cover Design: The Killion Group, Inc

Invasion is a work of fiction. The characters, descriptions, events
and dialogues in this book are of the author's imagination and
are not to be construed as real. Any resemblance to persons,
either living or dead, is coincidental.

Published and Printed in the United States

DEDICATION

Hoffwn gyflwyno'r argraffiad hwn i'm cyfeillion yng Nghymru sydd wedi fy nghefnogi ers i fi symud yno ac ers i fi symud i ffwrdd.
I would like to offer this edition to my friends in Wales who have supported me since I moved there and since I moved away.

Ac yn arbennig, i'm hannwylaf ŵr a'n meibion am eu holl amynedd a chariad. Fe wddoch ba mor bwysig ag ydych i fi.
And especially, to my dearest husband and our sons for their patience and love. You know how important you are to me.

Also by Lily Dewaruile

Traitor's Daughter (The Tywi: Book One) 2011
Invasion: Book 1, Pendyffryn: The Conquerors, 2012
Salvation: Book 2, Pendyffryn: The Conquerors, 2013
Betrayal: Book 3, Pendyffryn: The Conquerors, March 2013
Revival: Book 4, Pendyffryn: The Conquerors, June 2013
Forthcoming in the *Pendyffryn: The Conquerors* Series
Reconciliation, Book 5 Summer 2013
Forthcoming in *The Tywi* Series
Vengeance's Son Fall 2013 *(The Tywi: Book Two)*
Forthcoming in 2014
Pendyffryn: The Inheritors
Justice
Blame
Worth
Merit
Virtue
Redemption

ACKNOWLEDGMENTS

I bob un o'm cyfeillion yn *Hearts Through History*, *Celtic Hearts*, *Maine RWA* a *San Francisco Area RWA* am eu cefnogaeth dros y blynyddoedd ers i fi ddechrau ysgrifennu'r nofelau hyn am Gymru.
Every one of my friends in Hearts Through History, Celtic Hearts, Maine RWA a San Francisco Area RWA for their support and encouragement over the years since I began writing novels about Wales.

Nearly three hundred years since the Godoðin were defeated, by the year AD875, Rhodri Mawr had earned the friendship of Charles, the king of the Franks, by defeating the Vikings and extended his kingdom from beyond the Menai to the Tywi, from Offa's Dyke to the Irish Sea. Until Aethelfrith had driven his sword into the heart of Powys, Cymraeg was the language of Scotland south of the Highlands, England, Brittany and Cornwall. More than a hundred years had passed since the enemy to the east had silenced the protests of Pengwern and slaughtered Cynddylan. Cyngen's pillar cross of Llangollen stood as proud testament to the hero, Elise.

ONE

Gwennan made the last stitches in the work she intended for her husband's wedding shirt. She had begun the work on the eve of her fourteenth birthday, when the father of her first suitor came to Pendyffryn. Her pleasure in the work was not diminished when he, like every father and suitor after him, had been sent from the house and the suitor's meager virtues were dismissed by her father. Though she had worked on the piece for eight years, the skill of the needlewoman had been joy and solace for the daughter of Daran Pendyffryn, the *pendefig* of the largest *ystad* in the region.

The threads she bought from the harvest markets were as bright on that spring morning as on the day she had selected them. The design was as fresh and as meaningful to her at twenty-two as at fourteen. The ravenous hounds were still entwined across the dyed fabric to cover her husband's torso with her promise of love and fidelity—the two virtues she had learned from her parents' long union.

Though her mother had died days after her birth, Gwennan's father spoke of his wife as though she was beside him at every crossroads in their daughter's life. "Your mother has always had misgivings about this family," Daran Pendyffryn had said of her first suitor. "Blaenant spawns excellent warriors and they are loyal to Pendyffryn, but ambition clouds their judgment. The boy they have proposed to me will command an army—I can see that in him—but he will not be your husband."

Derwyn Blaenant was handsome, dark-haired with bright, blue eyes that enflamed whomever he studied. Gwennan had known him from her earliest childhood when her father fostered him as his groom. He was older but near enough to her age for the two of them to have become friends but she had accepted her father's assessment of him. The colors she had chosen for the tunic were for another man, a different man from any she knew.

Gwennan had lost count of the men who had asked for her. As she clipped the last golden thread and loosened the spruce green linen from the frame, her father's voice boomed from his office two flights below her turret room. She smoothed the tunic and folded it so that the embroidery, upon which she had lavished so much of her skill and imbued with hopes for her future, was protected and laid the wedding garment on top of all the linens she had prepared for her own home. *I will be too old to wed and all these will be dust.*

From the window ledge at the second turning of the stairs, Gwennan watched as Elgan Maergwn, the most recent unsuccessful suitor, strode from Daran's office. Her father was forthright in his assessment when he told his daughter his reasons for refusing him.

"He is an adequate warrior and nothing else. He cannot manage the Gaer farm because he is too busy making mead to drink and betting on his hunting dogs. I will replace him when I find a man more capable. *That* man may be your husband."

"Does Elgan have any redeeming characteristics to recommend him?" she asked, dismissing the scrap of hope her father offered. He had been similarly scathing about every other suitor and as vague about her future. No one, in his eyes, was fit to be husband to the daughter who would inherit Pendyffryn.

"He has one."

"And that one is?" She had taken the seat on the bench beside his chair in the office where he spent most of his time when he was at home. Since her eighteenth birthday, her father had spent more time away. His reason was the war surging toward their mountainous homeland from the East. He had returned only weeks ahead of an army that was devastating their neighbors, all along the border with the *Saeson*.

"You will never discover that one characteristic, Gwennan, for which you will thank me," was the warrior-prince's response as he laid his arm across her shoulders and planted a kiss on her temple. "Even this one quality was not enough to prevent me from kicking him down the stairs as I have all the others who have had the audacity to think they were worthy of you."

"Is there one man in all the world you would approve?"

"He must be extraordinary, Gwennan. When I see this man, I will send him to you myself."

"I will not hold my breath, Tada." Gwennan rose, brushed her tunic and strode from her father's company. "I would be dead before I could breathe again," she said over her shoulder.

"If he is not good enough," her father shouted, "he is not!"

"No one is perfect," she replied, turning before she opened the door.

"Gwennan, he must be perfect for you."

"In your opinion, Tada. I have my own ideas of perfection."

"I know. But in this, my expectations are paramount. You will know him." When she turned away from him, he said, "You will know the man meant to be your husband, as all women know in their hearts, the moment he sets foot on this soil."

"Tada, I have expectations too," she murmured, aware that the house did not guarantee a private conversation even in her father's office. "All my cousins are wed. They think there is something wrong with me." She was as tall as most men, taking her height and ashen hair from her father's line. If she gained anything from her mother, Gwennan did not believe it was Cerith's renowned beauty—only her skill with a needle was equal.

"If they think at all," Daran Pendyffryn answered. "They are fools. They are jealous."

Gwennan escaped to her haven at the river bank below the house perched on the slope of the mountain. Stripping out of her tunic and linen frock, she swam to the center of the pool and washed the feel of the midwife's fingers from her long legs. Each time, the man was gone before negotiations came to the matter of the virgin's honor price.

The sun's heat, filtered by the budding leaves, soothed her spirit as much as her flesh as she lay on the riverbank, away from the prying eyes and whispers of her father's household. Gwennan trusted that the midwife never disclosed her reason for attending her, but there was no hiding that her attendance coincided with the arrival of a suitor.

Years past twenty and still a maiden. Her father delayed and made excuses but she was incapable of finding fault with the father she adored. *He has good reasons.* Gwennan twisted the water from her hair and tossed the long braid over her shoulder. For a time, she sat with her arms around her knees, watching the river's current swirl in the pool and flow on. *How can I know the man, if I am here, with no sight of any who may venture near?*

She dove again into the pool, taking long strokes and turning onto her back to watch the sky through the canopy of spring buds. Above her, her father's rambling house spilled over the gorse-festooned mountainside. With the purple of the heather and the wide swathes of grass, the bright yellow amidst the granite rejoiced in new life after the gray of so many winter months and the insistent threat of war.

The king of Powys left no heir and Rhodri Mawr ruled north, west and east. Like most of her neighbors and friends, Gwennan lived her life beneath the notice of rulers. Their actions earned *her* notice only when they changed her life. The Mercian king was keen to push his thegns further west and the *gelyn* were moving steadily, hungry for the land. Their success in the east against farmers and tradesmen encouraged them to look toward the formidable mountains of Gwennan's home, with avid speculation about its Roman gold mines and fertile farmland. One after another of her neighbors on both sides of Offa's Dyke lost their lands and now it was Daran Pendyffryn who watched the morning horizon.

The man who had been thrown from her father's *llys* that morning was the commander of the Gaer, from a family with a long history of service to Pendyffryn. Elgan Maergwn lived at the southern entrance to the valley, in the house that had been her father's birthplace and had sheltered three generations of his family before him.

Gwennan's birth, his only child after fifteen years, marked an end to her father's expectations of a large family. When Cerith Gernant died soon afterward, he abandoned his plans to demolish the Gaer house to build a stronger hill fort. The house that had stood on the spot from the earliest generations of his family now accommodated garrison commanders, not families or young wives with *baban* or dreams of a home to raise them.

The Gaer's farmland was the most productive of the *ystad*. Its wide river plain flooded in early spring when the lake in the high mountains above Pendyffryn's house deposited its fertile wealth in the Gaer's soil. The woodlands surrounding the river plain provided all the timber he needed to build houses for his people and were the hunting grounds that fed them in winter. In spring and summer, the waterways were crowded with so much trout, the fish had to leap to find space and could be caught in a man's hand.

If there was to be an invasion, the Gaer was crucial to their survival.

"I can hold the Gaer," she told the canopy of trees above her refuge.

Two weeks after Elgan Maergwn had been thrown from Daran Pendyffryn's *llys*, Gwennan declined an opportunity to travel with her father to attend a council of the *pendefig* of the southern districts. Although the talk was certain to be of war, Gwennan told her father she preferred to spend the early summer days where she had some influence—gathering herbs and making soap. Her father lifted his close-cropped gray head and gazed at his daughter across the table.

"You have always enjoyed the *Seiat*," he commented, a frown in his blue eyes. "What is wrong?"

"I see no point in my being there, Tada. No one has ever listened to what I have to say. You do not listen, why should they?"

"Can you blame them, *blodyn*? Warriors experienced in battle do not take well to lessons in tactics from girls still with half their milk teeth. Sometimes, it is better to listen." He reached his hand toward her and scowled when she withdrew. "Gwennan, come with me."

"What purpose would that serve?"

"Because you enjoy it and you will learn something. You always do."

"I have better things to do."

On the day Daran Pendyffryn rode away from his home in the mountains, Gwennan stood in the archway of the *porth* and raised her hand in farewell. For the first time in her life, she was glad to see her father go without her and in the afternoon, she left her father's house.

"You are a strange woman, Gwennan Pendyffryn," Elgan Maergwn said when he greeted her in the thatched hall of the Gaer stockade. Gwennan pushed back the hood of her brown cloak to reveal her ash blonde hair, festooned with green cords and gold beads. "Your father has changed his mind?" The forty year old warrior gestured for her to take the lesser of the two chairs by the table.

"I am of an age to make my own decisions, Elgan."

"You are," he agreed. "I see, but if—. I would be foolish to defy your father's wishes in any matter. Pendyffryn did not favor my proposal, *boneddiges*."

What one quality does this man have that my father says I will be grateful not to discover? The man standing in front of her was the same age her father had been when she was born. Like her father, he was vigorous and strongly-built. He was fair-haired and handsome though his face was ruddy and weathered. The stupor of his eyes confirmed her father's assessment of his character. The hands on her arms were trembling and his kiss was ale-tainted. She recanted her initial decision. "I know nothing of your proposal to my father, Elgan. I have come as *pennaeth*—to manage the Gaer and command its army."

"Take the house," he said, backing away as though she was poisonous. "I have no women to serve you, *boneddiges*."

Gwennan crossed the bridge that spanned the narrow ravine between the Gaer's *buarth* and the steep path up the hill that led to the house. At the *porth*, she turned back. The man she had considered and rejected in one breath lifted a tankard to his mouth and gulped the liquor down his throat. As she entered the house, her heart clenched in her chest. Rotting food sat in bowls and on platters from one end of the table to the other. Dogs gnawed on the half-eaten joints they stole from the cold spit. There was no square of the stone-covered floor that was not littered with their leavings. A boy lay sprawled in the alcove. She recognized his father in the boy's flaccid mouth. Oswin Elgan opened an eye to look at her when the dogs stirred, turned away and grumbled.

"I will not complain," Gwennan declared under her breath as she climbed the stone staircase to the sleeping area built below the rafters of the house. "I may regret, but I will not complain." She found two girls sleeping near the pantry and directed one to wash the crockery and the other to burn everything in the lower hall that was not useful. Taking a straw broom, she swept the rushes and vermin into the hearth and set it alight. While it burned away the stench of the house, she chased the hunting dogs down the hill to the *buarth*.

"My father will not let you drive his dogs from the house," Oswin laughed. "He will chase you out and bring them back."

"There are clean clothes for you on that chest. Take a bath and come back to have your supper."

"I will have my supper now," he replied. "I do not take orders from you."

"You *did* not but you will now. I am *pennaeth* and you need a bath."

"My father is *pennaeth* here. You do not order me," the boy said, running out.

"You will need help, Gwennan Pendyffryn," a fair-haired woman said from the doorway. "I am Siriol Pendryw."

"And I am Aine Tudwal," a shorter, older woman said. "There are four other women here who will choose to be in your household, but you will have to command all but one of them to come."

"I am grateful," Gwennan said, inclining her head toward the two, neither of whom needed to be told their duties.

In the next weeks, after her father had returned from the war *seiat*, the only communication she had with him was through Derwyn Blaenant, whom her father sent from his army to join Elgan's war band. "Daran Pendyffryn congratulates you on your choice of husband and regrets he could not attend the celebrations."

Gwennan smiled at her childhood friend, now a man worthy of her father's esteem but not as her husband. He avoided her gaze. "Thank you," she answered, laying her hand on his arm. "But Elgan is not—."

Derwyn looked down at her hand. "As you have chosen Elgan Maergwn, I will serve him faithfully, Gwennan."

"Derwyn," she sighed, "will you—?" Before she finished her offer of friendship, Derwyn gave her a sharp bow and left her.

Derwyn and his aunt, Galar, Gwennan's nurse as a child, were her only links to her father. Derwyn's passion for life was a tonic for her regret. Her father had sent Derwyn to her as an admonishment, the fulfillment of his promise to send a man worthy of her but Gwennan's heart did not know him. The wedding tunic remained folded in her chest of linens. If there was a man worthy of *her* esteem, she was unlikely to know him when he set foot on the soil of her homeland. She kept the garment as a reminder of her lack of faith in her father's judgment.

For six months, Gwennan lived in the Gaer house and governed the farm as *pennaeth*. She had not discovered the one quality that her father claimed made Elgan Maergwn less unworthy than other men. Despite her disappointment in her judgment, Gwennan enjoyed the work of the farm. She cherished the camaraderie and friendship of the other women as they gleaned and spun, milked and embroidered. Her six months as *pennaeth* of the Gaer were filled with work and laughter more often than regret.

Within days of the harvest festivals, when the grain was weighed, apportioned and stored, Elgan dressed in his leather jerkin and armor, met Gwennan's gaze for a long moment and led his war band to join others among the Cymry in the borderlands to fight the *gelyn*. Derwyn rode beside Elgan, splendid in the green *trwsus* that Gwennan had made for him. Her thoughts followed the path that the sight of Derwyn Blaenant often took her and she watched as he rode away from her, his strong back straight, painted with the totem animals another woman had drawn on his skin.

While the warriors remaining to guard the Gaer prepared themselves for battle, the women gathered in the house above them and prepared for their war. Only the youngest of them, Menna, had no experience of war. She sat in the lower room with the others and listened with wide eyes as Aine Tudwal said, "If our men cannot keep these murderers from the Gaer, we will all be dead long before *Calan Gaeaf*. They will not spare any of us. Better that we are all dead before they reach the gates."

"There is no reason for you to stay here," Gwennan said to her friends and companions. "Take everything you can carry and go to the caverns. You will be safe there for weeks. There is plenty of food."

Menna glanced from one face to the next but no one agreed to the plan.

"I will stay with you," Siriol said, wrapping her arm around her daughter while her six year old son slept with his head in her lap. "There will be wounded and the warriors will need our help."

"I'll go," Madlen said.

"Me too," added Ruth. "There is no sense in all of us staying here."

"Ach, you two are no surprise," Aine snapped at them.

"I want to go too," Branwen murmured without looking at her *pennaeth*, cradling her two-year old son in her arms. "Iago is with Elgan and I do not know what has happened to him."

"May I go, *boneddiges*?" Menna asked.

"I think that is best," Gwennan said, "until we know what this *gelyn* plans, the fewer who are here, the better. If you are needed, I will send for you."

"Gwennan," Siriol began but Gwennan raised her hand.

"You and Aine will also go. Until we know." When she climbed to her room, Siriol followed. "I know what you are going to say, Siriol. You and Aine must go with them," Gwennan murmured, "or they will eat all that we have worked so hard to preserve. Take Oswin as well."

"Why should you stay?" Siriol demanded.

"It is my duty. I am responsible—until Elgan returns—I am responsible."

"I do not like this," Siriol said, combing her fingers through the length of her friend's hair. "You should not be here alone."

"Galar will be with me and I have sent word to my father."

"He is at war, Gwennan, like the rest of the *pendefig* in this region. And Galar cannot defend you if—."

"Siriol, I know," Gwennan sighed. "But, it is my responsibility. I must be here."

When all of the women of her household were safely away, Gwennan gazed into the small hearth, a smoke-stained gap in the stone wall, resting her hands on the mantle. For months, she had worked to restore the house and the Gaer to good repair and order. There was no man or woman who was without clean clothing. There were no dogs or rats in the house. Elgan Maergwn had gone to war in a clean shirt and fine tunic. Gwennan Pendyffryn didn't regret what she had achieved; only that the man for whom she had worked was not a man she wanted to call her husband. Through her thoughts ran the words that she had held in her heart watching Elgan lead his war band out of the Gaer. *I am responsible. If Elgan is killed, I am responsible.*

two

"What will stop them?"

"Brace the walls," Tudwal told her.

"We have no other option for now," Gwennan Pendyffryn agreed. "There are too many of us to escape to the gorge. Our harvest will be stolen."

"There's nothing more you can do, *pennaeth*. There's no time to bring more of the families into the Gaer. You've done all you can. The household guard, while I live, will never open the gates."

Gwennan covered her eyes for a moment, feeling the exhaustion of the past days surge through her and pushed herself again to take command. "We must attack this army from below, out-flanked them."

The timber walls of the Gaer were no stronger barrier than parchment. The gates were as formidable as linen. The two watchtowers tottered and the food she had ordered stored in the caverns below the house was not enough to see them through the next weeks, never through the winter. Without access to the hunting grounds, a siege would end in annihilation. Elgan's disregard, as commander, was known to all the warriors left to defend the Gaer and anxiety shadowed their eyes as they piled rubble against the walls, bracing the gates with cross beams. All she had been able to accomplish was not enough. The Mercian thegn was driving his sword into the heart of her home. Her country was bleeding.

"How long before they come?"

"Hours, *pennaeth*. You can smell them."

That night, Gwennan paced the walls, watching for the invading army. At dawn, the first of the *gelyn* appeared on the brow of the foothills and their army flowed into the valley south of the Gaer. Her heart faltered at the sight of their black and gold banners, spilling over the hills like a swollen river. Dust mingled with the smoke from the fires they set in the thatch of the hovels as they marched northwestward. Her breath ceased at the sight of their triumphant confidence. Their backs were straight and their weapons ready, disciplined, ferocious. Across their chests, they wore wide, gold-colored bands and their black flannel shirts glistened with dew. Every one of them carried a shining *pafais*, shields bearing the crest of their commander—a gold crescent moon with three stars in the black sky. The *pafais* reached from their shoulders to their knees and they beat a rhythm on the edge with the blades of their swords—a thunder that silenced the dawn.

"Your father will not abandon the Gaer."

"My father has already done so, Tudwal." Gwennan returned her attention to the army that was building its camp around the three exposed sides of the Gaer, trampling through the harvested fields and churning the dust of the farmland. "Unless we resist their attacks, we will be dead by twilight."

"We will not surrender, Gwennan."

"We will withstand, Tudwal. We must study them and delay until we can maneuver into position. We will negotiate with them, convince them of our intention to meet their terms until we can defeat them."

"These men will take all we have, Gwennan Pendyffryn, and kill everyone in their way. We cannot prevent their butchery."

"If what you say is true, Tudwal, we are walking in our shrouds already and may as well open the gates to die quickly rather than resist and watch our children starve to death."

"We can resist until Elgan returns. We can resist until Pendyffryn comes."

"When they come, our bones will be dry and picked clean."

"Pennaeth," Tudwal said, extending his hand to the young woman who had commanded the household guard of her father's childhood home for eight nights, "have you no faith in your father or Elgan?"

"I have faith, Tudwal," Gwennan replied, *the commander of this army will bring his warriors to my gates.* "I have faith," *his army will celebrate their victory in my hall.*

"Then you know we will be safe."

"Yes. But until they come, we must hold this place. How many can you spare to attack this army from the woodlands? We have bowmen whose skill—."

"We are a hundred, Gwennan. You ask for the hand of God." When Tudwal requested that the mead stores be opened, Gwennan nodded without hesitation and helped to carry them to the tables in the common hall for the soldiers to drink on the eve of their battle. Through the hours before dawn, Gwennan Pendyffryn watched the *gelyn* army from the southeastern watchtower. Another, larger banner of black and gold flew among the others, bearing the same crescent moon and three stars.

Jehan-Emíl deFreveille stood at the opening of his tent at the center of the encampment, a crust of bread in one hand, a flagon in the other. He gazed at the gates of the Gaer and ate his meal. He straddled the earth beneath his feet, planning his tactics to save his men by killing others. Food he needed to keep his army fed through the winter was being eaten from the stores within the walls. His scouts assured him the siege was destined to be brief. He had already noted the walls were feeble.

Certain of his victory, the *gelyn* commander studied the weakest points in the timbers. His army needed to eat and rest. Taunt the people he held captive with threats and, in a day or two, order the gates battered down—a good plan, unworthy of him and his army. Perhaps, consider ending the slaughter before all of the people inside were dead, save the useful ones—farmers and woodcutters, millers, the cooks and the women, always useful to an army, until food was scarce.

Jehan-Emíl turned to the raven-haired warrior beside him. "I do not understand this, my friend. Everything we have been told about this thegn, all we know, has prepared us for a fight. This is murder."

"There will be a fight, Jehan." Maides smiled from behind a day's growth of beard.

The commander cocked his head and nodded. "But not a good one. We will not earn our victory, Maides."

"Terror works as well as strength. The guard is weak. With so many women and children, perhaps they will surrender." Maides lifted his ice-colored eyes to the watchtower nearest their position. "Their commander has no heart for killing, Jehan."

"I have no appetite for this slaughter, Maides. We will talk our way into the warmth of their hall, drink to peace and spend the winter in comfort." He held his flagon to salute the commander of the Gaer. When he threw back his head in laughter, the corner of his friend's mouth twisted. "I know you prefer a fight. I will be content with a bath and bed that does not reek of my own sweat. I will be happy for one night's sleep under a roof that has no leaks."

"You're expectations have altered."

"Pendyffryn has made this too easy. I do not understand the man—he must have known we would strike here."

"Underestimate his strategy at your peril, my friend. These Welsh have secrets."

"I know his secret," Jehan-Emíl replied. "Knowing does not make the task any less distasteful. You know my purpose."

"This place is a poor choice," Maides replied. "Feeble reward for all these years of war."

"The reward I seek is worth any risk, my friend. I will bring my children to this house or I will die on the threshold."

The dark one departed but the commander turned again to study the walls and flimsy gates. His scowl was deep. He disliked what he saw as much as she disliked her weaknesses. *Though they are all to his benefit, he is not happy to do this. We are no challenge to this man.* She laughed aloud. Moments later, the *gelyn* commander retreated to his tent—ready to sleep through the night in peace.

Gwennan sank to the platform of the watchtower, resting her shoulder on the slatted wall, still watching through the cracks until the bonfires dwindled and only a few *gelyn* staggered between them and the command tent. *What manner of man is he that he can laugh before he lifts his sword to kill women and children? What manner of man smiles when he knows he asks men to die?* For eight nights she had commanded and for eight nights she had not slept, neither through the night nor in peace. *What does he expect to gain here? What drives him to murder?*

Before she found the answers she needed, the storm in the mountains drove the *gelyn* army and her friends to shelter but the rain clung to the skies. He was like any other warrior she had known: confident, powerful, certain. And yet, by the time she reached the *porth* of her house, another question planted itself in her thoughts—one that strengthened her certainty this man could be defeated. *What troubles him?*

While the *gelyn* commander rested his army, drank and laughed with his friends, studying the walls of the Gaer, Tudwal watched from the tower. There were no signs the army, encamped less than the throwing distance of his weakest spearman, had any intention of honoring their challenge. The captain of the household guard prepared his men for a siege, certain Daran Pendyffryn did not mean to abandon his home and only child to the commander of a ragged army intent on drink and plunder.

"We had given you up, Derwyn," Tudwal said, greeting the black-bearded warrior on the wall above the gates. "The *pennaeth* is in the house. Elgan is not with you? The others?"

"Elgan is dead. And others. Some are prisoners," Derwyn told his superior officer. "We may all die tomorrow, Tudwal.

The commander of this army is a fool but his army is strong. He knows how few we are to defend this place. When they strike, we can hold them until the last few of our men are dead. I will tell you all I know but first I must prepare Gwennan for the worst."

"Where is Pendyffryn?" Tudwal asked, following Derwyn toward the house.

"He is north, fighting another army, bigger still. *Gelyn* have reached Cwmdu."

Tudwal hesitated a moment, taking a breath. "Does Pendyffryn know this army threatens the Gaer? His daughter?"

"He sent us back to strengthen you, but he must have known what we would find."

"Then he must believe we will prevail," Tudwal said. "The *pendefig* would not send only ten if more were needed— not with his daughter's life at risk." He clapped his hand on the young warrior's shoulder and grinned. "We will not die tomorrow, Blaenant. The Gaer is safe."

Derwyn continued his climb to the stone house. At the door of Gwennan's room, he listened but heard nothing before he pounded on the door.

"I knew nothing could prevent you from returning," Gwennan said, gazing up at him from the lower hall. "Is Elgan with you?"

"Why are you here? Why are you not with the other women?" He jumped from the staircase to stand before her, meeting her gaze.

"That is not my place." There were great dark smudges beneath his blue eyes and his strong body trembled with fatigue. "Derwyn, what can be done to stop this army?"

"Fight them. And die," he answered. "Your husband is dead. Your father has ordered me to take you from here—to safety. I will return to fight. Pendyffryn said to tell you he has kept his promise to you."

She lifted her eyes to Derwyn's handsome face, a spark of hope at the corners of her mouth brought a smile that faded before he noticed. Although she sought confirmation of her father's promise in the eyes of her childhood friend, she did not see the man worthy of her esteem in Derwyn's narrowed gaze. When she raised her arms to embrace his weary shoulders, he held her away from him.

"You made your choice, Gwennan. Your husband is dead."

"We are no longer friends?"

Blaenant turned aside, shrugging off the hand on his shoulder. "I have seen their prisoners—all the warriors from every *ystad* these scurrying rats have conquered—in chains," Derwyn hissed. "Our kinsmen are there, like animals."

"We can hold them here, Derwyn. We can release our kinsmen—." She extended her hand to him, but withdrew when he stared at her.

"How do you plan to do this, against hundreds more warriors than we have?"

"While we argue, they rest."

"You know nothing of war, Gwennan. Let men do as they are trained."

"Does my father think I will abandon these people? And the Gaer?"

"You can do nothing to stop this army. Tomos is waiting for you in the gorge."

"I will not leave these people to die."

"If you refuse, I cannot force you. You cannot plague me as you did Elgan," Derwyn replied. "You defy your father, Gwennan, and risk the lives of a hundred men for your pride."

"The Gaer is my home," she said. "These are my friends—they depend on my help to survive this. I cannot abandon them for my own safety. I don't expect you or Tudwal to protect me from this army and I won't run away because my father has no faith in me or because my presence here is an annoyance to you. My father prefers to forget that I, if I live, will be *pendefig*. How can I throw my skirts over my head now and hope my warriors and my friends will forget my cowardice when it comes my time to lead them?"

"Tomorrow, we will win or die." A flare in the sky signaled the first heavy rain of the autumn, breaking the tension building in the mountains.

"We will not die. We will do whatever we must to live, as my father expects. Send Tomos to Pendyffryn for fifty bowmen. We can harass this *gelyn* from the tops of the trees until they beg——."

"By the time your bowmen come, Gwennan Pendyffryn, this *gelyn* will have driven his sword through your body." Derwyn hesitated only a moment before his strides thundered over the worn flagstones and he leapt across the ravine to rejoin his command.

The warmth the day promised was already steaming from the muddied ground. Derwyn, in battledress from first light, stalked the *buarth* like a wolf, his black hair braided back from his forehead, his helmet under his arm. The *gelyn* did not come forward and Tudwal refused to let his subordinate dictate the terms of war. Derwyn wanted combat. He received a peaceful, golden autumn morning and nothing to do with his rage but pace.

"Tell me the moment they move," Derwyn told his superior. When he slipped through the door into the lower hall, he was enraged to see the hearth alight and the table strewn with trinkets.

As he turned to ascend the staircase, Gwennan entered the hall from the kitchen, her hands behind her head to fasten her war braids in a brass pin. She stood erect when Derwyn stared at her and let her hands fall to her sides. She was draped in her black shawl. Beneath it, she wore a padded battle jerkin like his. Her studded body armor stood by the bench. Turning her attention to the objects on the table, Gwennan opened her mouth to speak.

"What are you doing?" he demanded. "This is no time for women's games. While you sort your baubles, your warriors wait to hear your words."

"Derwyn." She forgave his disrespect, as a friend, and motioned him to join her at the table. "I have a solution."

"Are you mad? Your warriors will fight to the death for you and you refuse to speak?"

"I have been considering this plan all through the night—."

"*Uffern*," he hissed, grabbing her shoulders. "Go down. Tell them what they wait to hear. Give them reason to fight."

"You have seen what waits for us. If we fight, more will be killed. This is another way. We can defeat this army, if we are prepared to wait."

"You can return to this entertainment when we are all dead," he declared, propelling her toward the door. "And take that off." Scattered pieces of her battle plan fell to the floor. "Sorrow will not inspire your warriors to kill this enemy. Mourn the loss of Elgan Maergwn when this *gelyn* is dead."

"Killing is unnecessary. I have studied the commander of this army and we need not accept death. He is willing to bargain. We have means—."

"Killing is what you have, Gwennan. Either that or death," he replied, "and worse for you and your women." He stared into her hazel eyes. When he reached for her, she fell into his embrace, still searching for the man her father had promised. "I will not let that happen to you, Gwennan. If you know I am dead, use this," he said, handing her the smaller of his daggers.

Gwennan stared at the weapon lying in her palm, its blade directed at her heart. When she raised her eyes again to the face of a man who had once asked to be her husband, his eyes held only a demand for her death. She slipped the dagger between the cinched laces of the jerkin and strode to the *buarth*.

"I do not expect your deaths today," she told her war band of thirty, meeting the gaze of each man in turn. "I expect you to resist this enemy, to survive to live on this land, our land. For your families. Live today to live tomorrow."

Derwyn raised his sword. Tudwal shook his head as his household guard and the survivors of Derwyn's war band shouted their challenge to the *gelyn*. The older warrior glanced at the house he had shared with Aine and gave his voice to the battle cry of his friends.

Before the *gelyn* had kicked off their blankets or rubbed the drunkenness from their eyes, the gates of the Gaer flew open with a roar from the warriors behind them. The Cymry charged forward, flooding into the encampment with their swords and axes soaring above their heads. The bowmen were the first to fall and the foot soldiers were trampled beneath the hooves of the Cymry's maddened warhorses. The horses, with their chalk-whitened manes standing on end, screamed and snorted in the faces of the *gelyn*. Their riders swept the unwary out of their way like chaff, driving toward the center of the encampment.

The *gelyn* commander threw his breakfast behind him and lunged for his weapons, calling for his horse while his dark friend leapt onto the back of his stallion and thrashed forward into the sea of tattooed Cymry, swinging his sword in an arc over his head, slicing through the bodies in his path. The *gelyn* commander rode behind, bringing the blunt edge of his battleaxe down on their backs while his warriors mounted and charged to encircle them.

Time ended as each man in her army lifted his weapon and was struck down. No one within the Gaer walls took breath as Gwennan's men fought to stay mounted while the *gelyn* surrounded them and pointed their weapons to the ground. Derwyn surveyed the *gelyn* army as bowmen aimed their arrows at his war band.

"Surrender. Live," Gwennan urged him, but, when the mounted *gelyn* warriors turned toward the gates, Derwyn commanded his men to fight to hold them back. Gwennan threw her body against the planks of the watchtower, peering through the gaps as the Cymry were taken prisoner. "Kill them," she shouted at the boy soldiers along the walls. She reached for the longbow. "Kill them all." She took aim for the *gelyn* commander's back. When he turned his horse to face her, Gwennan's hand trembled. "*You will know the man meant to be your husband…*"

The bowstring snapped across her cheek and the arrow sliced across his arm, piercing the shoulder of another *gelyn* warrior. A storm of arrows struck on both sides of the Gaer walls. The commander turned his men away from the Cymry, ordering them to charge the gates. "Run," Gwennan commanded the boys. "Hide your weapons. There are too many. We will fight tomorrow."

The boys jumped from the walls into the mud of the *buarth*. They ran in every direction as the first of the *gelyn* warriors hurtled over the collapsing gates. Their horses crashed into the stockade like an avalanche of boulders, crushing everything in their way, chasing anyone they found. Their swords and axes shrieked through the air. The watchtower shuddered, crumbled beneath her. The ground shook with the onslaught of hooves and soldiers maddened with hatred. Gwennan landed behind the wall of the dairy and lay in the splinters of the tower. When she could breathe, she turned onto her side and witnessed the slaughter she had feared.

The *gelyn* commander sailed over the rubble of the ruined gates on his golden warhorse and, with his sword high above his head, shouted a word she did not recognize. Except for the snorting of the excited animals and the wail of a woman, there was no other sound. She held her breath as the commander spoke to his warriors, gave orders and rode through the *buarth* to the door of the common hall. A boy followed and leapt from his horse, taking the reins the *gelyn* tossed to him, standing erect as his commander dismounted and strode into the hall. Though blood ran down his arm, the wound she had inflicted had not stopped him, had not caused him a moment's hesitation.

"Find your children," she hissed at the women near her. "Hide."

Before the *gelyn* warriors reached her, Gwennan dragged to her feet and slid along the wall to watch the gates. There was no killing inside the Gaer once the *gelyn* commander had shouted his orders. Women, children and boy soldiers were herded toward the hall, corralled by foot soldiers and forced to huddle in the dirt while the warriors followed their commander into the long, stone hall.

Three

If Derwyn or any others were alive, they were beyond her help, outside the Gaer walls, lying in their own blood and that of other men—*gelyn* and friend. If they were alive, they winced at the brightness of the sun, retching at the odor its heat drew up from the saturated earth. If they lived, they gazed at the blueness of the sky and wondered how long they would lie in the filth of other men's wretched deaths before death came.

Gwennan Pendyffryn had seen war. Her father came home from war with scars and tales of his army's bravery. She had lifted men from the blood-sodden earth where they had fallen. She had washed their bodies and dressed their wounds. She had held them close while they died and held them down when they were delirious with pain.

The *gelyn* foot soldiers were filling the opening and the broken timbers were hoisted to enclose the Gaer once more. The *gelyn* began to strip the dead, stealing their weapons and clothing, as she had done for her father's army. She murmured prayers for her friends. The encampment was filled with screams and shouting, silenced as *gelyn* picked their way through the bodies. As the pickers came closer, Gwennan crept back, hiding amidst the bodies of the dead and wounded, crawling through the ruins of the walls toward the scullery yard, and into the kitchen where she could watch the *gelyn* while they celebrated.

"How can you think of sparing them?" a blond warrior demanded of his commander. He spoke the flat language of the *Saeson* market traders.

"I have given my orders, Alrick. Bring in the wounded and see to them. Find the women and bring them here to cook." The *gelyn* commander's accent was unknown to her, his skin was sun-darkened and the unruly curls on his head were too dark for *Sais. Mercenary.*

"I suppose we are to leave the women alone as well?"

"For now, there will be no more war." The commander sank back against the chair near the hearth, crossed his ankles and planted his boot-heels on the grate irons. He drank wine and continued his dictation in a different language from the one he spoke to his officer. Someone had tied a strip of cloth around his upper arm but the wound was still oozing. He ran his blood-stained hand through his wild hair and watched Alrick pace. Beneath the streaks of sweat-thinned blood and many days' growth of beard, his face was hard, but he looked around him in thought.

What troubles him? Gwennan scoured the thought from her concerns, also watching the younger warrior. He was impatient to taste the glory and plundering that came with victory. He had not had enough of bloodshed. When the commander's dark friend brought the farm women into the hall, the blond man lunged, eager to exact the toll their men had paid. Gwennan's breath caught. Two of her women stood among them. The women and girls screamed as one and huddled together. The commander rose to his feet and spoke.

"Jehan-Emíl deFreveille is *pennaeth* here now," the dark warrior said in her language.

Gwennan sucked her breath hard into her lungs. *How has he learned this?*

"Prepare a meal for your new masters. A *meddyg* will tend your wounded." Though he had dismissed them, they shook their heads but soon responded to the dark man's icy glare and ran like sheep toward the kitchen. The man called Jehan-Emíl deFreveille clasped a full skin of wine and filled his cup, beckoning his friend to join him. The commander questioned and laughed. The dark warrior answered and frowned.

Gwennan hushed the women and girls seeking her counsel, sending them to hide and disappeared herself into the confusion of the *buarth*. His soldiers were already drunk on the liquor they found, called to order by their comrades when their madness threatened to bring the wrath of the officers on their heads. Gwennan heard the *gelyn* commander's name growled as a curse among his men. She wrapped a ragged shawl around her and searched for friends among the wounded.

When none of the women reappeared from the kitchen with the food the warriors demanded, Alrick burst from the hall with a shout for a hunt. A younger warrior straightened his legs as he stood in Alrick's path. "They are scattered in all directions," the lean man said. "I'll get the cook."

"I want the women, Wode. You saw where they went—bring them now. I've had too many bellyaches from the cook's food."

"What makes you think these women won't poison you?" Wode had turned his head to scan the stockade and glanced back at Alrick. "I wouldn't trust any of those I saw. Not to cook for me."

"We think alike," Alrick laughed. "Bring two. That will be enough for me tonight."

"You heard Freveille's orders."

"He'll have his own woman tonight. We've earned as much. Make sure she's young," Alrick said as Wode walked away, "with teeth in her head."

The man whose head Gwennan held in her lap groaned and she covered his mouth with her hand, bending low over him.

Alrick re-entered the hall, shouting, "Wode has gone after them, Freveille. You won't be hungry for long." Laughter filled the hall. "There is not a warrior here who mistakes your meaning, Freveille. A hard battle deserves a full belly."

"This was no battle, Alrick," the commander replied. "You will have no belly to fill as reward for such meager effort. Find the cook or starve."

"As you starve, Commander, so shall we all, gladly." Another shout of laughter followed the banter.

Gwennan bandaged the man's head. When a small, dark-haired man came into the stockade from the encampment, she crawled further into the shadows. With him were boys whom he directed with flailing arms and a soft-pitched voice. Gwennan left her patient in the *gelyn* physician's care.

The hands that had killed their friends were greasy with the food that was meant to feed the Gaer through winter. Madlen and Ruth lingered at the door of the kitchen, serving meat and drink, giggling together. Seething in anger at their stupidity and outrage at the *gelyn* commander's arrogance, Gwennan forced calm and thought to rule her, resisting every urge to lunge into the hall and take his heart with the cleaver she gripped. The man dressed in black seated at the table continued his discussion with his friend, lifting his cup to drink, turning his eyes on his warriors with no sign of distraction from his conversation. The dark one spoke in response to his commander's question, repeating her father's name.

"DeFreveille wishes to know if you have been told your *pennaeth* is dead?"

Madlen and Ruth glanced in the warrior's direction but Gwennan concentrated her attention on the commander.

"This is a foolish thing you are doing, *blodyn*," Galar hissed between her teeth, her gnarled fingers digging into Gwennan's wrist. "You should have stayed where you were safe."

Gwennan moved away from the old woman but Galar followed and the dark one replied to another of deFreveille's questions. The *gelyn* commander grinned. His smile broke into a deep laugh that spread through the hall. Gwennan clenched her jaw, straightening her back and slipping out of sight into the larder. Laughter followed in her wake. Galar hobbled after her.

Ruth brought empty platters that moments ago she had set before the *gelyn*. "We were caught," Ruth replied to her *pennaeth's* narrowed glare. "We were only worried for you, alone here. What will they do to us, Gwennan?"

"Keep out of their way." She slammed the lid of the empty iron pot and glared at the wall. Galar pinched her arm, forcing Gwennan to look at her.

"Give me the dagger," Galar hissed. "Regret is useless now, *blodyn*," the old woman snapped. "They have seen you and know who you are. They know you are alone here. Derwyn put your only escape in your hands. Best you use it now, before their commander or the *Diawl* does so."

"I am not a coward," Gwennan hissed, wondering why Galar had brought their attention to her. "If Tudwal is dead, if Elgan is dead, I am still responsible. I cannot desert these people."

"And if Derwyn lives?"

"I will live."

"Do you think he will want you when they have finished? There is Derwyn's answer, Gwennan. " Galar pointed at the hidden dagger. "Better you are dead. You will be dead to my nephew forever…if you live through this night."

"As God wills, Galar," Gwennan replied, straightening her back. "If Derwyn means for me to die, let it be by his own hand."

"Gwennan, *blodyn*," the old woman began, softening her tone. "Go to the house. You will be safe there for a few hours. Think of what you do, how your father will suffer to learn the manner of your death at the hands of these animals. You do not know. You have never seen what happens to women in war."

"I have seen what happens to men. I cannot be less brave," she said, taking an empty jug from the shelf above the door. "I am not a coward."

"What are you doing?" Galar restrained Gwennan with the head of her stick.

"They are drinking my mead."

The air in the hall was fetid with the odors of sweat, damp ash and blood as the fires smoldered. When Gwennan began to empty their cups into the jugs, they protested to their commander and were silenced. But, when Gwennan reached for Jehan-Emíl deFreveille's cup, he brought his hand down over hers, speaking in a low voice as she fought him for possession.

"The commander will allow you to reclaim your *pennaeth's* drink, but the wine in his cup is his own," the dark one said.

Gwennan loosened her grip on the commander's cup but he imprisoned her hand. She twisted her wrist to escape, wrenching away and falling against one of the men behind her. An arm whipped around her waist and lifted her from the floor. The hall resounded with cheering and laughter. The arm tightened and pain swept through her.

"This one is dressed for battle. I am ready for the fight you have demanded, Commander."

"Alrick." DeFreveille took a swallow of his wine before he set the cup on the table. "I have given my orders. This woman is not your concern."

Gwennan's captor loosened his arm and she slid down his body until her feet touched the ground. "If you want this one, choose one for me, Freveille. I, as well as my command, have earned a woman as much as you and Maides." His arm dropped away from her.

Gwennan lunged at the table, slapping her hands on either side of the jug of mead, pain overwhelmed by rage. The commander met her eyes for a moment before his gaze dropped to study her hands. "You will not be here long enough to hurt us," she hissed at him, calming her nausea with anger. "When you have finished *your* wine, leave this house."

His eyes narrowed when he grasped her chin, turning her head to examine her cheek. The tone of his voice sharpened. Gwennan covered the place with her hand but Freveille pushed her hand away. His thumb pressed beneath her chin to raise her head but she kept her eyes averted. The commander smiled at her, leaning back in his chair while he spoke to the one called Maides. "*Menyw,* Jehan-Emíl invites you to sit with him."

"I will never dishonor my friends by sitting near this pig."

The commander fixed his eyes on her face and spoke. Gwennan studied her enemy with keen eyes, trained to learn what she had to know to survive. Though she did not like what she saw, he had reasons not to kill her. She stood, drawing her body erect, secure in her understanding—he had a use for her. He was not a generous man.

"For now, your friends are prisoners. When they are healed, they will have opportunity to gain their freedom. Their choice will be simple. Jehan-Emíl offers the women this same choice. War between you and his army can end now, or continue. That is for you to decide."

"That is no choice." Gwennan answered as her strength returned.

"Nonetheless, that is your position. If you do not sit with him, *menyw*," Maides warned, "these others will find a use for you. As a rule, they are happy to share their good fortune."

"You dare threaten me?"

"You have a choice, *menyw*. One man or forty." Maides turned his attention to his commander for a moment. "Jehan-Emíl understands your reluctance but, for your own safety, he insists that you sit by him."

"And if I do not?"

"He will force you to do so."

"Let him try," she hissed, turning her back to return to the kitchen. She had taken two steps when the commander leapt over the table and landed behind her, clasping her around the waist and dragging her to a stool by his chair.

"My friend does not take no for answer, *menyw*," Maides said, returning her pain-sickened glare with a smile, speaking to the *gelyn* warriors. "This woman thinks she can defeat Freveille though her warriors could not." They thrashed the tables with their flagons and shouted ways she could be punished. "No one here understands your language, nor do they understand what Jehan-Emíl says to me," Maides told Gwennan. "What he says to you and how you reply will be between us."

"I have nothing to say to *him*." Taking long breaths to quell her pain, Gwennan saw Galar from the corner of her eye. The old woman stared in return and shook her head.

"Jehan-Emíl," Maides said, "is delighted with your promise of silence after such a noisy day. He wishes to assure you no harm will come to you…for now." Freveille's words drew another smile from Maides. "Jehan-Emíl deFreveille asks you to consider us as guests." The commander clasped and kissed Gwennan's hand. "Those women whose husbands have survived will be re-united with them soon. For these, the war is ended."

Gwennan looked down at the hand holding hers. His fingers were long and his grip was strong but he exerted no pressure. When she pulled her hand free, he let her go and poured a cup of wine for her, speaking to Maides.

"Jehan-Emíl asks if you have eaten today."

"Yes," she replied, keeping her eyes on the glowering face of the old woman. The commander spoke again and a boy, the same boy she had seen holding the *gelyn's* warhorse and acting as his scribe, ran into the kitchen. Gwennan pushed up from the stool. Freveille caught her wrist.

"The boy is Artur, Jehan-Emíl's groom. He will bring your meal since you do not answer truthfully."

Gwennan stared into the brown eyes of her captor. He smiled and put the cup of wine into her free hand, closing his fingers over hers until she accepted the cup. The boy returned with a small platter of meat, cheese and bread, an apple and a handful of walnuts. When Artur set the platter in front of her, he bowed. Gwennan bit her lips together. "This is too much."

"It is your food, *menyw*. That old woman has not eaten. Share with her if you wish."

"I do not accept the leavings of dogs. Better to throw it into the cesspit," Galar spat in Gwennan's direction. "A dead woman has no reason to eat."

"Why does the old one call you a dead woman?"

"She is old," Gwennan said.

"And you will never be," Galar cursed. "Do as you are bid. You have your father's promise. Derwyn put your future in your hands. You bring shame to this house with your cowardice. Take the way you must. You are dead to all who loved you."

"Your guest, Jehan-Emíl, with your permission, wishes that you eat. He has sworn no harm will come to you," Maides said after a long discussion with his friend. "If the old woman threatens you again, she will be confined. For your safety."

"Dog," Galar hissed. "You think you can have my girl and no harm will come." Galar struggled to her feet and shook her stick at the men at the table. "You are dead men."

"Sit down, old one," Maides said. "You will cause yourself an injury."

Galar lifted the stick over her head and hissed another curse under her breath. "You will see what harm comes of this night," she murmured. "*You* will see," she hissed at Gwennan, "and die."

Jehan-Emíl shrugged when Maides interpreted the old woman's curse. He pushed the platter closer to Gwennan, urging her to eat. She closed her eyes for a moment. She had already refused death by her own hand. While she hesitated, Freveille took one of the walnuts, rolled it in his hand and, when he had found its weakness, crushed the shell in his palm. As he opened one hand to offer her the meat, he released her from the constraint of the other. Taking what he offered to her from his own hand was impossible. Gwennan ignored the gesture, taking an apple and biting into it, staring into his eyes.

Her captor shrugged again and tossed the two halves of the walnut onto the platter. The men at the table were quiet for several moments. Jehan-Emíl deFreveille leaned back in the chair, contemplating his cup and his captive in turn. When he spoke again, his voice was low and Gwennan stopped eating, the apple suspended near her mouth. His voice was calm, soothing—so deep and soft that it felt as though he spoke to her as he would a child. She waited for the interpreter to speak. When Maides remained silent, she glanced at him.

"Do you want to know what Jehan-Emíl has said?"

"If it concerns me or my friends, I have a right—."

"—While it concerns you, it is not in Jehan-Emíl's interests for me to speak, therefore..."

She bit hard into the flesh of the apple and took a swallow of the wine.

The central pit had reduced to coals and the empty iron spit was glowing. The hall was as hot as a bonfire and the faces of the warriors glowed with sweat and the blood of her friends. DeFreveille flexed his wounded arm but gave no other sign that it troubled him. The strip of cloth glistened. More of their own drink was brought in from the *gelyn's* supplies. They lounged in groups scattered around the hall, watching their commander, grinning as they speculated on her fate.

DeFreveille gulped down another mouthful of wine. He drew his dagger, studied the food on the platter and stabbed a chunk of meat. Plucking the apple from her hands, he dropped the meat into them, gesturing for Gwennan to accept the food he offered.

"I am capable of selecting what I want to eat," she said as she tossed the meat onto the platter. He shrugged and spoke to his friend.

"Jehan-Emíl will not allow you to starve yourself in order to punish him."

"I would not do that. I would not give him, or any of you, the satisfaction."

"You will not starve or you will not punish him?"

"Interpret in whatever way you choose," she said. "You will lie for your own reasons."

Maides leaned close to her, glancing at deFreveille before he murmured, "You are mistaken if you think I lie to Jehan-Emíl, *menyw*. I may not tell him every word you say, but he will always know I speak truly. We will not gain if you die. Neither will you. Punishing Jehan-Emíl will gain nothing for either of you. Make what you wish of your circumstances. This is what you have—a man who is eager for your friendship—."

"Friendship?" she demanded. "You cannot believe that is possible."

"—Who is also a man who has taken all you value and made it his own."

"You will not stay here," she said, pushing to her feet. "We will fight and take back everything you have stolen." Gwennan moved to the front of the table and whisked the platter away. Slamming it down on the board in the kitchen larder, she covered her face with her hands. *This is my fault. I brought this on myself, on all of us.*

"*Menyw?*" Artur bowed at the waist. She folded thick pads of cloth to lift the iron pot onto a hook above the fire. "*Menyw,*" the boy said with a bow, taking the pads from her.

"Thank you."

The boy cocked his head and followed her, lifting and carrying as soon as she reached for an object, speaking in a conversational tone but in no language she understood. While she made work, she considered what she had learned and observed. After a moment, the boy extended his hand toward the hall, saying his commander's name. In the *gelyn's* language, he said, "I have not learned your way of speaking." He shrugged and bowed again. "DeFreveille waits for you."

"Let him wait," she said under her breath.

"Artur," deFreveille called to the boy, making a slight gesture. The foreigner strode to the door of the larder and watched while she found occupation to keep her back to him, avoiding his eyes when she turned in his direction.

"Gwennan?"

Although his accent was heavy, she recognized her name and her hand shook as she reached to the shelf above her head. *How does he know me?* She dropped her hand to her side as the foreigner took a step toward her. While he studied her, casting his eyes over her from the top of her head to her boots, every muscle in her body trembled. He spoke in a quiet voice, approaching steadily until he was within arm's reach. He laid his hand on her arm and spoke in a low voice. Beads of moisture stood out on her temples, dampening the wisps of hair around her face. Extending his open hand, he said her name again at the end of a long question, laying his hand over her cheek while his other hand slid down her arm and captured her hand. Her heart pounded so hard its drumming deafened her to the steady murmur of his voice. As he bowed his head and kissed her mouth, Gwennan held her breath, motionless. When he drew his head away, she swayed and he held her against him. She fought to breathe again. Her heart was still battering the wall of her chest and, for a moment, her brow dropped to his shoulder. He spoke again.

"Jehan wants to know your age, *menyw*," Maides said from the doorway.

"That is not your concern," she murmured, withdrawing and returned to her work, listening but unable to decipher the language they spoke.

"DeFreveille has decided you will go to your house. He will find you when his work is done."

Gwennan stared at the two men. "He has no right to command me."

"As I told you, *menyw*, he is responsible for you, for all of you. The choice for you is simple. Jehan-Emíl or forty."

"I will not submit—."

"Submission is not required," Maides said. "This is what will be."

The dark mercenary walked her as his prisoner to the house, ignoring the drunken advice of the warriors, holding her by the arm as he searched every room. When he released her, he said, "Do not underestimate us, *menyw*. There is no escape for you to your friends in the caverns." His cold smile darkened as she realized the certainty of his knowledge. "We know all we need to hold this place. We know how Derwyn Blaenant returned. We know how Pendyffryn meant to defeat us. Do not mistake Jehan-Emíl's generosity for weakness nor his concern for regard."

Clenching her fists in her hair, Gwennan paced the lower room until she commanded calm. When the sun's glow was gone from the mountains, she stripped out of her mud-encrusted gown and shift, gasping with each small movement and cried out when she examined the damage to her body. She bathed and gazed at the angry abrasion on her cheek from the bowstring that had sent an arrow through her enemy's arm. She could hear the laughter and singing in the common hall, the crackling of the bonfires beyond the gates and the cries of wounded men.

The sensation of the foreigner's hand on her cheek and his lips on her mouth lingered. Gwennan scrubbed away the feel of him with the back of her hand but she could not erase the memory. Even the sting of the abrasions did not relieve her sense of shame. She had not used Derwyn's weapon to threaten the man whose hair sprung in wild curls, whose eyes were soft, whose deep voice stilled her terror, whose laughter…. Growling at her cowardice, Gwennan secured Derwyn's small dagger in her clothing. For a moment, she kept her hand clenched around the carved handle. *One of us will die.*

She built the fire in the lower hall to a thunderous blaze to drown the joy of their victory and stared at the objects that remained on the table. With trembling fingers, her hand fell on the peg that represented Derwyn's position but she did not move it. *You should have listened.* Refusing the tears that stung her eyes and closed her throat, she gathered the pieces from the stones and studied the awl that was the foreign commander. She clenched the tool with such rage that it gouged into her palm, leaving a mark that persisted until the logs on the grate fell to embers. She dropped the awl back to its original position in her battle plan. *He is not Sais.*

She had no doubt, had Derwyn Blaenant followed her plan, the foreigner would not have succeeded in crushing her defenses so soon. She had no doubt he would not have lifted a finger against her until his army was rested and fed. She had no doubt her bowmen would have tormented him for a day. Gwennan laid her head on her arm, gazing at the field of battle as she had foreseen. *Fool. He is paid to kill. Paid well.*

Moments later, her eyes bolted open, her heart crushing the wall of her chest. A chair scraped along the floor behind her. A man growled, whistled low, threw a log onto the grate. Except for the soft crackle as the log caught and the bark flared, the *gelyn* was still. She kept her head down, searching for the invader. He stood with his back to the room, resting his head on his fist at the mantel. After a while, he glanced at the floor above and Gwennan held her breath but he returned his gaze to the fire. He sat in the *pennaeth's* chair at the hearth, wrapping a long cloak around him, settling as though to sleep. *What is his plan?*

Believing he intended to sleep by the fire, Gwennan began to doze until he cursed and his hobnailed boots scraped on the stone staircase to her room. Her gaze darted to the *porth*. He stumbled on the worn stair and cursed under his breath. Gwennan remained still, breathless. The foreigner stood outside the door for several moments before his hand fell on the latch. The door sprang open from the force of his shoulder and she pressed her lips together to keep from laughing when the powerful warrior tumbled into the dark room and raised a finger to his lips. He whispered her name amidst his scolding.

He's drunk. Very drunk. She sought the reassurance of the dagger. When he stumbled back to the lower hall and stared at the flames for what seemed like hours, Gwennan watched him as he studied the flames licking at the log he had added but was half asleep when deFreveille stood by her, one hand resting on the table as he studied her battle plan.

She felt his eyes shift from her battle plan to her face, but she showed no sign of waking until he bowed over her and brushed her bruised cheek with a kiss. A moment later, he swept the peg from the table and flung it away. Gwennan cried out, falling to her knees, hunting for it among the kindling. When the *gelyn* stood over her, crouched and plunged his fingers into the splinters of wood, she covered her face, restraining the sob that threatened to escape. He drew her hand away from her eyes and held the peg before her, covering the mark the awl had made on her palm with his long fingers. He spoke but she refused to look at him.

He held her hand until her throat ceased to ache. When she was calm, he drew her hair away from her cheek, cupping her chin until she allowed him to turn her face toward him but she did not lift her eyes when he said her name. After a time, he pulled her to her feet and led her to the table.

"This is good," he said in the flat language she understood, "but I am glad this warrior lost his nerve." Gwennan kept her head bowed and her eyes on the battle plan as he set the peg within the Gaer. "If this warrior and these had succeeded in this plan, I would not be here tonight. Tomorrow, perhaps. Two days if this warrior had believed in his plan, but here I am. Here I will stay, Gwennan." He moved the pieces as he spoke, showing her how well he understood the plan and how he would have defeated her. In spite of herself, she smiled when he chose the awl and placed it within the Gaer. "This warrior," he said, picking up the peg and rolling it between his fingers before he offered it to her, "will not trouble me. He does not have the nerve to withstand me."

Gwennan stared at the wooden piece, trembling when she plucked it from his grasp. *Derwyn did not listen. I am not as foolish.*

"This warrior cannot stop me. He is already defeated. If he makes another attempt, I will deal with him but for now, I have had enough of war."

His clothes still reeked of burning and the blood of men he had killed. His face and hands were clean. His hair was damp, curling close to his forehead, springing free as it dried. The pungent scent of power filled her body though she hardly breathed. He stroked her hair, slid his arm around her and held her against him, bowing his head to murmur against her temple. "You and I will have another battle, but not tonight. You are as weary as I am." His breath whispered against her damaged cheek. "I will enjoy you another time, woman. Tonight, we both need sleep and tenderness."

She meant to scream to bring witnesses but her throat constricted and no sound emerged—there was no one near to hear her. She meant to kill him with Derwyn's weapon but doubted she had the strength to drive the blade deep enough to do any damage other than make him angry. She could use the blade as Derwyn intended. While her assailant filled his senses with the silk of her hair, the perfume of her skin and the glistening of her eyes, Gwennan's fingers crept to grasp the hilt with relief. When he noticed that she held a weapon, he smiled into her eyes, inviting her best effort to end his life. She turned the blade toward her heart. DeFreveille's eyes widened and he put his palm between the tip of the blade and her breast.

"No, Gwennan, this will not be." He cursed, closing his hand around the blade, throwing it away from him. "No. *Inferni*," he said. "*Deus*." He pointed to the ceiling of the room. "How can I make you understand? *Inferni*," he said, pointing to the floor. "You will not do this, woman. *God, Deus?*"

"*Duw*."

"*God, Duw? Inferni?*"

"*Uffern*."

The *gelyn* sighed, combing his fingers through the loose waves of her hair around her neck. "*Duw*," he murmured and reverted to his own language for several sentences, finishing, "… *inferni. Uffern*."

Gwennan clasped his wrists to drag his hands away from her face.

"*Uffern*, Gwennan," he repeated. "No." He tilted her chin and planted a kiss on her lips, locking his arms around her. "Gwennan," he whispered, scolding her with a wagging finger, tightening his arms for a moment.

She felt his sigh reverberate in her body and he relaxed though he still held her fast. When his breathing deepened and his grip on her softened, she opened her eyes to stare at his face. "*Duw*," she cried under her breath, as she studied his quiet, ordinary face in the glow of the fire. *My friends want me to die. My father has abandoned me. My enemy insists I live.*

As if he understood her thoughts, Jehan-Emíl smiled and slipped his arm under her knees. "Tonight, we sleep, Gwennan. Tomorrow will be different."

He stole the last of her strength in the struggle to escape him as he climbed the stairs to her room. She struck him once but had no strength for another blow. When he laid her exhausted body on the bed, his breath stirred in her hair. Standing in front of the small hearth, he spoke her name again. Gwennan stared into his warm, earnest eyes. *I cannot be such a coward. I must be mad with grief.*

"I have given you my word," he said. "I will have you, Gwennan Pendyffryn, but not as you expect, nor even as you want me tonight."

The *gelyn* words were as foreign to him as they were hateful to her but she could not let him know she understood. *This man cannot be worthy.* She could not cower or acknowledge the threat.

"I am not like these men you hate. What I will have from you is more than you are prepared to give, but once we are friends, you will not deny me."

For one night, exhaustion defeated her. Until the sun crested the eastern hills, she was insensible but, at dawn, truth yanked Gwennan from her bed. Her room was empty. She sought sanctuary in the room in which her father had spent the first years of his childhood. Burying her face in her hands, she made no sound as the shame of truth possessed her. *If he was not my enemy, Ieuan Emyr would be a man worthy of my esteem.* She blamed grief and dismay that she had given him a name to cherish.

Derwyn, the man whom she had once thought to wed, was lying beyond the gates but she had not thought of him while she lay in the arms of the invader. "I am insane with grief," she said aloud. She bathed in the cold water, soothed and bandaged her body.

If the *gelyn* won, his army would take as they wanted, absorb her country into theirs and call her 'Welsh'. *I will defeat that man.* Gwennan lifted her head to stare at the carved screed wall protecting her from Jehan-Emíl deFreveille. *But this man, Ieuan Emyr, this man I will know better before I decide whether to kill him.*

FOUR

Jehan-Emíl opened his eyes when a beam of sunlight crept up his arm and penetrated his eyelid. He took a deep breath and grimaced, shielding his eyes against the single ray of light cutting across his face, though the rest of the room was dim. He concentrated his senses on the sounds of the house, turning his attention to the staircase leading to the *pennaeth's* room. As soon as his eyes fell on the door, he threw off the cloak across his legs and took the stairs at a run. Even one night sleeping in a chair was not his idea of victory.

Gwennan opened the door and backed away, eyes narrowed, snarling at him.

He cocked his head to one side, not to understand her better, but in amusement. She had no fear of him. This could be bad but she had no weapon to hurt him enough to stop him, if he chose to make good his promise to bed her. That he wanted her was apparent the moment he reached the door but she did not lower her eyes from his face. That he wanted a woman as much as he did was no surprise—Alrick was not alone in his hunger to taste the pleasures of success.

That he was hungry for this woman surprised him. She was tall. And strong. And determined. If it had not been for the fight she gave him, he had thought to break his word and have her as he wanted. But, he was not a man to win a woman by force. Land. War. Yes. A battle of this kind required other skills.

She was dangerous. Jehan-Emíl rubbed his jaw. She had left no mark, but her will to do so was plain and had made him pause. The moment she was subdued, if he took her, the chance of another night with her was non-existent. Why he should want her more than one night, he dismissed. He was not a man who needed a lot of women. He was a man who needed a lot of one woman. And he had not had that for many years, not since his wife betrayed him.

She backed further away, into the small room, refusing to speak any word he understood. Her hair was still damp, loose around her shoulders. Her heavy linen frock and shapeless, black woolen tunic concealed more than her slender body. Confusion? A blush? He took a deep breath and looked around him. She had lead him into a trap, a good room for children but no escape. Something better crossed his mind and he smiled, catching her with one arm.

She pushed him away. *Yes, a blush, from this throat to these eyes. Hazel eyes.* He strode to the wooden tub in the corner of the room, holding her soap in his hand, inhaling its fragrance. He grinned, gesturing for her to come to him. He lunged but she escaped.

The water was cold. Though the bath had not been prepared for him, Jehan-Emíl stripped and stepped into the tub, watching her over his shoulder. He kept his eyes fixed on her as he soaked a cloth and lathered the soap.

"You prefer your lovers clean?" He detected no recognition—not as he had when he spoke the Saxon tongue—and continued in the language of his country. "If I had not seen you last night—, it is no matter now. Years ago, months ago, yes, the one with red-gold hair, she would have done for me. But, no. Once I saw into your eyes, no mortal man could keep me from you. Your father will want my head for what I will do." He scrubbed his back, chest and arms, studying her face. "Gwennan. I like this name." His eyes moved slowly over her body.

Gwennan ignored his scrutiny, keeping her eyes lowered while he washed the smears of blood from his body, frowning at the scars on his arms and torso. Before she turned away, she made a mental calculation of the length of his thighs, his narrow hips, the power of the muscles rippling beneath his skin. He washed the evidence of his part in the deaths of her friends from his body, soothing his weary muscles.

He bathed away what remained of the filth of battle and took linen to dry himself. His hands were strong and rough on his body, rubbing the skin of his torso, arms and legs, heedless of the wound on his arm. Her heart pounded hard in her chest. He spoke again and she recognized the names of his groom, his friend and her own but she did not respond.

Their meager understanding of the previous night was forgotten. Gwennan had no sense that he remembered her threat to end his life and she did not want to remind him by repeating the few words he had learned of her language. He wrapped the linen around his waist and lathered his face, taking Derwyn's dagger from his belt. Standing before the polished *drych,* he studied his ordinary face and scraped the tawny growth from his jaw.

Gwennan lifted her arms to gather her hair into a braid but had only twisted the first strand when he growled, turning sharply to look at her. He questioned her but she shrugged in response. While her eyes were lowered, he caught her around the waist and raised his hand to her cheek, repeating the question. Without letting her go, he laid his hand on the tub and gave it its Latin name, demanding an answer. Gwennan responded with its name in her language. He pointed to the fresh scar on his upper arm, now surrounded by a bruise. He struggled to find the Latin word for the mark and Gwennan said, "*Clais.*"

"Yes," he sighed, again touching her face. "*Clais,* Gwennan. You have *clais.*" He turned her to face the *drych,* pulling her hair away from her face. "Who has done this?" he asked, meeting her eyes in the reflection.

Gwennan raised a trembling hand to her face, examining the angry mark on her cheek, the dark bruise spreading around it, evidence of her failure to kill him. *Such a fool you are. He will learn the truth.* When the foreigner laid his hand over hers, she was shocked to see their reflections in the polished surface, recognizing the concern in his expression—concern she had never seen in Derwyn's eyes. "*Uffern,*" she cursed, covering her face with her hands.

"Who has hurt you?" Jehan-Emíl demanded. "Who is in this house, Gwennan? Who?" He turned her in his arms and tried to drag her hands from her face but she fought to stay hidden. "I will find him, Gwennan," he murmured, taking her into his arms and holding her head against his shoulder. "I will find him."

Though she could not understand him, there was an element in his tone that comforted her. This foreigner, who had known her for less than a day, had more compassion for her than the man she had loved as a friend since childhood. *Had.* She cursed again. This man, who caused the deaths of so many she had known and some she had loved, held her in his arms and comforted her for a bruise she earned by her reluctance to kill him.

Though she could not accept his kindness—because he, more than those who wanted her to die, was her enemy—she allowed Ieuan Emyr to hold her until her anger subsided, until she turned her head away from him. Still allowing him to stroke her hair and murmur, she drew deep breaths of the scent of her own soap, mingled with his warm skin, into her lungs. She had no excuse to lean against him. *I should have killed him when I had opportunity.*

She raised her head and stepped back, without meeting his gaze, and went to her room. She listened while he lathered his face again. When he returned to the *pennaeth's* room, his chin and jaw were smooth. He was not as handsome as either Derwyn or Elgan, but he was pleasant to look at. He was well-formed with cheerful features that belied his brutality. *He is a hired killer. Murder is his profession.*

He strode to the pile of his blood-stained clothes and clasped them in one hand. Gwennan lifted the lid of her linen chest and handed him a fresh shirt, tunic and *trwsus.* His

51

eyebrows knit together in doubt but she waved him away to dress, picking up her wooden comb and sinking onto the stool by the hearth to wait for him to leave. She stole a glance at her enemy from under her lashes as he slipped the tunic over his shoulders.

The foreigner examined and stroked his hand over the fine stitching on the front of the tunic. But when he raised his head to look at her, Gwennan's face was turned to the heat of the flames, astonished the drunken brute appreciated the work of a woman's needle. With a laugh, deFreveille clasped her around the waist, unlacing the front of her somber tunic. She shoved his hand away. "I will bathe you now, woman," he commanded, pointing to the buckets of cold water on the hearthstone.

"No," she said, slapping his hand away.

When he persisted, she lifted his hand and bit it. With a hiss, he pulled his hand back to stop her. She threw up her arm to ward off a blow and, at the same time, went limp in his embrace. Jehan-Emíl set her firmly on her feet but kept his arms around her waist.

"You have no reason to fear me, Gwennan," he said. "I do not beat women. I am not an animal like the one who did this to you," he whispered, moving his lips over her bruised cheek. When he said her name, her apprehension gathered in a tight fist around her heart, intensifying as his lips touched her throat and his hand caressed her hair. His mouth was warm, his breath steamy and his hands powerful, eager when he pressed his palm over her breast. He whispered as his lips moved slowly over the tender skin of her throat. "I want you, but I am content to wait, Gwennan. My men will understand that you are mine. When you are ready—soon, I think," he murmured, gazing into her wide, hazel eyes, "we will make love."

Her body was so tense she could not breathe. Her heart thundered, hammering against her breast, and, if his arms had not supported her, she would have fallen as she fainted.

"I will leave you alone to wash away the stink of me in peace," Jehan-Emíl laughed as he lowered her to the floor and let her head rest on the bed. He bellowed his orders as he ran down the stone staircase and into the *buarth*.

Gwennan lifted her head and listened to another voice in the hall.

"*Menyw?*"

"Yes?" she answered, calming her voice, recognizing the voice of the foreigner's groom. "Yes?" The boy trotted up the staircase. When he knocked on the door, she pushed herself to her feet and moved away from the bed. "What is it? What do you want?" All the muscles of her torso ached and clenched, sending tremors through her.

"*Menyw,*" he began but had no words in her language to explain. "Commander deFreveille."

She cringed at the name but stepped closer to the door.

"*Menyw,*" he said, "The commander has ordered that I stay with you. All day."

Gwennan detected a note of displeasure in his young voice and remained silent.

"I have your breakfast, *menyw.*" When she did not respond, he left the tray on the narrow landing, clattering the dishes to alert her.

As soon as he returned to the lower hall, Gwennan opened the door a crack and dragged the tray toward her. She took the breakfast of *uwd*, apples and walnuts to the stool by the hearth. Smiling at the halved walnuts, she spooned the *uwd* into her mouth while she considered her plan. Before she went to the dormitory to examine the damage Ieuan Emyr had shown her, she ate every morsel and put the walnut shells in a row on the mantle. *You are a fool if you think he will not retaliate,* she warned her reflection. She pressed a cold cloth to her face, loosened her hair to conceal the damage and bound her injured ribs.

She hid the *gelyn* commander's blood-stained clothing and emptied the tub down the drain hole in the corner of the dormitory. When her father's grandparents had built the stone house, it offered a natural defense. A steep hill rose on three sides, dropping sharply on the fourth into the gorge. Gwennan was proud to return to her great-grandparents' home. She didn't ask her father for her mother's tapestries, cushions and *carthen*. She did not live in the house as a wife.

At the end of the afternoon, she emerged from her room and was surprised to see Artur at the table, studying sheaves of small quires. The groom jumped to his feet when the door opened. With a slight frown, he came to the bottom of the staircase and bowed. "*Menyw.*"

Gwennan inclined her head in greeting and walked to the table to look at the sheaves. "What is this? You can read?" she asked, picking up the palm-sized vellum sheaves and turning back to the first, hand-written one. "And write? What is this? I have never seen this."

Artur shrugged.

She turned another sheaf but the words were in an unfamiliar language and she closed the leather cover. "You are *ysgolor*," she said. "A scholar?"

Artur's brow furrowed for a moment and his face brightened. "Yes," he replied with a broad smile. "I understand. Scholar, *ysgolor*," he repeated, continuing in his clerical Latin. "We have traveled very far in five years and I make these—."

"Slow," she laughed. "I am *not* a scholar!"

Artur took a deep breath and continued at a pace she could follow, stopping to explain a word or phrase. "I make these notes of what I have seen. Maides made this codex for me from waste quires he couldn't use. I had no reading or writing at first but Commander deFreveille and Maides have taught me. And I have some schooling with monks. These are not very good. I do not understand everything I see."

"You are his foster son?"

"Pardon? What is 'foster'?"

"Your parents have paid deFreveille to train you?"

"No, my parents are dead. The commander is my employer—he pays me," the boy laughed, "when he can."

Gwennan smiled at him for a moment, storing the fragments of information he gave her. "What does your writing say about this place?" Artur blushed and looked at the table. "You don't have to tell me. What do you write about your home?"

"I can remember what I wrote even now." When Gwennan encouraged him, even at the slow pace he was forced to go, Artur sat by her at the table and began. "My house was very small, on the estate deFreveille. The father of my employer, Emíl deFreveille, he was there and his wife. We lived very well until I was eight years old and my father was ill. The doctor would not come."

"Why?"

"He would not be paid so my father died. My mother was very sad. Very angry with the master, the father of deFreveille. She told him she would leave and he told her to go. On the day that my mother finished packing all of our possessions, the master was dead. His wife was distraught and my mother stayed to help her. My house was empty. The servants had all gone from the master's house and stolen many things. Commander deFreveille came but there was nothing he could do. Everything was gone." The boy stopped for a moment to catch his breath. "The bailiffs had come to take the estate to pay the master's debts, even his wife's dresses. Commander deFreveille was very angry."

"Why was he angry?" Gwennan asked, loosening the black and gray shawl around her shoulders.

"His mother died that night, like his father. The commander's wife was also very angry, when he told her everything was gone."

"Perhaps, you should not be telling me this," Gwennan murmured in her own language.

"Pardon, *menyw?*"

"Nothing," she said. "I did not mean to interrupt you." If the foreigner did not want her to know his private affairs, he should not have sent an intelligent, talkative boy to keep her company.

"After that, we had no place to live. When my mother died, Commander deFreveille's wife—Helene—told him to put me with the monks but he had no money to pay them, so I stayed. And Commander Maides stayed, of course. Everyone else, all his friends, gone."

"Maides is also an employee?"

"No, they are friends, like brothers, from very young. There is nothing they will not do for one another. Even when Commander deFreveille was very wild and killed that man, Maides protected him from the man's family and saved his life many times. The commander has done the same for Maides. Like this," he said, clasping his hands together hard.

"Who was this man he killed?"

"The lover of his wife," Artur murmured, turning red. "*I should not tell you,*" he gasped. "*I—. This is bad,*" he cried, leaping up from the bench and pointing a finger at her. "*You are bad.*"

Gwennan understood his exclamation. He blamed her for his indiscretions. She looked away for a moment. "I'm sorry, Artur," she said as he grabbed his little codex from the table and tied its leather cord with such force it snapped.

"That was not fair," he complained as he threw himself against the stone wall of the staircase and slumped to the floor to glare at her. "Not fair," he repeated in Latin.

Gwennan bit her lip. "*Mia culpa.*"

"What have you done?" Jehan-Emíl asked from the doorway of the house. He glanced from one to the other as Artur jumped to his feet.

"I have—," Artur began and hung his head.

"I am to blame," Gwennan said, also on her feet. "I am to blame." She strode to the hearth and glared into the low burning embers. Courage deserted her.

The foreigner frowned in Artur's direction but followed Gwennan. "What?" he asked quietly. "What, Gwennan?" When he tried to make her look at him, she resisted so forcefully that he let her go, opening his arms wide. She sank to the chair and kept her face averted. "What happened?" he asked of Artur. "What is all this *culpa* and these tears?"

Artur hung his head for a moment. "I have been very foolish, sir. She asked me about my home. I told her too much...about you."

Jehan-Emíl was silent for a long time. Gwennan glanced from master to groom. Artur was watching deFreveille from under his lowered brow, his unkempt, sandy hair like a curtain. His employer was staring at the floor, a fire iron gripped in his hand. He raised it for a moment to look at it and gripped the head in his other hand. Gwennan straightened her back and stood, throwing off the hindrance of the shawl.

"This is not Artur's fault," she said. Her courage had not returned but her duty to justice took its place.

The foreigner turned his head to look at her, letting the iron swing from his hand. He turned his attention to Artur. "Thank you for telling me," he said to his groom. "Go to the hall and have your meal. After, bring back a good meal for this woman and for me."

"Yes, sir."

"Artur. No more tales of home."

"Yes, sir." The boy ran from the house. Gwennan watched him go, her lips pressed hard together.

"Now, Gwennan," Jehan-Emíl said, turning on her. "You are smart, I think. Too smart for boys." He hung the fire iron from its hook beneath the mantle and sat, straddling the bench, bracing his hands on his knees. "I have had a very good day, so far, Gwennan. I think you have as well," he commented, peering at her around the fall of her hair. He spoke to her at a pace she could not begin to decipher even the simplest of words that she might have recognized from their similarity to her language or to their distant Latin origins. That he had forestalled beating her with the iron gave her little comfort. She stood in front of him, expectant, and when he invited her to sit with him on the bench, she moved further away. He shrugged.

"I have been looking at this place," he said with a yawn and stretched the muscles of his arms and shoulders. "I have to admit that I have begun to call this my home. From the wall, I have scanned the whole stretch of land for any suitable spot to build another, better house but there is no place in the landscape, in any direction. I will ask Maides to work miracles where my house now stands. This is inconvenient, especially for you, Gwennan, but there is nothing I can do. You will stay here, of course, and when my children arrive, they will live here also." He raised his eyes to her face, cocked his head at her and smiled. "Maides has assured me that he can turn this dereliction into a fit place for a man to live," he told her. "He has drawn plans for the house and says the outer walls will be strengthened soon."

Since he made no effort to speak so that she understood him, Gwennan listened to the sound of his voice, thinking how strange it was that they had begun the day in the way of other people—bathing, dressing, planning. Now, at the end of a day, he seemed to tell her what he had done while he was away from her. She placed her hand on the mantle and stared into the grate, watching the embers spark life into flames that struggled to catch in the green wood from the woodlands he— her enemy—was cutting down to rebuild what he had destroyed.

"So," he sighed, "our knowledge of one another's misfortunes is equal. This is not a good thing but perhaps you will understand better what drives me." He rubbed his thighs for a moment. "Tomorrow, I will let you tend to your wounded. More live than have died but graves have already been dug…where they will not be a reminder. I will find a way of uniting your people with my own. I will include you in my plans, in some way. I accept my responsibility for the deaths of your friends," he said, examining the stitching on his chest, "but you will see how I rebuild—life will be better."

"I want you to understand," Gwennan said, "that I have spent the day plotting against you." Though he peered at her steadily, he understood her words no better than she had understood his.

Five

"I like the way you have left your hair," he said, "soft, like you. Is it to please me or to hide what this man—whoever he is—has done to you?" He rose to his feet, running his hand over the front of his tunic. "I wanted to thank you for the loan of these clothes. The warrior for whom you made them is a fortunate man."

Gwennan turned her face toward him, wondering what his purpose was in allowing her to understand these of all the words he had spoken.

He took a step toward her, continuing in the *gelyn's* flat words. "Is he alive, Gwennan? Did you love him?"

Gwennan looked at him for a long moment. The clothes fit him well, as if they had been made for him. The color of the tunic—a dye she had mixed herself to turn the wool the color of spruce—suited him. The length of the linen shirt sleeves with their delicate chained embroidery was the exact length of his arms and rested on his wrists as though she had measured him. The *trwsus* sheathed his muscular thighs as well as a pair of fine gloves. The skill and artistry of the embroiderer was an expression of love for a man she had once thought to wed. *Had.* As she studied the foreigner, she realized her life had changed forever, whether Derwyn was alive or dead. Adding to her confusion, he wore Derwyn's smaller dagger in his wide leather belt, next to his own, a reminder of her choice to live.

"Who is the man for whom you made these clothes, Gwennan?" he asked, laying his hands on her shoulders, peering into her eyes. "We have a register of the dead," he continued, staring hard into her hazel eyes. "If his name is there, perhaps you will regret allowing me to wear his clothes."

She met his gaze with a blank stare.

"Did your husband know you had a lover?"

Gwennan glanced away for a moment, reminding herself of the information that Artur had given her. His tone told her what his words did not. *This man is jealous.* She met his gaze again. *Never let him know you understand.*

DeFreveille grasped her arms at the elbows and pulled her toward him. "Do not think that knowing one thing," he said, "means you know all." She held her breath as he kissed her temple. "I have never been generous. Helene complained of it." He traced the curve of her cheek. "I am man enough for you," he whispered, capturing her mouth. His arms slid around her waist. "I am more man than you have ever had, Gwennan. You will not want this lover again once you have tasted love in my arms." He loosened the cord at the neck of her frock and traced his fingers along the edge of the opening until they reached the swell of her breast. His mouth followed the path of his fingertips. Sliding his hand over her hip, he gathered the heavy fabric of her gown, caressing her thigh.

"No." Her voice trembled. She pushed hard against his shoulders but his blood was surging through his body and his breathing was ragged as he held her against him. Lust swelled in his groin. "No."

"Gwennan."

DeFreveille raised his head, staring into his captive's clear eyes. Gwennan turned her face toward the speaker. The foreigner clenched his arms around her waist and straightened his back, keeping her hard against him while he glared at the golden-haired woman standing in the doorway of the kitchen.

Siriol ran to the hearth and threatened him with the fire iron. When she struck at him, the foreigner caught the iron in midflight and held it high above her head until she released her hold.

"Who is this woman, Gwennan?" he asked, grinning.

"Siriol, what are you doing here?" she demanded, a frown creasing her brow.

"I came to help you," Siriol answered. "What has he done to you?"

"Nothing. I'm all right," Gwennan said, pushing at the foreigner's shoulders again.

He tightened his grip and, after a moment, he frowned and turned her in his arms to face the blonde woman, keeping his arm around her waist, relieving the pressure on her ribcage. Gwennan felt his blood cooling and bowed her head for a moment to conceal her amusement.

"Oswin told us this animal was in the house last night. Blessed God, look what he's done to you," she exclaimed, reaching to touch Gwennan's cheek. Before she could, deFreveille held up his hand to warn her away. Gwennan turned the bruised side of her face away from her friend.

"It's not what you think," she said, pushing his arm away from her when the pressure hurt her. He loosened his grip and stepped back when Artur entered the house with their meal. "Why have you come, Siriol?" Gwennan asked, laying her hands on her friend's arms. "You were all safe where you were. Now, he knows you are here."

"Have you seen Pendryw, Tudwal? Are they alive?" Siriol asked under her breath, searching Gwennan's face. "Does Derwyn know what has happened to you?"

"If Derwyn is alive, he knows where I am," Gwennan replied. The foreigner's presence near her was a comfort. "I will find him."

As she spoke, Aine, Menna and Branwen crowded into the doorway between the kitchen and the lower hall. They craned their necks around one another to stare at the foreign commander. When deFreveille moved away, Gwennan watched him out of the corner of her eye as he sat in the chair by the hearth and rested his chin on his fist. While he studied the group of women and three children with them, he began to smile. When his smile became a laugh, Gwennan turned her face toward the hearth, forcing her lips into a straight line before she turned a severe glare on her friends.

"You have been foolish," she accused them under her breath.

"Gwennan," he said when his laughed quieted. Gwennan glanced over her shoulder as he made a gesture toward the women.

"These are the wives of my warriors," she answered.

Jehan-Emíl frowned at the women for several moments and spoke to Artur. The groom ran from the house and, while he was gone, the commander helped himself to more of Elgan's mead, still watching the group in the doorway. He held the jug by the neck, pouring the fragrant liquid into the cup and kept one eye on them. When Aine and Siriol moved toward the staircase, he said, "No, you will not," and continued speaking for several moments until he set the jug on the table. He made a sharp gesture away from the stairs and pointed to a place by the table.

"What does he mean?" Aine demanded under her breath.

"He means he will not allow you to go to my room."

"How dare he?" Siriol exclaimed, glaring at him.

"You allow him to command here?" Aine asked, her frown deepening.

Gwennan crossed the hall and laid her hand on her friend's arm and said, "For now, Aine, we are alone here. This man commands an army and we cannot fight him, yet."

"Tudwal will never allow this—."

"Aine," Gwennan peered into the older woman's eyes. "I am sorry…"

"No," Aine gasped. "No." Her knees collapsed from under her. Siriol and Gwennan helped her to sit on the floor and held her in their arms. Gwennan saw the commander lean forward in his chair, bowing his head for a moment. When he met her eyes, his earlier amusement was gone. Gwennan looked away, gathering her friend in her arms. When Ieuan Emyr's spoke again, he was talking to Maides.

"*Boneddiges*," the mercenary said to her, "Commander deFreveille wishes to express his condolences to you and this woman for the death of her husband. He regrets the loss of a brave warrior."

"He kills our husbands and you dare—," Branwen hissed at Gwennan.

Gwennan raised her hand in a sharp gesture. "You will not accuse me of any wrong without evidence. If you have complaint of my actions, you may present your case to the Adjudicator when he holds his next *llys*."

"Oh," Branwen scoffed, "as if your own father—."

"Be silent," Siriol snapped, pinching the woman's arm. "You forget what has happened and that Gwennan has faced these men alone—for your sake."

The commander spoke again to Maides. When Gwennan felt the raven-haired mercenary close to her, she turned her head and lifted her eyes to his icy blue gaze. Ieuan Emyr continued to speak but the mercenary, although attentive to the commander, kept his eyes on Gwennan's face.

"*Boneddiges*, I am instructed to take this woman to her husband. The other women and their children will be accommodated as necessary."

"Where is my husband?" Siriol asked him.

"And mine?" Branwen pleaded.

"If they live," Maides replied, "they are prisoners of war."

Siriol looked at Gwennan for the answer to her question.

"I did not see him, Siriol," she answered, "only Tudwal."

Maides crouched before Aine. "Come with me, *menyw*." He did not offer to help her to stand, turning on his heel to lead the way from the house, after another brief exchange with Jehan-Emíl. Siriol followed but when Gwennan also turned to go, the commander caught her arm and shook his head. Gwennan stared at his hand.

"Artur," deFreveille called and spoke rapidly to the boy.

"Your husband is not there," the young groom told her. "You will not go."

"Gwennan," Menna wailed, "what will happen to us?" She covered her face and sank to the floor.

"It is war, Menna," Gwennan said quietly. "Go to the kitchen and stay there."

The *gelyn* commander gave an order to his groom. The only woman remaining in the hall cowered in the alcove by the hearth with the three children. The *gelyn* commander glanced at Branwen and pointed toward the door of the kitchen. Without a pause, the four scurried out of his sight to join Menna.

"You do not command me," Gwennan said to Ieuan Emyr, a man worthy of her esteem whose presence in her house threatened all she trusted and held close to her heart, facing him squarely when he came to stand near her. "No one commands me. No one has ever commanded me. If there was ever a man who thought he did, that man was my father and he ceased to believe in his ability to control me long before I became a woman. You will cease even to consider the possibility soon. The only way to stop me is to kill me. If that is not yet clear to you, it will be."

During the time that she spoke, Ieuan Emyr watched her mouth for a few moments then allowed his gaze to drift from the top of her head, her face and over her body, coming to rest again on her mouth when she was silent. He lifted his hand and she allowed him to trace his fingers over the line of her jaw and to slide them into the loose plait at the nape of her neck. When he bowed his head to kiss her, Gwennan allowed him to hold her still for the purpose but when his lips grazed her mouth, she ripped herself away from him with enough force to convey her displeasure. Although he did not release her, the *gelyn* commander lifted his head and met her eyes.

"If, *if* I ever want you," Gwennan said, "you will know." She removed his hand, releasing it as she would an object that disgusted her and turned away from him. Over her shoulder, she said, "Elgan Maergwn was a violent drunkard. I never allowed him near me. I have never regretted that decision. I will not give myself up easily, Ieuan, and, in your case, never is more likely." He took a step toward her and she raised her hand to halt his movement without turning. "You have more need of me than I have of you, Ieuan Emyr," Gwennan warned him. "Since you already know this, we will, eventually, come to an arrangement—either you will go…or you will stay. Either will be my decision. But first," she concluded, turning toward him with a slight smile—a smile that brought a deeper frown to his already puzzled expression, "I shall know more about you." With a broad smile she darted through the *porth*.

"Gwennan," he bellowed, followed by a string of curses, as he ran after her but was too late to prevent her from descending into the turmoil.

She remained motionless for a moment as she surveyed the carnage before her eyes. The *buarth* was strewn with the bodies of wounded men from both armies. All the men looked the same, bloody, broken, in pain. Artur had run after her on Ieuan's shouted order. When she recovered with a cry and ran into the chaos, her heavy, buckled boots clattering on the planked walkways through the mud, the groom followed. Several of the women watched from a distance as she searched the face of one man after another, a few whispered, "Derwyn."

Aine knelt by Tudwal's body, weeping over him, bathing his face and preparing his body for burial. Branwen's husband, Iago, was able to sit, his back against the wall. Siriol's husband, Pendryw, was also alive. Others of her friends survived but she moved on, attracting the attention of the *meddyg*.

The small physician caught sight of her as he lifted his eyes from the face of a young boy soldier whom he had tended most of the night. He stood and walked toward her. The foreigner descended the hill and crossed the *buarth* with Maides.

"*Boneddiges,* these are all our own men," the physician, Rocaille, told her as he helped her to her feet. "Who is it you want?" The commander stood behind him.

"Derwyn," she whispered her call again. "Derwyn, my—. My—," she said, reluctant to finish with the commander glaring at her over the physician's head. "A tall man, with a black beard." Gwennan touched Rocaille's arm, her keen eyes sweeping across the bodies strewn on the ground around them.

"There is one like that over there, near the tannery. I have done what I can for him."

Gwennan had already spun away and ran in the direction he indicated. Though his hair and beard were matted with blood, his face bruised and swollen, Gwennan knew him. The cry of Gwennan's bereavement chilled the blood of the *gelyn* as she flung herself upon the body of the man she called friend. Lifting the bloody hand splayed across his chest, Gwennan's sorrow drowned all other sound. She held Derwyn's hand to her breast and cursed all who had struck him.

"What does the woman say, Rocaille?" deFreveille asked.

"Grief, Commander," the physician responded with a frown.

"My girl calls the wrath of all her family to the ninth cousin upon the men who have robbed her," the old woman hissed at their backs. Galar laid her stick on deFreveille's shoulder. Her hand trembled but her voice was steadied by the emotion behind it. "Beware the nights and the grief of my girl, warrior of Satan. What she cannot do, I will make sure of."

The three men watched the bent woman kneel by the side of the Celt warrior. Keeping his eyes on Gwennan, deFreveille raised his hand to his shoulder where the stick had touched him and moved the bone and muscle as though to relieve an ache.

"I have been insulted, doctor? Threatened?"

"Yes, Commander."

Gwennan sat with Derwyn, chafing his hands to warm them and washing away the blood from his hair and beard, soothing his handsome face. Galar held a bowl of water for her chick and, whenever it was passed to her, wrung the cloth in her withered hands. While the old nurse rinsed the cloth, Gwennan bent over the man and kissed his lips and forehead, smoothing his war braids free of debris, his head resting in her lap. Taking the cloth again, she prepared him for *Annwn*, her tears wetting his cheeks.

Jehan-Emíl moved closer to observe her lover—a man younger than himself, but handsome, as strongly built. "Rocaille, see that the woman does not grieve herself to death," he said over his shoulder and joined Maides at the gates. He rolled his shoulders and forced himself to turn his attention to other, more urgent matters. He took a last look at Gwennan mourning the man whose death was his responsibility and strode through the gates with Maides to the encampment. He stroked the fine needlework of the spruce-colored tunic with the flat of his whole hand. It was not the first time he had admired the needlework while he had worked with his friend that day, but it was the first time he lost his smile as he did so.

The physician drew a *carthen* over the young woman's shoulders and knelt beside her. Intent on her preparations, Gwennan did not notice him. Galar narrowed her eyes but said nothing. Rocaille stretched his hand over the warrior's chest and raised an eyebrow. Jumping to his feet, he moved to the other side so the women were not in his way. He listened to the man's heart and ran his pale, experienced hands along his arms and legs. Awakening to the *meddyg's* actions, Gwennan grabbed his hand.

"He lives?"

"Yes, *boneddiges,* but barely," Rocaille responded.

"Please, you must save him."

"We will take him to the infirmary. We will get these filthy rags off him and I can better see what I am doing." Rocaille called three soldiers to lift Derwyn onto a pallet.

"We will take him to my house," she commanded, shaking off her distress and helping Galar to her feet.

Rocaille frowned but when Gwennan attempted to lift the man herself, the physician ordered the soldiers to carry Derwyn to the house. When they reached the lower hall, his wounds had opened. The physician refused to let the soldiers carry him further. While Gwennan made him comfortable and Rocaille worked to save his life, the old nurse keened and beat her breast, hissing curses on the man she blamed for each wound inflicted on the body of her nephew. "For every bloody wound, the warrior of Satan will suffer defeat and misery. For every bruise on this saint's body, the warrior of Satan will lose his dearest wish until he begs to die. He will see his family slaughtered before his eyes. The man who struck this boy will fear the coming of every day as each misery piles upon the former."

Staunching his wounds was their first task but for a man who had lost so much blood and lain without help, Rocaille thought him robust. He said nothing to the women but he had few doubts about the man's life—his will had kept him alive. Gazing at the face of the woman who tended him, the physician did not wonder at the warrior's desire to survive.

"What is wrong? Why do you shake your head? Is he worse?"

"No, it is nothing. This man will live. He has a strong will to do so and I cannot blame him, *boneddiges*. A man who has the love of a faithful woman—."

Gwennan stopped him with a hand held before the foreigner *meddyg's* face. "He lives because he is strong."

"Yes, he is strong, *boneddiges*. But even strong men can wish for death, many times."

"Derwyn Blaenant will live because he wills it. And he will kill the man who has done this to him," she murmured, "or he will be killed. Either way, *meddyg*, the loss will be great and war will never cease."

"*Boneddiges*, if I can—."

Again, Gwennan stilled his voice, gazing into his deep brown eyes. "You are kind," she murmured, but could not reveal her thoughts to him. "I will need your friendship."

"Anything," the small physician offered, clenching his jaw as he glanced at her bruised cheek. "I am your servant."

Ruth did not speak as Alrick yanked her after him into his tent. "I am not an animal to take a woman for all to see," he told her. She did not understand what he was saying but she understood what he intended to happen to her. She lunged for his dagger but he prevented her from laying her hands on it and was fatigued by the battle before he won. He lay on his back after she had run from the tent, savoring his triumph. Before he had taken a long breath, he was kicked from the cot and stared into Maides's dark, icy grin.

"Have you come to share my victory?" Alrick grinned back at his comrade.

"Your victory is short-lived, Alrick. Your spoil has run to complain to her friends."

Alrick shrugged. "What can they do to me?" Behind the mercenary, the *gelyn* captain saw that Maides had brought with him six of his own command, all men with whom, in the recent past, he had shared the rewards of victory. They were not grinning. With a single gesture from the dark one, they dragged Alrick to the common hall where deFreveille was already hearing accusations against him.

Alrick straightened his back and shook his hair from his eyes. The woman was not in the hall but two Gaer warriors spoke through the physician, Paul Rocaille, in Maides's absence. Alrick did not hear any word that was not the truth of his action. He grinned at his fellow warriors.

Pendryw, the taller of the two Cymry, stepped forward. "Rape is a crime that demands reparation," he declared. "In our country, we do not punish the woman for the crime committed against her as the *gelyn* do. She is not beaten or driven away or blamed for a man's violence against her."

"This is war," Alrick hissed before deFreveille gestured for him to be silenced.

"What reparation is fitting?" deFreveille queried, studying the two men who had made the complaint—at risk to themselves and with no assurance of justice for the woman. He was responsible for putting the women in the way of his second captain, deFreveille had an obligation to meet the Cymry's demands, though he had nothing of value that would come near what he believed they would expect. And if the woman was impregnated—, deFreveille let the unwelcome thought fade from his mind. They had no expectation of justice from a man who had, as they thought, taken Pendyffryn's daughter in the same manner as Alrick had taken this woman. DeFreveille's innocence was only a matter of degree—his intent had been the same as Alrick's. For a moment, he wondered why no one had spoken of reparation for Gwennan.

"You do not deny that you took this woman against her will?" deFreveille demanded of his captain.

"I took her as my reward for victory," Alrick replied.

"Then you have had your reward."

Alrick's smile at his commander's pronouncement was broad and met with the grins of the *gelyn* army crowded into the common hall to see their commander punish the Cymry for their audacity.

"For disobeying my order," deFreveille continued, "you will receive fifty lashes and a fortnight at labor under Commander Maides."

A low hiss broke the tension in the hall.

"For breaking the law of *this* land, you will pay reparation according to Welsh custom to the woman and her kindred."

Pendryw smiled and Iago Brynteg bowed his head but did not conceal his wide grin. Maides clamped his hand on Alrick's shoulder as the fair-haired captain's knees buckled. He ripped away and lunged at his commander.

"Who will give *you* the lash, Freveille?" Alrick hissed. A simple, dismissive gesture was the only answer he received as deFreveille rose from his chair at the center of the table and motioned for his third captain, Wode, to follow him.

Exacting a price for their victory from the vanquished was their due—the price of failure that the womenfolk of the Gaer warriors were expected to pay. Though only Alrick had disobeyed his orders, deFreveille's decision to punish him was unpopular among the highborn *gelyn* warriors and they resented the separate rule that the foreign commander had made for himself. His friends and the soldiers he commanded accepted the difference as his due. He glanced at the house above the stockade with some guilt in his smile. His innocence was irrelevant—and temporary.

Wode stood at his commanding officer's shoulder with his back straight and his hands clasped behind him, fixing his eyes on the scene that Jehan-Emíl deFreveille also observed. The other surviving warriors were carried into the infirmary tents, erected in the encampment for the wounded of both armies. Menna and Branwen appeared in the *buarth* with the two-year-old Pedr *mab* Iago and Siriol's children, hungry and frightened. The judgment against Alrick gave the women of the Gaer liberty to continue their work unmolested.

When his work was done for the day and the din of the common hall and *buarth* were disagreeable, the commander climbed to the house. In the hall, Rocaille had returned to tend Derwyn Blaenant with both Gwennan and the old woman quick to do his bidding. Gwennan bathed her lover. DeFreveille did not need to exercise his imagination to guess how the Welshman had come to be in his house and not in the infirmary as he ordered. Her hands caressed the younger man's body with tenderness.

The man she loved was his junior by perhaps six or seven years. He was fit, well-formed and handsome. He had not yet seen much of war though Maides had said the young warrior was bold, fearless in battle. Except for the wounds inflicted by deFreveille's men, the Welshman's body was much less scarred than his own. The fearsome blue, green and red paintings of wild animals were smeared. Wherever his wounds, the paintings had been washed away, leaving dismembered heads and limbs on his torso and back. Though deFreveille made a ritual of blocking the memories of his battles once they were over, he recalled the Welshman as the Gaer warriors hurtled from the gates in their surprise assault. He was a natural leader and making a friend of him—if the man loved Gwennan as much as he was loved—required more thought than deFreveille was prepared to give at that moment.

He washed his hands and face at the table, beckoning Gwennan and the old woman to come to him. He was not surprised that the old woman shunned him nor that Gwennan complied, though her attention was fixed on the physician's work and her lover's face. "This evening," deFreveille murmured, "I will forgive this display of devotion to one of your warriors. Later, tomorrow and every day after, will be different, woman."

Gwennan did not bother to turn her head to look at him or attempt to decipher by his expression what he might mean. As a matter of defiance, she rejected his language and deliberately turned her cheek away from him when he raised his hand to brush a stray wisp of her hair back to its place.

"We are not friends as yet, woman, but that will change," deFreveille laughed softly as he turned his head to speak for some time to Maides. As the mercenary translated to her, the *gelyn* studied her face.

"That is within the law," Gwennan replied when Maides explained deFreveille's decision to punish Alrick for his assault on one of her women. As the dark mercenary interpreted her answer to the foreign commander, deFreveille frowned, clenching his jaw and spoke at length to his friend. "Why do you look at me like that?" she demanded of Ieuan Emyr.

"DeFreveille wants to know if you think he is a fool."

Gwennan's bitter laugh filled the lower hall. DeFreveille's frown deepened for a moment—she had not given the angry response to his crimes against her for which he had prepared and he suspected a trick—but the sound of laughter, even derisive, forced his scowl to crack.

"That I think he *is* a fool is not in question," Gwennan said to Maides, when she had recovered enough to speak. "Though I would like it better if the animal was put down, the fact your commander has punished him at all is of some comfort but will never be reparation enough for Ruth's suffering." Gwennan glanced away, her expression once again revealing her distress under the weight of her responsibilities. The laws of her country did not favor a woman who accused a man without witnesses. Ruth had called on no one to help her. Since it was a matter of the *gelyn* captain's word against hers, the judgment of law could have fallen on the side of the *gelyn*, despite the complaint brought against him by Pendryw and Iago Brynteg—both had accepted Ruth's word without evidence.

"DeFreveille wants you to know that he will punish the man and ensure that he makes recompense according to your custom. Alrick does not deny his guilt, *boneddiges*, and he disobeyed orders. DeFreveille had commanded that the women were not to be molested."

Gwennan bit her lip for a moment. When she turned her narrowed eyes on Ieuan Emyr, she met his gaze steadily as she said, "I will convey this news to Ruth. She will rejoice, I'm sure, at the *gelyn* commander's fine sense of equality in justice."

DeFreveille did not take his eyes from her face as Maides told him what she had said. For a moment, he didn't understand but his eyes narrowed though he did not drop his gaze or bow his head in any admission of his guilt toward her. Excusing herself from their company at the table, Gwennan returned to her lover. Waging a campaign against men intent on the destruction of all she valued was more difficult than expressing her ideas to her father's bored and indulgent friends. Protecting her people from violent men was more difficult than managing a neglected farm.

At the end of the evening, deFreveille rose from his chair. The fire had gone to coals and he sent Artur to put more logs on the hearth while he went himself to see how the Celt responded to the care he received. The old woman slept in a heap in a corner. Gwennan rested at Derwyn's feet, her head and shoulders leaning against the alcove wall, her eyes turned with dull fascination on Derwyn's motionless body. DeFreveille stepped closer to lift her into his arms but the physician restrained him with a hand on his sleeve.

"Commander, this woman needs rest. Leave her to me, she's no use to you dead and she will be that if she isn't given an opportunity to heal."

"What is wrong, Rocaille?"

"You would know better than I," the physician replied, his expression angry and unguarded. "She is feverish."

"Then she is better in a bed," deFreveille said, shrugging off Rocaille's hand. "What of the warrior?"

"You can see for yourself, Commander. He will live if we keep him quiet. His wounds are mending and he is strong," Rocaille replied.

"What more will you do tonight?"

"He will sleep and I will see how he fares in the morning," the physician replied.

"Then go to your other patients or to bed." DeFreveille ignored Rocaille's warning and lifted Gwennan. The physician stood to protest. "I am responsible for the woman, Paul. Whatever she needs, I will provide." She showed no sign of the spirit that had challenged him earlier. "See to the warrior. Tomorrow, move him to the infirmary with the others."

The commander turned on his heel to mount the staircase. His actions brought shame on her in the eyes of her friends. Their unforgiving hearts were plain when he met them earlier that day. Their hatred for him was obvious but they also cast blame on her. Although he was innocent of an assault, she was entitled to complain of his intrusion in her home—but she did not. The man that deFreveille assumed to be her lover was in the hall below. She was in his arms and he was as hungry for her as he had been the previous night. He unbuckled her shoes and put them by the fire, dragged the thick woolen gown free of her body, leaving the linen frock and delicate chemise.

Draping her with the *carthen*, he built the small fire until it roared. After he had undressed, folding the clothes, he stood by the blaze to warm his skin. Laying his hand on the mantle, he knocked one of the walnut shells to the floor. Jehan-Emíl picked it up, found its mate and held them together again in the palm of his hand. A slow smile crossed his features as he lay down beside her. He yawned, settling his weary body against her and slept untroubled.

six

Rising in the morning before his companion, Jehan-Emíl washed in the cold water of the bucket, dressed in the clothes Gwennan had made for her lover and went down to the hall to see how the warrior had fared during the night. He woke Artur with a pat on his fuzzy cheek, sending the boy to the larder in the common hall to get breakfast for the household while he rebuilt the fire in the hearth. When the old woman awoke, he was decanting ale he had found in one of the many nooks in the walls of the house. The unbending of her withered frame was painful to watch. He poured her a cup of the drink, handing it to her when she became aware of him.

"You!" she spat. "Been at my girl again, have you? I tell you to leave her be. She will never be for you."

"What do you say, old woman?" he asked, smiling. Not for a moment did he think that the old woman was exchanging pleasantries but his mood allowed him to express his natural generosity despite his denial of the characteristic. "Good morning, old mother." He bowed and saluted her with his own cup. The old woman refused to drink with him but drank the ale when he looked away.

Artur returned, carrying a large platter of bread, meat and apples, set it on the table and ran back to bring more. On his second trip, he informed his commander that Maides requested to speak with him but would wait until the commander joined him in the common hall.

The old woman had helped herself to bread and was struggling to cut an apple. Jehan-Emíl extended his own dagger to her, assuring her that the edge was sharp enough for any work she had in mind. He examined her knife and gave it to Artur. "See that this is honed well so that the old woman will not be inconvenienced again."

He sat on the bench beside Galar, with his back to the table so that he could watch the warrior as well as the staircase. The old woman's sudden screech caused him no concern though he looked at her in mock surprise.

"You have stolen it." Galar grabbed for her nephew's small dagger in the *gelyn's* belt but deFreveille covered the hilt with his hand. "I knew she would not choose to live after what you have done to her. You have robbed her of her honor. There is only one course that will restore her name to her father's esteem and Galar must do this, for her chick."

When the door to the chamber rasped open on its hinges, the old woman stabbed his dagger into the table with all her might.

"Touch Galar's girl again and you will die by this!"

Working the blade free, he wiped it clean on the heel of his hand and grinned at her before turning his head to watch Gwennan descend the staircase to him. When she stepped onto the landing at the head of the staircase, her eyes sought him, not the warrior. Her eyes followed him as he crossed the stone floor to greet her. Only once did she take her eyes from his face, to look over his shoulder at the old woman. When she had reached the bottom step, resting her hand against the wall to steady herself, deFreveille offered his hand to her but, after another glance at the old woman, she ignored his offer.

Gwennan took a deep breath and walked slowly past him to sit at the knees of the crone and lay her head in the rough skirts, accepting the caresses of withered hands. Though she meant to resist, she looked for Ieuan Emyr in the hall from beneath her lashes, allowing Galar to pet and soothe her, combing fingers through her thick hair and plaiting it into a single cord before she even looked at Derwyn. DeFreveille had turned as she walked past and watched her with Galar, his curly head cocked as if he tried to understand their conversation.

"What does this dog do to you at night that you cannot take your eyes from him in the morning?" Galar demanded though her tone was soft and appeasing. "Does he live here now? Do you allow him the part of *pennaeth* in your house. Does this dog rule here now? Have you abandoned your hope of being Derwyn's wife and returning to your home because of what this one has done to you?"

"No." *I am mad with grief. I am a coward.*

"Why do you not kill him in his sleep? You have the means. There is no other way for you, *blodyn*. You must kill him."

At Derwyn's first stirring, Gwennan rose and went to him. She pressed a damp cloth to his forehead. He opened his eyes for a moment, lifted his hand from the pallet but could do no more.

"Quiet, Derwyn, you must rest."

"Lost," he moaned.

"We are alive," she replied and leaned her cheek against his. Still groggy, she remembered falling asleep at Derwyn's feet but she could not remember waking to go to her bed. She had not slept alone but there was no sign of the foreigner in the room or in the children's chamber beyond. Turning onto her back to face the room, she had been disappointed that Ieuan was not waiting for her to wake.

Lying in the warmth of her bed, she had called into her mind the feel of his body—so hard and unyielding that she could not have left any mark on him in the way his arms and legs marked her wherever they had held her through the night. His scent was everywhere on her body and she drew deep breaths to take this small part of him into her. She stared at the empty place in the bed where he had slept, alarmed by her thoughts of him.

When she had opened the door, saw that he waited for her and that Galar was in the hall, her alarm turned to shame. This man, for whose touch her body ached, had allowed one of her women to be ruined, yet she could not take her eyes from his face. Though Derwyn lay at the hearth, alive, she was proud and reckless with Ieuan Emyr's eyes on her, eager to make love with him. He offered his hand. Every fiber in her body reached toward him.

She could not recall an ache to be near Derwyn. The moment she was assured of his safety, a deep loneliness overwhelmed her. Derwyn was alive and yet her eyes searched the hall for Ieuan. He lounged at the far side of the hearth at the table, his head bowed. *What troubles him* ? A fierce blush took her breath away. Galar was right. He did act the part of *pennaeth* in her house but not with arrogance. He was confident and his confidence strengthened her. If Galar had not beckoned, she would have taken the hand he offered to her at the foot of the stairs and hastened into his embrace, regardless of consequences.

She clung instead, chastised, first to Galar because the old nurse was the only mother she had ever known, and then to Derwyn because her father had sent him to her. The *gelyn* commander was not worthy—would never be worthy in her father's eyes—but the feel of his hand on her cheek, his body seeking her embrace, his lips on her skin were more pleasant than anything she had ever experienced or known was possible to feel for a man. Her mother had felt the same for her father, had given her life for *her* life and for love of Daran Pendyffryn. Cerith Gernant would understand why her daughter contemplated betraying all she had ever known.

"Gwennan?" Once more, Derwyn attempted to raise his hand from the pallet.

She tore her eyes away from Ieuan Emyr and leaned toward Derwyn, covering his bruised fingers and lowering her head to kiss his forehead. His shoulder and arm were bandaged. He had defended himself against blows that tore his flesh and might have been, for a weaker man, fatal. He would mend and be fit before winter. His first thought would be to kill the man who had defeated him.

Raising her free hand, Gwennan brushed the heavy dark locks of hair from his forehead, smoothed his beard and fought to keep from imagining his hair was shorter, of a warmer hue, had more curls. She wished him beardless and his jaw harder; his face less handsome, but kinder. The two were near in size and strength. The foreigner made her tremble. There was no hunger or warmth in Derwyn's eyes. Her concern, sorrow for his pain were no less than for the others who were wounded, as friends, as brothers, and no more. "Hush, Derwyn. You must rest."

Rocaille stood in the doorway at the entrance to the house and asked deFreveille's permission to enter. The commander nodded his ascent. He had finished his breakfast but sat on the bench, idly slicing an apple in thin wedges. He laid each slice on his tongue, letting the juice trickle down his throat before he swallowed the flesh. The old woman stayed by him, her faded eyes flicking from his profile to the couple near the hearth but she did not pester deFreveille with her threats. From the corner of his eye, he could see her expression waver between satisfaction and puzzlement. His own attention was more often fixed on Gwennan.

"You see, Rocaille, both have survived the night in my care," deFreveille commented, seething with anger. "Even this old woman lives one more day."

"I see, Commander." Rocaille bowed. "May I attend the Celt?"

DeFreveille granted the request with a nod and returned his dagger to his belt. He poured another cup of ale and pushed it into the hands of the old woman. She pushed it back. "For the woman, old mother," he said, "Gwennan," gesturing for her to take the cup. "For Gwennan."

"Galar does not like that you are attentive to this girl. She does not like that you are so confident, so deep," the old woman complained to him. "She hates that you have no fear Gwennan will leave you." Under her breath, she said, "Galar is stronger than you. Galar will do what must be done."

DeFreveille listened to her voice, half his attention on the lovers at the hearth and his physician. "I do not fear this boy," he told the old woman. "He is no threat to me." He leaned forward, resting his arms on his knees and looked back at her over his shoulder. No one in the room but Artur and Rocaille could understand him and their opinions were unimportant. His smile was broad when he said, "Forget your plans for Gwennan, old woman. I have my own and she will accept them."

"Galar reads your eyes, *gelyn*. You think you will have all that is not yours but you are wrong. You will die here, alone and cursed by Derwyn Blaenant for your crimes." Galar tossed the drink back into the jug and, with shaking hands, poured a cup for Gwennan. DeFreveille laughed at her defiance and shrugged. As Galar carried the ale to Gwennan, he stacked a small platter with slices of bread, cold meat, an apple and a handful of walnuts he split for her. Calling Artur to him, he gestured for the boy to take the platter to Gwennan and was satisfied that she accepted it from his groom. She laid the platter in her lap and ate while she watched the physician at his work.

Galar thrust the ale into Gwennan's grasp, urging her to drink deep. "This will do. This will do."

Two women burst into the hall but stopped when they saw deFreveille. "What do you want?" Jehan-Emíl demanded of Branwen and Menna. "Why have you come?"

Gwennan jumped at the sound of his anger, the contents of her platter tumbling into the ashes. As the women backed to the doorway, she stretched her hand into the hearth to retrieve her breakfast.

"Leave it!" DeFreveille sent the bench flying as he leapt to prevent her from putting her hand in the embers. Gwennan threw her arm over her face as he grabbed her wrist and yanked her away from the fire.

"Commander!" Rocaille cried, leaping to his feet.

DeFreveille ignored them all as he examined each of her fingers and turned her palm upwards in his own. He brushed the ashes from her fingertips, lifted her from her knees and pushed her toward the table. "Artur! Prepare another breakfast for this woman."

While the boy did his employer's bidding, deFreveille turned to face the physician. "I have told you, Rocaille, the woman is my responsibility, not your concern. See to this warrior. Get him out of my house. And tell those women they must seek permission to enter." When he was satisfied that Rocaille acted on his orders, deFreveille directed Gwennan to sit at the table while he retrieved her platter and the food that had fallen into the ashes of the hearth. "Artur, deal with this, if you will," deFreveille said, thrusting the gray heap at him.

Though Rocaille had told them what they must do, Branwen and Menna stood, their mouths agape, still staring at their *pennaeth* and at the *gelyn* commander. Finally, the youngest one cleared her throat. Gwennan looked up at her.

"We came to see Derwyn, *boneddiges*," Menna said and took a step forward with Branwen into the hall.

"Physician, did you not tell them what I expect?" he demanded.

"Commander deFreveille requests that you show proper respect for his house. You may not enter without his permission."

Both women were silent when they curtsied to him, their eyes wide with fear. DeFreveille decided to be generous once more and accepted the curtsies as fulfillment of his requirements. He beckoned them forward but did not allow Gwennan to join them at the warrior's side, gesturing for her to eat her breakfast.

"All the men are improving, Gwennan," Branwen whispered behind her cupped hand. "The *meddyg* has been kind." She glanced at her companion who had knelt beside Derwyn and was holding his hand. "We thought Derwyn had died when he was not brought to the infirmary with the others."

"He has not and will not," Gwennan said. "You can see for yourself." She pushed deFreveille's hand from her shoulder and knelt on the other side of the warrior. "Derwyn cannot be killed by men like these." The youngest one looked down on the dark face of the Celt and her eyes filled with tears. "Tears will not help him, Menna," Gwennan warned and urged Branwen to take the girl away. "And remember you must ask permission to enter this house again."

Gwennan fell back on her heels when they had gone and covered her face with her hands, ashamed of the outburst that had prompted her to accept Ieuan's rule. *I am still mad, but this is not grief. Why am I jealous?* Gwennan dropped her hands into her lap. The answer to her question was in Derwyn's eyes, in Elgan's indifference, in her father's reason for rejecting every suitor. *Ieuan Emyr is like these others.* Once he understood she was the warrior whose battle plan he admired, once he knew she was the tactician, once he knew she had aimed the arrow meant to kill him, she had no hope of love. *How can it be that I want him?*

Jehan-Emíl did not need the physician's help to interpret the words spoken during the scene before him to understand the warrior had won the heart of more than one woman in the place and there was jealousy between them. "Rocaille, the sooner this warrior is moved to the infirmary, the better," he growled. "I will have my house in order without these intrusions. You understand? Today."

Work progressed on the repair of the outer wall. Nothing could be done to replace the timber with stone until the spring. Even the strongest of his men could not dig enough in the quarry to rebuild the wall. They could not slaughter enough of the cattle to yield the offal for the mortar without risking starvation during the winter months.

Jehan-Emíl awaited word from his employer, Haelsted, whose campaign against the Welsh was eternal. He awaited the arrival of his children. He worked alongside his men to fell the forest so that it would offer less shelter to enemies so close to his home. The green timber was used to strengthen the towers, reinforce the walls, and provide shelter for his soldiers along the outside walls of the common hall. With the smaller branches, he ordered lean-tos to be built in the *buarth* to shelter the families who remained within the walls and to provide shelter for all who must come in, if the marauding bands reached them.

After another day of constant tending, the black-bearded Celt was still not fit to be moved and deFreveille began to suspect that the physician conspired to keep the man under his nose. He did not allow Gwennan to fall asleep another night by the warrior's pallet. He was enough enraged by her constant attention to the man during the day.

On the fourth morning, Gwennan awakened alone, dressed and felt disappointment when the only greeting for her at the bottom of the staircase was Galar's frowning, red-rimmed gaze. Shame filled her heart when disappointment was her response to seeing that the only man in the hall was Derwyn. She had fed, bathed and tended his wounds from morning to evening, willing him to improve. When Rocaille assured her that he was, she willed him to mend more quickly. Each day, she grew ever more groggy, struggling harder to keep her eyes open, to be wake when Ieuan Emyr joined her.

The night before, she was awake. He undressed by the fire, warming his body as before. His skin glowed in the ruddy light of the embers, his muscular torso defined against the dark stone wall. When he turned toward her, Gwennan held her breath. The line of hair that marked the center of his body drew her eyes to his dark loins. He did not bother to conceal from her, as he had from Siriol, the evidence of his lust. When he slid beneath the *carthen*, he met her gaze and said nothing when he pulled her against him, dropping his thigh over her legs to pin her to the mattress. She closed her eyes, aching to feel his hand on her breast, anticipating the feel of his lips on her throat, holding her breath to taste his kiss, eager for his body to weigh down on her. Ieuan Emyr had left her before she awoke at daylight.

Derwyn was awake when she opened the door. Galar's tired eyes followed her progress down the stairs but, except for giving her ale to drink, she did not impede Gwennan from going directly to her nephew.

"I am glad you're alive," she said, easing to her knees beside him.

"Gwennan," he murmured, opening his hand to her though he could not yet lift his arm. She cradled his hand in hers and clasped it to her heart.

"Derwyn, you have been so ill. I thought you would die."

"Who else lives?"

"Pendryw and Iago," she told him. "Tudwal was killed. Bedwyn was injured but the *meddyg* is confident for him."

"Are they all we have? Four warriors?"

"There are others," she said, lowering his hand to her lap. "At least twenty. Many were wounded, some worse than others. Only two are dead that I know."

"Find out. Exactly," he said. When she stared at him, he growled, "I must know if we are strong enough to fight."

"Not yet. None of you are fit."

"The longer we wait, the stronger the *gelyn* will be also."

"They have ten, twenty times that number, Derwyn."

"Are you sure? Have you counted?"

"No, but—."

"Count them," he told her. "Tell me all you discover."

"Derwyn," she murmured. "It's no good. They are already rebuilding. They have taken everything. The Gaer is theirs."

"Who commands this *gelyn* army?"

Gwennan searched his face but could not find the compassion she sought. "I believed you were dead." Derwyn pulled his hand from her grasp with such force that she was unbalanced, hitting the side of her head on the hearth wall.

"If you thought I was dead, why are you living?"

Gwennan stared at her empty hands. "I had hope," she whispered.

"Tell me who commands the *gelyn.*"

"A mercenary," she answered. Derwyn grabbed her wrist. "I have been by your side while you have been unconscious, every waking moment to keep you alive. You ask me questions I cannot answer." *But you do not ask if I am well.* The bitterness drove deep in her thoughts. "Derwyn, you must recover. This vexing does not help us."

"Our patient is thriving," Rocaille said as he crouched beside her and smiled at the young man.

"Keep your filthy hands off me," Derwyn hissed.

"Derwyn," Gwennan pleaded, "Paul has saved your life."

"Do not be concerned, *boneddiges,*" the small physician said, patting her hand. "I am used to the ingratitude of my patients."

Derwyn reached across Gwennan and grabbed the front of Rocaille's tunic. "Keep your hands off her, *gelyn* pig." When he thrust the *meddyg* away, his fist jutted back and grazed Gwennan's chin. "Touch her again and I will kill you."

"Derwyn, please, if not for the *meddyg,* you and all the others would be dead, or crippled," Gwennan said. "This is not his fault."

"It is the fortunes of men, *boneddiges,*" Rocaille murmured, studying Derwyn. When he turned his eyes back to her face, he frowned at the new injuries since he had last seen her, regretting his loyalty to the man he held responsible. "And women."

Derwyn glowered at the physician and would not allow Rocaille to examine the wounds the *gelyn* army had inflicted on him. Paul walked away and sat on the bench by the table, studying his other patient as the old woman took his place by the Welshman.

Gwennan pressed her fingers over her lips, closing her eyes for a moment. "If you will not allow the *meddyg* to help you, I will do all I can but I am not trained."

"Galar is," Derwyn replied, "better one of my own than the *gelyn*. Or one who has sympathy for them," he hissed.

"I—. How can you accuse me?"

Derwyn made no answer, turning his eyes on the old woman. Galar took the younger woman's place, preparing fresh dressings for his wounds. When Derwyn fell asleep, the old nurse turned her piercing eyes on her chick.

"Galar warned you," the old one whispered near her girl's ear. "You lie with the *gelyn* and you have become the *gelyn* to the man you love. Go to your room, my *blodyn*, and pray that your father never hears what shame you have brought on his family." Gwennan stared wide-eyed at her nurse. Galar made a dismissive gesture, shoving her away. "I will see that this warrior is fit to take back what belongs to us since you would give it to our enemy. Go lie at that dog's feet like the whoring bitch you have become. You are dead to all who loved you."

"Galar," Gwennan pleaded, "I have done nothing wrong. Nothing has happened. He ..." But she could not say that Ieuan Emyr did not want her. Derwyn did not want her any more than any man had ever wanted her—never enough to defy her father. Without her father's blessing, she was of no value to men who wanted land.

The old woman pushed Gwennan to the rushes and Rocaille leapt to his feet to intervene, wrapping his arms around her and helping her to stand.

"You are not well, *boneddiges*. I have seen this coming for several days," he said. "You must rest. I will give you a drink to help you sleep and—."

"I am all right," she said, dusting her skirt. "I have been worried. I'm a little tired." When he led her to the table, she sank to the chair and accepted a cup of mead from him, glancing once at Derwyn and Galar. "I am a little tired," she repeated.

"*Boneddiges*, if you are injured," the physician offered, searching her face, "I can only help if you tell me." Though the offer was disloyal to a man he respected, Paul Rocaille continued, "I cannot ignore what is obvious, *boneddiges*—. I am a friend."

"Thank you, Paul," Gwennan replied. "Your concern is unnecessary."

The physician observed her for the rest of the morning, but did not press her again to accept treatment.

When he woke in the afternoon, Derwyn was restless and listened for every sound of the *gelyn* soldiers, as they came and went in the *buarth* below. The work on the outer wall plagued him and his questions to Galar were endless.

Unable to resist sleep any longer, Gwennan drifted into unconsciousness.

Jehan-Emíl entered the house accompanied by Maides and Wode. The commander laughed to see that the Celt sat upright with his back against the stone firebox.

"I see the Celt is ready to fight again, Commander," Wode said.

Gwennan raised her head at the sound of Ieuan's deep voice and the laughter around her. She glanced at the back of the chair, realizing that she had not fallen asleep on his shoulder as she had dreamed. She did not hear the commander approach until the *meddyg's* eyes warned her. Confused, she leapt to her feet to stand by Derwyn.

DeFreveille beckoned Maides to follow when he went to the Welshman's pallet and began to speak to the convalescent in a cheerful tone.

"My commander wishes you to know that we are glad you have recovered," Maides said. "Your healing has been a source of concern to all of us, not the least the woman of this house. Both she and our own *meddyg* have worked tirelessly for your recovery."

Jehan-Emíl's hand closed on Gwennan's wrist and he drew her to stand by him, staring into her eyes before he sent her to the table, as had become their custom, to await him. He smiled as she responded to his unspoken wishes. Artur began preparing their meal. This was the orderly household he required for his children. This gave him the freedom to be generous with his enemies. With Gwennan seated in her place at the table, he could afford to be magnanimous toward her lover.

"Your petulance is a disappointment, my young friend," Maides continued as deFreveille spoke. "You have a hot temper but deFreveille believes this is youth. You are raw. With experience, you will become an asset."

"Tell the *gelyn* pig I will see him dead before that."

Maides informed Jehan-Emíl of Derwyn's response. "DeFreveille accepts your reluctance under the circumstances. With time, this will change. For now, you will find the company of your friends in the infirmary an aid to the recovery of your full strength."

While Maides finished, deFreveille strode to the table and slumped into his chair, a man grateful to be in his home. Artur brought him a basin of hot water and a cloth. While the commander washed his face and hands, he praised the boy for his good work and watched the warrior receive and react to his orders. As soon as the message was delivered, he turned his attention to Gwennan as she accepted another warm, damp cloth Artur held out to her. He leaned toward her. "You are quiet, Gwennan." Although she turned her eyes on his face, she did not answer. His eyes narrowed but he said nothing to her about the new bruises on her chin and temple. The commander gestured to his groom and the meal was served.

"This warrior is my third in command. He is a good man," deFreveille told her. She glanced at him but he did not intend her to understand and she made no effort to listen. "Unlike my second in command," deFreveille continued, speaking close to her ear, "this one can be trusted to follow my orders. I would give you my first officer, but as you see, Maides is essential to me now. This one will keep you safe when I cannot." He clasped her fingers. When she pulled away, he loosened his grip. "Wode," he said in the *gelyn* language, "this is Gwennan daughter of Daran Pendyffryn. Her safety is essential to our success to keep this estate."

"Yes, Commander?" the young warrior replied, a puzzled frown creased his forehead.

"Without her, we will never convince her father to accept our terms."

"Yes, Commander," Wode replied, his frown disappearing.

"Gwennan, *cariad*," deFreveille murmured and smiled when she met his gaze. "I have made a start to find many words," he whispered against her cheek, "to say to you when we are alone." His breath was soft and its warmth on her throat radiated to her heart. His command of her language was worse than his primitive Latin, but he had made an effort and she wondered who among her friends had helped him with such an intimate promise. "I want you to meet Gethin Wode, he will be—."

"Gethin?" Gwennan asked.

"Yes, mistress," Wode replied, leaning back in surprise.

"How did you come to be called by a Celt name?" she asked, her voice barely above a whisper. "Your mother?"

"I do not understand her, Commander."

"Where were you born?" she asked. "Who were your grandparents? What *ystad*?"

DeFreveille clasped her hands and said so that Wode could understand, "There will be time enough for your questions, Gwennan." To her, in his own language, he asked, "Why are you so eager? What about this man excites you?" He raised her fingers to his lips. "Must I be jealous of every man I bring to this house?"

He held her hands so that she found it difficult to pursue her interest in Wode. She was too tired to care.

An hour into the meal and still early in the evening, deFreveille disengaged himself from his discussion with Maides and turned toward her again, clasping her hands to his chest. "The physician commands that I ensure you rest. Go to bed, woman. I will come to you before long." He spoke softly in her ear. Gwennan understood his meaning when he propelled her toward the staircase. He remained standing as he watched her ascend the stairs. She climbed slowly, using the wall for support.

Gwennan was grateful for the escape but when someone came after her, she struggled to be released. Her terror did not diminish when she realized the man carrying her into the room was Ieuan. She clawed his fingers with her free hand, digging into his flesh with her nails but his strength was too much for her. Her feeble pummeling of his back when he lifted her over his shoulder had no effect. He slammed the collapsing door behind him.

He dropped her feet to the floor, studying his hand. There was a smile on his lips as he licked his wounds. His wrist and several fingers of his right hand were bleeding. He licked away the small drops of blood. She, in turn, rubbed her wrist. When he stepped toward her, she fled to safety further from him. "It is not enough for you to flaunt your lover in this house," he growled, "but you must also seek comfort from my men?"

Sheltering behind the chair by the fire, she hissed, "You have no cause to be angry with me. I have done nothing wrong." She sank against the rough surface, too weak to fight him. "After all our nights together," she continued under her breath, "you frighten me. I will not let you beat me." He did not approach her but shouted at her and pointed to the bed. "No."

"My own physician and now my captain?" He lifted his hands, beckoning her to him. "Do you want me to go mad?" She pressed harder against the wall. "Gwennan, I want you to come to me, willingly, but I am not prepared to wait forever. You know I want you. You know what it costs me to respect your refusal. An indefinite wait is unthinkable. I do not want to force you but I have no words you understand," he sighed, watching her, like a trapped animal, desperate to escape. Jehan-Emíl dropped his arms helplessly to his sides. "Gwennan."

Gwennan gasped in ragged breaths. "No."

"Go to bed," he ordered, pointing to the bed again. As he threw his tunic on the stool, he shouted again. When she refused to comply, he blew out the flame of the oil lamp. He tore his shirt over his head.

She did not take her eyes off him. Her body sagged, ready to slump into a chair. The fire was dim. Before her eyes had adjusted to the dark, he sprang at her and threw her down on the bed. She could not fight him or scream aloud. *Don't do this. I will not let you do this.*

Trapping her hands above her head with one arm, he loosened the laces on her gown. He yanked it down her body and threw it across the room. Gwennan watched it slide off the chest onto the floor like a rag. DeFreveille threw the *carthen* over them both and held her down, whispering something in her ear, stroking her shoulder.

"Now be still," he commanded. He held her as he had the first night, his weight enough to quiet her. Her muscles loosened. He caressed her arm and shoulder, loosening the bodice and cuffs of her linen frock. Her body tensed once more but he continued to soothe her until her fatigue overcame her.

Despite her terror, her body welcomed the familiar weight and she drifted to sleep, drawing warmth from him, feeling safe with him again. With no strength left to resist, Gwennan made no protest when he worked her frock above her waist and over her head. She was asleep before it followed her gown to the floor.

Jehan-Emíl's eyes adjusted to the dimness and he watched the contours of her face soften as her sleep deepened. "Are you clever," he asked, "or is your lover an imbecile?" Jehan-Emíl traced the curve of her breasts through the fragile cloth of the chemise. "Is he careless, Gwennan? Why have you taken this boy for your lover?" he wondered, pressing his hand on her abdomen. "Do you believe this Welshman is better for you than I will be?" He stroked her shoulder and kissed the palm of her hand. "I will not allow you to play this game with me," he murmured as his blood surged through his body like fire. His hands trembled as he gathered the fragile cloth of the chemise in his fingers, drawing the fabric over her thighs. "Wake, Gwennan. Wake," he whispered, "I will make love to you." His hand came to rest and he forced his fingers to be still, caressing her as softly as a sigh but she refused to be awakened. "You challenge me, *cariad,* but I will win. Not tonight, but soon. I will persist until I break your will to refuse me. Then, Gwennan, you will forget these other men."

SEVEN

At dawn, Gwennan awoke. Her leg stretched across deFreveille's thighs and her arms encircled his neck. The sun had begun its climb to the crest of the hills in the distance, casting a gray pallor over the room. Her cheek rested on his chest and her fingers were locked in the riot of curls at the nape of his neck. Only his arm around her waist restrained her, but she held him fast. *If I wake him, if I stay in his embrace, if I encourage him with a sigh, a kiss...* Dismayed by her desire and her refusal to kill him as her friends urged, Gwennan dragged herself away. His arm clenched when she moved against it and she was still, holding her breath.

"*Menyw*," he sighed, sliding his hand down her back and over her hip to hold her, pulling her leg higher over his thighs. Her chemise had risen above her hips. He slid his hand over her skin to the tender flesh of her inner thigh.

"Leave me alone," she commanded, raising her head from his shoulder.

"Leave *me* alone," he repeated, grinning as she dragged her arms from around his neck. "I told you, *menyw*, I warned you," he murmured, pinning her to the bed beneath him, his hips settling heavily between her thighs. Of its own accord, her body reached for him, opened and sought his manhood as he touched her. "Now?" he whispered, thrusting once, caressing her tingling flesh, moistening her with his first emission of arousal. "Now?" Gwennan felt the heat of his secretion reach her excited flesh.

"No, please," she begged, shame surfacing against the overwhelming desire of her body to conceive, to mate with him, to carry a child in her womb, to feel a man's desire satiate her own.

"No?" he laughed, pushing against her. "Please?" He kissed her throat, sliding his hands under her hips and lifting her up to him. "Please, Gwennan?" Planting his hands on either side of her, he raised his upper body, nudging against her. "We make love together, *cariad*? Now? Please?"

"No," she growled, pulling away, pressing her thighs together and dragging her chemise to cover her bruised body. "No." He did not move when she pushed herself to lean against the headboard, holding himself above her on his extended arms and lowering his head to kiss her. She turned her face away and his lips moved over her chin. His breath seared through the thin fabric of her chemise as he kissed her breast, dragging the garment away from her skin with his teeth.

"Now?"

"No."

With a groan and a laugh, he threw himself onto his back, kicking the *carthen* to the floor, his breath hissing from his body as he willed his lust to subside. "No is no," he said. "No is yes, soon." He swung his legs over the side of the bed and sat on the edge. He glanced at her over his shoulder and grinned. "No will be yes," he declared and disappeared into the children's dormitory.

When she lowered her gown over her shoulders and tightened the lacings, her terror subsided and relief swelled in her heart. Though only a few of the eyelets were torn, he had the power to overpower her—if he chose to use it. *How can I kill him*, she asked, a faint smile crossing her pale lips, *until I know what make of man he is*?

The door creaked faintly on its cold hinges but the sound did not alert deFreveille. Derwyn slept with his arm trailing on the hearthstone, blue with cold. Gwennan made her way to him.

He had more color. He would live and, if she were fortunate, he would not know she had never loved him.

Artur, who was so quick to anticipate deFreveille's needs, was still asleep on his cot near the kitchen. Gwennan lowered herself to sit by the pallet and lifted Derwyn's arm to put it under the *carthen*.

"I have come to say good-bye," she whispered against his cheek. Derwyn woke, and, turning onto his side, clasped her against him with his good arm. Gwennan wept. He said nothing at first but when she had stopped, he stroked her hair and whispered in her ear.

"Hush, Gwennan. I swear, once I am able to stand, I will kill this pig who has dishonored you. That is the least I can do for you," he said, pushing himself to a sitting position. "I will avenge you, Gwennan, it is my duty."

"What are you saying?" Using the bench for support, she struggled to stand before him, searching his face. "Your duty? Is that all you have for me? Your duty?"

"Hush, *menyw*, that jackal will hear you." Derwyn glanced toward the top of the staircase.

"I did not open the gates to let the *gelyn* into my home," she said. "I did not leave women and children unprotected while I sought glory. All that has happened to me and others is not *my* doing."

"You blame me?" he demanded, under his breath, glancing again at the door above and with narrowed eyes at the sleeping groom.

"Tudwal did not give the order," Gwennan accused him.

"You preferred a slow death for every man and woman in this place. *You* had chosen for children to starve to death in their mothers' arms. I gave you the choice of an honorable death but you chose to bring shame on your father."

"You cannot speak for my father." She reached for the support of the table. "He will rejoice that I am alive."

"You have seen him? You know that *he* is alive? You dishonored him when you defied his wishes. You dishonor him now with his enemy."

Gwennan swayed, despite the firm grip she had taken on the edge of the table.

"While you played at being *pennaeth*, your father grieved. While you have been a whore for this *gelyn* pig, your father lies dead, food for wolves."

"You have no right—no right to judge me. You do not know what has happened. You do not know—."

"Your father is dead and you have let his murderer make you his whore."

"Do not say that to me," she gasped, swaying and slipping to her knees. "I have never wished you harm—." Derwyn warded off the hand she raised to touch his face. She lost her balance and fell to the rushes with a cry, landing on her hands. She dragged her hair from her face and stared at him. "You wanted me dead," she said. "I lived for your sake—in case you needed me."

"I do not need a whore." He raised his fist. "We have no future, Gwennan, not since you took the *gelyn* into your—."

The door of the bedchamber flew open and deFreveille leapt from the landing, stalking toward the Welsh warrior, his dagger ready. Gwennan raised her hand to stop him. He stood over her and pointed his dagger at the man. "Touch her again, Welshman, you will die." He crouched and gathered her into his arms, brushing her hair back from her brow. "This is the last time, Gwennan," he hissed at her. "You will not do this to me."

"Ieuan." She searched his face for a moment and closed her eyes.

He lifted her limp body from the floor and carried her back to their bed, flinging the *carthen* over her. "You will *not* make a fool of me, woman."

When he returned to the lower hall, he studied the warrior. Derwyn had fallen back against the firebox and Artur was standing over him. DeFreveille grasped the iron that Siriol had raised against him and swung it hard at the warrior's head. The warrior did not flinch or raise a hand to defend himself. The foreign commander threw the iron to the side and smiled.

"Striking you dead is as easy for me as striking that woman is for you," he said. "But I am not like you. When you are strong again, we will see if you are man enough to take Gwennan from me," deFreveille said with a broad smile, "but I know you have already lost her. Today, you leave my house, Welshman. Go back to sleep. I have much to do."

"We will win, *gelyn,*" Derwyn hurled at him. "You will not last a year ruling with the sword. You may kill all of us, but we will never be conquered. We will change you—forever. Gwennan is dead to me now—she is of no use to a decent man."

"Gwennan is mine," deFreveille smiled at the warrior, "for now." Turning to the table and rolling out the maps of the lands that he held, he studied the markings made from his men's reconnaissance. With the added lands of Cwmdu and the whole of Pendyffryn, he would have an estate of immense value, one to repay Maides, if he chose to take one of the outlying strongholds for his own. Here was his home, a space on the parchment larger than anything he had imagined. He needed only to secure it and his children would be with him once again.

At least part of his battle for Pendyffryn would be won if he could persuade the Welsh to join under his command. Keeping them in chains was wasteful, foolish, when their knowledge of the country and the language were useful to him. DeFreveille sent Artur to rouse his captains and paced the floor while he waited for them to come. Christophe Maides entered the house within minutes of the call.

"What do you think, my friend, can I walk up to these warriors and ask for their help?"

"You may ask, Jehan, but I doubt you will receive the answer you want." Maides poured a flagon of ale and stretched his long legs toward the hearth. "That one will be the key," he said, nodding toward Derwyn Blaenant.

"So I think as well. I have thought better of killing him."

"Will you give the woman back to him?" the mercenary asked.

"She will not go back to him," Jehan-Emíl replied with a glance at the door.

"I see," Maides said with a brief, cold smile.

When the others came through the door, deFreveille strode to the table. He pointed to the maps. "Wode. All of you. We have rested long enough. Now our real work begins." He watched them glance from one to another, aware that they were as exhausted by their toil as he was. "Bown, gather the boys and set them to work in the kitchens. Wode, take all the soldiers who are fit and bring the camp into order. This place will be a garrison before breakfast is served. Maides, your men will clear the rest of the woods. You know what to do with your prisoner, Alrick," he said. "The others will be carpenters. If there are any among the Welsh who have skills, put them to work. Now go," he bellowed. When they had left to do his bidding, he swung on Derwyn.

DeFreveille smiled. "You are wondering what I have planned. I think even you will approve. Although it will cost you, in particular, most of what you value, in the end all will be better." He pulled a stool closer to the warrior. "Perhaps you are wondering what I plan for Gwennan." He smiled again when he saw Derwyn's head jerk at the sound of the woman's name on his lips. "I am aware of the feeling you have for her. I have decided to keep her. My employer will not like that but Haelsted is not a good man for a woman like her."

DeFreveille stared at his hands for a moment. "I have known worse but I—. You do not need to know what I have done to keep my family alive," deFreveille murmured. "You will understand this: Gwennan is mine and I will separate her from you. It is a flaw in my nature," Jehan-Emíl grinned. "I was never generous. My wife complained of it. She was inclined to be too generous. I ended that. I will do the same here. I have children." He slapped his knees and leaned forward. "Ah, you will like my sons. Jehan-Batiste is bright, not much of a soldier but Marshal warrants his name. He is a born warrior, very like you, I see." Rising from the stool, the commander glanced at the bedroom door. "Now, I have work. You are banished to the infirmary. Before breakfast, I think."

DeFreveille rolled the parchment map and replaced the leather circlet that bound it. He ignored the warrior's stare as he climbed the staircase to his room. He wanted another bath but there was no time and she slept so heavily, he chose not to wake her even to bid her well for the day.

Gwennan woke for the second time to the familiar sound of women and children running, laughing through the chamber to the dormitory beyond. For a moment, she forgot all that had happened in the past days and enjoyed the warmth beneath the *carthen*. Listening to a child's laughter, she wondered that she could have dreamt such sadness. Aine's ragged face, when it appeared at the opening of the bed hangings, chased away all Gwennan's happy thoughts and her sorrow swept over her again.

"Gwennan, why have you not risen?" Aine questioned. "Four of us have been sent back to the house. I do not know why or what will become of the others. They have no respect for our laws. And that commander, that barbarian, is changing everything. He acts the master here. Ach, even Pendryw approves. I cannot understand why they will not fight."

Her smile was distant as she turned her face away from Aine to stare at the walnut shells on the mantle. When Siriol came, Gwennan's view was blocked but she stared as though she could see through her friend's body.

"What is wrong, Gwennan? Are you in pain?"

She did not answer their questions. The two brought water in a cup but she refused it. They pressed a cool cloth to her forehead and encouraged her to drink an infusion. "Ieuan?"

"You have a fever, Gwennan," Siriol told her. "Galar prepared this for you."

"Go."

Siriol bent over her. "What can I do, Gwennan?"

"Ieuan?" She swallowed more of the infusion, overcome with fatigue. "Go. Leave me."

"She knows what she is doing," Aine said, folding the *carthen* close to Gwennan's chin. "Let her rest. We will come back, Gwennan, when you have slept more."

They covered her with another *carthen*, pulled the hangings closed and left her in peace. The sickness that had begun as an ache in her back, a discomfort low in her belly, had increased so that she steeled herself against the pain to breathe. *Ieuan is here*. The room darkened and she drifted into unconsciousness.

Siriol descended to the hall in search of Galar but the old woman had gone to the infirmary with Derwyn, thinking better of arousing his fear for Gwennan. She returned to the rooms above. The other women were busy comparing their experiences. Only Aine had suffered the loss of her husband.

Before darkness fell, Artur knocked on the door of the room, to request the presence of the women at the last meal of the day. Aine and Siriol held back to speak without the others hearing.

"Should we tell Derwyn that she is ill?" Siriol asked.

"What can he do?"

"We must tell someone. The *meddyg*? He will help."

"She is better off without his help. Leave it to God, Siriol. After what she has suffered, she is better dead."

"You would let her die? What if Gwennan does not wish that?"

"It is better out of our hands. She will not thank you, Siriol. She wants to be left alone, as she told you. Let her die in peace." Aine descended to the family hall and took her place at the table.

Siriol was given a place between her children. The presence of the *gelyn* in the family hall subdued Eira and Gareth. Siriol's meal was quiet. She observed the foreign commander, watching him turn his brown eyes toward the door to Gwennan's room and then to study Aine's face. For the remainder of the meal, deFreveille was unconcerned by Gwennan's absence. He spoke with the raven-haired man, but otherwise, he drank and ate in silence, watching the women though he appeared not to notice them.

Before the end of the evening meal, as soon as Artur cleared his trencher, deFreveille left the table and the hall. Carrying a jug of his own wine and two cups, he climbed the staircase to the door of the chamber. Both Aine and Siriol stared after him. The door was ajar and deFreveille nudged it with his foot, slipped through the gap, shoving it closed with his shoulder. One day more, his carpenters had promised, and the stairwell to the second chamber would be finished according to Maides's plan for the old house. He had allowed them back to the house—another gesture to win their favor.

Placing the jug and cups on the mantle he built up the fire to take the chill from the air. He removed his new tunic and untied his shirt at the neck and cuffs, running his hand over his damaged arm. "A bath would be a good thing," he said aloud with a shrug, "but not possible." Sinking into the chair with a cup of wine in his hand, he stretched his legs in the glow of the flames and glanced at the bed on the other side of the room behind him, frowning when he noticed that the heavy hangings were closed.

He drained his cup, filled it again and the other. Jehan-Emíl was satisfied with the progress of the day, the improvements he made were winning a few of the Welsh to him, some joined for the sake of their families. His confidence in the steps he had taken during the day to win their approval of his management fueled his pride. Striding to the enclosed bed, he pushed the curtain aside with his elbow and stepped onto the platform. Gwennan's back was turned to him. He placed the cups on the chest behind him while he lit the taper in the brass holder. "Tonight," he murmured, "you will say yes, *cariad*." As he began to drag the shirt over his head, he saw that she slept in her gown. Her breath was shallow and quick. When he turned her onto her back, he saw the fever stains high on her cheeks. Her skin burned to his touch.

"Artur!" Jehan-Emíl bellowed and sent the boy in search of Rocaille. While he waited for the physician, he dampened a cloth in the bucket of cold water near the hearth and folded it across her forehead. He was dragging her gown off her shoulders when the physician entered. Together they removed her clothing. Jehan-Emíl cursed when the physician brought more light. He backed away and turned to the mantle, fixing his gaze on the row of walnut shells.

"A fever, Commander," Rocaille informed him, taking his hand from her brow. The doctor let out his breath. "Also hemorrhage."

Jehan-Emíl turned to face the physician. His eyes were red. Rocaille frowned and Jehan-Emíl grabbed the front of the small man's tunic, his fierce, dark eyes flashing.

"You think *I* did this," deFreveille accused the physician.

"What should I believe?" Rocaille asked quietly. "I am a doctor. She has been—."

"This woman is essential to my plans, physician," deFreveille hissed. "See that she is well." Releasing his grip, the commander let the physician stumble back against the chair and strode to the bed. The violence of his grip on the frame shook the bed despite its massive weight. "What has happened do you think, Paul?"

"I know little of these matters. I mend the wounds that men inflict—in war. This is for women. Let me send for a nurse among her friends. They will know better what to do. "

"As you see fit," the commander murmured, crouching by the bed to study Gwennan's face, averting his eyes from her bruised body. "Gwennan?" he smoothed a lock of her hair from her bare shoulder. "I'm here. You should have told me," he said. "I would not have allowed you to work so hard for that boy."

Siriol was waiting when Rocaille opened the door. Galar stood at the bottom of the staircase, alerted by the call for the *meddyg*. The physician nodded, stepping aside as Siriol darted to the bed. She met deFreveille's eyes when she knelt on the opposite side. The foreigner rose to his feet and the old woman shoved him out of the way when she took his place.

"They will not allow us to stay, Commander," the doctor whispered. Jehan-Emíl turned his head to stare into the doctor's eyes as the two women opened the curtains around the bed. Rocaille continued in a low voice, "This is for women, my friend."

Jehan-Emíl shook off the physician's hand on his arm and stayed by the bed.

Galar cursed him, but Siriol faced him, "You cannot stay. We have work and you cannot be here."

DeFreveille looked down at her and turned his eyes back to Gwennan's face. "I am at fault," he murmured. "I let this happen."

"She says we must go," Rocaille said. "They cannot do what they must if you stand in the way, Jehan."

Jehan-Emíl stared at his physician for several moments. "No, Paul, Gwennan knows she is safe when I am here."

Jehan-Emíl looked beyond the golden-haired woman as Galar bent over Gwennan and began to waken her. He watched as the old woman lifted Gwennan's shoulders and shook her. His impulse was to interfere but his head urged him to let the women be. He lunged at the old woman, but pulled back when Siriol put her own body in his way. After searching her eyes for a long time, he relented and stepped away. Rocaille touched his arm. Once Jehan-Emíl had gazed again at Gwennan's pale, tranquil face, he followed the physician from the room, closing the door behind him. Before he reached the bottom of the staircase, the other women and children scattered to seek refuge in the kitchen.

Gwennan woke with a moan and stared into the narrowed face of her childhood nurse.

"Did you think you could hide evidence of your betrayal? You must die, *blodyn*," the old woman whispered in her ear. "Galar found the bloody evidence of the *gelyn's* crime. You have no courage. Tonight, your father's honor is restored."

As the old woman raised her shoulders from the pillow, Gwennan was hit by a wave of nausea that radiated like fire from her abdomen and reached the tips of her fingers. Her low, strangled cry was heard through the house. She searched with dimming vision but Siriol was not in the room.

Nausea overwhelmed her when the old woman pulled her from the bed and made her walk the floor of the chamber. A convulsion collapsed her against the bedpost and Galar cackled. When she could stand again, Galar made her walk. When Siriol returned, she held the hot infusion of willow bark to Gwennan's lips. Though she begged to be allowed to return to the bed to sleep and complained that she was too cold to pace the room, Galar refused. She wept, "Why are you so cruel?"

The small fire that the *gelyn* commander had built was cold at first light.

"There is the work of that dog," Galar hissed, wrapping the bundle of deFreveille's bloody clothing in linen. "That one has done this to your *baban*, Gwennan. That one has murdered Derwyn's son. Pendyffryn's heir. That one has murdered my chick."

Siriol stared into the old woman's face but remained silent. She bathed her friend of the sweat covering her body, dressed her in a clean chemise, tugging the garment over her hips. She changed the bedding and tucked the *carthen* close around Gwennan's legs. With a warm, damp cloth, she soothed her friend's face, studying her with a frown.

"Take that away, Galar," she said. "Burn it." When the room was empty but for the two of them, Siriol leaned over Gwennan, smiling into eyes that were wild and dark. "Do not listen to Galar. No matter what has happened between you and this *gelyn*, you have not lost a child. You will not die. All these bruises will heal, Gwennan. They are fading already."

"Ieu ..." Gwennan began, forcing her eyes to focus on Siriol's face.

"Hush, Gwennan. You need to rest."

"No," Gwennan whispered. "Is Ieuan here?"

"I'm sorry," Siriol said. "I'm so sorry. If I had known what that monster was doing to you—."

"No," Gwennan whimpered, clasping Siriol's hand. "No. Ieuan. I—." *I want him. I need ... I need to tell him ... something ...*

"Do not fret, Gwennan. You are safe now," Siriol declared, biting her lips together and shaking her head. "That man will not come here again. He will not hurt you again. I promise."

Galar carried the linen shroud cradled in her arms. When she reached the family hall, deFreveille raised his eyes from the flames and peered across the distance between them, questioning her with red-rimmed eyes.

"Here is your work, Fiend, the death of all Pendyffryn's future," Galar snarled. "Here is the evidence of your evil to my girl but Galar has saved her." She held out the linen bundle to him but deFreveille did not react to her. Galar cursed him and stalked away through the door. He rested his brow on his fist against the mantle. Rocaille asked permission to see the woman. Jehan-Emíl nodded and slumped into a chair. When Siriol replaced the *meddyg* in the hall, the commander glared at her, daring her to blame him, until she retreated to the kitchen with the others. He climbed the stairs to the chamber just as the physician closed the curtains around the bed.

"Nature has done what is best for her. Gwennan will sleep now," Rocaille told his commander. "When she wakes, I will know more."

"Then you may go to your other patients, Rocaille." Jehan-Emíl said.

The physician recognized the dismissal but was reluctant to leave. "She will need attention. Care."

"I will see to her."

"You?" the little man scoffed, heedless of the other's fury.

"Physician, I have told you. Now go." DeFreveille's command was charged with violence. Rocaille rolled down his sleeves, gathered his instruments and left the chamber.

Siriol watched the doctor descend and started toward him but was restrained by Aine's strong hand. Breakfast was finished. None of the women had asked what happened in the night.

"Keep to your own, Siriol."

"He will tell us what needs to be done."

"That one works for the *diawl*. Leave Gwennan to them."

Siriol stole up the staircase with only Aine's eyes upon her. The *gelyn* commander slouched in the chair by the fire, his arms hanging at his sides, staring into the flames. Siriol slipped past him and behind the bed hangings though she was seen. Bending over her friend, Siriol touched Gwennan's still feverish cheek. "I do not understand what Galar has done," she murmured. After straightening the *carthen*, Siriol turned the damp cloth on Gwennan's forehead and sat by her, holding her dry hand. Assured that Gwennan was comfortable and sleeping, Siriol stepped down from the platform and into the room, pulling the hangings closed behind her.

DeFreveille glared at the golden-haired woman but did not rise from his chair. Outside, the wind raged against the walls of the sagging house, sweeping through the gaps in the small window and lifting the hangings on the bed enclosure. Though he had put more logs on the fire, the room was bitter beyond the circle of the hearth. He had only to stretch his hand at arm's length and feel the cold. Siriol remained standing near the bed, her hands folded at her waist. When the *gelyn* commander turned to meet her challenge, she took a step toward him.

"I promised Gwennan that you would not come near her," Siriol said, "but you do. You are not ashamed of what you have done. You don't care how you have hurt her, taken her from a man who loved her, brought shame on her and cut her out of the heart of her people." When his only reaction was to stand, she continued, "If she recovers from this, I will see that you make reparation. If she does not, I will see that you are hunted until you are driven away or mad."

"Woman," deFreveille began in a quiet voice, "I can understand you are full of anger toward me. I do not wonder at that," he said, smiling. "I would feel the same." He extended his arms to the side, inviting her attack. "I am guilty of the invasion of your homeland. For that, I accept your anger." He bowed his head to her. "But," he said, raising his hand, "I will make amends. I have promised compensation for this woman whom Alrick has assaulted, but Gwennan…" When Siriol glared at him at the sound of her friend's name, he made a slight bow. "I will do more. This will be a good place to live again, I promise you." DeFreveille took a step toward her and Siriol retreated a step onto the platform.

"My children will arrive in a few days. You will see what manner of man I am through them. I am not a coward like the man who has hurt Gwennan." Siriol glared at him. "Of that, I am not guilty. What has happened is done. I will strive to make recompense for your loss but I will not give up what I have won. Nor will I let Gwennan die." As he walked toward her, Siriol stepped back once and then stood her ground.

"If you think I will let you—."

"Woman," he said, grasping her arms and lifting her to the side, "I know your purpose but you will not stand in my way." He set her on the floor and turned her in the direction of the door. "See to your children and we will talk later." With one hand, he dragged the hangings aside and stepped onto the platform. Resting his shoulder against the post, Jehan-Emíl gazed down on the daughter of Daran Pendyffryn. The cups of wine still waited on the chest and a new taper flickered sporadically as the wick shuddered in the draft he had admitted. Gwennan seemed to breathe easier, though still quick and uneven. The stains of fever on her cheeks were fading.

"I will not go," Siriol told him.

DeFreveille glanced at her but made no move to eject her from the room. "Bring water," he commanded. "For, Gwennan, water." He made a gesture of drinking. "Water. You know, thirst," he urged her. When she refused to understand he crossed the room and brought water from the bucket. "Water."

"*Dŵr*, Commander." Siriol held out a cup. DeFreveille sat by Gwennan's shoulder and let water drip from the cup between her parted lips.

"*Dŵr, menyw,*" he said with a smile. "*Dŵr* for Gwennan."

"You are strange," Siriol commented, a frown in her eyes.

After a long interval of silence, Siriol studied every move he made and every expression on his face. When he took the damp cloth from Gwennan's brow and turned it to the cooler side, Siriol lowered her eyes for a moment. When he slipped his fingers into Gwennan's hand and she closed her grip around them, Siriol frowned.

"I will leave Gwennan in your care," he said as he handed her the cup. "I know only how to watch men die and beg for death myself. My friends would not let me die so I am still here—to plague you," he smiled. "You will not let Gwennan die, that is good. That is what I want." He withdrew his fingers and for a moment, laid his hand over Gwennan's, kissing her temple. "Rocaille will come whenever you need him."

When he left the room, Siriol stared at the door. "He is strange," she said, placing a chair by the bed to continue giving water to her friend and refreshing the cloth on her brow.

At the end of the day, the *meddyg* knocked on the door and entered when Siriol answered. "I am informed that the *boneddiges* is resting," Rocaille said with a doubtful smile.

"She is quiet and breathes easier. I think her fever is down," Siriol replied. "*Meddyg*, you must tell your commander not to come here."

Rocaille glanced at the blonde woman. "I will do what is possible, *boneddiges*, but deFreveille is his own law. If he wants to be here, no one can stop him."

"Then I will be here as well, for Gwennan's sake."

Rocaille finished his examination. "*Boneddiges* Gwennan is no worse, perhaps she is able to rest now. I think she may improve soon. I will explain to deFreveille but you must understand, *Boneddiges* Siriol, he commands and he will do as he believes is best."

Jehan-Emíl climbed the steep grade to the house after most of his command and the whole of the household had gone to their beds. His letters were written and dispatched. The garrison he had ordered was standing and the meal he had shared with Maides had been accompanied by discussion that gave him hope for the success of his strategy. He climbed the stairs to the room with a sense of accomplishment. His hand was still on the latch when he noticed Siriol in the chair by the bed. He pointed in the direction of the dormitory but she folded her arms. He pointed again but she shook her head.

"If you are here," Siriol said pointing at him and the chair, "then I am here. If you are *not* here, I am here."

"Of course," he replied, lowering his brow. "I had hoped for a quiet rest and a moment to speak with Gwennan but since you do not trust my good will, I will make the best of what you allow me," deFreveille told her. "Rocaille has told me that she is, in his opinion, out of danger. I have taken a bold step based on that information," he continued, secure in Siriol's ignorance of his language. He sat on the edge of the bed and drew Gwennan's hand into his, directing his spoken thoughts to her while Siriol refreshed the damp cloth. "A bold step, Gwennan, but one I think you will approve. I have sent Maides to meet with your father. He will be told that you are ill and will be assured that you are receiving the best care that any man can offer. He will not be told you have miscarried—so I will not be accused, at least by him, of a crime I did not commit." He stroked her hand, smiling at the scratches she had left on his own. "I have not left as much as a hair out of place on your body, Gwennan," he murmured, "but I cannot be unhappy that I will not be forced to watch you grow round with another man's child in your body."

Pressing her hand to his chest, he removed her gold ring and put the plain band on the smallest finger of his hand. "I am called Jehan-Emíl. One day," he whispered against her fingertips, "*cariad*, you will call me by name to this bed to be your lover." He sealed the command with a kiss on her parted lips. When he lifted his head, he turned his eyes on Siriol. "I have said what needs to be said. I will not interfere with your care. When Gwennan is fit to receive visitors, Rocaille will inform me." He gathered his belongings and Derwyn's dagger, bowed to Siriol and took a last look at Gwennan before he left the room.

eight

On a morning three days later, the sound of the carpenters' hammers woke Jehan-Emíl as they erected the sides of the stairwell. The carpenters were fitting the first of the two timber walls which would support the risers and landing and worked in the neglected garden, carrying the sections into the hall when they were ready. DeFreveille planted his feet on the carpet of his campaign tent and pushed himself to stand. "I am too old for this," he complained aloud. Artur's head appeared from beneath the flap and his employer beckoned him to enter. "Well, your report?"

"Nothing, Commander. There is no change—none for the worse, none for the better. The children and the women are curious about the work the carpenters are doing. There is a boy—." DeFreveille frowned. "An angry boy in your house."

"Ah, yes. What about him?"

"He is there. He sleeps in a room below your bedchamber. He is Elgan's son. The women do as he tells them—a very arrogant, violent boy, sir. He has struck two that I have seen."

"I will deal with him, Artur. Have you seen Gwennan?"

"No, sir. She sleeps all day. But I have heard her voice in the night."

"In conversation with Siriol?"

"No, sir. She calls for her mother," Artur said.

"Her mother is dead."

"She also calls for her father…and another name."

"The Welshman? Elgan Maergwn?"

"No, sir."

DeFreveille turned his back to tie the waist of his *trwsus*. "What does Siriol say?"

"She does not know this name, Commander. She told Rocaille that she would bring the man immediately, if she knew him."

"What name does Gwennan call?" deFreveille asked as he dragged a black tunic over his head. When the boy remained silent, he met his eyes and smiled. "If Gwennan calls for a friend, Artur, it is an act of kindness to search for him."

"She does not speak clearly, sir," Artur replied, "and there is no one by that name here."

"What is the name, Artur?" deFreveille insisted, taking one stroke with his razor on his chin. "Perhaps we can find this unknown man for her."

"It sounds like—, it is hard for me to say these words, they are strange to me. It sounds like 'yay-ahn'."

DeFreveille's hand shook and he sucked his breath back with the sting of the cut. He dropped his razor on the table. "After these nights on this cot, my hands are not steady enough to avoid slitting my throat, Artur," he laughed.

"Rocaille says it is not a Welsh name that he knows," Artur said. "No one has heard of this friend. They say she is delirious."

"Finish this shave for me so we can begin our search for this man, eh?"

"But, sir," Artur said, picking up the razor and whisking off his employer's growth of beard with confident strokes, "Siriol says there is no one here by that name."

"There is, Artur," Jehan-Emíl replied, "or Gwennan would not call for him."

"Perhaps she calls on one of their gods, Commander," Artur offered. DeFreveille turned to study his groom. "Yes, sir, I am sure you are right."

Jehan-Emíl stretched his arms wide when he emerged from his tent, glanced once at the house with a grin and strode into the *buarth* to have his breakfast in the hall with his army. Artur stood by him as he had on the previous mornings his employer had chosen to sleep in the camp. Wode was near the house. Alrick was still confined. The warriors who had recovered enough to leave the infirmary were under guard in the *buarth*, either beneath the canopies that stretched from the timber walls or in the tent erected as a jail, with *gelyn* soldiers at each corner. When he had finished the breakfast of *uwd* and ale that was served to all of his army and the prisoners of war, Jehan-Emíl inspected the progress of the rebuilding and the tree felling.

Near the end of the afternoon, Maides returned and deFreveille found an excuse to go to the house. When they both entered, unannounced, he smiled to see the children running through the hall and out through the kitchen. Even the youngest boy, Pedr Iago, joined in the chase. Oswin was lounging by the hearth, stirring the ashes. DeFreveille took his chair at the table, glanced once at the door above him and nodded. Maides caught Oswin by the scruff of the neck and propelled him to stand in front of the *gelyn* commander.

"I have heard from witnesses," Maides began his verbatim translation of deFreveille's words, "that you have struck two of the women of my household. I have seen the evidence with my own eyes."

Several of the women appeared at the door of the kitchen but did not venture into the hall. Oswin glared at the *gelyn* for a moment, cocking his head with a defiant sneer on his face as he glanced at the women of his father's household. Branwen and Aine lowered their eyes.

"What have you to say in your defense," Maides continued, "before I pass judgment, sentence you and hand you down for punishment?"

There were sudden gasps from the kitchen doorway and the boy sneered, taking a step backwards. Maides laid his hand on Oswin's shoulder, clamping him to the spot. "You have no authority to punish me. I am *pennaeth* now, not you, *gelyn* pig."

Maides repeated the boy's words, accompanied by a slight upward turn at the corner of his mouth.

"If your father was alive, I would punish him as well. I understand that you have had bad influences but I do not accept these as an excuse for your own behavior." DeFreveille leaned back in his chair and gestured for Branwen to bring him a jug of ale. When she did as he bid, Oswin lurched at her and Iago's wife scurried back to the kitchen. "You are guilty, by your own laws, of striking a woman with no lawful provocation," the dark mercenary said for deFreveille. "You are hereby sentenced to serve in the kitchen of the common hall and to be under the supervision of the woman called Betsan, as her servant."

"You cannot do that," Oswin shrieked. DeFreveille raised his finger to his lips.

"If you learn and serve well, your sentence will be shortened. If you do not, your sentence will be reviewed and prolonged, perhaps, made more severe."

Oswin twisted in the mercenary's grip.

"DeFreveille has been lenient with you, boy, in consideration of your age, but do not think he will give you any opportunity to hurt any woman of this house again."

"He dares," Aine whispered to her companions, "accuse Oswin of his own crime."

"Oswin hit me this morning," Menna murmured.

"Be silent, girl. Disloyalty has its consequences—as Gwennan will know, if she ever recovers from the beatings this wretch has given her."

"Elgan threatened her," Branwen said under her breath, and added, "also."

"She has a sharp tongue," Aine hissed, "and has never learned to curb it."

"So do I, but Iago has never hit me for it," Branwen said, lifting her chin. "That is unlawful."

"Perhaps he should," Aine retorted, turning her back as deFreveille ordered that Oswin's belongings be removed from his room and taken to the common hall where he would sleep with the other kitchen staff.

When the boy was gone, escorted by Wode, deFreveille glanced at the women and turned his attention to his friend. Both men walked out of the short passageway into the neglected garden at the side of the house. "What did Pendyffryn say?"

"He is not as Haelsted believes," Maides paused, considering his answer. "There is nothing old or feeble about the man. He was not surprised you sent an emissary."

"No? Did he expect an army?"

"He was ready for any move, knowing you as he does. If he comes to reclaim the Gaer, he will call on more than ten times the men we have."

"Worthy and formidable."

"He is not the thegn of this estate because he is a kindly old man, Jehan."

"What will he do? Wait or fight?"

"You have his daughter. He values her more highly than this patch of farmland."

DeFreveille looked out over the wide expanse of harvested fields, forest woodlands and pastures. "Why did he allow her to remain here with none but that low man to protect her?"

Maides shrugged. "He did not say. While you hold her hostage, he will not move against you, of that I am certain."

"Once she has regained her strength, she will not remain my 'hostage' for long, my friend," deFreveille laughed. "Did you have any sense that he had knowledge of these events?"

"He seems to have spies everywhere, Jehan. He keeps them close but they do not know or reveal everything." Encouraged to speak at will, Maides said, "Pendyffryn is skilled at concealment, but he could not hide his dismay at her illness nor his concern for her. She is his weakness."

"Then I have won, Christophe," Jehan-Emíl said, clapping his hand on Maides's shoulder, "but, we will not celebrate yet. Pendyffryn's daughter is as skilled as her father and I expect worthy opposition from both before we claim the prize. And you," the Gaer commander said, grinning at Maides and squeezing his shoulder with affection, "my friend, are the key to our ultimate success."

Maides gazed at his friend, no smile coming to his eyes to match Jehan-Emíl's affection, but a brief turn upwards at the corner of his mouth conveyed his amusement.

"Now," Jehan-Emíl announced, "you will begin to teach me more of this language."

The following morning, deFreveille stood by the fine, planed wall of the new stairwell. The fragrance of the hewn timber amid the aroma from the roasting meat on the hearth spit and the rushes on the floor was far more pleasant to his nostrils than the smell of decay everywhere in the neglected farmstead. The opening was cut in the dormitory floor, fitted with cross timbers and a bolt. The door in the timber screed between the dormitory and his bedchamber was fitted with a bolt and padlock on his side to ensure his privacy.

He had already sent Artur on several errands while he inspected the carpenters' good work. The wall that reached to the beams supporting the chamber floor, strengthening them, was already raised into place. The stairs were built and stood between the new timber wall and the wall of the house ready to be bolted into the stone and pegged to the timber. He turned toward the center of the hall as two children tumbled into the hall from the garden, the vanguard for the carpenters carrying the final section of the staircase.

"Your mother has no concern for your safety among these men, I see," deFreveille commented, the sound of his voice rooting Eira and her brother where they stood. The girl lifted her eyes to the door above the stone staircase but it did not open. "You will like these changes." He scowled for a moment before he ventured to pronounce the word for which he searched. "*Plantos.*" Their startled expressions did not tell him whether he had used or pronounced the word for children correctly but he continued, "This will make the house better for all—."

"Why are you here?" Siriol asked from halfway down the stone staircase. "Why have you come?" she demanded under her breath, glancing at the door above her. "She will not see you," Siriol told him as she came down to the hall. "I thought you understood."

Jehan-Emíl smiled at her for a moment. "This is my house, *menyw*," he said and sat down at the table.

"There has been enough disturbance with these carpenters without your bellowing. How can you expect Gwennan to convalesce under these circumstances?"

"Gwennan improves?" he asked, her name the only word he understood in Siriol's speech. "Gwennan is better?" he asked, cobbling together the few words he had learned from Maides.

"No! She is not. How can you believe she could get better——." Siriol looked at him with suspicion. "And how have you learned——? Who has taught you these words?"

"No?" he queried, jumping to his feet. "Why? What is wrong? Artur!" When the boy appeared, he said, "Bring Rocaille at once."

"Bellowing for the *meddyg* won't help either," Siriol snapped at him.

The moment the physician arrived at the door of the house, deFreveille flung his arm toward the bedchamber. "See what is wrong. This woman says Gwennan is not well."

"I saw her this morning, Jehan," Paul Rocaille said. "Her fever is nearly gone. She was better though still not——."

"Go, see for yourself and tell me," the commander said, sinking to his chair again. He studied Siriol for several moments while his physician remained in the bedchamber. He took the small loaf of hot barley bread offered to him and bit through the crust to the soft flesh. Glancing toward the top of the stone staircase, he beckoned Siriol to sit at the table with him. When she refused, he said, "Your opinion of me is unimportant, woman. Irrelevant. This is how it will be."

He leaned forward and studied her for several minutes. "I have decided to take this place and that woman." With another glance at the door, he continued. "Many women since my wife's death have made assaults on me. I have enough children and no difficulty luring a woman to my bed when I want one. I do not need a wife. However, I need land and a place for my children to call home. This place is good, better than I expected, so you are part of my children's future." After a long pause, in which he contemplated his loaf of bread, he said, "That woman is also part of what I have now planned. Nothing," he said in a clear, deep voice, "nothing will come between my children and their future here. Do you understand me? Nothing."

Though Rocaille assured deFreveille that Daran Pendyffryn's daughter was improving, Siriol prevented him from approaching the stairs and took her meal with him, leaving Aine with the *pendefig's* daughter. As often as she cajoled deFreveille to leave the house while the *meddyg* was there to speak for her, his determination to be in the house defeated Siriol and she left him and the physician to relieve Aine of her vigil.

"Has she woken?" Siriol asked, "Even once? A flicker of her eyelids?"

"No, nothing. She murmurs but says nothing intelligible. Only this name, 'Ieuan'. Who does she mean?" Aine wondered. "Someone at Pendyffryn?"

"I don't know," Siriol answered. "She has never mentioned anyone there but her father."

"She weeps when she says this name."

"Perhaps he is dead," Siriol offered.

"As are all our best," Aine replied, walking through the door to the dormitory.

Siriol brought a chair to the side of the bed. When she took her seat, Gwennan sighed as if in a dream and threw her arm over her head. The burning taper shivered, splashing her bare forearm with hot wax. Siriol blew out the flame and removed the candle, leaving the bed enclosure in darkness. "Gwennan?" she whispered. "You have slept four days. The *meddyg* believes you are getting well. Derwyn is stronger every day. Most of our warriors are ready to fight again." The fire in the hearth smoldered, making a meager effort to illuminate the wide room. "We only wait for your command." Siriol turned the cloth on Gwennan's forehead and shook her shoulder. "Gwennan, wake now. Any longer and the *gelyn* will never be driven away. Already, that man has changed everything—even this house. In another few days, you will not recognize your home."

With no light to watch her patient and nothing to do to occupy her hand to keep her awake, Siriol left the bed and made herself comfortable in the chair by the fire. For nearly an hour, she kept her vigilant eye on her patient but when the embers died, the room was dark, a bitter wind crept through the low window and chilled her neck driving her to the dormitory for a shawl. When she returned, Gwennan had turned onto her side away from the door and her upper body was exposed to the cold.

"Ieuan?" Gwennan Pendyffryn sighed as strong fingers slid into her hand.

"Who is this 'Ieuan'? Where can he be found, Gwennan?" Siriol pleaded.

"Go to bed, *boneddiges*," deFreveille said as he closed the door from the lower hall. He crossed the room and lifted Siriol with his arms around her waist, planting her on the opposite side of the screed partition and closed the door.

"You cannot do this!" she hissed through the latticed partition, pushing against the door with all her strength. DeFreveille wedged a chair against it and closed the hangings around the bed nearest the timber screed. "You cannot do this! You monster," Siriol hissed. "She is sick, you animal. Leave her alone. Please," she begged.

"I'm here," Jehan-Emíl whispered when he had taken Siriol's place at Gwennan's side. He stroked her cheek and brushed her hair away from her face. "You have not done well without me," he said, kissing the corner of her mouth. "If this is the way you behave in my absence, I will not leave you again,

Gwennan." He stretched his long body on the bed behind her and pulled her into his arms. "Have you ever been across the sea? It is a treacherous journey, in a ship much less than the size of this room. Swaying in the darkness and the wind like the devil's own harridans baying for a man's blood. My children were so frightened, *cariad*, even Jehan-Batiste cried. I will not ask them to live through such torment again."

For several moments, he listened to her breathing and studied her face. As soon as he was silent, the hissing from the dormitory began again. "I have a daughter, did I tell you?" he asked, keeping his voice low but loud enough to quiet Siriol. "I do not know her well, I regret to say. Like your father, I have had too many concerns with war and killing to give her the attention a girl needs. For a time, I was not sure that Cecilé was my child but—you will see when you meet her. She is much prettier than her father," he laughed softly. "You know that my wife is dead. I am somewhat to blame for that. After the death of her lover—Artur has given you this information and I give you credit for finding a use for it so soon—but, between my father's gambling and Helene's infidelities, ah yes, more than once, Gwennan—this is not behavior that I condone or tolerate."

He was silent again for a time while he lifted her hand to his lips. "Between these two, my children have suffered. And so, I have caused the suffering of the children of other men." He paused for a moment. "I am eager to meet your father again. I think he and I will be strong friends. I have you, his only child." He kissed her palm. "He will not like the circumstances—nor would I if a man like me held my daughter—but he will be reconciled to what must be." He brushed the *carthen* away from her body and dragged his fingers over her, from shoulder to thigh, settling his hand on her hip. "You will be reconciled as well, *cariad*. I promised you would call me to this bed to be your lover and you have. I will honor that. Neither you nor I will regret that we have met."

Artur climbed the staircase to the commander's chamber slowly, a tankard of ale in one hand and a letter for deFreveille from Haelsted in the other. Artur stood to the side as his commander drank the brew and read the letter. His commander had now spent two nights in his bedchamber, and a short time during each day, when he returned from inspecting the work in the wood or on the walls.

DeFreveille dressed in his shirt and *trwsus*, stamping into his high-topped boots. For the third morning in a row, he ordered Artur to bring nothing but ale. Artur returned to the kitchen for a salver of bread, nuts and fish for the two women in the room. The other women and the children went down to the hall for breakfast using the stairwell, whenever they pleased, no longer confined to the dormitory at the commander's discretion. The physician was admitted and left again, looking less grave than on the two previous mornings.

DeFreveille called Maides and Wode to the house as soon as he finished dressing but Artur was not privileged to hear what they discussed. He guessed that Haelsted had confirmed deFreveille's claim on the Gaer.

When Maides and Wode returned to the *buarth*, they formed small units to bring more of the farmers and the cattle into the farmstead. The work parties were increased to finish repairing the walls. The Welsh were given work to do. Those who refused sat by the fire in the common hall and sent threatening looks in the direction of the *gelyn*. Bown and others of the *gelyn* were all summoned but the commander did not come down to the long common hall or ride out that day.

When Artur was called again, it was already dark and everyone else had eaten. He cajoled the cook to prepare a meal. He wanted to go to his bed but he would be kept waiting for another hour while the commander finished the meal. Siriol, in a dark gown, opened the door to him as soon as he tapped it with his elbow, she had been in the commander's bedchamber each time Artur came. Artur did not see the commander in the room and assumed he was within the bed enclosure with Gwennan Pendyffryn who had not been seen for a week.

119

Siriol pointed to a stool by the hearth where Artur placed the trencher of roasted pork, oat porridge and the jug of ale. He took a close, surreptitious look at her. As he was leaving the room, the woman pulled aside the hangings surrounding the bed. Artur caught a glimpse of his commander but was satisfied that there was nothing to the taunts of the other grooms. His mentor was not dead.

Siriol touched the commander on the shoulder and beckoned him to come away. He did not turn at first but continued to stroke Gwennan's brow with the cloth. When he did turn, he looked at Siriol as though he saw her for the first time. Drawing the curtain further back, she indicated the trencher of food. With the cloth in her own hands, she took his place at the bedside.

Though she still believed deFreveille was responsible for Gwennan's illness, Siriol could not make up her mind about him. His attention to her friend was as steadfast and devoted as any husband. Although she believed he was prompted by guilt, Siriol had come to like him though they did no more than gesture to one another and teach one another a few words during the past few days.

For two days he had waited for Gwennan to prove Rocaille's declaration that she was well. And, for two days, Rocaille had shrugged, frowned, and gone away. He had worked, discussed, planned with his men. He had inspected the repairs, assured himself of the quality of the improvements. He had seen with his own eyes that the women of the household approved his changes. Finally, the letter for which he had waited had come that morning but Gwennan did not respond.

Jehan-Emíl ate none of the food or drink, standing motionless in the center of the room waiting for Siriol to finish so that he could take his place again. Everything was ready for the arrival of his children. He should have been content—all that he had worked for was within his grasp. Not since his father's gambling debts and foolish investments had destroyed the future he had expected from Emíl deFreveille's estate had Jehan-Emíl been able to provide security for his family. When

Siriol again gestured toward the meal brought for him, he stepped onto the platform and took the cloth from her hands.

She backed away and turned to sit by the hearth to eat while she watched him.

"I have kept my children with me as much as possible," he told Gwennan, sitting on the edge of the bed, with her hand cradled in his palms. "Their mother could not bear the sight of either of the boys—they are so like me. Jehan-Batiste, who had always adored her, was rejected though Helene tolerated him better than Marshal. She claimed he was my spy though the boy also loved her very much." He lifted his fingers to her cheek for a moment. "It is good you do not understand me," he commented with a slight laugh, straightening the bodice of her chemise over her shoulder. "I have not sought the company of women of my own rank since Helene's death. They are too troublesome while I have been preoccupied with saving my family from destruction. Whores have taken care of my physical needs. I confess Charlotte, my daughter's nurse, was also accommodating." He smiled. "Now, with my goal within reach, you will understand that I have been lonely." Jehan-Emíl studied Gwennan's face for a long moment. "I have not thought about this, Gwennan. I have been too busy taking what I must for my children's sakes, but," he said, laughing aloud, "I am a family man. I want my life as it was when I was a young man and held my firstborn in my arms. Is that too much to ask?"

"She cannot hear you," Siriol said. "She understands nothing you say."

DeFreveille glanced over his shoulder at his companion of the last few days and shrugged. He returned Gwennan's hand to its place beneath the *carthen* and relinquished his place beside her to Siriol while he washed his face and hands.

"She understands that I am here," he grumbled to himself, scrubbing his face dry with the small towel set by the basin for him. When he turned back to the room, Siriol was frowning at him though she had not understood what he said, either to Gwennan or to himself. "Go to bed, Siriol. I will watch tonight." He searched Gwennan's face. "Do you think she has improved? I have noticed some change, I think."

Siriol shook her head and would not leave the room. When Rocaille came into the room moments later, he nodded to his commander and stepped onto the platform. DeFreveille raised a flagon of ale to his lips. Rocaille felt his patient's brow, listened to her heart and held her wrist.

"You should rest. You can do nothing here, Commander. Go. I will sit with her."

"I will only take a walk, Rocaille," he said. "My children will be here soon."

"That will make you happy."

Jehan-Emíl retreated to the lower hall, facing the hearth, allowing its heat to warm him, and found some pleasure in it. A jug stood on the table. He reached for it, filled a cup for Artur and one for himself. When Artur accepted the drink, deFreveille saluted him and swallowed the contents before turning to face the hearth again. He laid his arm across the mantle and his brow on his forearm, staring into the flames.

"I am a man," he said, "like any other."

Artur lowered his eyes from his employer's face. "Yes, Commander."

When Jehan-Emíl returned to his room, Rocaille and Siriol had finished bathing Gwennan and the linen on the bed had been changed.

"You were right. She is improved." Rocaille took his cloak and crossed to the door. "She may awaken in the morning."

"Thank you, Rocaille. You will be rewarded for this."

"May you also be rewarded, for your part."

The physician held him accountable but deFreveille was too joyful to reprimand him. He motioned Siriol out of the room, secured the screed door and knelt by the bed. Taking Gwennan's hand in both of his, he rested his brow on them. Her fingers moved in his grasp, but when he looked up, she was still sleeping. He kissed each of her fingertips in turn and extinguished the tapers. Undressing by the light of the fire,

Jehan-Emíl washed away the tension of three nights' vigil in the cool water left by the hearth and lay down beside her.

The siege camp was alerted to the arrival of deFreveille's children, their attendants and the remaining score of his soldiers by the clamor of horses, laughter and trumpets. The company travelled by torchlight through the earliest hours of the morning at Jehan-Batiste's insistence. The soldiers with them were heavily armed. Jehan-Batiste, in his twelfth year, leapt from his horse just beyond the walls in the *buarth* and bounded past the rows of canvas tents to the door of the common hall. Marshal was close on his heels.

"Father!" they shouted together, crashing through the entrance to the hall and coming to an abrupt stop. "Father?" the oldest boy called in a weaker voice, his confidence drained at the sight of so many strange faces peering at him from every corner. "Where is Jehan-Emíl deFreveille, my father?" he demanded of the prisoners. Spying Maides at the hearth, the boy stiffened his back and strode through the ranks of his father's enemies. "Commander Maides, where is deFreveille?"

The mercenary gazed at the tall, lean, dark-haired boy for a few moments. "Where should he be, Jehan-Batiste?"

"Of course," Marshal shouted and turned toward the house. His brother followed.

DeFreveille met his sons at the top of the bridge and stooped to accept their embraces, enquiring after their sister. Jehan-Batiste told his father that she was coming and both boys began to question him about his victory. "Your first concern must always be for the women left in your charge. Bring your sister to me," he admonished. "Then I will tell you what I can remember. It was all a very long time ago."

"Oh, Father, you are teasing us," Jehan-Batiste complained but he withdrew to bring his sister as he was told. Marshal, two years younger, refused to go.

"Why do you not do as I say?"

"Is this where we are to live, Father?"

"Yes, for a while. It is large enough for us, no?"

"I want to go home, Father. I do not understand why we have come all this way. I have had many fights and the people do not speak so I understand."

"They speak a different language, Marshal. I do not always understand them but I am learning. We will have many fights, my boy, but we are together now. This will be better, yes?"

"Yes, Father," Marshal replied.

Charlotte led Cecilé by the hand and stood at the foot of the bridge, waiting for deFreveille to cross to them. He first kissed his daughter's cheek, acknowledging the nurse with a nod, but his scowl was deep.

"You had a safe journey, Cecilé?" he whispered, lifting the little girl into his arms as the three of them ascended the steep slope. Cecilé clung to her father's neck when she saw how far the drop was from the bridge to the ravine.

"Of course, Commander," Charlotte answered for the blonde child in her charge. "Jehan-Batiste was very insistent that we arrive today and not tomorrow." Charlotte's light laughter echoed against the stone of the crumbling garden wall. She raised her large eyes to study the house and frowned behind her employer's back. "You are looking well. I am very glad to see you again."

"You must be hungry," Jehan-Emíl said, "and tired. I will have the cook prepare food for you. I have already eaten." He lowered Cecilé to stand amid the rushes on the hall's stone floor. His five-year-old daughter still clung to his hand. "The house is small, Charlotte," he found himself apologizing. "But the hearth is kept alight."

Jehan-Emíl climbed the staircase once again, leaving his daughter below, to call Siriol. The door was opened to him before he knocked and the golden-haired woman came out onto the small landing, standing in his way. He frowned and bit his lip, glancing over his shoulder at the group below. Though they had come to understand one another well enough over the days during which they had kept vigil, he could not explain the complexities of his family as easily as he had indicated that he wanted a cloth for Gwennan or food for himself.

"My children, Siriol, *plantos*," he began, becoming aware of movement in the bed enclosure to the left of the door. Prevented from moving around Siriol, he picked her up, setting her to one side. Flinging the hangings apart, holding them wide with both hands, he stood above Gwennan. His heart raced, filled with joy to see her awake and broken to see her so altered. She clasped the *carthen* to her chin but could not hide her trembling limbs or pale face or darkened, sunken eyes. "I have much joy in seeing you are well, *boneddiges*."

Gwennan turned her head to the side and closed her eyes.

"I was concerned. I am happy," he said, helplessly. "I am happy," he said again, dropping his arms to his sides.

"I think he is trying to tell you," Siriol said from the other side of the bed as she straightened the cushions beneath her friend's thin, listless shoulders, "that he is glad you have recovered."

Gwennan said nothing but a faint, flickering smile enlivened her gaunt face for a moment. Jehan-Emíl laid his hand on the headboard, smiling first at Siriol and again at Gwennan who, though she did not look at him long, had not shown displeasure.

"*Boneddiges?*" he murmured, lowering himself to one knee beside the bed and sliding his hand between her curled fingers. Grateful that she neither resisted nor withdrew from his touch, he raised her hand to his lips. "Gwennan," he said, closing his eyes, unable, otherwise, to curb his joy.

"Derwyn?" Gwennan whispered to Siriol.

"Pardon?" DeFreveille glared at the blonde woman.

"Derwyn," Siriol replied, meeting the commander's frown. "She asks for Derwyn."

"No." DeFreveille's hand tightened on Gwennan's fingers. "Finished. He will not come here. Finished."

"Derwyn is well, Gwennan," Siriol said. "You do not have to worry." She turned to face the *gelyn*. "Gwennan wants to see Derwyn."

"No. No," he said again. "He will not come here."

"Friends," Siriol insisted, struggling to remember words they had taught each other to ease their own communication. "Derwyn. Gwennan. Friends—you understand? Friends."

"Friends." DeFreveille gazed at the woman. He did not see in her eyes that she lied to him but he did not believe her. "No. Finished. No friends." He shook his head and laid Gwennan's hand flat on the mattress beside her. Rising, he stood down from the platform before he made an emphatic gesture and said again, "No friends."

"*He* will not allow Derwyn to come here," Siriol explained. "I will take a message for you."

Gwennan lifted her fingers from the mattress and let them fall again, all the energy she had to make a gesture of dismissal and drifted back to sleep, glad the agitation was over.

"She sleeps?" DeFreveille moved back toward the bed and peered into her face. "Good. Now, *boneddiges*, my children. *Plantos*."

"*Plantos*? You have children here?"

"Of course, *boneddiges*," he laughed at the expression of shock on her face. "I am father. Three!" He held up the number of fingers on his right hand with pride. "Three, no? Chamber. They need room. To sleep? Yes?"

"There are only two rooms, Commander. As you know. This and," Siriol gestured to the screed, "that. Which for your children? Where are we to sleep? Branwen, Menna, Aine and myself? Our children?"

"That," he commanded, dismissing further discussion because he did not understand her complaint. The room was large enough, at least temporarily, for all the women and children. She and the other women did not need privacy or protection from his children. He ended their conversation, pointing his finger at her. "No friends!"

Siriol curtsied with sarcasm and flung herself into the chair by the hearth to take up her sewing. When deFreveille left the room, she laid the cloth down and returned to the bedside but it was several hours before Gwennan woke again.

NINE

Jehan-Emíl was halfway down the staircase before he realized his children watched him. Charlotte also watched. He could see questions in her eyes though she had quickly covered her puzzlement with a smile. She had seen him wrestle at the door with Siriol. *Let her wonder.* He fixed a broad smile for his children.

"Now, my children! We eat. This cook is very good. The food is very good and the company is excellent." He was pleased to see that the three other women had come into the hall with their children. The two groups of women and children stood on opposite sides of the hearth, eyeing each other with caution. "*Menywod*, good morning! Come, eat," he invited the women to which they responded with reluctance.

"Father," Jehan-Batiste said, "you cannot mean we are to share a meal with them. They are our enemies. They must be kept imprisoned. Why do you allow them this freedom? Why do you speak to them in their language?"

"Who commands here?" deFreveille asked his son quietly.

"You, of course, Father."

"Then do as I tell you. These women are in my household, under my protection. You will treat them and all here with the respect due to them."

"I understand, Father." Jehan-Batiste awaited his father's direction to sit at the table but was distressed to see the women and children take seats without invitation and to compound their disrespect by helping themselves to his father's food without permission, before his father had seated himself.

Jehan-Emíl patted his eldest son's shoulder, understanding his consternation. "Sit, Jehan. You will enjoy your meal much more." After he had directed Charlotte to a stool next to Cecilé, he nodded for Marshal to sit near Jehan-Batiste. "After you have eaten, I will introduce you to these women and their children. We must all be friends in our new home."

"Yes, Father." Cecilé agreed with a yawn, staring at the enormous platter of food placed in front of her and her father.

"It will not be easy to become friends with these…people, but we will all do our best, will we not, Cecilé?" her nurse asked, leaning over the little girl and stroking her blonde curls. Her own strawberry blonde hair swept in waves across her shoulders and down her back, unrestrained. Charlotte de Guidry tossed her head and returned the gaze of the other women with her own haughty scrutiny. Her smile beamed with confidence when she spoke to Cecilé, casting her blue-eyed gaze on deFreveille.

"I hope you will not find it as difficult as that, Charlotte," Jehan-Emíl said, leaning back in his chair. Aware that the women speculated among themselves about his relationship with the nurse, deFreveille ignored Charlotte's smile and soon excused himself from her company, taking his sons with him to see their home. "You will find enough to do, I am sure, with Cecilé. She is a very sleepy girl, no?" He dismissed Charlotte, kissed his daughter and left the house.

Aine rose from her place at the table and returned to the dormitory by the stairwell. The door between the two upper rooms was open. She burst through to accost Siriol as she sat sewing beside Gwennan.

"He has brought his family here."

"Yes, he told me," Siriol replied. "They are to sleep there."

"What of us? What of her?" Aine demanded, pointing at her *pennaeth*.

"Gwennan is much better," Siriol answered.

"That fiend has brought his family. His wife."

Siriol dropped her hands into her lap and stared at Aine for several moments before both women turned to look at the woman asleep in what they both had come to accept was the commander's bed.

"He said nothing to me about a wife," Siriol murmured. "Only his children."

"But she is here," Aine said.

"The children are to sleep in that room," Siriol repeated. "We will have to find pallets for them." She folded her work and stood. "I suppose we should have guessed that he would not make so many changes for our benefit. When he returns, we will ask him to have our possessions moved. For now, let Gwennan sleep. She does not need to know that he...of his deceit."

"How much worse can it be for her to be abused by a man who has a wife than one without?" Aine demanded. "Do you think he cared he was unfaithful to his wife when he did this to her? Do you think Gwennan will feel the sting of her dishonor that much worse because he did not tell her he was wed? She will rejoice that he will torment her no more."

Siriol did not reply for a time. "Stay with her while I have my breakfast." Aine nodded and took the stool that Siriol had vacated. "Leave her in peace for now. She does not have to know everything the moment she wakes." Siriol tidied her hair and descended to the hall, keeping her eyes away from the woman she had seen from the top of the staircase. She sat at the table to the left of the commander's chair and was gratified that Artur came immediately to serve her. With him also she had learned to communicate by necessity and employed their familiarity to ease her own disquiet.

The foreign woman sat in a chair by the hearth with deFreveille's daughter at her knee. She raked her fingers through the little girl's hair as she gazed first at the flames and then at the others in the room. Her eyes fell upon Siriol more than once as did Siriol's upon her but neither woman betrayed anything more than mild curiosity. The child neither moved nor spoke, mesmerized by the constant petting.

As soon as Siriol had eaten, she followed the other women up the stairwell and explained to them the changes to be made. Until deFreveille returned, she assumed nothing more than what he had told her. She replaced Aine at Gwennan's side.

"Siriol." Hearing her name spoken with such a sense of comfort and assurance made Siriol smile before she turned to greet her friend.

"You have slept well, Gwennan."

"How well?" she asked, searching the room trying to tell the number of hours and days by its contents. There were no man's clothes on the chest now. The bed linen was fresh, the pillows straightened. Everything was as it had always been. Her brow knit closely and she bit her lip, wondering if it had been a dream. The one question to ask to make all else clear she could not ask of Siriol. "A meddyg?" she questioned, safer than asking if there had been a man with warm brown eyes and hair that curled around her fingers. "There is a *meddyg*?"

"Yes."

"Derwyn is well?"

"Very well. This *meddyg* has done well for all."

"Will you ask Derwyn to come?"

"I cannot, Gwennan. He is not allowed to come to the house."

"Why?"

"He will not be given permission. DeFreveille has forbidden him to come here."

Everything that she remembered was real. Elgan was dead and she did not grieve. Derwyn was forbidden to visit her and she did not care. She stared at her thin hands and body. "The *meddyg*, Siriol. Bring the *meddyg*."

Artur ran over the bridge at full tilt, the sleeves and tail of his dusty woolen coat, flapping behind him as he dashed across the hardened *buarth* to the infirmary. When he emerged more slowly with Rocaille close beside him, gesturing excitedly toward the house, still trotting while the physician kept pace with him, deFreveille followed the boy's progress with anxiety.

Distracting his sons with the treat of being allowed to stay with the soldiers, he followed in their wake but was too late to catch the physician before he entered the house. By the time he reached the hall, there was no sign of the physician, Artur or Siriol. Charlotte rose when he entered, approaching him with her hands extended. Aine and the others watched from the inglenook where they were sewing by the light of the flames. Jehan-Emíl dismissed the nurse and bounded up the staircase.

The door, when he reached it, was closed. He heard voices, laid his hand on the latch for a moment. Bracing his hands on the wooden frame, he bent his head to listen. Rocaille's voice was clear but deFreveille could not distinguish the physician's words or the women's voices from one another. He raised his fist and brought it down on the door with less force than his intention. Hearing the bar raised, he tried it again but met Siriol. This time her expression told him that she would not be moved.

"Gwennan?" he questioned, dropping his hands from the frame and peering into the pretty face turned up to him. Her slight smile relieved some of his anxiety.

"The *meddyg* sees her now. You must wait."

"No, I do not wait," he hissed.

"You *will* wait." Siriol pushed his shoulders slightly and watched as he stiffened. "After. When he is finished. She is well," she added to reassure him. She glanced beyond him to see this other woman watching them. DeFreveille attempted once more to slip past Siriol but she closed the door and leaned against it, her defiance tempered with a laugh as she looked up at him. He raised his hands in a shrug, a thin smile crossing his mouth in capitulation to her superior maneuvers.

"Your children? A room?" Siriol asked to distract him, slipping her arm through his and starting down the staircase.

"Ah, of course," he murmured, glancing over his shoulder at the door before accompanying Siriol to the hall.

"You must tell me the worst," Gwennan demanded. "Everything."

"*Boneddiges*, you are recovering well. I have listened to your heart," Rocaille tapped his brass ear-cone on his hand and smiled. "You are strong. In two days, three, you can rise but not to work. You must still be careful."

"I want to know," she sighed, grasping his arm. "I cannot remember what happened." Though she could have asked Siriol or Aine the same questions and received truthful answers, she depended on the physician because he was a stranger.

"Ah, *boneddiges*, you were very sick. A fever. I do not know what caused it. There was nothing anyone could do to save the *baban*." The physician could not look at her.

"But…you say I have lost a *baban*?"

"Yes, *boneddiges*. The *baban* is gone. Stillborn. A boy."

"Who told you this?"

"The old woman, Galar, *boneddiges*."

"It is not possible," Gwennan told him.

"These things happen, *boneddiges*. You must accept that…considering all that has happened," Rocaille frowned. "You have worked very hard to save your friend. That and your injuries, the trouble since the battle ended, all of this has not helped."

"Where is the evidence?" Gwennan asked.

"The child is buried, *boneddiges*. Do not think of it," he murmured, clasping her hand in his. "*Boneddiges*, you are young. Perhaps, in time, when you are well," Rocaille faltered. In his own language he growled, "If I were a warrior, if I even had a dagger, I could kill my commander though I would regret the act always." To her, he said, "You must rest. DeFreveille has been here every day. I know he regrets what has happened. You are still weak. These feelings you have will go when you are stronger and have begun again."

"I could, you say, in time, have a child?"

"No one can say with certainty, *boneddiges*, even without such injuries. It is possible, in time. A good husband, gentle, yes, in time."

Gwennan gazed into his dark eyes. "My father—," she began but ended with a laugh. "You will not believe how I have longed to have a child."

"*Boneddiges* ... there is no need for you to tell me these things. You will heal. You are strong."

"I do not care what you know. My women know, but they do not speak of it. I have not lost a child."

"Perhaps you did not realize, perhaps because of all the sadness and upheaval—."

"Think as you want. I am too tired to argue." Gwennan slipped down in the bed, pulling the *carthen* over her shoulder as she turned away from the physician.

"*Boneddiges*, if there was anything I could have done to prevent—."

"Do not blame yourself," she said. "I have not lost a child."

"*Boneddiges*, it is better that you accept what has happened. I know you cannot yet forgive Commander deFreveille but I can assure you that he is truly repentant—he regrets most deeply what he has done to cause you harm." Gwennan turned her head to look at Rocaille over her shoulder. "He is, yes, a man of violence, war is his profession. But I swear to you, *boneddiges*, I have never known him to deliberately hurt anyone weaker than himself. I do not understand all that the old woman claims against him but a man who loves his children as much as deFreveille does, could not kill like this...he has been by your side, day and night. I know you cannot forget but, perhaps, one day, forgive him?"

"Forgive him? *Meddyg*, it is not for me to forgive him." *A man who loves his children ...*

Jehan-Batiste and Marshal returned to the house, bored with the ordinary work of the soldiers. They had not been entertained by sewing tunics, polishing boots or repairing the leather straps on shields. The boys sat staring at the other children while their father attempted to hold a conversation with Charlotte and the other blonde woman.

DeFreveille struggled to translate so that Siriol understood what Charlotte said. His mind was not on the task, glancing often at the bedchamber door. Charlotte said nothing that the other woman needed to hear, only babble about how long their trip had been, how tired she was and how she longed for a bath. For a moment, he allowed himself to gaze at Charlotte and to remember what the sight of her had done, in the past, to raise his spirits. She had removed her cloak and was leaning back comfortably in the large chair. Both he and Siriol were seated on stools. Cecilé sat on his thigh, leaning heavily against his chest.

He stroked his daughter's curly hair. When she looked up at him, he smiled into her brown eyes. "You are much prettier than your father," he whispered against her ear.

Cecilé cupped his face in her tiny hands and shook her head so that her curls bounced in a way that made him laugh. "My father," she whispered earnestly in return, "is very handsome." She cuddled into his shoulder and was nearly asleep when the bedchamber door opened.

Without thinking, Jehan-Emíl deposited Cecilé in Siriol's lap and met the physician at the bottom of the staircase.

"A new crisis, Rocaille?" he asked, feigning levity to hide his concern but thought better of it under the physician's appraising stare. "How is *Boneddiges* Gwennan?"

"She is improved."

"Will she be well? Soon?" He spoke so that Charlotte and his children did not understand his conversation. He clasped the small man's arm and moved toward the outer door. "Is it possible to have—ah, to celebrate the arrival of my family? We have musicians, to entertain her…and the others."

"I cannot judge the rate of her recovery. She is better. She is stronger, but she may never fully recover."

"What do you mean?" He stared into the physician's eyes. "What?"

"I cannot be certain. Much depends on her strength. And will. It is early yet, there may be more." He stopped at the path to the bridge.

"What more? What more do you mean?"

"I am unable to tell what your...interference has caused."

"My interference?" DeFreveille stared at the patch of dirt under his feet. The garden had been trodden and left fallow for so long, he did not think it would bear fruit in spring. "I do not blame you for your concern," he sighed. "Thank you, Rocaille, for all you have done."

"I have only done what I am meant to do. If all men did likewise, *Boneddiges* Gwennan would not have suffered." Rocaille bowed and began the perilous descent. "Remember, Jehan, *Boneddiges* Gwennan has been delivered of an infant. She will need time to recover. You understand?"

"How much time? A week?" Jehan-Emíl asked. The physician glared at him and frowned. "More, I remember."

"Charlotte is particularly pretty this morning. You will be content with her."

"Paul," deFreveille began, pulling himself to his full height, "you know me as well as any man. If you believe I am capable of such crimes, you are at liberty to leave my employ." He laid his hand on the physician's shoulder. "I would be sorry to lose you. It is not a great offense to tell another when you believe he has transgressed and I do not fault you for that or your concern for this woman. I admire your ferocity for her sake, but," he warned, "you will not comment on my domestic arrangements." He smiled at his friend. "I depend upon you to bring *Boneddiges* Gwennan back to full health. In that, I will not interfere. Come to the house as you feel is necessary, and whenever she calls you."

"I will, Jehan, depend on that."

"And Paul," Jehan-Emíl ended, "do not accuse me again of a crime, without evidence. You will know if I am guilty." The physician descended. When the bridge was clear he shouted for his sons and had already reached the *buarth* when they followed, running from the house down the steep hill and across the bridge before they could be stopped by the nurse's strident questions. DeFreveille beamed when he saw them, proud of their exuberance, relieved that their long separation had not weakened their affection for him. He welcomed them into his arms and waited with them while Artur saddled horses, his hands clasped behind his back, staring at the western mountains. The sun was bright overhead and the day warm. Artur offered to ride with them but deFreveille asked him to go to the house instead. "If Gwennan requires anything, see that she has it."

"Yes, Commander," Artur replied, unable to conceal his disappointment.

"If this was not important, Artur, I would entrust these tasks to Michel or another."

"Thank you, sir," Artur replied with a bow.

"And," deFreveille said out of earshot of his sons, "you will take your orders from either Siriol or Gwennan—no one else. Do you understand?"

Artur nodded, turning on his heel and trotting toward the house.

"Now, my sons, I will show you our new home."

"Will we live here long, Father?" Marshal asked urging his horse forward. Marshal deFreveille was a miniature of his father, from his straight back and square shoulders to his long legs. Jehan-Batiste had his mother's eyes and his grandfather's dark hair. The commander glanced at his firstborn, riding sedately behind him, his blue eyes scanning the landscape with hawk-like attention, darting from one hill to another, peering into the depths of the forests that swept down to the riverbank.

"What do you think, Jehan-Batiste?"

"Where are the vineyards, Father?"

"The Welsh have no need of vineyards," Jehan-Emíl laughed.

"They have no wine?"

"They make a drink of honey—."

"That is for children," Jehan-Batiste scoffed.

"We will see if you think this when you wake one morning with a bad head as I have on several occasions. This mead is potent enough, even for you." He rubbed his son's serious head. "It is all very different, my son, but we will learn."

"Why should we learn, Father? It is for them to learn from us."

"That is a foolish thought, Jehan-Batiste, and unworthy of a boy with your intelligence." Jehan-Emíl patted the boy's shoulder. "We have been too long apart and I am to blame for that. Tell me, my young scholar," he said with a broad smile, "if you have never been in a place before and there are men who have twenty score times your knowledge, who would you expect to understand better how to make your crops grow and the fish to jump from the river?"

"Crops grow, Father and fish are netted," Jehan-Batiste replied.

"You have much to learn," Jehan-Emíl said. "I was the same. For now, we will watch and learn, yes?"

"Yes, Father."

"You will like this place better as you come to know it and make friends."

"Friends, Father?" the twelve year old demanded.

"Friends, my sons," he told them. "Both of you. We cannot hope to make our home where we have no friends." When Jehan-Batiste opened his mouth to argue, his father lifted his hand. "Friends, no excuse, no complaint. Understood?" When they agreed, he said, "Tomorrow you will begin your work here but for today, we will have some fun together." He spurred his golden warhorse to a cantor and led the two boys toward the few remaining inhabited *hafodydd* in the wood beyond. As they came up beside him, he pointed upstream to the head of the valley. "The castle of the thegn of this district is there, beyond those trees, high in the mountains."

"But you are thegn, Father," Marshal exclaimed.

"Not yet, my boy."

"When will you take this castle?" Jehan-Batiste inquired.

"I have already taken what this man values most," his father answered. "The rest will follow, soon." As he spoke, he saw his sons straighten in their saddles but he glanced above them to the house on the edge of the cliff that hung over him. From the riverbank, he could see part of the garden wall and the

upper level of the house with its thatched roof jutting out over
the heavily overgrown cliff face, hanging precariously over the
gorge. "Soon," he said again, turning toward the broad
woodlands stretching as far as his eyes could see.

Although the quiet knock on the door surprised her, Gwennan
remained silent. As she dragged the *carthen* from around her
legs, she heard footsteps trotting up the stone staircase, too
light to be a man. Drawing the curtain half closed, she waited
to see who came to her room with no interference from her
friends. The door opened and the floor boards protested the
light footsteps as someone entered, closed the door with care,
added logs to the fire, filled a cup from the bucket and set it on
the chest by the bed. Artur crept across the room toward the
screed wall. As he slowly closed the door and bolted it, she
drew the curtain open, watching him fix a padlock to it. He
turned with the key in his fist and met her eyes.

"Artur," Gwennan said softly, with a smile.

The boy's knees buckled and he wiped his brow.
Swallowing hard, he advanced one step toward her and bowed.
She pulled the curtain back further and her thin hand clung to
it.

"*Boneddiges*?" he breathed.

"Come," she said, gesturing with her other hand.

"*Boneddiges*?" he asked more urgently, moving forward.
"Water? Food?"

"No." She fell back on the cushions but did not take her
eyes off the boy, her hand slipping along the edge of the
curtain to hang listless down the side of the bed.

"*Boneddiges* Siriol?" he begged, edging toward the hearth.

"Ieuan?" she asked.

"Ah no, *boneddiges*. No Ieuan. I am sorry," he answered.
"*Boneddiges* Siriol has said. No Ieuan, yes? The commander has
searched but no Ieuan is here. You understand?"

"Yes." Gwennan did not have the energy to close the
curtain again as her body sank into the sagging mattress and
her eyes closed.

Artur finished his tasks and raced from the room, escaping before Gwennan opened her sunken eyes again. Once halfway down the staircase, he stopped and breathed a sigh of relief. Siriol waited for him at the bottom of the staircase. Since he had been told to give her a message, the boy was grateful that she had come to meet him. Her rosy face was a welcome change from what he had just seen.

"*Boneddiges* Gwennan?" she demanded of him.

"Well," he said, confident he did not lie. "The commander orders."

"Yes, what does he want?" Siriol had been waiting for this message since the early morning. She crossed her arms at her waist.

"The commander says *Boneddiges* Menna and *Boneddiges* Branwen, her child, go to the hall with husbands. Now. He says Cecilé, there," Artur pointed to the dormitory, "with you. Jehan-Batiste and Marshal, here, this room." He nodded toward the room Oswin had left.

"And *Boneddiges* Gwennan?"

The boy shrugged and frowned. "She, there." He nodded toward the commander's bedchamber. "No change."

"The commander?" The boy shrugged again and shook his head. "His wife?" Artur crinkled his brow and pursed his lips. "He did not say where his wife was to sleep?"

"Ah. Wife?" When Siriol nodded, he continued, "The wife of deFreveille is dead, *boneddiges*, many years."

"But…" Siriol frowned. "And her?" she asked, nodding toward Charlotte. "Where will she sleep?"

"Charlotte?" he whispered, a bright color appearing at the neckline of his shirt and shooting up to his ears. "There," he pointed to the dormitory, "with daughter of deFreveille."

"*Her* daughter?" Siriol asked under her breath.

"No," Artur said with a laugh. "No." The boy blushed hard again and complained. "*You are bad.*"

Siriol studied him for a moment. "What did you say?"

"Nothing, *boneddiges*," he replied, dropping his head for a moment.

"Thank you, Artur. Is that all?"

"Yes, *boneddiges*. All." He bowed to the golden-haired woman and approached Charlotte.

Jehan-Batiste and Marshal had returned from their day with their father, still damp-haired from swimming and ready for a meal. They greeted their father's groom as a friend they admired and were full of questions for him. Artur's duties came first. "'*Moiselle* Charlotte," Artur began, once he had freed himself of his employer's sons. "DeFreveille has sent me to show you and his children where you will be sleeping. And I am to ask you which of the chests you will need."

Charlotte nodded haughtily to the boy. "Thank you, Artur, I am grateful that Commander deFreveille has sent you and does not expect me to direct these barbarians to help poor Cecilé." Artur bowed slightly, a frown crossing his usually cheerful face when he did not see the little girl in the hall.

"If you require any assistance, Siriol is castellan in this house until Gwennan Pendyffryn is well—."

"Gwennan! What an ugly name," Charlotte laughed, encouraging Jehan-Batiste and Marshal to agree with her.

"Gwennan Pendyffryn," Artur began, standing erect and looking directly into Charlotte's eyes, "*Boneddiges* Gwennan is the daughter of the *pendefig*."

"What is that?" Charlotte scoffed, wrinkling her nose at the strange words Artur used. "What does that matter to us?"

"The *pendefig* is very powerful, very important. He is a prince," Artur assured the nurse and deFreveille's sons, repeating what he had learned from the Welsh grooms with whom he had become friends.

"My father has already told us that the ruler here has been defeated," Jehan-Batiste, adopting Charlotte's arrogant tone. Artur looked at the boy and shook his head. "You are disloyal to my father if you say otherwise."

"You will discover for yourself what is right to do," Artur told the commander's eldest son. "*Boneddiges* Gwennan is important to deFreveille. He has great respect for her and her father."

"These barbarians?" Charlotte laughed.

"They will be our friends," Marshal said, "as Father has told us."

"Yes, Marshal," Artur said, "our friends."

Charlotte waved her hand in ten year old Marshal's face. Rising to her feet, she brushed and fluffed her skirts, swept her hair from around her neck and nodded once again for Artur to lead the way. When the boy servant turned on his heel toward the wooden stairwell, Charlotte inhaled deeply, "As Jehan-Emíl has ordered," she commented to herself, "for now." With her back straight and her head held high, Charlotte followed the boy up the narrow stairs out of sight of the barbarians and through the hole in the floor to the dormitory.

The boys stood together at the door of the room they were to share. When Artur returned, he helped them to make the bed that they were to share.

"Artur," Jehan-Batiste asked, "where does my father sleep?"

The young groom handed over the pile of *carthen* and said, "He has a campaign tent in the camp, Jehan." This was true and Jehan-Batiste was satisfied. "I will be sleeping here in the house too," he continued, "until you are all settled. I have one more task and I will return when that is done."

While Artur explained to Branwen that she was to be reunited with her husband and that Menna would help the *meddyg*, Charlotte stood rigid at the trapdoor, her sparkling blue eyes fixed on the screed wall. As soon as she was alone, Charlotte crossed the room and tried the door. Realizing that it had been bolted, she kicked it and flounced onto the bed farthest from it.

ten

A fine autumn day greeted Gwennan Pendyffryn when she opened her eyes, startled awake by a sharp, high-pitched voice in the dormitory. "Good day." Gwennan recognized the language, but not the voice or the words. Although the hangings on the side of the bed nearest the screed wall were closed, she stared at them for several minutes expecting them to be opened to reveal the owner of the voice. She judged the owner to be someone near to her in age, possibly younger from the chatter that followed. Gwennan heard Siriol speak but did not hear what was said and the other woman spoke too fast for her to make any sense of her words.

Beams of sunshine shot across the floor, divided by the legs of the chair in front of the small window, trapping sparks of dust in a shaft of light that climbed the foot of the bed. When it reached her arm, its warmth brought a lazy smile to her face as she listened to the voices in the other room. Not until the voice was silent and she heard the screed door being closed did she begin to question who its owner could be. After so many days of illness, she was slow to comprehend and confusion beset her thinking as she watched the beam cross her chest. Her thoughts found clarity in the memory of Ieuan's hands on her body, as warm, as pleasurable as the sun beam.

Gwennan's smile faded as she heard the latch scrape from its hook and a woman's hand grasped the edge of the door. Sensing that someone entered by stealth, Gwennan slid beneath the *carthen* and turned her head away. She reached beneath the cushions for Derwyn's dagger but could not find it before she was forced to close her eyes. Concentrating her other senses on the intruder, Gwennan heard the door to the staircase close. Half opening her eyes, she watched the woman—a small woman with red-gold hair—as she wandered through the room, touching everything within her reach.

For a while, the intruder studied the documents and maps on the table. Gwennan saw that she did not understand what she studied and was soon moving on to finger Ieuan's clothing, folding some items with a shake of her head that implied she was familiar with the task and fond of their owner. When the woman picked up the spruce-colored tunic, Gwennan had to hold her breath to keep from protesting. The intruder examined the stitching and poked her finger at something. She held the gray-green tunic in front of her eyes, wrinkling her nose in disdain at the pattern of embroidered shapes. She spoke under her breath, sneering at what she examined, picking at the gold and green chain border along the hem. She pulled a thread loose and let it unravel with her prodding before she crumpled the garment and tossed it on the edge of the chest. When she turned, the tunic fell to the floor.

The intruder continued her search of the room. When she gazed at her reflection in the *drych* Ieuan used to shave, the woman sighed and examined herself with obvious satisfaction. When she turned toward the room again, she sighed, but now with a sense of indulgence. When she turned her attention to the occupant of the room, she stole to the bed and stepped onto the platform. Before she could touch her, Gwennan turned onto her back and glared at the meddling woman. The woman smiled. "Often I have also desired to sleep away the day after a night with deFreveille."

"Who are you?" the *pennaeth* of the Gaer demanded, dragging her hair out of her eyes with a thin, trembling hand.

The intruder laughed. "But you do not even come close to the image I had conjured. So pale, starved, and very long, a very long creature. He has treated you badly, I see. Oh dear," the woman pouted. "I am called Charlotte, and you?" she asked cheerfully. "We are going to be good friends," she bubbled, straightening the *carthen* around the Gwennan's extraordinarily long, thin body. "If you are the best he could find, we can be very good friends. You will see."

Gwennan stared as the woman spoke to her and touched her. The woman was solicitous, happy and beautiful, round, soft and glowing. Her clothes were rich, embroidered. Her hair floated around her like a beaded scarf. Gwennan watched as she returned to straightening and rearranging the room. Although offended by the presumption, she had no energy to stop the woman and crept again beneath the *carthen*, watching with unwelcome agitation. Nothing was left in its place when the woman went once again to the bedside and patted Gwennan on her drawn up knees. "Now, Jehan-Emíl will be more comfortable in this stable."

Alone again, Gwennan lay back and let her legs drop to the mattress again. "That will not happen again," she said aloud, glaring at the door. "Siriol. Aine." Struggling to sit up in the bed, she was surprised that the room was soon crowded with women. "Is there anything the *meddyg* will allow me to eat?"

"Whatever you like, Gwennan," Siriol said, dashing from the room and calling Artur.

"If there is anything left after these *gelyn* have raided our stores," Aine complained, helping Gwennan to sit.

"None of you look starved to me," Gwennan replied to the older woman. "Are you well, Aine?" she asked, searching the woman's face.

"As well as you, Gwennan."

"I am mending. Are you?"

"I had no wounds to heal that any can see. Bereavement is no less to me than to you. We will all rejoice when these men are gone."

"I do not think they will go soon."

"You at least can rejoice the *gelyn* will not trouble you again. His wife has come, and his children. Soon, we will all be sleeping with the soldiers."

"Wife," Gwennan murmured and glanced at the changed room, all her belongings, gowns, ornaments, even her shoes moved so that she could not find them. An arrogant wife, a wife sure of her husband, Gwennan mused, not bothering to conceal her smile. *A dead wife?* she pondered, recalling Artur's tales.

Siriol entered the room with a platter piled high with meat and bread. Artur followed with a jug of mead and cups on a tray. Menna and Branwen gathered at the foot of the bed, Siriol's children near them.

"Your hand is much needed again, Gwennan," Aine said. "Madlen and Ruth go to the beds of these men."

"What is it you want me to say, Aine? I have no authority to make them chaste."

"You are not to blame! Even when you are ill, that one comes here! He is here with Siriol and she does nothing to help you."

"Who is here?" Gwennan asked. "That one? Who do you mean?"

"When I am here, nothing happens to you," Siriol protested. "What would you have me do when he sends me out, Aine? Am I to kill him in his sleep and be a murderer— worse than the *gelyn*?" Siriol slumped onto the bed and pleaded to her friend. "The commander has been kind—to all of us. All these days and nights he has been as concerned for you as my husband for me."

"Because he is to blame, you fool. He does not want to burn in hell for killing Elgan's child with his lechery."

Neither had seemed to notice that she had asked a question. Gwennan held a small loaf of bread in her hands. "It does not matter now, Aine. If Madlen and Ruth go to these men, it is a matter for them. Perhaps they will be fortunate but they must know that lone women with bastards to feed are not welcome when food is scarce."

"You would not throw them out!" Branwen gasped. "Not when you share their shame."

"What shame do you mean?" she asked, looking from one to another as each dropped her eyes to avoid making a direct accusation. "It is not for me to decide. They are grown women with their own concerns." Although she was no longer hungry, she bit into the bread and clasped the cup of mead, forcing herself to eat and drink. "Go. The rest of you. I am too tired to talk anymore." When the others had left the room, she beckoned Siriol to her and held her hand. "Tell me everything that has happened so that I will know how to fight."

As Siriol told the tale from the day she had become ill, Gwennan watched her friend's face, stopping her only once in a while to ask questions about their friends.

"And Derwyn has remained in the infirmary since that time?"

"He is with the other warriors who were badly wounded."

"What are his plans? Has he decided his next move?"

"DeFreveille?" Siriol asked.

"No," Gwennan said, examining her friend's pensive face for some time before she continued. "Has Derwyn thought? What will he do to fight?"

"I do not believe any of them have thought—they are defeated."

"My father is not defeated," Gwennan said. "If he is not, we are not. I must get a message to him somehow."

"DeFreveille has done so."

"What?" Gwennan demanded. "This is the *gelyn* commander?"

"He is," Siriol answered, cocking her head slightly. "He has sent an emissary to Pendyffryn. You do not remember him?"

"What has my father done?"

"No army has come to support our warriors, Gwennan. None of your father's men have been seen here since before the *gelyn* came. Pendryw says we are alone."

"We are not alone," Gwennan replied. "As long as my father is alive, we will not be alone. He waits to hear what I will do."

"How can you get a message to him, Gwennan? All the roads are under guard, more of deFreveille's soldiers arrive every day. There are so many—."

"They do not have even half the men that my father commands," Gwennan assured her friend. "When he knows that I am ready to fight, he will move against the *gelyn*."

"But—," Siriol did not complete her protest and when Gwennan searched her face, she lowered her eyes.

"You have changed," Gwennan commented. "You like him, this *gelyn* commander."

"No, Gwennan. I am not...I haven't betrayed you. He has been kind—. Some people feel confident, safe," Siriol said, biting her lips together.

"He is our enemy," Gwennan reminded her, "the *gelyn*. Our men are in chains and women have been assaulted. What of them?"

"Gwennan," Siriol murmured, "I know. These are terrible things...I do not blame you for seeking revenge."

"This is not revenge, Siriol. This is justice. War. Tell Oswin that I want to talk to him."

"He is not here. DeFreveille has sent him to work in the kitchen as Betsan's servant."

"What? But he is Elgan's son. Who is this man?"

"DeFreveille has punished him for his behavior...toward the women of his household."

"Oswin is not a threat to them...or my father. We do not need the protection of our enemy," Gwennan replied, contemplating the bread in her hand.

"You have it, regardless," Siriol said, rising to her feet.

"Ieuan? Is he here?" she asked, studying her friend.

"Who is this man, Gwennan? We do not know him—if we had, we would have brought him to you—you called him so often."

"It does not matter now." Satisfied Siriol had not guessed the identity of the man she sought, Gwennan's determination to prove Ieuan Emyr worthy did not falter. Her body was not capable of sustaining the level of energy her plans demanded and, by early afternoon, she had fallen asleep once again, refreshed by a warm bath and a change of bedding. When she woke again, the room was dim, with only the glow of the hearth and the crackle of the flames to keep her company.

From the lower hall, Gwennan heard the faint voices of women, voices she recognized and the shrill voice that was new to her. By the light in the small window, she judged the hour was not late. She could not distinguish any words spoken but there seemed to be no anger expressed in any of them. From the dormitory, the breathing of sleeping children soothed her. *Ieuan Emyr's children?* Gwennan turned her head to stare at the open door in the timber wall.

The pre-dawn chill woke deFreveille from his stupor. He lay on his back sprawled across the narrow cot like a dead man knocked from his horse. Sitting up on the edge of the cot, he held his head in his hands until it stopped spinning and eventually staggered between the tents in the camp to the *buarth*. Outside, the air was clear and froze his breath. He took deep breaths, clearing his head. The red sun was cresting the hills to the east when he climbed to the house.

He frowned, seeing no sign of his sons, vaguely remembering what he had told Artur to do. With a shrug, he began the long climb to his bedchamber, resting against the wall when his head spun too fast and he was in danger of falling to the rushes below. He slumped against the door frame, laying his head and back against the cool stones, sucking in deep breaths to still the nausea. *Too much mead.* When he could, he laid a trembling hand on the latch of the door and lifted it.

The light from the fire was feeble but good enough for him to avoid falling over any of the furniture. Nothing was the way he had left it the previous morning. His clothes, maps, shaving blade were all put away. Even Gwennan's belongings had been moved, the chairs, boxes and chests rearranged. His frown was deep when he reached the hearth and threw more logs onto the grate. Turning toward the bed, he tore his shirt free of his *trwsus* and ripped his tunic over his head. He knew

Gwennan could not have put his things in order or changed the room. None of the other women dared.

He yanked his boots off and flung them at the screed wall, then dragged the chair from its new position back to where it belonged near the hearth. He sat with one leg hanging over the arm, watching Gwennan sleep, wondering how long he would have to wait until she woke and turned to him. Anger had sobered him. He had slept long enough in the tent from drink and did not need to disturb her with his cold body or steal her warmth. With a heavy sigh, he allowed his anger to subside. He lit a taper, set it on the narrow table and spread out his maps.

Days and nights lying in bed, however sick she had been, had left Gwennan restless. Sleeping long hours was no longer possible and she was exasperated to find herself wide awake before the day had dawned. She had heard every step and snarl Ieuan made entering the house and ascending the staircase. She crept deeper into the *carthen*, covering her head, and struggled to stay quiet as he entered the room.

She could not see him with her back to the fire but she sensed his anger and stiffened when he threw objects. Her last conscious memory of him was the morning she woke with her arms around him. The memory was shameful and she blushed, recalling how her body had betrayed her. Both Siriol and Rocaille had told her the *gelyn* had been near her while she was ill, she had no clear memory of it, only a sense of someone close to her. She could not pretend to be asleep forever.

Her heavy sigh brought Jehan-Emíl back from his contemplation of his maps as though he had been caught by a grappling hook. He leaned back in the chair, laid his head against it and turned his face toward the bed. He watched her struggle onto her back and her arm drop above her head listlessly. She was awake but she did not open her eyes.

Gwennan could not tell whether he was awake or had fallen asleep in the chair, he was so quiet. She had hoped that by moving, she could force him to respond. Through her eyelashes, she could see the taper's flame splutter and flicker and, by the fire burning down, that he sat in his chair, silent, motionless, and she could stand it no longer. Mustering her small reserve of energy, she sat up and leaned back on her hands, staring across the room into his quiet face.

He stood and crossed the room toward her, keeping his eyes locked on hers. Kneeling on one knee beside her, he placed his hands on her shoulders and pushed her back against the cushions. He smoothed the fabric of her chemise and caressed her neck and shoulders. "Gwennan," he murmured, taking her hand and raising it to his lips. "You are so changed," he whispered against her palm.

"Do you think that knowing a few words to say to me will make a difference?" she asked, laying her free hand on his wrist. When he raised his eyes to her face, she was free to speak as she felt, without fear that he would understand too much. "Where have you been, Ieuan? What have you done that I will have to undo?" She spoke too fast for his limited ability and she studied the frown on his pleasant, ordinary face. "You know I must fight you. I have no option now." Though he could not understand, Gwennan kept her voice low so that none of the women in the next room could hear her. "If you had come unarmed, if you had not killed my friends, if you did not threaten my father, if you had asked," she sighed, turning her cheek toward his hand.

"Tell me," he said in the Latin he knew she understood, but she shook her head, a tear coursing over her cheek and falling into her hair. "Tell me, Gwennan." He caught the next tear in the crook of his finger and kissed her temple, tasting the third on his lips. Glancing at the hangings around the bed, secure that they were not observed by anyone from beyond the screed wall, he stretched his body on the bed next to her, closing his arms around her.

"I cannot tell you," she said, refusing to let him understand her. "I can never tell you," she whispered as his lips brushed her throat. For a moment, she locked her fingers in the curls at the back of his neck. "Ieuan."

"*Menyw*," he murmured, sweeping the *carthen* away from her body. His hands trembled as he lifted the chemise from her thighs, tracing his fingers over her silky skin to her hip, slipping around her thigh to draw her leg over him. "Gwennan. You make—," he hissed against her throat. "No, I cannot! I cannot," he repeated, though his grip on her leg tightened. "I am—. Rocaille tells me I cannot," he said turning his head to look into her eyes. "You understand? I want. I need, but no." His eyes turned away to study the smoke-blackened thatch. Raising his finger to his lips, he said, "I am good. Quiet. I can."

Gwennan lowered her head so that he did not see the smile she forced away from her lips as she watched him struggle to regain his composure, expressing his determination to control himself in a language in which he spoke as simply as a small child. "Ieuan," she murmured, laying her fingers on his wrist and tracing the veins that carried his blood, feeling the pulse of his heartbeat.

"Gwennan," he sighed, turning toward her again. "No, *cariad.*" He touched her cheek and bent his head to kiss her forehead but she tilted her head back and caught his mouth, parting her lips as his arms clenched around her waist. "You are bad," he murmured against her mouth. For several moments, he responded to her invitation. When she lifted her hands to open the neck of his shirt, he disentangled himself from her embrace and covered her legs again, tugging the chemise over her breasts. Turning onto his back to stare at the blackness of the thatched roof, he said, "No," and pulled her hands away from him.

"Now? Please?" she teased him with his own words, sliding her hand under the cords of his shirt and tugging at the knot.

"No," he laughed under his breath. "This is not possible," he continued in a low voice. "Not possible. Everything has changed, Gwennan. Everything."

"You refuse?" she demanded. "You repudiate me now?" Gwennan saw from his expression that he struggled to comprehend her. "You have ruined my life and you will not accept your responsibility to me?"

"What? Explain to me," he said. When she turned her face away from him, he sat at the edge of the bed and hissed, "It does not matter what you say. I have decided what will happen to you." She stretched her fingers toward his face. "No," he repeated, drawing the *carthen* over her arms. He extinguished the taper, gathered his clothes and left the room.

Gwennan lay beneath the *carthen*, watching the sky change colors through the window in the opposite wall. Morning broke into the room, the first companion to end her solitude. From the kitchen, the sounds of another day and the quizzical voices of children in the dormitory cheered her. A woman's voice she now recognized responded angrily to a chirped greeting. Gwennan turned her back to the screed and slept until midday.

The blackened thatch above her seemed to descend as she opened her eyes in the afternoon. The rosy light that had filled her room at dawn had changed to a dull, grayish brown. Gwennan drew back the hangings on the side of the bed nearest the dormitory. The bolt and padlock were in place. If any of her friends, or others, were to come into the room, they would enter from the lower hall. Listening for voices, she held her breath for a moment and released it slowly. Although the house was quiet, she had only had to let the rings of the bed hangings clink against one another for her wakefulness to receive a response. The knock on the door was tentative.

"Come in," she replied, curious to see who was on guard now. Gwennan smiled when Artur opened the door and peeped around the edge. "Good afternoon, Artur."

"Good afternoon, *boneddiges*."

"What are your instructions today?"

"I am to do as you require. Do you want a meal now?"

"Yes, thank you. Walnuts are welcome," she said, pushing herself to sit against the headboard, "with cheese and *cawl*?" The groom turned on his heel, returning in a few minutes with what she had ordered. "The walnuts are not cracked," she said with a pout.

"*Boneddiges,* deFreveille is not in the Gaer today," Artur apologized, setting the tray on her lap. "I have brought this instead." He held a small tool in his hand and grinned.

"I hope you know how to use it," Gwennan laughed.

"Oh yes, *boneddiges,* deFreveille has taught me—for just such an occasion, but he does not use it."

"I know," Gwennan replied, taking the two halves of the first walnut the boy opened into her hand. "You speak very well," she commented. "Much better than your employer."

"He does not have much time, *boneddiges.* DeFreveille has many responsibilities."

"He only has himself to blame, Artur. He was the one who decided to take the Gaer. No one asked him to do that." Artur looked at her for some time and when she smiled into his earnest fourteen-year-old face, he frowned slightly. "You are a good friend to him, I see."

"Yes, *boneddiges.*"

"With whom is he studying to learn this language?"

"Many people are assisting," Artur replied, sitting up straight on the stool by the side of the bed. "At first, only Commander Maides, then the *meddyg. Boneddiges* Siriol, of course. Many of the warriors also, Pendryw, Iago, Tomos—."

"Derwyn?"

"Ah, no, *boneddiges.* The Celt is very angry. He does not speak to deFreveille. He does not speak to anyone but the Cymry."

"He would learn more if he did," Gwennan replied, lifting the bowl of *cawl* to her lips.

"DeFreveille?"

"Both," she answered, smiling. "DeFreveille's children are here."

"Yes, *boneddiges.* The boys are in the room below. The girl is there—with her nurse."

"What is her name?"

"The girl is Cecilé."

"And the nurse?"

"Charlotte, *boneddiges*. She has been nurse to the children since before Cecilé was born—a friend to… the commander's wife."

"Helene. I have met this nurse," Gwennan admitted.

"She will not come to this room again," Artur assured her, taking the tray to the table.

"Why?"

"DeFreveille has told her that she is forbidden."

"He was very angry…" Gwennan murmured. "With me?"

"Ah, no, *boneddiges*, with her. She should not be here. He told her, before he came, she was not to come."

"But, she did." The groom nodded, bowing his head. Although Gwennan knew he was uncomfortable discussing his employer, she said, "Charlotte is very beautiful. He must have been glad to see her after the welcome he received here."

"I do not understand," Artur replied. Gwennan smiled at his valiant effort at discretion. "*Boneddiges*, deFreveille has told me I must answer all your questions. I do not like to talk about him, but if you ask, I will tell you."

"You have told me all I need to know, Artur. I have no more questions." The boy heaved a great sigh and bowed from the waist. "Please tell Siriol that I am awake."

On an early winter day, when even the ravens refused to fly against the bitter gale, Gwennan Pendyffryn listened to the chatter of the women in the dormitory as they exchanged news from the stockade and the house. Derwyn, Menna told the others, was now in the common hall with the rest of the warriors. As on another day, more than a week before, deFreveille bellowed in the lower hall for one or the other of his sons, neither of whom had she yet seen, though the little girl was often in the dormitory—a shadow for Siriol's daughter, Eira,—when her nurse was not close.

A handful of days had passed but autumn had become winter, during which Gwennan had seen no one but Artur, Siriol, Aine and Rocaille. The *gelyn* commander called his little daughter by name and laughed when the child ran down the stairs into his waiting arms. Taking another shirt from the pile on the small table by her chair, Gwennan spread it across her knees, examining the work she had completed on the previous evening before fatigue had sent her to bed. There were still four others that needed to have their collars turned and the cuffs sewn. Several only required hemming before they were ready to be handed out to the soldiers in the garrison.

Though several of the women had refused to work on any shirt that might be given as winter garb to one of the *gelyn*, Gwennan made no distinction between soldiers who had served in Elgan's command and those who served Ieuan Emyr. After so many weeks of occupation, the lines were blurred with many of Elgan's men, some only from boredom, deciding that activity was more to their taste than staring at the whitewashed walls of the common hall.

"Pendryw," Siriol said as she took a seat near Gwennan, "is captain of a war band." Gwennan glanced at her friend for a moment. "He has never been able to remain idle while others work," Siriol continued by way of apology. "When deFre— when he was offered the promotion, he didn't hesitate. I have only heard it from Menna this moment. Are you very angry?"

"No," Gwennan replied. "How many of the soldiers will need coats this winter?"

"Nearly half, if not more."

"How many?" Gwennan asked, folding the shirt with care and laying it on the chest with others to be distributed. When Siriol still had not answered her question, Gwennan lifted her eyes to her friend's face and followed the direction of her gaze. "What is it? What do you see?"

"Nothing."

"Of course, you do. Bring it here." Siriol stooped and plucked the spruce-colored tunic from the floor. Gwennan took it from her, shaking the dust from it. "This will be suitable for Pendryw in his new rank."

"You can't give it to him," Siriol gasped.

"Why not? I can give to anyone I please."

"But—."

"But what, Siriol? I will repair this damage now and you will give it to your husband, with my compliments on his promotion."

"If he is seen, Gwennan—."

"By whom?" Gwennan demanded. "In fact, Siriol, invite him here. This evening. I will present it myself."

"But what about the commander, Gwennan? He has worn this tunic, he—."

"Invite Bedwyn and Iago as well."

"They will not be allowed to come to the house."

"This is my house, Siriol, and I will have the guests I choose. If you will not do as I ask, I will go myself to invite them, if I have to crawl."

"That is unkind, Gwennan. You know I will go."

"Then do. Come back to help me dress."

During the time that Siriol was gone from the house, Gwennan examined the tunic. From her box of threads, she chose colors to repair the pulled stitches. When the repair was finished, she lifted the tunic close to her but it had lain on the floor too long. The only scent she detected was dust. She held the tunic to her heart for a moment before folding it into a length of plain cloth and tying a cord around it. While she was still alone, she wrote the message she had for her father.

DeFreveille watched Siriol don her cloak as she walked down the staircase. Though she glanced at him, she did not stop to explain her errand and he did not interfere. This was only his second visit to the house in eight days to be with his daughter. His sons stood with him at the hearth as Jehan-Emíl held Cecilé on his knee. Only for a moment did he follow Siriol's departure with a quick glance at the door of his bedchamber. He knew Charlotte observed him. He concealed his frown in Cecilé's curly hair and a laugh when she tickled his chin.

"Artur," he called. When the groom emerged from the kitchen, he said, "Tell the cook that we will all have our meal together tonight, in the house. Invite Aine and Siriol, and, of course, *Boneddiges* Gwennan."

Paul Rocaille bowed when he stood at the door from the entry passage of the large room.

"You were called?" deFreveille asked the physician, making no effort to conceal his interest though he concealed his words so that neither his children nor the nurse understood.

"I was not called. I come at this time most days."

"I was not told of this," deFreveille said. "Is the *boneddiges* well?"

"She is still very weak. Very weak, *bonheddig*."

"Will she be able to dine with me—with us, tonight?" His self-imposed ban had begun to grate and the physician's freedom annoyed him.

"Oh no, *bonheddig*, not for a long time. A long time." The physician bowed again and dashed up the staircase. Rocaille knocked on the door but deFreveille did not hear Gwennan's voice inviting him to enter, before the physician slipped into the room, saying, "Good day, Gwennan. You look—," and closed the door.

"Father," Jehan-Batiste began, touching his father's shoulder, "why do you speak to Artur and your physician in this language?"

"Because I can, Jehan," he replied and set his daughter on her feet in front of him. "Artur, ensure that you deliver the invitation to the *boneddiges* Gwennan personally."

"I will, *bonheddig*."

Rocaille finished his brief examination of his patient but his frown was deep when he put his brass instruments into his pouch and took the seat she offered by the fire. "You look well," he commented, "but you are pushing too fast." Gwennan dismissed his observation with a curt wave of her hand and brushed her hair back from her eyes, bending her head over the last shirt to be hemmed. "Jehan-Emíl is concerned for you, Gwennan. We have had this conversation many times over the past days. There is no reason for you to rush to your duties. *Boneddiges* Siriol is as capable. She keeps the house in order," he laughed, "as well as the children. Every one of them is fed and bathed as they should be. To be honest, she is a better nurse to them than Charlotte has been at the best of times. You need to rest," he insisted, "and not to worry so much. When you are well, there will be time enough to re-establish your authority in the house. No one is keener than deFreveille for this to happen."

Gwennan raised her eyes to the *meddyg's* face but her smile did not convey to him what she was thinking, only what he wanted to believe.

"Good," he sighed. "We are agreed. Another week, perhaps a few days longer and I will give you my blessing to leave this room." He rose to his feet and took her hand. "Now, I must tell deFreveille that he will have to wait longer to see you again. It gives me pleasure to see him huff and puff with impatience."

"Does he wish to be rid of me, Paul?" Gwennan asked, fingering the cord on the cloth parcel.

"On the contrary, *boneddiges*," Rocaille chuckled. "I think that is the furthest thought from his mind where you are concerned."

Before Rocaille left her, they were joined by Artur. The groom sat on a stool in the corner of the room, waiting for the physician to finish. As he had no other business with Gwennan, the small man bowed to her at the door and skipped down the steps under the scrutiny of his commander.

"You are cheerful, Rocaille," deFreveille commented.

"It is a beautiful day, *bonheddig*."

"And the *boneddiges*?"

"Also beautiful, as you know."

"You overstep, Paul," deFreveille said. "Do not."

"I state only what is common knowledge, *bonheddig*. Would you prefer that I am blinded?" he asked. "Will you order that my eyes are burned out?"

"You tread dangerously."

"As do you, *bonheddig*. If you are not content with my service, I will go but I will not abandon the *boneddiges* nor will I be false to you. The *boneddiges* is my patient and is not strong enough to deal with you. I will tell you the moment she is. I am as eager for that moment as you are."

"Why is that, Paul?" deFreveille asked with a smile.

"It is your due, *bonheddig*," Paul Rocaille replied with a bow and a grin.

"We have no conflict, *meddyg*," the commander replied, "as long as you concern yourself with her good health."

"What has brought you here, Artur?" Gwennan asked, setting her work aside and studying the young groom. "You are never here voluntarily," she laughed.

"I am not unwilling, *boneddiges*," he protested.

"Do I frighten you?"

"No," Artur said and hung his head. "Yes."

"I'm sorry, Artur," she laughed again. "Now, why have you come this time?"

"Commander deFreveille, *boneddiges*, has asked— wishes you to join him tonight for the meal. He also invites *Boneddiges* Aine and *Boneddiges* Siriol, their children also, to join with his children."

Gwennan left her shawls draped over the back of the large chair and turned her back to him, crossing the room to sit on the edge of the bed, wrapping her still thin hand around the bedpost. She studied her fingers for a long time. Artur also rose to his feet but did not move from the spot in the corner. Gwennan looked up at him. His black tunic with its gold crest over his heart was frayed along the hem and his *trwsus* were thinning at the knees. The collar of his linen shirt was torn. The cord at his neck had broken. On his feet, he wore boots that were run down at the heels but were of high quality leather. At one time, all of his garments were excellent. His bearing was proud. In another month, he would be too tall for anything he wore that morning. She could see that his wrists dangled from the shirt sleeves and the cuffs were too tight.

"I cannot accept this invitation," Gwennan replied. "I have already made an arrangement with my friends."

"What should I tell deFreveille?" he asked.

"Tell him that his presence in my house is not welcome, nor is that of his children or any of his household. Tell him that I await their removal without delay."

"*Boneddiges*, I cannot tell him this."

"Then I will tell him myself," Gwennan answered as Siriol came into the room from the lower hall. "Siriol, this will amuse you. The wolf has invited us to share a meal with him tonight."

"Oh," Siriol said, turning on her heel, "I will tell the others to come another night."

"You will not," Gwennan declared though her voice was low. "I will not be put out of my house. If he wants to use my house to entertain his friends, he must ask *my* permission. I do not ask his." She turned suddenly to fix Artur to the spot in which he was standing. "I do not want to cause you any difficulty with your employer," she said with a gentle smile. "Tell deFreveille that I have guests tonight and *my* house will not be at his disposal."

"Gwennan," Siriol sighed, "this is not like you."

"Artur, please tell Aine that I will want a bath later, in this room."

When the groom had left, Siriol turned on Gwennan. "You do not know this man and you are deliberately courting his anger. What has come over you?"

"Sense," Gwennan replied. "I was a fool to be so complacent, to depend on Derwyn to protect us. I almost committed the worst of all sins because of my reliance on him. If not for this wolf, I would be dead. And because of this wolf, I have lost my home—for a while. I intend to reclaim it."

"He is here, Gwennan. He will not go away because you tell him to leave."

"You would be surprised what a man will do," she said, lowering herself to lie on the bed, "given good reason."

"Look at you," Siriol complained, "you can barely stand and you begin a fight with a man twice your size."

"Even if he was five times my size, I would fight him for what is mine. Help me or step aside."

"You know I will help you," Siriol replied, sitting by her friend, "but I beg you not to put Pendryw in deFreveille's way. Pen is a simple man, a good and kind man. If you play him against the *gelyn*, my husband will not understand his part and deFreveille will punish him. Pen does not deserve to be used for your revenge."

"Forgive me, Siriol. You are right. It will be much better for me to be direct. Pendryw will have to make do with my good wishes. Now," Gwennan said, "what shall I wear tonight?"

After she had made her choice of garment, Gwennan finished the mending of a few of the warriors' tunics for the remainder of the afternoon and sorted through her box of clasps and ornaments. As she was putting the box back onto the mantle shelf, she discovered a key and handed it to Siriol.

"Good," her friend exclaimed. "We will have no more of this locking of doors between us. Aine has not felt confident of visiting you since deFreveille put this lock against us." Siriol swept across the room to the door, removed the lock and dropped it with its key on top of the parchment maps and documents still strewn across the small table where they too had been abandoned. She unbolted the door and wedged it open. "Now, we can all come and go as we please, Gwennan. Even Rocaille cannot keep you a prisoner," she laughed. But when she turned back to the room, Gwennan had crawled back into her bed. Siriol laid a good fire, blew out the taper and went down the staircase to the hall to join Aine and her own children. DeFreveille's forlorn little girl stood with her brothers, watching Eira and Gareth. Her father turned from his conversation with Artur and glared at Siriol but did not interfere with her tasks.

ELEVEN

By the time the wooden tub was moved from the dormitory to the bedchamber, deFreveille was pacing the lower hall like a bear. As the buckets of steaming water were carried up the stone steps, he came to his senses, made his apologies to his children and left the house. When deFreveille returned in the evening, accompanied by Maides, Artur bowed his head once and continued with his duties as he had been directed by the *boneddiges* as well as those that the commander had given him, despite the conflict between them.

As Pendryw, Iago and Bedwyn entered the house, deFreveille greeted them with a nod and sent one of the girls to them with cups filled with Elgan's mead. Aine entered from the stairwell but she was prevented from retreating when deFreveille approached her with a bow, extending his hand to her. "Thank you for joining me," he said. Covering her cold hand with his own warmer one, he drew her toward the hearth where he encouraged her to sit in the chair he used—the *pennaeth's* chair.

When Charlotte, who had taken care to dress in pale blue and fine muslin, swept from the opening of the stairwell, her entrance was noted by Maides with an upward turn of his mouth and by Aine with a frown. Jehan-Emíl glanced at her and growled, "Where is my daughter?"

"She is very sleepy."

"Bring her, dressed for the occasion."

"But—."

"Do as you are told or find another employer," he hissed, turning away at the sound of the new door to his bedchamber swinging open on stiff hinges. He reached the bottom of the staircase just as Siriol stepped onto the landing.

"Oh, no," she whispered to Gwennan, "deFreveille is here."

"Did you expect otherwise?" Gwennan asked, joining her friend at the opening of the door. Before she also stepped onto the landing and into view, she took a deep breath, bracing her hand on the door jamb.

"You knew?"

"What else would he do?" she said with a smile as she released her grip and emerged, for the first time in weeks, into the view of her friends and enemies. Of all the gowns she inherited from her mother, none fit her better in her weakened condition than the one her mother had worn the first time she met Daran Pendyffryn—the wild, impetuous warrior-prince her family had contracted as her husband. The shimmering gray-green brought out her hazel eyes and gave her ash-colored hair a golden sheen.

Though she was still too pale and the darkness around her eyes had only begun to fade, the signs of her illness could not overshadow the proud grace with which she descended the staircase under the watchful eye of her friend and the steady gaze of Ieuan Emyr. The panels of the gown clung to her body, accentuating her stature and disguising her frailties. Although her hair was plaited, Siriol had kept it loose so that wisps of silvery gold floated around her cheeks as she walked and rested like delicate lace around her throat. When she reached the next to last stair and was still above the *gelyn* commander, keeping her eyes on his, she extended her hand outward. "Bedwyn, if you please."

The young warrior sucked his breath and came forward, lifting his hand to take hers onto his arm. Gwennan turned her head to smile at him and descended the last step to the floor of the hall. Siriol came quickly after her, meeting deFreveille's angry glare before she went to her husband's side. In less than a blink of an eye, deFreveille smiled, turned on his heel, following Gwennan and her chosen escort to the center of the hall where the *boneddiges* had taken a seat beside Aine. Bedwyn stood to one side.

Jehan-Emíl stood in front of her and bowed, taking the hand that she had offered to the young, fair-haired Welshman and kissed her fingers before calling on Artur to bring him a chair. The *gelyn* commander positioned the chair in front of Gwennan, making conversation with her awkward for everyone else. Gwennan met his opposition with a smile but she reserved her energy for another battle. DeFreveille leaned forward and struck up his own, one-sided, conversation.

When Jehan-Batiste and Marshal came from their room and were joined by their sister, the three joined their father, gathering around him as a sanctuary of familiarity in the midst of the hostility they met in the faces of the others in the room. DeFreveille welcomed his children but did not allow their presence to break the flow of his discourse. He spoke to Gwennan as though she understood every word, as though they had learned to communicate with one another in his language.

"—And you will be pleased to know that all of your warriors are now fit. As you know, many of them have accepted commissions in my army. Others will do so by the end of this week. I regret the necessity of this war between us, but I do not regret that it has allowed our meeting." He kept his voice low and his words were too vague for Jehan-Batiste to comprehend his true meaning. Marshal openly stared at the woman his father treated with respect. Cecilé insinuated herself between her father and the woman she had glimpsed from the door in the screed wall whenever she shadowed Eira's movements.

Gwennan avoided meeting deFreveille's eyes and ignored the children. Her senses were trained on the reactions of her friends, upon whom she knew she would have to depend if she were to launch a campaign of resistance to the rule of the foreigner. In the hidden pocket of her gown, her letter to her father waited for an opportunity to be delivered to her messenger. For a moment, Gwennan was attracted to the nurse, who also came to stand near the commander—completing an intimate family group. DeFreveille did not turn his head to acknowledge her presence as he had the children but his momentary scowl did not escape Gwennan's quiet notice.

The arrival of the meal was preceded by its aromas emanating from the steaming heat of the kitchen. Everything that Gwennan had requested for the meal began to appear in greater quantities than she had stipulated. The smile that she bestowed on her adversary was greeted with a cocked bow of his head and a similar smile. By the time he had sent his children to their places at the smaller of the two tables, Gwennan had taken Bedwyn's arm and advanced to the long table intent on taking the *pennaeth's* chair at the center. When Bedwyn pulled the armed chair out for her, deFreveille was there to take her arm. He granted her the privilege of assuming the authority of the household but when Gwennan offered the chair to her right to Bedwyn as her companion, the *gelyn* commander made a sharp gesture toward the young Welshman and Bedwyn relinquished the place at the table to deFreveille.

Pendryw, as her most senior guest was seated to Gwennan's left, accompanied by his wife. The unhappiest partaker of the family meal sat with all the children at a separate table, glowering at her employer and faithless lover with blue eyes cold with hatred and hot for revenge. While Charlotte filled her thoughts with scheming, her laughter with the children filled the hall. Her beautiful smile filled both Jehan-Batiste and his brother with shy confidence as they entertained Charlotte with tales of their exploits.

"And what do you think, my little pretty one?" Charlotte asked the commander's daughter as she stroked Cecilé's small head. "Do you think as these boys or are you of the opinion, as am I, that a word," Charlotte said, lowering her voice to a whisper in the little girl's ear, "a glance, a touch are enough to conquer even the ugliest of barbarian women? Such women are easy prey for men like your father, are they not? A man who dominates will snap such creatures like twigs. You will see, he will break this one to his will and leave her for his men to finish." When the little girl whimpered, Charlotte scolded in a soft voice, patting the tearful girl's head. "Oh, you are a silly child. Eat your meal, my darling. I know it is tasteless, but it is the best that these wretched people have to offer your poor father and his darling children."

Jehan-Batiste glanced at the long table and pressed his lips together when his father clasped the barbarian woman's hand and raised it to his lips.

"You are pale, Gwennan," he commented, at liberty to speak so she understood him. "Very pale, very thin. The smallest wind will lift you like a feather. I am sad to see you so changed—but I cannot be sad to see you. So beautiful." He kissed her fingers again. "I do not have words," he complained. "You are angry, I know that. We—you and I—we, one day, are better, yes? Friends? Is possible," he assured her, releasing her hand.

They had finished their meal when Gwennan caught the eye of one of the girls and murmured her instructions. When the girl returned with a parcel wrapped in vellum, Gwennan tossed it on the table in front of the *gelyn* commander.

"What is this?" the commander asked. Beyond Pendryw, Jehan-Emíl saw Siriol's eyes widen and her expression change from confusion to alarm. "What is this?"

"Commander Maides," Gwennan said in a clear voice, loud enough for everyone in the hall to hear her, "tell this man that this tunic is not fit for any of my warriors. He may treat it with as much disrespect as he has shown members of my household. Tell him he is not welcome in my house." While Maides murmured the translation so that deFreveille's children would not know that the woman had insulted their father in front of his enemies, deFreveille watched Gwennan's face. "Bedwyn," she called as the last word was spoken.

The young warrior was at her side the instant deFreveille was on his feet. With dignity, Gwennan pushed herself from her chair, refusing Bedwyn's help though her effort was arduous. Siriol dashed to her friend but was waved away. Gwennan grasped Bedwyn's sleeve and pulled herself toward him.

Though still stunned by her speech, deFreveille witnessed Gwennan's exchange with the young warrior. Bedwyn clasped her arm and was assisting his *pennaeth* to the staircase when deFreveille gave an order to Maides. At the foot of the stairs, Gwennan began her climb alone.

When deFreveille joined Bedwyn, he laid his hand on the young man's shoulder. "Go with your commanding officer." Bedwyn drew back but Maides was already behind him. Jehan-Emíl followed Gwennan and was a step below her when she turned. Sweeping her into his arms, he carried her into the bedchamber and kicked the door shut behind them with such force that the latch fell into place and barred the entrance to anyone who came after. Within seconds, he heard shouting in the hall and Siriol was at the door.

"You are unhappy, Gwennan?" he asked with confidence in her language, peering into her dark rimmed eyes.

When he spoke, she let her arms fall listless and turned her face away. He carried her, without resistance, to the bed. He had not been near her for weeks and indulged his pleasure in holding her, knowing she would have him the next time he came to her bed. Though he knew that she was still too frail to bear him, he began to count the end of his separation from her in days. His arms tightened around her as he remembered the feel of her caress, her fingers in his hair, the taste of her throat. His heart stopped, and then shot ahead like a catapult, as he watched her chest rise with her breath. His fingers stretched to close over her breast.

She wrenched herself free of his hand as though she had been burned, crying out. DeFreveille caught her before she fell from his arms. While he struggled to keep her from falling, Gwennan drew back her arm and, with all the force of her anger and humiliation, slapped the side of his face.

Siriol screamed.

The blow's strength so stunned deFreveille that he could only stare at the hand that delivered it. His jaw stung and the palm of her hand reddened. He heard Charlotte's laughter. His back stiffened. "Out!" he shouted without looking at the nurse standing in the open door of the dormitory.

DeFreveille laid Gwennan on the bed and lunged at Charlotte, shoving her through the screed door and slamming it in her face. Whirling at the other door, "Away," he shouted, pounding the table with his fist. He grabbed the lock and held it before Gwennan's eyes, his fist clenched around it so that she would know that his anger was for her as well. He snapped the lock in his hand and rammed it closed on the bolted door. "Away! All away!"

"Please," Siriol pleaded, slapping the door with her open hands. "Don't do this. Don't do this. "

"Commander," Pendryw said, knocking on the door.

"He is worse than the *Diawl* who rides with him" Aine muttered, as she backed down several stairs. "Now you see his true character. Now you see."

"Away," deFreveille growled.

Gwennan slid from the bed and along the wall to escape.

"Woman," he hissed, slamming the crossbar into place. He raised his fist and smashed it against the thick planks of the door but when he turned his eyes on her, there was no anger in them.

Unable to see him beyond the corner of the staircase alcove, her breath caught when she heard his fist crash on the door. Her strength was giving out, her knees buckled and she held herself upright with her fingers finding holds in the gaps between the wooden planks. Gwennan pressed her head against the rough wall, her body wedged into the alcove next to her linen chest. She screamed when he leapt at her and threw her arms over her face, sliding to the floor boards.

Siriol pounded on the door, hurling curses at him and then begging him to be merciful. Rocaille had arrived in the hall and ran up into the dormitory but he could not break through the heavy iron bolt across the door. "Commander," he said, still calm. "Gwennan is not yet well. Be patient. Gentle." He turned his smoldering eyes on Charlotte who stood near the screed.

"Rocaille, I hope he will not kill her," she gasped. "But such a barbaric thing, to strike a man when he is defenseless…"

"You had better hope that he does not harm that woman." Rocaille pounded on the door and called the commander by name but there was no response after Gwennan's scream. Rocaille knocked more quietly, pleading with his superior to open the door but he could hear only Siriol's begging.

Jehan-Emíl stood above Gwennan, his fists on his hips, calming himself with deep breaths while he considered his next move. The screeching from the other side of both doors did not help him to convince the woman crumpled on the floor, hiding her face, that he was not going to hurt her. The protests from Siriol and the physician subsided as they listened for his next action. He crouched in front of Gwennan and dragged her arms away from her face. She twisted her head to the wall.

"Gwennan," he murmured. She attempted to yank her arms free of his grasp but he refused to release her. She tugged again, this time snarling. "Be still, *menyw*. Hush." Her breathing was heavy and came in gasps. Jehan-Emíl clasped her wrists in one hand and dragged her hair away from her face with the other. "Be still, Gwennan."

He stroked her hair and let his hand slide down her back and around her waist until he was able to draw her toward him. Resting his back against the bedpost, he sat on the platform and cradled her between his thighs. She caught her breath with every move he made and gasped to breathe but her body began to relax. He bent his head over the back of her neck, sighing as his lips brushed her fragrant skin, and was taken by surprise when she cursed him.

Instantly, the pounding at both doors resumed and Jehan-Emíl threw his head back against the post, defeated. The sounds of his children's anxious voices were the final blow. He pushed himself to his feet, pulling her with him. Without releasing her, he raised the crossbar and opened the staircase door only as wide as his hand and glared at Siriol. Behind her,

Aine glared back at him and his sons pushed past. Pendryw met his gaze.

"Leave *Boneddiges* Gwennan in peace." Jehan-Emíl commanded. "Now," he told Siriol. To his sons, he said, "Go to your sister, stay with her until I call for you. Wash your faces." He stared at the two women on the stairs until they backed down and did as they had been told. He glared at the other door. "*Meddyg*. Go back to your patients. *Boneddiges* Gwennan has no further need of you. Take the nurse with you. She neglects her duty to my children." He turned again on Gwennan. "And now, *boneddiges*, we will try again."

He ran his fingers down the long row of toggles along her spine. "You make a show of defiance for your warriors," he murmured. "I understand this." From the nape of her neck, he unfastened each toggle in turn, "But you dress for me. I understand this also." He pushed the gown from her shoulders and, when it floated to the floor, he gathered it in one hand and draped it over the back of the chair. "We, I think, will be happy together, *cariad*. We are well-matched—worthy opponents in the eyes of others, passionate lovers when we are alone. This suits me, for now, Gwennan," he whispered, pinning her beneath him on the bed.

Gwennan wrenched her body to the side but he planted his knees on either side of her, trapping her under his weight. He crossed her wrists and held them with his left hand while his right brushed her hair from her face and caressed the tender underside of her arm to her breast. One slow tug at a time, he unknotted the thin cord at the neck of her chemise and pushed the fabric aside. Pressing his palm over her flesh, he cupped her breast in his hand and drew it into his mouth, stroking her ribs with his thumb.

Gwennan pressed herself into the mattress, resisting him with all that remained of her strength, but the deeper she pressed, the harder he sank onto her, every movement she made bringing a low, hungry moan from him. He lifted his thigh and pressed it between hers, bringing the pressure of his hip down on her belly. Even through the thickness of his clothing, she could feel him thrusting against her. He groaned again and murmured something without taking his mouth from her breast.

"Can a man have no peace?" deFreveille complained when the pounding began again at the staircase door. With his teeth, he dragged the front of her chemise to cover her and lifted his head, grinning. His grin broadened when her eyes widened. He shrugged his shoulders, kissed her breastbone and pushed her hair off her cheeks. His own face was flushed. He relaxed his grip on her wrists, snapping his hand closed when she threatened to pull away and shaking his finger in her face. "No, *boneddiges*. You do not run. You stay."

Gwennan stared at the hand before her eyes and Jehan-Emíl smiled. "What have you done? Why did you steal my ring?"

"Ring? Ah yes." He released his hold on her and rolled onto the mattress. "Ah, this bed. It is impossible. We need better, no?"

"My ring?"

"Shh, *Boneddiges* Siriol hears." He looped the cords of her chemise together over her breasts and pushed the *carthen* up to her chin, raising his finger to his lips. "Shh. I tell no one, I swear, what we do together, *boneddiges*." He winked and leapt from the bed, tossing up the crossbar and tugging the door wide. "Ah, *Boneddiges* Siriol, as you see *Boneddiges* Gwennan is well."

Siriol studied Gwennan's face, though her friend kept her eyes downcast, seeing no evidence that Gwennan was hurt and the expression on her face was amusement not fear. Her cheeks were pink. Siriol frowned. She could see the red mark on deFreveille's jaw.

"Now, you are satisfied and will leave us in peace," Ieuan Emyr said, preventing Siriol from stepping into the room. Without force, he pressed the door closed and lowered the crossbar, grinning at Gwennan over his shoulder. He dragged the hangings back on two sides of the bed and laid logs on the fire.

Gwennan raised trembling hands to tie her bodice tighter. Her adversary stood at the hearth, his gaze unwavering but Gwennan kept her eyes lowered, blushing. Ieuan Emyr laughed aloud, so full of joy and life—nothing of the triumph he felt.

"All right," deFreveille sighed. "We have some understanding." He sat beside her on the bed, draping an arm around her shoulders. "Tomorrow, we will have more," he yawned, stretching comfortably along the length of the bed. Despite the sagging mattress and rough straw in his back, it was more comfortable than the cot in his tent and he had not slept well for weeks. He turned toward her and laid his head on her shoulder, picking up the ends of the cord on her chemise and tossing them in his hand. "Very, very pretty," he sighed. "Very pretty."

Once deFreveille had fallen asleep, nothing that Gwennan did made any difference to him. She rolled him into the middle of the mattress so she could get out from under him and he slept on, mumbling his complaint but stretching out as before on the bed. Gwennan threw a *carthen* over him and closed the curtains. She opened the door and stepped onto the landing.

"What will you do?" Siriol whispered as Gwennan descended to the lower hall.

"Let him sleep. The longer he is here, the safer Bedwyn will be."

"Bedwyn is with Maides. He was arrested and Pendryw took him to the stockade."

"I will have to find another way to reach my father," Gwennan sighed, sinking into the chair by the hearth.

"Can you not see—? Ach, Gwennan, Bedwyn has been loyal to you...and now he will pay the price. DeFreveille may have him tortured."

"Bedwyn knew the risk," Gwennan said, "and he has his orders." Recognizing the disapproval in Siriol's eyes, she said, "I know what I am doing."

"I pray you do," Siriol replied. "Do you want me to bring the *meddyg*? Has he hurt you?"

"I no longer need the *meddyg*."

"Shall I stay with you?"

"That will not be necessary now, Siriol. I am in no danger from this man."

"You are very sure, Gwennan."

"He dares not. Go back to your husband. Celebrate his good fortune with my blessing."

Gwennan sat at her desk, finishing her accounts by candlelight. On the arm of the chair, she had left her needlework, the dim light of the fire was too feeble for her to make a good job of her mending. The material she had worked was bulky and she used a coarse thread in a large needle to close the seam under the arm of the tunic. The garment had been washed and she recognized it as one which had belonged to Tudwal. She had made a darn beneath the breast that marked the blow that had ended his life. She did not know where his body now lay but she prayed that his soul rested. She also prayed that the man who struck the blow would not be the one to wear his tunic.

The back of deFreveille's crooked finger on her cheek catching one of her tears was the first she knew that he had awakened. He laid his hand on the tunic, gathered the cloth in his fist and released it.

"The Celt?" he asked. He did not want to bring her Welsh lover always between them, but neither could he ignore her sorrow. "Derwyn?"

Gwennan shook her head and wiped away her tears with her fingertips. "Too many are dead." She turned her attention back to her ledger.

"Who?" he asked, pointing to the garment.

"Tudwal, Aine's husband."

"I am sorry. I was...late," he said. "Too late." DeFreveille covered her hand. "Have you pain, *boneddiges*?"

Gwennan's only excuse when he closed his arms around her and accepted the comfort he offered was to keep him away

173

from Bedwyn as long as possible. She allowed him the liberties he took for the sake of her messenger. Tudwal's tunic lay where the *gelyn* commander had let it fall from his hand, clasping Gwennan against him. His mouth moved, languid and warm, over her lips. When he carried her to the bed, she lay down with him. Her arms encircled his neck and her fingers entwined in his hair at the back of his neck.

DeFreveille took a long, deep breath, studying her face in the glow of the oil lamp. Gwennan felt his body tense as he closed his eyes, clenching his arms and drawing another deep breath. She lifted her chin. Where she had struck him, she brushed his jaw with her lips. He turned his head, capturing her mouth, urging her to open her body to him. When her lips parted, he encouraged her to take him deeper, pressing her shoulder to the bed and sliding his hands under her, spreading her legs apart to take him. He pulled her knee across his back. "This is how it will be, Gwennan, when we make love." Pulling her chemise clear of her thighs, he stroked her soft flesh. Gwennan held her breath, withstanding his efforts to seduce her. "You are hard to resist," he murmured, nudging the thin fabric of her bodice away from her breasts. "I want to be inside you. I want you to take me," he hissed, thrusting between her legs. "Do you feel me, Gwennan? Do you want me as I want you?" He lifted his head from her throat. "Yes? Yes, Gwennan? I think, yes, but Paul will have my head on a spike if I damage you after all his effort to make you well, *cariad*. When you are strong, nothing will stop me."

He pushed her leg away from him as though its meager weight annoyed him and turned onto his back. For a moment, she remained facing him. Unnoticed, her arms slipped away from his shoulders. After a while, he rose from the bed, straightened his clothing and combed his fingers through his thick curls. He did not look back when he gathered his documents and maps from the table and left the room.

"What does he say?" deFreveille demanded as he entered his campaign tent.

The mercenary shrugged. "He refuses to speak," Maides replied, turning away from Bedwyn to greet his friend. "We have had a long conversation but he has avoided making any confession...yet."

"Take the letter from him," deFreveille said, sinking into the chair behind his desk and laying his broad hand on the vellum parcel Artur had brought from the hall. Maides reached inside Bedwyn's tunic, fending off the young Welshman's attempt to prevent the theft. "Read it," Jehan-Emíl said. Maides studied the document and handed it to the commander. Jehan-Emíl glanced at the small square of vellum and the confident scrawl. "What does she say?"

"She writes to her father, Jehan. She tells him she is well and asks if he will visit before the feast of the Nativity, as is his habit. She signs this note as 'Your loving daughter, Gwennan.'"

"That is all?"

"That is all that is written."

"There is a message here that the father will understand, yes, Christophe?"

"No doubt."

Jehan-Emíl folded the message and gave it back to Gwennan's spy. "Deliver your message, Bedwyn," he said, "as the *boneddiges* has commanded you." Once he had dismissed the warrior, he leaned back in his chair and contemplated the parcel. "If this is an invitation to bring an army, we will be ready. If it is something else, my friend, we will be entertained."

TWELVE

"Rail as you please, Paul, as long and as loudly as you like," Gwennan laughed, pushing her foot into her suede boot and tightening the buckle around her ankle. "I am not a prisoner in this house. I have duties and work." So much had she improved over the further eight nights she had been left alone that she leapt from the chair and whirled into the fur-trimmed woolen cloak Siriol held up for her, snapped the clasp and raised the hood over her plaited hair. "I am *pennaeth* here until I am replaced and my work has been neglected for far too long."

"But, *boneddiges*," the *meddyg* protested. "The day is bitter and worse where you go. You have only begun to…"

"To walk," she laughed again. "Now, I want to run."

"Exactly," Rocaille commented. He had no serious medical objections to her venture. This gaiety was fragile. He did not believe that she would find anything beyond the walls of the house to sustain her. "You have not yet taken my advice to walk out in the garden for a few days and here you are insisting you are well enough to visit the infirmary as well as take up your duties as *pennaeth*."

"We will all starve if I do not."

"I do not dispute the possibility, *boneddiges*. I only argue that, if you insist, and do yourself harm, we will indeed starve."

"Look at me, Paul," she chided. "Am I someone who claims to be too weak to lift a finger when there is need of a whole hand?"

"No, Gwennan."

"Then stop your fussing and help me do what I must." With a nod to Siriol, Gwennan passed through the doorway and descended the staircase. Tugging red-dyed gloves over her hands, Gwennan led her small retinue from the house and stood with her back erect at the top of the hill while she surveyed the army in the stockade. In every direction was evidence of all she had expected to see—activity, order, renewal, hope. For a moment, she bowed her head to contain the swell of pride for the man who had achieved so much in the weeks that she had relinquished her responsibilities to him.

She crossed the newly strengthened bridge, the hem of her cloak trailing behind her, with both Siriol and the *meddyg* close at hand. Noting with some curiosity that the still poorly clothed soldiers looked up as she descended, spoke among themselves and parted without argument as she approached, Gwennan strode past the common hall directly to the infirmary.

Paul Rocaille walked beside her, explaining how many still lingered in the tents and what might be done to aid their recoveries. Gwennan also noted that the gates were open as they passed through to the encampment. The commander and his captains were in the camp or had business elsewhere but there was no hope that she could muster enough strength among Elgan's warriors to keep deFreveille from returning when so many of his soldiers resided within the stockade. She allowed the seed of the plan to settle where it could rest and find nourishment until the sun might shine upon it.

"We had despaired of seeing you, Gwennan," Menna and Branwen cried together. "We heard so many rumors…" Though Branwen's husband had left the infirmary many days ago, there was no house for them. Pedr Iago sat amid the pallets of the patients, playing with a stick as a sword.

"You have been ill for a long time," Menna said. The strain of her survival outside the safety of the household had taken its toll on the girl. She had no husband to protect or console her.

"You should be in the house," Gwennan murmured, clasping Menna's hand. "Go when you are ready."

"But the Commander—."

"It is my house, Menna. You are welcome."

"And your *baban*—dead!" Branwen wailed. "What kind of man kills that way?" She looked directly at the *meddyg*, though she knew he understood her, defying him to tell his commander that she, as well as many others, accused him.

Rocaille waited for Gwennan to refute the accusation against deFreveille, but she was silent. He frowned at her back but said nothing for the other women to hear. Siriol, who, of anyone, knew as much of the truth as Gwennan, also remained silent.

The physician was not a warrior but he discerned the lines of battle and understood the terms of war when he saw them. Curiously, he did not blame them for their anger—they had been invaded and their land stolen, women abused, husbands killed. Their struggle against deFreveille was hopeless but Paul Rocaille understood they were less in their own eyes if they did not attempt to throw off the yoke, no matter how well-fitted or easy to carry it was.

When Gwennan turned to go to the common hall, the few of her warriors who had suffered from a lack of spirit and those who had lingered in the infirmary for lack of purpose, followed her to the hall to take their places among their comrades. Iago Brynteg stepped forward and stood with Gwennan and Siriol in the center of the hall.

Derwyn sat with Bedwyn, sprawled before the hearth at the farthest end of the long building among the other young and fit warriors who had left the infirmary weeks before.

Only a few of the *gelyn's* captains were there but their presence in their possessions was plain. Gwennan's eyes quickly assessed which of the possessions were stolen from her own people. There was not much amid the clothing, brushes, ornaments, even weaponry that was alien to her. The *gelyn* had come with very little and gained much from their pillaging.

Although, as on the first day of battle, it was her place to speak to them, she chose to converse quietly amongst her warriors, assessing their condition and their spirit for another fight. She considered waiting for another to speak. The only one among them who was likely to do so watched her with a glare so hate-filled, its murderous intent passed through her like a blacksmith's rod. She laid her hood back from her plaited hair, folding it to lie across her shoulders.

Iago was reluctant to speak before the enemy soldiers present. The *gelyn* had been quick to notice the entrance of Pendyffryn's daughter. They were on guard, though their prisoners gave them no cause for excitement. One of the *gelyn*, whom Gwennan recognized as Gethin Wode, followed her into the hall, and watched as she stood with her group near the doorway. He spoke to her but she refused to understand the question and did not respond any more than to glance at him. His voice alerted his comrades who moved to watch the group. The *gelyn* did not feel threatened by two women and a single warrior, but when Derwyn jumped to his feet, followed by the fittest of the Cymry, the *gelyn* also leapt.

"Gwennan," the black-bearded warrior said, striding forward with his retinue in his wake. Despite the warmth of his greeting, his opinion of her had not changed. He loathed the sight of her. Behind him, Galar sat at the hearth. The fury of the old woman's glare told Gwennan as much as the indirectness of Derwyn's own eyes when he clasped her hand. *They want me dead.* The realization had no power; she had known from the day the *gelyn* appeared. Only the *gelyn* urged her to live.

"Your choice is not forgotten," he told her, standing at her side while the other warriors gathered around them.

"I am glad to see you are well, Derwyn." She met Bedwyn's gaze and their brief exchange reassured her that he had accomplished his mission for her.

"I am pained for your loss of the *pendefig's* grandson," Derwyn said. "Yet you live."

"Thank you for your sympathy."

"A child of your body would have put fire in our cause to beat these pigs back to the sea." Derwyn peered into her face.

"DeFreveille," she admitted, "is intelligent enough to have known that."

"Before I kill him, I will slice open his belly for the *baban*."

But not for me. Recklessly, looking into his blue eyes, because she had once believed she loved him and cared for him as a friend still, Gwennan raised a hand to his long, shining hair to push it away from his brow as she had when he was injured and could not prevent her.

Derwyn caught her wrist and shoved her hand away from him. He bent his head and spoke under his breath. "What was, is no longer. What might have been will never be. Your hand is soiled on the flesh of my enemy and your body is of no use to me now, *menyw*."

Gwennan neither gasped nor stepped back from the assault of his words. Her head remained high, her eyes softening as she studied him and she closed the fingers of the hand he held, not into a fist but an empty embrace. When Derwyn released her, she drew her hand under her cloak and smiled at him. His expression did not change and his anger was tainted with disgust.

Though he remained standing beside her while the other warriors pledged their fealty to fight for Daran Pendyffryn, Derwyn forced himself not to look at Gwennan, but his senses acknowledged her fragrance, her proud stance and her slender, graceful form. He drove his aspiration of being her husband out of his thoughts. Galar had told him that she welcomed the *gelyn* to her bed again, after he had murdered the *baban*— and that could never be forgiven. Derwyn's feeling for her died with his respect. She was as wanton as any of the whores he bedded in her stead.

DeFreveille, flanked by Maides and Pendryw, stood in the doorway of the thatched hall, watching the performance before him with keen interest. He drew his long, glistening dagger from his belt. Pendryw stepped forward, his hand clenched on the hilt of the dagger in his belt. DeFreveille held him back and stabbed a crust of bread, lifting it from the platter on the table and plucking it from the blade before sinking his teeth into it.

Gethin Wode's worried frown subsided and he sighed his held breath when his commander was unconcerned by the event.

"They pledge to an old man!" Bown jeered.

"Allow them their hopeful moment," deFreveille commented.

An icy cord whipped around Gwennan's heart and stiffened her back, otherwise she showed no sign she knew Ieuan was present. Siriol swung her head around to stare at the black-garbed trinity by the door, meeting her husband's eyes for a moment before she looked away and stepped closer to her friend.

Gwennan raised her hand to Bedwyn's arm, grateful that her limbs did not betray her with useless trembling. Derwyn's desertion and change of heart had not hurt her—she had been prepared; she expected his lack of faith in her. There was nothing anyone could do to destroy her dignity. "Thank you," she murmured to the young warrior as he clasped her hand and drew her away from Derwyn's side.

"*Boneddiges*," Bedwyn said as he bent his blond head toward her, "deFreveille knows. He knew that night."

"I would have been surprised if he did not, Bedwyn," she replied with a warm smile. "Did he question you?" She moved further away from Derwyn and the others, keeping her hand on Bedwyn's arm, avoiding looking in the direction of her adversary, though his eyes sought her. She leaned closer to Bedwyn and looked into his earnest face.

"No, *boneddiges*. The *gelyn* told me to deliver your message."

Gwennan thought for a moment. "What did my father say to you?"

"The *pendefig* has accepted your invitation," Bedwyn replied. "He also told me to express his condolences on the loss of your home."

Gwennan laughed at her father's insult and asked, "Does deFreveille know that my father will come?"

"If he does, I did not tell him," Bedwyn declared, pulling himself more erect. "I told the *pendefig* that deFreveille knew my message. I would have told you but I have not been allowed near the house since my return."

"Were you mistreated the night you were arrested? I have heard nothing."

"No, *boneddiges*. Maides talked to me, we drank the Commander's wine and when deFreveille came, they took your message from me—Maides knew where I had hidden it. There was nothing I could do to prevent them from reading it. I was prepared for worse," he told her with a smile in his blue eyes. "If I have failed you—." Bedwyn bowed his head for a moment.

"You have not. Did my father say anything else—when you told him that deFreveille knew I had sent you?"

"He said he wanted to see this man before he was forced to kill him."

Gwennan trembled as her hand clenched on Bedwyn's arm. "I would be surprised if he hadn't promised that." The young warrior put his arm around her for a moment, to steady her, and dropped his arm as soon as he met the *gelyn* commander's narrowed glare.

"Your father's army is fearsome, *boneddiges*," Bedwyn murmured, close to her ear. "I would not like to face them, but this *gelyn* is not afraid."

"With my father's help, there will be no reason for a fight—we will be rid of the *gelyn* by the winter solstice." Before she turned to leave the hall, Gwennan raised the hood to cover her hair and slid her hands into her gloves.

"There is always reason to fight dogs like these," Derwyn hissed, catching her arm. "Your lover will be killed and his head hoisted on a pike outside these walls for sending the *Diawl* to kill Alun Cwmdu and all your Gernant cousins. There will be a fight, Gwennan. Your father will kill this dog," he whispered, "for taking you. He may also kill you for allowing his land to be stolen and whoring with his enemy."

"These are my father's walls, Derwyn, walls that this man has rebuilt," Gwennan replied, prying his fingers from her arm.

"It could as easily be your head on the pike—for wishing me dead."

Derwyn lurched toward her with a sharp breath and his eyes narrowed, the question in his eyes was not the one he asked aloud. "Is the father of your murdered child here? We will mourn with him."

"You will never know," Gwennan whispered, so close to Derwyn's lips that he took a breath from her body, "but that he is the only man I have ever known worthy of my esteem." Feeling deFreveille take a step nearer, she pressed against the handsome Celt and murmured, "You will never know why or for whom I chose to live and that uncertainty will haunt you." She avoided the sudden movement of his hand, tossed her head and walked away from him.

"Why do you taunt him?" Siriol demanded. "He has always loved you."

"Has he?" Gwennan asked. "Bedwyn, I am grateful for your help. I will repay your kindness." The young warrior bowed his head, keeping an eye on the *gelyn* commander. Giving Siriol a curt nod, Gwennan turned to face the men blocking their exit.

As they approached, both Maides and Pendryw stepped aside but the commander remained in their path. Ieuan Emyr smiled when Gwennan came near. Glancing once over her shoulder at her hot-headed lover, he bowed to her. "He will never threaten you again, *cariad*," he murmured, laying his hand on her arm and drawing her close to him. "Troublesome and intelligent as well as—." He smiled for a moment, studying her, from her half hidden face to the red gloves covering her slender fingers. "What I have to say to you, Gwennan Pendyffryn, I will say when we are next alone. Soon."

He turned to Maides. "This charade has required deliberation, my friend. Our young warrior would not have the presence of mind to orchestrate such a grand pretense of undermining our efforts to persuade the Welsh to join us." He smiled again into Gwennan's eyes. "*Menyw*, you are a feast for a well-fed man. For a man who is starving, you are the gift of life itself." He clasped her hand, peeling back the cuff of the glove to kiss the underside of her wrist. For all to hear, he said, "Thank you, *boneddiges*. Good. Very good. I am grateful for your assistance." Jehan-Emíl allowed her to leave. When, after observing her walk across the muddy ground toward the bridge, he turned back to the hall, watching the fiery Welshman.

Derwyn Blaenant also followed the departure of the tall woman and her companion. Before Derwyn turned his eyes on him, deFreveille frowned to see that the man's expression was not one of admiration. The expression Jehan-Emíl recognized in Derwyn's eyes was one of hatred—the degree of hatred he himself had felt toward a woman who betrayed him with another man—and the determination to take revenge. It did not take much searching of his imagination to envision what revenge the warrior considered appropriate for a beautiful woman who had no claim on his honor or his protection.

"Do these men seem less hostile to you, Christophe?"

"To me? No, Jehan. Everyone is hostile to the soldier, except perhaps the whore who collects his pay for her services."

"Nor to me," deFreveille pondered. "This scene was touching, yes? So heartily they swear to one who is not here to lead them or able to provide means for their survival."

"Perhaps they hope this warrior will lead them."

"This warrior cannot lead them. He vows only to kill," DeFreveille commented. "He is cunning, but he is not thoughtful nor particularly honorable, although he holds his own sense of honor very high."

"I would not trust him, Jehan—a man with so much hatred in his heart is capable of anything."

"I would rather put my life in Gwennan Pendyffryn's hands," the commander laughed. "At least my death will be swift." The commander turned on his heel and left the hall, beckoning Christophe Maides to follow. Under the low sun of the bitter day, the stockade seemed as desolate as when it was strewn with the bodies of the wounded and dying. DeFreveille glanced up at the house on the hill. Gwennan had already disappeared. "Let us decide the next step, my friend," he said, clasping Maides around the shoulders and drawing him away from the hearing of the soldiers. "You, I know, and some others, prefer the sword, but we cannot kill all of them. Besides, that is now against my policy."

"Can we not even kill the ones we know to remain our enemies?" Maides asked with a raised eyebrow.

"They are all our enemies, Christophe. From the youngest child to the oldest soldier. Idle men are more dangerous than men who are kept too busy to lift their swords. Pick the best of them and give them command of my soldiers. Making themselves understood will give them enough to do for now. The rest will take orders from our own captains. Give this hot-headed warrior a full company of men and set him to bringing into the Gaer every head of grain and every living thing on the whole of the farm. Set Iago to assist you to command the repairs and Pendryw will oversee the digging of a dry moat beyond the stockade. I have a special task for Bedwyn, our spy."

"Now, Jehan?"

"Of course, Maides," the commander laughed. "There are hours yet of daylight in which we can fatigue these rebels. We exhaust ourselves for their benefit while they fatten and grow fit. If these Welsh do not kill us in our sleep, marauders will. Winter makes all men desperate. Some of our own countrymen will be seeking shelter soon." He hunched his shoulders deeper into his cloak. "Now go. Tell Wode what I have decided. He will be grateful for the activity. And, if Alrick is sufficiently chastened, put him on duty to care for the horses. He will have to prove himself worthy to rise above the office of stable boy."

The smell of smoke and the fire in another village drew the attention of the women in the house above the Gaer. For a week, *gelyn* soldiers and their Gaer commanders had gathered stores and villagers. Gwennan, Siriol and Aine stood at the back of the walled garden and watched the flames consume the thatched roofs. The women returned to their inventory in the caverns when they saw the soldiers and farmers emerging from the wood and picking their way through the stumps of felled trees.

Gwennan recognized the green of Derwyn's livery—every stitch her own. He rode ahead of his command and deFreveille's black and gold standard was held high above the soldiers' heads. Most of the soldiers were not much beyond fourteen or fifteen years. Some of Elgan's own field hands had joined deFreveille's service.

None of the women were eager to return to the storage caverns dug into the steep face of the cliff. The caverns were thick with rats that skittered away to gnaw at the other barrels of grain while the three women rolled them toward the entrance. To save as much as they could of the grain, the worst of the barrels had to be replaced. The oil lamps spluttered and the air was fetid with the stench of mold and rot. The earthen floors were slick with the slime of trampled fungus. They hitched their skirts into their belts under wide aprons to keep them clean but their wooden shoes and ankles were muddied.

The racks of mead jugs were only half full, dusty and festooned with cobwebs which clung to their hair as they counted the wax-sealed jugs, taking down those that showed signs of decay, to be consumed before they spoiled. The light visible at the entrance to the caverns was fading as Gwennan and her friends, covered from head to foot in grime, began to carry the jugs and smaller baskets of edible food up the path and through the back gate of the garden to the kitchen. Menna was assigned the lightest duty of keeping count of their work, making signs and scratches on the slate to represent barrels, jugs and sacks.

They had made two trips and were returning from a third when they heard the voices of the commander and his captains in the family hall. Bown prevented them from finishing the task, herding all four along the garden wall and through the kitchen doorway. DeFreveille, wearing another black tunic bearing his crest, sat in the chair by the hearth with his sons on either side of him and his daughter on his knee. Charlotte stood close behind the chair. She was smiling and laughed at the smudged faces, dirty hands and soiled clothing of the barbarian women.

"Now, we see them as they really are," she murmured near the commander's ear.

Gwennan released the skirt of her plain brown frock from the belt around her hips and smoothed the fullness with dignity. She ignored the dirt on her face and clothes as well as the spider's web clinging to the untidy plaits coiled around her head. Siriol and Menna hid themselves from the laughter in the *gelyn's* eyes.

"Commander deFreveille has been told of your thieving, woman," Bown said to Gwennan, "and his consort has complained of your threats to her and the commander's daughter."

Gwennan stared at Bown for a moment, understanding his flat language better than he would ever understand hers. *Consort?* "You may tell the wolf that his whore is a liar."

"Gwennan," Siriol and Aine exclaimed under their breaths. Menna giggled.

"Ach, he cannot understand even the simplest insult." She met the glare of the red-faced warrior. "Can you, horse-eating *gelyn* pig bastard son of a—."

"Bown cannot," deFreveille said, "but I can."

"Good! —bastard son of a horseman's dinner."

The laughter that burst first from deFreveille and Wode brought stares of dismay from Bown and Charlotte. Pendryw and Siriol dropped their heads to conceal their grins. Menna held her sides but could not stand up when a flare of scarlet burst across Gethin Wode's cheeks when his laugh crippled him. Gwennan glanced at the half-Cymro. *Who has taught him to understand us?*

Cecilé and her brothers glanced at their father. The boys smiled and frowned but the little girl's laughter brought a smile to Gwennan's face that her outrage could not subdue. Though she turned her face away, her eyes met Ieuan Emyr's smiling gaze for an instant.

"I have work to do," she declared, glowering in Ieuan's direction but not meeting his eyes again. "If you have nothing else to say, I will return to it."

"I can see," he began and called Maides to come closer. The mercenary murmured and stood nearby. "You work too hard, Gwennan." He stroked Cecilé's small head, bent to kiss her brow. "You do not steal, I hope."

"Steal? How can I steal what belongs to me?" she demanded, storming toward him, her arms straight at her sides. "If there is a thief here—." She stood within a few feet of him but his captains had stepped forward as well as his sons. DeFreveille rose, still holding his youngest child in his arms. "I am not the thief here," she said with disdain, "I have not taken what does not belong to me or hurt anyone to take what is theirs. I have not murdered and my hands are not made bloody with greed."

DeFreveille handed his daughter to Charlotte. His movements were so measured that Gwennan was surprised when he lunged at her, grabbing her arms above the elbow and yanking her against him. Siriol gasped and stepped forward but was warned back when Pendryw lifted a finger to still her.

"Enough," deFreveille hissed. "Do not push me, Gwennan." At the same time, his grip on her arms loosened. He leaned toward her and the grin he showed her was the same she had seen two weeks before when he raised his head from her breast. Gwennan's knees buckled. "Do this work," he ordered, pinching her chin between his finger and thumb. "I see after. Tonight." For good measure, he pushed her away from him and pointed to the doorway. "Go, but do not work too hard, *blodyn*. You are not strong enough…yet."

"Why do you force me, and your *daughter*, to suffer these long days and nights among these Welsh? They will kill us both!"

"Why are you here?" Jehan-Emíl growled at Cecilé's nurse when all the others had left the house and his daughter had been taken in tow by her brothers.

"What do you mean, Jehan-Emíl?" Charlotte cooed, caressing his arm as she slid close to him. "I am always here when you want me."

"We agreed, Charlotte," he said, granting her the intimacy, "you were to accept the employment offered to you in Haelsted's household."

"Jehan," she sighed, laying her head on his chest. "I know you so well." She lifted her face to him. "We have been together for many years. You spoke in anger. We were both angry."

"Yes, I spoke in anger *and* I meant what I said, Charlotte."

"How can you possibly do without me?" she laughed, pressing against him, encouraging his body to reawaken to her beauty. "There is no one here to care for your sweet little daughter. There is no one here who will love her as her own child, no one to teach her to become a woman, a wife fit for a great man and his household. Have I not always kept your house in order, Jehan? Have you ever had any reason to complain of my ability in your house," she asked, "or in your bed?"

DeFreveille looked down into her pretty eyes. "Your interference is causing too much trouble."

"Interference, Jehan?" she sighed, wrapping her arms around his chest, caressing the muscles of his back with experienced hands. "How can I have interfered when you do not let me near you?" Her hands moved over the small of his back and he caught them before she reached his thighs, pushing her away from him to arms' length. "I had begun to believe that you were unmanned by these heathens but I see you are as eager for me as you were when we made love in the garden of Haelsted's stronghold," she murmured, straining toward him. "Do you remember, Jehan, how you begged—."

"Interpret as you please, Charlotte. Lust is nothing of which I am ashamed. Your services are as useful as any other whore."

"Then use me, Jehan," she murmured. "I am here, willing. I ache for you. Why do you abandon me?" Charlotte's tears glistened in her eyes and sparkled on her rosy cheeks in the glow of the fire. "You have grown tired of this filthy Welsh woman…" Charlotte complained. "You do not use her at all now. You have not used her since you killed the Welshman's bastard."

DeFreveille eyes narrowed. He released her arms as though she was infested and strode from the house to the garden. He sent the boys back to the stockade and carried his daughter up the ladder and stone steps to the top of the walled enclosure of the garden. His banner whipped crazily above their heads in the sharp gusts of wind. A fine mist hung over the gorge. The voices of Gwennan and the women of her household drifted up to him from beneath the canopy of trees. Jehan-Emíl wondered what new emblem he could put on it to represent his changed circumstances. He pointed out to his daughter the felled forests and scorched fields, anything that might interest her five-year-old mind. Because she was quiet, he could not tell if she was intelligent and he had not yet had time to give her the attention he could give her brothers who needed to learn what he had to teach them.

"There is another girl here, Cecilé."

"Yes, Father."

"Does she also have a doll. Does she play with you?"

"No, Father."

"Do you not wish to play with this girl?" He had seen his daughter follow Eira, with her eyes. Cecilé did not answer. "Does she not offer to play with you?"

"I do not know, Father. She is not allowed to speak to me."

"Her mother has forbidden this?" he demanded, already angry with Siriol.

"I do not know, Father. Mistress Charlotte—." She stopped abruptly, glanced at her father and away.

"Charlotte will not be with you tonight, Cecilé. Speak and do as you please."

When the women returned to the hall, their clothes and bodies were even more filthy than when deFreveille had seen them. Charlotte turned her nose up at them and, through the girl servant she had brought with her, told them to keep their distance. "Charlotte de Guidry regrets you will not be able to have baths this evening," the girl told them. "She requires one herself as she is to dine with deFreveille. She is accustomed to very long baths. No one will fetch or heat water for you."

Between them and Siriol's two children, they carried enough water to the cauldron to be kept warm in the domed bath house. Siriol helped Gwennan to undress and was glad to see that no marks of her long illness remained on her body. With the exception of a few tiny scars, she was as unblemished as she was the day she arrived unescorted to become *pennaeth*. Gwennan combed the tangles from Menna's soft hair, glad she had brought the girl back to the house. Her happy laughter was a pleasant diversion.

When Gwennan bathed, Eira held the soap and leaned on her mother's shoulder, learning some of her adult duties by performing them. When it was Siriol's turn to bathe, Gwennan insisted on giving her friend the same care, helping her daughter to untie the laces on her mother's gown and shift. Eira was familiar with her mother's preferences and went to her tasks. Gwennan was absorbed in watching the girl and doing as she was instructed.

Gareth steadfastly resisted his sister's attempts to entice him to wash. Eira was the first to notice the curly-headed girl near the low door. She nudged Gwennan who glanced up from scrubbing Siriol's ankle. The *pennaeth* smiled at the little girl and gestured toward her but Cecilé did not venture further into the bath house.

Gwennan began to sing a rhyme from her childhood and to teach the children the words. After Eira and Gareth had repeated a verse and the chorus a few times, they sang with Gwennan. Their voices were augmented by the tune murmured by the commander's daughter. Not wishing to embarrass the child, Gwennan did not turn around when Ceceilé slid a few steps closer to the bathers but Gareth swung around with his hands on his hips.

"The words are easy," he said and began to sing the whole of the first verse and the chorus. Gwennan and Siriol joined in the final few lines and Cecilé sang the last with them. "That's right," Gareth said. "Ho! Ho! Ho! I know another one. *Mae gen i ga—*!"

Gwennan clapped her hand over the six-year-old boy's mouth with a gasp. "Gareth, you will not teach that to a little girl!"

"May I teach it to Marshal?"

"No."

Cecilé gazed up at Gwennan with a slight pout, tears already welling in her brown eyes. Gwennan crouched in front of her. "Your dad would not want you to boast of your manly prowess," she said with a smile. "I doubt he would appreciate such boasting from his ten-year-old son either but it is a funny song all the same. Are you hungry, *blodyn*?" She gestured to explain before taking the child's hand and leading her to the house.

The glow of the small fire was the only light in the room. Siriol sat in the chair, her children asleep on the bed with deFreveille's daughter between them, and Gwennan sat on a stool at her knees while Siriol took the cords from her hair and unbraided the two plaits. Neither woman had said much since returning from the hall after their meal, nothing at least that was not related to taking an inventory of the food supplies, cloth and mending needs and the health of the children. The meal the women of the household had taken together was as silent as vespers. Only Siriol's children and deFreveille's daughter were talkative at their small table away from the women.

Gwennan's venture that day to perform her duties as *pennaeth* had not been as futile as her venture to garner support for her father. She was aware of the stores available to the household for the winter months. She included in the needs of the household all her women, their children and husbands wherever they resided, as well as the farmers, their wives and all the children, whoever their father. Their survival depended on

Ieuan Emyr and the good will that she had endangered to avenge herself. By engaging her father's help, she had set Elgan's warriors once more against Ieuan, endangered his life and all who stood with him, as well as exposed herself to his anger and her friends' distrust.

Uffern, if I am truthful, I miss him. She hated his indifference more than she resented his governance. She had foreseen Derwyn's desertion, its sting was nothing in comparison to the ache at the mention of Ieuan's name. Though she willed herself to sleep without him, she still waited each night for his footfall on the staircase. Her room was now, without even his maps, an empty place. She stared into the fire and Siriol brushed her hair the way that Galar had always done until she had abandoned her.

"Do you want to return to your husband?" Gwennan asked suddenly, aware that her own troubles were nothing compared to what many of her women had suffered. "Do you miss him?"

"Of course. We have been wed for many years."

"Then, I want you to go back. You should be with him. Your children should be with their father."

"That will leave you alone here, with only Aine and Menna to help you," Siriol said, peering around Gwennan to look into her face. "You will have to deal with that wicked woman and the commander's children alone."

"The children are not difficult," Gwennan replied.

"I can see that, but what about his 'consort'?"

"I don't think she will be here often...now." When Siriol finished braiding her damp hair and wrapped the end with a narrow strip of linen, Gwennan spoke again. "If my father does not come, we will not survive if deFreveille is against us. My father will come but that may mean more death. And consider some of the others, Siriol. Is there one among them from whom we could expect anything but brutality?"

"Is not deFreveille brutal, Gwennan?"

"I know you will think the worst of me, as Derwyn does, and Galar, but he is not. He is fierce, but he is not brutal. None of the others care to make this a good place to live, for children. They want what they can take and then they will go, leaving us to starve. I trust deFreveille this far: he is not the wolf I have called him. He will not feed on us."

"Is that why he returned this?" Siriol held up the tunic Charlotte had damaged.

"I did not give it to him."

"What was in the parcel you thrust at him the night Bedwyn was arrested?"

"Another. One more akin to his station."

"Why do you do all in your power to provoke him? How can that help us?"

"I have given him a tunic that befits his place. He will interpret the significance of the gesture as he wishes. If he is provoked or incensed, that means nothing to me."

"You tell me we need him and yet you do all possible to make him your enemy."

"Siriol, until this man proves himself a friend, it is my duty—and privilege—to test him."

After Siriol went to her bed, Gwennan laid the tablets and parchments of her accounts, orderly and precise, on the table, ready to be examined. The nurse's noisy, happy return. Though deFreveille's daughter was not in her usual bed, the nurse did not notice. There was no footstep on the stone landing outside Gwennan's door. She banked the fire for the night, quietly lowering the crossbar over the door to the staircase and locked the screed door. Even so protected, she could not sleep. Every small sound set her heart to race.

Thirteen

Before dawn, she lifted her head from the cushion, surprised to find Cecilé still curled beside her beneath the *carthen*. Gwennan turned onto her back, draping her arm around the child and listened to the sounds in the house. Someone in the dormitory sighed and turned. Below her, in the room in which his sons now slept, a faint murmur as though in a dream disturbed her. A log fell from the grate in the hearth and a man cursed. Gwennan turned her head to watch the crossbar on the door. It remained in its place. No other sound came from the lower hall but she could not sleep again.

When Siriol knocked on the door, both Gwennan and Cecilé were dressed. Throughout the morning, she sat in the family hall near the hearth with Siriol. Though they could have remained in the upper chambers to work, Gwennan and Siriol repaired tunics and mended shirts in the chaos of children and servants.

The activity heartened her. She was delighted to hear the children's laughter and to watch them running after one another. DeFreveille's sons were apart but they were not taunted. Jehan-Batiste sat at the table concentrating on something he was writing. Marshal chased the girls at their work, tormented the dogs and watched Siriol's children as they renewed their acquaintance with Cecilé. When her nurse was not looking, all of them sang, as quietly as ghosts, the song Gwennan had taught them. The little girl was too quiet, not at all like Eira who used her six year old brother, Gareth, as a barrier to keep Marshal away from her. Moments later, she pushed Marshal off the back of the biggest of the wolfhounds and shook her fist in his face. The ten-year old leapt to his feet and lunged at her, his stocky chest thrust forward.

"Eira," her mother warned, glancing toward the door from the small *porth*.

"Father!" Marshal exclaimed, forgetting the girl's assault.

DeFreveille entered the house with Rocaille beside him. The physician crossed the stone floor toward the two women. DeFreveille waylaid Charlotte and lifted his daughter into his arms before he followed the *meddyg*. Near the hearth, he stopped and leaned against the mantle, whispering into the little girl's ear. Cecilé clung to his neck, giggled and pressed her lips to his cheek, whispering the song she had learned.

Though she greeted Rocaille with warmth, making room for him to sit beside her, Gwennan's concentration on her mending was intense.

"Are you well, *boneddiges*?"

"Very well, thank you, Paul," Gwennan replied. "Are you? I hoped you would return soon so that we might finish our game, Paul. Do you think you are fit to challenge me today?"

"No," the physician laughed. "I will never be as fit as that. Your game is too quick for my poor skill."

"It was not my game that trapped you between the fox and the geese." Gwennan lifted her head and gazed into his steady, soft eyes. Slipping her hand between his palms, she let her work drop into her lap. "I am sorry I cause you trouble. I promise to be a good patient and stay very quiet."

"*Boneddiges*," he murmured, raising her hand to his lips.

"Rocaille," deFreveille said. "I have not invited you here for this. Say what I have told you to this woman and be done with it."

"DeFreveille has asked me to speak to you. He does not yet have enough words to express his wishes. I will say what he has so far told me and give him your answer. Is this acceptable?" Gwennan nodded. "The commander requests that you resume your duties as *pennaeth*. Many of his men, the captains and soldiers alike, are in need of warmer clothing and the management of the Gaer is difficult, impossible, without knowledge of the needs of the people. DeFreveille would be grateful if you consider this proposal, at least until he can himself manage better."

"I have made an inventory of all the stores in the caverns below. I will make an accounting of the materials available for clothing. He may examine all the accounts—at his convenience," Gwennan said, hardening her jaw against the insult of the long night, waiting for him, "as well as the stores and material. As *pennaeth*, I will ensure my women, their children and all the rest are not left to starve."

Jehan-Emíl, though he pretended to play with his daughter, had not taken his eyes off Gwennan's face while Rocaille spoke. When she replied, he tried to read in her eyes what her words meant. When Rocaille told him what she said, he shrugged and commented.

"Your management will see that all are treated fairly," Rocaille translated.

"I am flattered that he believes me to be so fair, Paul."

DeFreveille spoke angrily, repeating the physician's given name several times with sarcasm. Rocaille bowed his head, suppressing a smile.

"What does he say?" Gwennan demanded.

"The commander does not think it appropriate for you to call me by my name."

"Does he not, Paul?" she asked, slipping her hand over the physician's long, delicate fingers. She could feel deFreveille's anger and heard his sharp intake of breath. "Tell your commander that it is none of his concern what I call you, Paul. Whether I call you 'Paul' or 'friend' or '*cariad*'," she murmured, leaning closer to the physician with each endearment.

"Gwennan…"

"Yes, Paul?"

"DeFreveille also wishes to know if you will manage his household," the doctor said, struggling to control the laugh in his voice.

"He already has someone to manage," she replied, pulling her hand away and returning to her work.

"Who else, *boneddiges*, is more capable than yourself?" Rocaille asked for his commander.

"I am not blind, Paul. Tell him," she answered, tossing her head in deFreveille's direction, "to command Charlotte to manage."

"Charlotte?" Ieuan Emyr frowned. "What is this about Charlotte, Rocaille?"

"Paul," Gwennan sighed, directing her reply to the physician. "The nurse has been manager of his household for years, has she not?" Rocaille shrugged. "Their relations are intimate." Rocaille reluctantly agreed. "I am not so dull-witted that I believe he truly requires my help."

Rocaille murmured her response to Ieuan whose eyes narrowed as he replied under his breath. "*Boneddiges*," the physician began, "deFreveille wants your answer to his request. Will you manage his household?"

Gwennan turned her eyes to her sewing and released an exasperated sigh. He was asking her to work with him, to cooperate and to submit herself and her friends to his governing. She knew her own answer but she could not answer for anyone else.

"I will discuss this with my friends, Paul," she said. "It will be more their fingers than mine to be pricked for his sake." What Ieuan Emyr said next to the physician was spoken with fierce control and through clenched teeth. "I will consider."

"DeFreveille is grateful for this dry crust you offer, *boneddiges*," Rocaille said, "but is saddened that you feel he is not equally concerned for the people of the Gaer. Your management will assure everyone of his equal commitment to them. Your management will guarantee their lives. Otherwise, many will die."

Gwennan caught her breath on the threat. "Then I have no choice. I agree. With one condition." DeFreveille nodded. "I manage without interference. He will have to trust that I do so fairly."

DeFreveille gave her a curt nod and, when she rose to speak with her friends, he raised her hand to his lips, but his expression was puzzled. He murmured his gratitude. Gwennan stared at him. *Remember, how easily he tricks you.* She turned her face away and met his eyes again, smiling at her from the tiny face of his daughter. Gwennan returned the smile, her expression softening. DeFreveille continued to hold Gwennan's hand while he spoke to Rocaille.

"DeFreveille asks if you will join him this evening to dine or do you prefer to rest?"

"I prefer to rest, Paul," she said, withdrawing her hand and turning away. When the physician had given her reply, Gwennan turned to see its affect. DeFreveille's jaw hardened but there was no other sign that he cared. She crossed the hall, the skirt of her red gown sweeping through the scented rushes.

"Cecilé," Jehan-Emíl whispered to his daughter, watching Gwennan's linen-bound plait sway across her hips. "Go with Gwennan. Take her hand. It is time you learned your duties. Gwennan will be your tutor." *Only smile once at me, Gwennan, as you smile at my daughter and my life is yours.* He watched Cecilé trot over the rushes, to catch the woman before she reached the stairs. *You send a child as your ambassador.* He turned half away, frowning at the self-derision in his thoughts, when Cecilé caught Gwennan's skirt in her small hand. Jehan-Emíl studied the woman's reaction, aware that he put his daughter into hands that would gleefully murder him.

"Cecilé," Charlotte snapped. "I have told you many times to keep away from these Welsh. They are not fit—"

"Do not forget your place, Charlotte. My daughter is no longer your concern."

"But, she is in danger. You cannot mean what you are saying. This is absurd. We discussed this—you agreed there is no one here fit to teach her," Charlotte began to purr, moving closer to him. "These women are devils. Our enemies. They do not even bathe properly, Jehan…" She bit her lip at the error of using his given name.

"You have duties, I presume," deFreveille sneered and turned his back, glimpsing his daughter as she climbed the staircase with Gwennan. The little girl watched him and he smiled to encourage her but his eyes were hard with rage.

"How did he kill his wife?" Madlen whispered in Ruth's ear as she combed her friend's hair. They had both searched for evidence that deFreveille resided in Gwennan's room though they all knew he now slept every night alone in his campaign tent in the camp.

"Who has killed his wife?" Gwennan asked.

"DeFreveille," Madlen volunteered. "He killed his wife and her lover."

"The Commander's wife died in childbirth," Siriol told them, tired of their chatter.

"How Siriol defends him," Aine said.

"Perhaps it is she who warms him at night now," Ruth taunted. "You were long alone with him when Gwennan was ill. Is he everything his warriors claim? Did you have to bite your fist to keep from crying out?"

"Everyone knows you have not the decency to bite yours, Ruth," Siriol retorted. "Your grunting is heard as far as Castell Pendyffryn."

"I do not grunt." Ruth jumped to her feet. "If I am a little weak, at least I do not chase men from my bed."

"You would not chase that *Diawl* from your bed," Aine murmured.

"And you are better? We all know what has been happening in this house. How was it to share deFreveille among the four of you and that nurse as well?"

"What good is it if we fight amongst ourselves?" Gwennan said. "Neither you nor Madlen have been in this house. You do not know what we have endured, nor do we know anything of your experience. We are here now and we have work to finish." She beckoned for deFreveille's daughter to come to her. Making room for her on a stool in front of the small hearth,

Gwennan offered to brush her hair. Cecilé sat quietly her arms folded around a wooden doll.

"I will not have it said of me that I have been with that *gelyn*," Aine exclaimed. "Only Gwennan is guilty and he abandoned her many weeks ago."

"Aine, you know no better than these what has happened in this room," Siriol chided.

Gwennan remained silent. Her friends as well as her enemies thought as they pleased, whatever she said to quell their chatter. The child, though she had been in Gwennan's company for several days, had not broken her silence, except to sing to herself. Gwennan ran her fingers slowly through the wild curls and bent her head close to her small brow. Suddenly tired, Gwennan dismissed all the women from the room. Sinking back in her chair, she gazed at the little girl. She smiled but had nothing to say. It was clever of deFreveille to put his children near her, to offer his daughter to her as a sacrifice. Stretching her legs toward the fire, she drifted to sleep. Cecilé remained quiet, hugging her doll.

"You are a mean, disobedient girl," Charlotte hissed, stealing into the room from the staircase.

Gwennan awoke when Cecilé jumped to her feet, the little girl's tears already stinging her bright eyes. Charlotte reached across the Welsh woman's knees and clasped the girl's arm, dragging her toward the door.

"What are you doing?" Gwennan asked, catching Charlotte's arm.

"I will not fight *you* for this child." Charlotte shoved Cecilé toward the Welsh woman.

Gwennan dropped her hands protectively around the girl's shoulders and glared after the nurse as she darted from the room through the screed door. Pulling the girl toward her, Gwennan hushed her, stroking her hair. Cecilé's eyes filled with tears but none of them fell.

"What is this, child?" deFreveille demanded, following Artur into the room. "Why are you crying?"

"I am not crying, Father."

"Then what are these?" he asked, touching a tear as it rolled to the edge of her lashes.

Artur laid the salver he carried on the table. Jehan-Batiste and Marshal stopped at the door, their eyes turned on the Welsh woman, waiting for their father to act.

"Have you been punished?"

"No, Father. I was only crying." Cecilé scrubbed her tears away. "Gwennan invited me to be here." She stood and put her hand in Gwennan's who responded by brushing the unruly locks, so like her father, of pale hair from the child's forehead.

"Do you think she will invite your brothers?"

Cecilé looked from her father to the *pennaeth* and said, "No, I do not think so, Father."

DeFreveille laughed, motioning Artur to finish while he closed and bolted the screed door without looking beyond at the women gathered there. Gesturing for Artur and his children to fill their trenchers and eat before the small fire, Jehan-Emíl filled a trencher and cup for Gwennan and placed them on a stool beside her.

"You must eat. I eat. We—together, *iawn?*" Although his attempts to speak her language embarrassed him, Gwennan smiled without looking at him and laid her temple against the fur pelt covering the back of her chair. He took her silence for consent and found a stool to sit near her. He watched his children, drinking the wine Artur poured for him. "You say no often. Why?"

"How can I say yes?"

"No." He finished the wine. "You say yes. All say yes. But, *you* say no. Why?"

"I cannot say yes for them." Gwennan lifted her head erect on the back of the chair.

"All say no?"

"No," she laughed, "some have said yes."

"Good," he exhaled and slapped his thighs. "Good." He reached across her knees and laid the trencher on her lap. From it, he speared a chunk of meat with his dagger and held it up before his eyes before taking it into his mouth. While he ate, he studied the children grouped before the fire, all four of their heads bowed together in a secret, whispered conversation. "I am happy," Ieuan Emyr told her.

She was also looking at the children but she had not touched any of the food. He called Artur and held his cup to be filled. He put a cup in her hands and urged her to drink while he chose a piece of meat and held it up to her, insisting that she take it into her mouth. When she parted her lips to protest, he urged her to open further and let the meat fall onto her tongue. As she closed her mouth, he lowered his hand to her neck, laying his thumb against her windpipe. He closed his eyes when she swallowed.

"You are strong enough now," he said, "you are well enough," but when he opened his eyes her cold glare was turned on him.

Though he did not take his hand from her, it trembled and Gwennan closed her eyes, shocked by the ease with which he could end her life. *Men have this advantage, always.* She should not have forgotten but she did. This reminder had been so gentle, she had almost thought he caressed her, had herself searched his face for any sign of his meaning only to be reminded that this gentle hand could snap her neck if she defied him.

He lay down on the skins before the fire, pretending to bite Cecilé's leg. She squealed, trying to get away though her laughter made her helpless. Jehan-Batiste and Artur moved to the side to give them room but Marshal attacked his father to rescue her, pounding the man mercilessly on the back and shoulders to force him to give up his prey and defend himself. Ieuan rose to his hands and knees above his tiny daughter and bent his head to bite her while she giggled and Marshal leapt on his back to steer him away. Cecilé was permitted to commit the most heinous crimes, kicking and biting her father, making him cry out in pain.

When he tired of the game, he flung himself onto his back and fended off the last of their blows, allowing them time for their excitement to cool. As they grew calm, he caressed and kissed them, calling Jehan-Batiste to him and gesturing for

Artur to clear away the food. "Take your brother and sister to their beds. I wish to discuss with Gwennan."

Cecilé was reluctant to go and offered to sit at Gwennan's feet and be quiet but her father dismissed her and she left, holding her brothers' hands.

He stretched his legs and folded his arm under his head, fixing his gaze on her face. He was content to lie on the floor, watching the fire light her eyes, washing her skin with its pale glow. She was the same woman who defied him so openly. His hand rested on her knee. When, at last, she met his gaze, he turned his eyes on the flames licking the blackened stones of the hearth. His hand slid from her knee, his palm spread over the gold crest.

"What is this song you have taught my daughter?"

"It is only a simple rhyme, to teach a child words and colors, a little grammar."

"Sing it," he commanded. Gwennan sang the verses of the rhyme and the chorus through to the end. "Again."

"I have no time—."

"Gwennan, sing again," he asked, kneeling in front of her, watching as she opened her mouth to sing the simple song. To her surprise, he sang some of the words with her and laughed when they came to the end together. "I like this song," he declared. "It is good. Very good. Sing again. Another perhaps. Do you know another song, Gwennan? What about this one about boys who boast of their prowess?" he asked, sliding his arm around her waist.

"How did you hear about that?" Gwennan laughed, pushing his arm away.

"It is funny, no? It will make you laugh to sing it," he said, persisting in his effort to embrace her.

"I will *not* sing that song."

"Why not? It is funny, a happy song."

"It is for men—and boys—to sing, when they are drunk."

"Then teach it to me so I can sing it to you," he murmured, brushing her hair away from her neck to kiss her below the ear. "I want to make love with you," he breathed against her throat.

"Real love, Gwennan. Teach me a song that will make that possible."

"Now what are you saying?"

DeFreveille began to hum softly. The tune was sweet but unfamiliar to Gwennan. He sang a few words in a whisper, holding her in his arms, smiling into her eyes. "You like this song?"

"It is pretty," she agreed. "Were you spying on me—on us? Is that how you know about this boy's song?"

"I—Yes ," he shrugged. "Yes, I admit. I confess," he grinned. "Do not be angry, Gwennan," he commanded, shaking a finger in her face. "For Cecilé—she is quiet. Too quiet. I leave my daughter with you and she is singing," he said, another grin brightening his face. "A little off-key, but happy. I do not see her happy, a long time. You forgive?" He pulled her hand to his lips, turning the palm upward and spreading her fingers. "She is happy so I am happy." He pressed a kiss in the center of her palm. "I am happy," he whispered, "since—. No, I am not happy since a long time. Gwennan," he breathed. "So...beautiful your name."

She pushed his arms away, no longer smiling. If the moment was not already too late, she would have begun to love him then. That she did love him was shameful. How could she have him, this *gelyn*, when all her friends, her father, every lesson she had learned of war urged her to kill him?

"What?" he asked. "What now?"

Gwennan rose from the chair and crossed to the bed. Her hair was still loose and she braided it before she unlaced the front of her gown, pushed it off her shoulders and folded it carefully before she laid it on the top of the chest. She closed the hangings all around the bed and was about to disappear behind them when he called her name. Glancing over her shoulder at him, she studied him from a safe distance.

He was stretched across the whole of the area before the hearth, the chair hid the lower half of his body from her eyes but she remembered him well enough. She missed him more, now that she was strong. She hungered for the weight of his large body beside her and to feel the power of his hands on her. From a safe distance, her face in shadow, she could recall the heat of his mouth, the ache of love.

Jehan-Emíl twisted her gold band on his little finger, interrogating his brain for some excuse to keep her talking but he could not keep his mind clear while his blood was so hot in his veins. He could not think what she meant by undressing in front of him and braiding her hair into a cord down her back, letting the oil lamp silhouette her body beneath her chemise. He turned onto his side to face the fire and cleared his throat.

"The old woman, Galar…" He flicked a charcoal into the flames. "Do you want her, Gwennan? As before. With you. In the house?"

"I am not sure," she answered honestly. "Does Galar wish to return?"

"She is old," he said. "Troublesome." Galar incited the Cymry, enflaming their hatred, encouraged their rebellion but that was not the reason he asked Gwennan if she wanted the woman with her. He sensed that the old woman wielded a powerful influence on both Gwennan and the hot-headed warrior, that she was part of the bond between them. Jehan-Emíl wanted to know if Gwennan meant to break that bond.

"She has been—she is the only mother I have ever known. If she is a trouble to you, I will care for her." She bent to extinguish the lamp and closed the hangings behind her.

The bed creaked as she lay down, but a long time passed before he moved. With his jaw clenched, his hand gripping the cup in a fist, Jehan-Emíl listened to the faint sounds in the house as his children and the other women settled into their beds. He finished the wine in the jug, waiting for the women to sleep.

Bedwyn ducked beneath the flap of the campaign tent and stood by the end of the desk, awaiting deFreveille's entry. Maides indicated the chair and the young warrior brought it forward. When deFreveille entered, he leapt to attention and was told to be at ease.

"We are friends here, Bedwyn," deFreveille said. "I have important work for you. I explain, Maides will tell you, *iawn*?"

"*Iawn*, Commander."

"As you know, the work in the Gaer has gone on for some time while the *boneddiges* has been ill." DeFreveille began while Maides translated. "Now she is well and will be more often among the soldiers to do her work, to manage what happens. I considered Wode for this position, but he has—he has other skills." DeFreveille tapped the desk for a moment while he thought. "You are already trusted by the *boneddiges*. It is my wish—my hope—that you will accept this commission for her sake. If you do, you will be my most trusted captain—after Maides, of course, but more than any of the others."

"I will not betray Gwennan Pendyffryn," Bedwyn said, starting to his feet.

"Sit. I do not ask you to betray." DeFreveille laid his hand over his chest. "I ask you to protect. She is not safe when she leaves the house. Maides cannot always be with her. I cannot be with her. I trust Wode—he is a good man. The *boneddiges* is too…smart for such a man." He smiled at the blond warrior. "Gwennan likes you, trusts you. I also trust you…"

"What do you want me to do?" Bedwyn asked.

"First," deFreveille replied, leaning forward, resting his forearms on the desk, "I want to talk to Daran Pendyffryn."

"I will not betray my *pendefig*."

"Talk, Bedwyn," Jehan-Emíl answered, opening his hands. "Only to talk, man to man—no armies, no warriors. I will go to him, unarmed, a truce."

"Why?"

"To talk, Bedwyn , between men. To see if we can agree. You can reach the *pendefig*—in secret?"

"Perhaps."

"Yes or no, Bedwyn?" DeFreveille placed his hands flat on the desk, leaning forward until the young warrior nodded. "Good. We go now. Get ready."

Within hours, deFreveille paced the sheltered *porth* between the hearth that was as large as a house and the open entry where horses and carts came into the lower hall of Castell Pendyffryn, delivering goods and information from all corners of the *ystad* to the *pendefig*. The *gelyn* commander had been waiting since before dawn for his application to meet Gwennan's father to be accepted. As far as he knew, the *pendefig* had not received Bedwyn. As far as he knew, Bedwyn was plotting to have him killed. As far as he knew, an army was already on the road to recapture the Gaer and his children murdered as they slept. These thoughts flashed through his mind. The moment they did, he questioned his reason for taking these risks.

He stopped in his tracks, a slow smile replaced his anxiety. He turned to face the man he had come to see. Haelsted's old and feeble enemy stood with his fists on his hips, his black boots straddling the stone flags near the hearth, his fur-lined cloak sweeping the polished floor and his close-cropped, silver hair standing out from his head like a crown. He did not look like his daughter. He studied deFreveille from clear blue eyes as he might appraise an inferior warhorse. Apart from a scar that crossed his right cheek from the bone beneath his eye to his chin, he was handsome.

Jehan-Emíl bowed his upper body slightly and was glad he had decided to wear his own livery. Daran Pendyffryn wore a tunic decorated with Gwennan's needlework similar to those she had given him.

Noting the direction of the *gelyn's* gaze, Pendyffryn smiled for a moment and stepped forward. Extending his hand, he indicated the chairs by the grate—large enough to roast the carcass of a buck, or a man. The *pendefig* swept his cloak out of his way as he took the larger chair and waited for his guest to sit.

"Breakfast will arrive soon," Daran said, leaning comfortably back, his feet set wide apart and his knees spread, resting his hands on the arms of the carved chair. "Why have you come, deFreveille?" he asked.

Pendyffryn's command of his language was a relief. "Why do you not ask what has taken me so long? Why have you not sent an army against me?"

"You have my daughter," Pendyffryn reminded the foreigner.

"You knew that before I sent Maides to you."

"If she needed me, she would have sent word."

DeFreveille also leaned back in his chair, his feet apart. "She has invited you to visit at Christmas," he said.

"Bedwyn told me you knew his message."

"I do not know what your reply to your daughter was, sir, but I also would like to invite you to the Gaer—at the same time as you visit your daughter, if you have accepted her invitation."

"I see no reason to refuse *your* invitation, deFreveille," Pendyffryn said, gesturing for the two women to set the breakfast on the table. One of the women brought his guest a flagon of ale. "I presume you do not include my army in your invitation as Gwennan has."

"Bring as many as you require. The number will make no difference to me or the circumstances of your stay." He drank the ale, took and bit into the honey-soaked bread the woman held out to him. "Gwennan has recovered well from the miscarriage and will manage any number of guests you insist are necessary." When he glanced at Pendyffryn, the older man's knuckles were white, gripping the arms of his chair. "You did not know that she has lost a child?"

The *pendefig* drew a long breath. "You disappoint me, deFreveille. I had not expected a man like you to lie."

"She did not tell you of this child," deFreveille speculated, "perhaps—I cannot be certain, but some believe the Welshman, Derwyn Blaenant—."

"He would not dare," Pendyffryn replied.

"This is not what the old nurse, Galar, has claimed. I had reason to believe...but once it was clear that Elgan Maergwn was not Gwennan's lover, Galar named Derwyn as the child's father."

"No," Pendyffryn growled. "You are lying to excuse your own—."

"I have done nothing for which I need make an excuse. I do not apologize to you or to Gwennan. I am satisfied that they were not—have never been lovers. This miscarriage remains a mystery," deFreveille commented, "however, I have come here to tell you that I intend to keep your daughter."

"As your hostage?" Pendyffryn inquired.

"As my wife."

Pendyffryn turned his attention to the food that was offered to him, smiling into the woman's pleasant face. "You confuse us with your allies, deFreveille. We do not sell our daughters to our enemies to make peace."

"For what reason did you sell Gwennan to a man so far her inferior?"

Pendyffryn's hand shook with rage but he gave no other sign the accusation angered him. "Women in our society are free to make their own decisions about such matters. My daughter would choose only the best man, and bed with him as it pleased her. If either Derwyn or Elgan gave her a child, only she would have determined which of them was worthy of that honor." Pendyffryn studied the *gelyn* commander for a moment. "She has not chosen you, deFreveille, or you would not be here to seek my blessing. What has Gwennan said to your proposal?"

"She will accept."

"You have not asked her," the *pendefig* laughed. "My daughter frightens you. I am not surprised by that. I have not yet found a man who was in any way worthy of her and many have asked—with better credentials to recommend them than you present. Since she was old enough to wed, I have kicked every jack of them down those stairs. The first was Derwyn. The last was Elgan. Both of them the best. The only reason my daughter went to the Gaer was to take command of my army there. Against my wishes, but she cannot be deterred when she knows she is right. If not for her management, I admit, there would have been nothing at the Gaer to attract your attention.

In the months she has governed, Gwennan has turned the place from a ruin to a thriving fortress—all without a single warrior knowing that Elgan took his orders from her. How can you hope that such a woman would consider relinquishing her power to you?"

"She will accept," deFreveille repeated, holding the flagon out to be refilled.

"When will this wedding take place, Commander deFreveille?" Pendyffryn asked with a laugh on the verge of bellowing from his chest.

"When you are ready to attend, *pendefig*."

"My daughter may refuse you, Commander. What will you do then?"

"Gwennan will be my wife," the foreigner answered.

"I will come to see this for myself."

"Your daughter will be happy to greet you."

"I will grant you two days, deFreveille, to perform this miracle."

FOURTEEN

Early on the day before the celebration of the Nativity, Gwennan was still dreaming though the sun had risen. The storm during the night left the acrid odor of sodden ashes in the room. Each day, she had worked with the other women from earliest light until late to finish as many simple tunics and cloaks as possible. Thick bolts of sand-colored wool leaned against the walls of the hall, coarse and rough to work, but the bolts diminished as the piles of clothing grew. Artur served as their model for the youngest soldiers and Gwennan, because she could judge the size by eye as she cut, chose Ieuan Emyr's measurements for the men. The tunics were not elaborate but each seam was finished to be as strong as the cloth.

Each night, while the others slept, Gwennan took from her chest her own cloth and, by the light of tapers and the small fire, she stitched a pattern she had known from childhood into the fine fabric of a gold tunic.

Cecilé, more frightened of her nurse than anyone else in the house, crept early from her bed and into Gwennan's. She made hardly any movement as she slipped under the covers but Gwennan became aware of her when the girl sought warmth. She pulled Cecilé into her arms and dozed again.

The clink of the wooden rings around the bed startled her awake and she looked up into Charlotte's face. Without a word, the nurse reached across the bed and shook Cecilé, dragging her free of Gwennan's embrace when deFreveille spoke.

"Why are you here?"

212

"Cecilé disturbs this woman," Charlotte replied in her light laughter.

"Leave her, Charlotte. I will see to my daughter."

"Of course, Jehan-Emíl," she said, using his name without regard in front of the Welsh woman. "But, Jehan-Emíl, please do not beat her this time. She is so little."

DeFreveille glared at Charlotte until she retreated.

"She wakes you."

"No. Let her sleep," Gwennan replied, dropping her arm lazily around the child and snuggling beneath the *carthen*.

Nudging Gwennan's arms away, he lifted Cecilé to his shoulder and woke her. Cecilé strained to be released and he quieted her. "Cecilé, stop now," he growled, setting her on the floor. "Go back where you belong." As the little girl left the room, dawdling as long as she dared, the commander sat down on the edge of the bed. "We talk."

Gwennan flung the *carthen* off and rose from the bed with her back to him, searching the room for her gown. DeFreveille stood between her and her chest and she attempted to move around him but he stopped her, his hand falling on her bare arm.

"What do you want with me now?" she demanded, refusing to look at him.

"Ah, what?" he asked. "What?"

"Let me go. I want to dress." She shoved his hand away but he held her with the other. Though she stared at his hand, his grip neither faltered nor tightened.

"Stay. We talk."

"How?" she sighed in exasperation. "How? About what?"

"Try. We will try."

"Let me dress."

"No," he murmured. "I like this." He drew her closer to him, slipping his hands around her waist. "It is enough." A languid, warm smile grew in his eyes as she tried to pull away from him, unable to conceal the effect he had on her. "It is too much." He slid the back of his hand over her breast and looped his fingers in the bow that held her chemise secure. "Only this," he whispered, tugging the cord ends free and pushing the material off her shoulder, "protects you from me, *cariad*. Only this and my plans for you."

"What do you want?" Gwennan forced herself to speak without pleading but she could not control the surge of heat or the ache for his caress to linger.

"When it is time for you to know, I will tell you. Of all here, you will be the last, I think." He raised his eyes from her shoulder, a knowing, sarcastic smile lifting the corners of his mouth. "I have your father. He is very old," he said, twisting the fabric of her chemise in his fingers, tightening it over her breasts.

"What do you want with my father?" She threw her head back to glare at him. His arm tightened around her. He shifted his weight so that his thigh rested between hers and dragged her upward, pulling her hard against him.

"I do not want him. I brought him to see you," deFreveille said.

"When?" Gwennan whispered, concealing her struggle to make herself immune to him. "When may I see him?"

"When you have earned his visit," Jehan-Emíl laughed. "A reward, if you behave, *blodyn*. I will decide."

"If I do not behave?"

"You will, for his sake, I think."

"You cannot hurt him," she pleaded, defeated. "Please."

"Please?" he repeated, his voice tainted with sarcasm. He dropped his hand from her shoulder and let it slide the length of her back to her thigh, his fingers tightening on her velvet flesh as he drew one leg free of the other to insinuate his thigh deeper between them. Her breathing quickened and her body tensed as he tugged the skirt of her thin chemise free of her legs and thrust his hand between her thighs, his powerful fingers plunging into her, lifting her with his forearm. "Please?"

With all her strength, Gwennan shoved herself free, lashed at his face before darting into the other chamber, taking refuge at Siriol's side and glaring back at her assailant.

His long strides brought him to the screed door only a moment behind her but he stopped when his daughter joined the formidable friends. Their combined, smoldering anger undermined his intent. He raised his hand in a fist at the two women. "Daran is old, *menyw*. Remember." When deFreveille turned away, his smile returned, his fingers tingling, still moist from her body. Lingering only long enough to ensure that neither Gwennan nor his daughter spoke of him, Jehan-Emíl strode through the room, critical of its tattered furnishing and, for the old bed, he had only a disdainful laugh.

Gwennan heard the laugh and turned away from her friend, hiding the uncertainty Ieuan drove through her heart. His shout for his sons to join him at the table—her table—stopped her breath but the light, giggling voice of his consort brought a growl from deep in her raging soul. "I would like nothing better than to tear him apart," she hissed at her curled, sharpened fingers until his daughter wrapped her arms around her legs. "But not you, *blodyn*. Never you."

"It will be good, yes, to spend this holiday with your children after so many years?" Charlotte murmured when Jehan-Emíl took his chair at the table. "And they are so happy to be with their fine father."

"Yes," he replied, stroking the side of the tankard Artur had placed in front of him.

"I am happy as well, Jehan-Emíl," Charlotte said, moving her own stool closer. "But I do not understand why you keep me so far away these days. I wait for you to send for me each night, but you have no time for me now."

"I have work," he said, leaning back in his chair. "I have all this," he swept his arm wide, "to command, to govern."

"Command me, Jehan-Emíl. I am yours to govern."

Hers was not the voice he wanted but the words from another would have sent his heart soaring.

"This Welsh woman," Charlotte continued, "why do you allow her to trouble you? Why do you not take her and be done?"

"That is your advice, Charlotte ?"

"I am not such a fool that I refuse to see that you want her. She is not without appeal," Charlotte commented, more generously than she intended. "Have her. Make a meal of her, Jehan-Emíl, and finish it," Charlotte said, her voice husky. "While you toy and dally with her, playing these tender games of seduction, and wait for her to come to you, she meets her lover in secret. They will laugh at you, when they meet tonight. Take what you want from her and throw her back to him. Then take me."

Making a fist on the arm of the chair, he closed the fingers of his hand into his palm, embracing the scent he had stolen from Gwennan. Drinking slowly from the tankard, he smiled at the nurse. "And then…what?"

"We will go on as we always have, yes?"

"Perhaps."

"Have you made an inventory?" Gwennan asked the raven-haired mercenary. "Can you write?"

"It will be better that the hand is yours, *boneddiges*," Maides replied.

"Then I will have more than enough to do," she sighed. "Derwyn also does not write."

"DeFreveille will be grateful, *boneddiges*," Maides said with a bow, untroubled by his commander's order that the two be brought together after weeks of enforcing their separation.

"I do this as *pennaeth*, not for deFreveille." Gwennan raised her hood again as she accompanied the mercenary out of the common hall and allowed him to draw her arm through his. In the far western corner of the stockade, Derwyn stood among the carts and barrels which had been brought in from the farmers. Though she did not avoid looking at him, Gwennan caught her breath when he approached and remained standing close to her. Maides was also near and, though they spoke freely, Maides's hand was on his dagger ready to kill him if he threatened her.

Derwyn gazed at Gwennan, openly assessing her body despite the presence of his commanding officer. Galar's accounts of Gwennan's wantonness burned deep into his hatred of deFreveille and enflamed his desire for revenge. Though the mercenary kept him away from her, Derwyn was careless, indiscreet. He did not care what the dark foreigner overheard.

"Have you forgotten me, Gwennan?" he asked, peering beyond the edge of her hood.

As he spoke, Maides stepped forward to stand behind her, so close to Gwennan that she could feel the heat of his body and his strength. She was safer with the dark-skinned mercenary than with the man she had once thought she loved.

"Is it likely that I would forget a friend?"

"I hurt you by my words, I know, but I have been mad with anxiety for you. You suffer at this demon's hands. He abuses you." Derwyn leaned closer to her in the heat of his passion. "I am ready to kill him the moment you order it. I am driven mad that he touches you when I have waited so long—and am not even allowed to see your face."

"Derwyn." She glanced at Maides.

"Why do you care what he hears? Are you ashamed that I, who was always meant to be your husband, want you? Are you afraid that you are so corrupted by this *gelyn* that I will not forgive you?"

"Derwyn, you are mistaken…"

"I will wait for you tonight. You know the place." When Derwyn tried to grasp her arm in his entreaty, Maides drew his dagger and stepped in front of Gwennan. Using the weapon's flat edge, he urged the Welshman to back away.

"*Boneddiges*," Cecilé called from the bridge and hurtled over the slippery planks. Before the little girl reached the opposite side of the ravine, Gwennan had turned toward the sound of her urgent voice and stooped to greet the supplicant. "*Boneddiges*, I have so much happiness to see you," Cecilé exclaimed in her peculiar mixture of languages.

"You have taught the little bitch our language," Derwyn hissed, lunging at her.

Maides's thrust was so quick, Gwennan did not see the blade but Derwyn leapt away as soon as the tip grazed him. Gwennan also leapt, in front of the mercenary, allowing Derwyn to escape. Maides, enraged by the urgency to protect her, shoved her aside to get at her assailant. Only her pleading repetition of his name reached him through his fury. He stood panting, held back by her hands on his forearms, the dagger, tipped with blood, clenched in his hand.

"Tonight, Gwennan." Derwyn called from a distance. "Tonight."

"Maides," Gwennan whispered, her voice tired and plaintive. "Please. Let him go." Still grasping his arms, Gwennan stared at the dagger between them, its glistening tip near her heart. She drew in her breath, but the mercenary turned the blade harmlessly downward. Raising her eyes, only the rock-hard line of his dark jaw told her he had seen what she thought to do and she could not let go of his arms, ashamed that she involved him in a moment of despair. The fire in the mercenary's eyes died and the cold, appraising expression returned as he wiped the blade clean on the sleeve of his black shirt.

"Where is my father?" she asked to cover her shame.

Maides rammed his dagger into his belt and pulled her hands away, setting her firmly on her feet. "Safe," he said. "The child is frightened, *boneddiges*. See to her."

Dropping to her knees, Gwennan took Cecilé into her arms and stroked her hair. "Be still, *blodyn*. Everything is all right. Are you cold?"

"I am not cold, *boneddiges*. May I stay with you?"

"Do you think you can help me, Cecilé?"

Maides swung around to lift Gwennan to her feet. She accepted the mercenary's directive to finish the inventory with Cecilé a happy partner in the accounting. When it was done, the three returned to the common hall.

Though the farmers protested that their food and grain was stolen from them to be added to the Gaer's stores, Gwennan ceased to listen. She rested her elbows on the planks of the table and stared at the accounts she had made. Discounting the food fit only for fodder, there was not enough to feed everyone through the long winter. She had been arrogant to think her tactics better than Elgan's warriors. Her punishment was to watch her friends and the people she intended to protect die in agony.

The cup of warmed mead by her hand, steaming with the aroma of spices, had been filled each time she drained it but its affect did nothing to deaden her sense of guilt. Across the dim hall, she met the eyes of Elgan's warriors and looked away.

"*Boneddiges*," Maides said, stepping toward her and offering his arm. "You have done enough for one day." He pulled her up from the chair and held her arm in his, leading her toward the door. She withdrew her arm from his grasp. Unwilling to risk her safety among the disgruntled farmers and the warriors who had watched with narrowed eyes while she redistributed the harvest, Maides clasped her wrist, wrapped her arm through his once more, smiling at her in his icy way and pulled her with him toward the door leading to the scullery yard.

"What is this?" deFreveille shouted. His thoughts were still wrestling with Charlotte's tales of treachery and deceit and he was weary from scouting the woods for marauders through the day. "What is this?" he asked, looking from his daughter to his friend, in a moment, allowing his eyes to settle on Gwennan's face.

Maides bent his head to speak to the woman. He glanced at his friend and returned his intense gaze to Gwennan's face. "*Boneddiges*, which will you choose? Stay or return to the house?"

Gwennan met the mercenary's eyes for the first time since the morning. Before she could speak, the commander had reached them, his hand on his own dagger. Exhausted by threats of violence, Gwennan tightened her grip on the mercenary's arm and sank toward him, turning her face away from deFreveille. The two men spoke quietly, and Maides said, "Sit, *Boneddiges.*"

"Sit, Gwennan," deFreveille commanded her, taking her gently from Maides's protective embrace. To his captains, he said, "All of you go. We will discuss later." He poured drink into her cup and drank most of it himself. "What? Tell me," he demanded, glancing first at her and then at the warriors gathered at the far end of the hall.

She pushed her accounts toward him, taking the cup from his hand and swallowed the cooled mead he left, watching for signs of his comprehension. He studied her list of calculations, understanding as he neared the bottom the reason for her distress.

"No good? Many die, yes?" She nodded, dropping her head onto her hand and staring at the worn oak of the chair arm. "I do not let people die, Gwennan," he said, lifting her by her arms to stand in front of him. "Some die every winter. That I cannot help. But none here will starve while I govern." Bowing his head, he gazed into her face, sorry to see that her eyes were again dark-rimmed with fatigue and worry. "And you manage." His smile was disarming, but Gwennan did not forget his ability to deceive. "Tonight and tomorrow we feast and after, we are more careful. Yes?"

No more than what they would eat was set out for the meal so that they would better appreciate the final feast of the winter months. DeFreveille's cook resented the Welsh woman's interference, but Betsan huffed around the kitchen with relief. The servants were told to slow their pace regardless of the complaints and the drink was not poured often. The rude awakening to the tight control Gwennan exerted stunned the commander and his captains.

"How can a man get drunk enough to sleep in this filthy place?"

"You will learn, Alrick," deFreveille replied, gazing with dissatisfaction at his own empty cup. "Soldiers may complain, captains may not." He was consoled for his acceptance of deprivation when Gwennan remained with him throughout the meal. When she took the place Jehan-Emíl offered beside him, all her fellow Cymry walked out. Oswin refused to serve at the commander's table.

"Do you stay to please me, Gwennan," he murmured, his lips brushing her cheek near her ear, "or to protect Daran Pendyffryn?"

"We have matters of importance to discuss, Commander deFreveille, but I will not pretend I have forgotten your threat to my father."

"You are honest," he said, with only a shrug of disappointment. "Though you are not pleased to be with me, having you near me pleases me, very much." He laid his broad hand over hers. "My name is Jehan-Emíl. It pleases me to hear my name on your lips."

"I know your name," Gwennan replied. "I hear it often enough on Charlotte's lips."

"And you will not say it," he laughed. "I hear your name spoken by many men, Gwennan, but saying it myself delights me no less."

"There is no man here who uses my name with any more meaning than a father or brother."

"No one, Gwennan? Are you certain?"

"Yes," Gwennan said, lowering her eyes and staring at her gold ring on his hand.

"Then you do not hear what I say to you when I say 'Gwennan'. I have no fatherly feeling for you, Gwennan. I mean you to understand that I am your lover, though you do not yet admit you want me."

"I do not want you. I do not want you," she said, dragging her hand from beneath his heavy grasp.

"No?" He allowed her to escape him while he peered once more into the empty cup. "Is there another man you prefer to me?"

"My father is imprisoned," Gwennan said after a pause. He was intent on tricking her into a confession of love, or guilt. "What more can you take from me?"

"I would take less if you gave more." His hand clenched the clay cup. The bowl shuddered with the stress exerted by his grip. Watching her sit back, he acknowledged she had defeated him again. He shrugged, accepted failure and grinned at her in return. "What matters are so important to discuss that you condemn yourself to be with me?"

Although deFreveille walked with her to the bridge, they said nothing more to one another about rotten grain barrels or rationing food or spoiled ale. When she started across, he caught her fingers and raised them to his lips. Taking another step toward the house, Gwennan did not turn to look at him. While he held her hand at the bridge, Jehan-Emíl debated. Maides had told him that Derwyn had arranged to meet with her. It was the confirmation of Charlotte's accusation he hoped had been nothing more than a vicious taunt.

Maides had reported everything that transpired in his company that afternoon. She was unhappy. He fought his impulse to comfort her as he would his daughter. He fought his desire to warn her. She left his company to walk into a trap he himself had set and would close if he had no choice. He held the tips of her fingers against his lips, silencing the violence in his own heart.

He released her fingers and she drew her hand into the warmth of her cloak before continuing her climb, feeling his eyes on her even though she disappeared in the heavy mist of the night. At the top, she turned back. The lower end of the bridge had dissolved in the fog, but Gwennan felt Ieuan Emyr was still on the other side, looking up, as unable to distinguish her figure as she was his. She wished for his footfall on the planks but shook the wish away.

Several minutes passed before he turned away from his vigil. The Cymry defied him. His daughter was in the house without his protection. DeFreveille stood aside from the bridge as Jehan-Batiste and Marshal ran toward him, their laughter filling him with pride and fear. Without a word of caution, he allowed them to leave the company of the soldiers to go to their beds in the house. He risked everything he valued on the hope that he had not set their future where they could never be wanted. Their laughing greeting for Gwennan Pendyffryn as they ran into the warmth of the family hall did nothing to allay his fear.

The family hall was decorated with boughs of ivy, fir, yew and berry-laden holly. The rushes were sprinkled with lavender. The other women of the Gaer had returned with their husbands and children to the house to be apart from deFreveille's army and Gwennan wondered at herself that she had not noticed their absence from the common hall while she shared her meal with Ieuan Emyr. As they discussed the food stores, Gwennan's attention was drawn continually to his face, the sound of his voice, his laughter, the intense expression of interest in his eyes when he looked at her and listened to her concerns.

Though the same rationing had been applied to the meal served in the house, the levity of the occupants was boisterous and unguarded, heard throughout the walled garden but she had not heard their celebrations as she climbed from the bridge.

Gwennan stood within the *porth* to watch her friends dance and laugh together as they had done a year before. Her heart ached for the same laughter she had shared at Pendyffryn, in her father's household, the same happy dancing and innocent games of the festival. She was not ashamed that she did not think of Derwyn. She was not ashamed of teasing Ieuan Emyr, knowing it would not be innocence that prompted her to sit on his knee during a game of Fox and Geese, as Siriol did with Pendryw.

Resting her shoulder against the wall of the short passageway into the house, Gwennan remained out of the light and indulged her guilty dreaming until she recalled that there was nothing innocent in deFreveille's threats against her father. She could never tease him, never dance or laugh with him however much she longed for his companionship, never lean comfortably against him, their bodies like two parts of one whole, fitted like walnuts, never reach for him or offer herself to him. She could never admit she loved a man who held her father's life in one hand and used that threat to caress her with the other.

When she entered the house, she was surprised to see Derwyn among the revelers. She had not expected him to be so daring. Though she did not welcome his sudden passionate attention, her past friendship made her go to him where he sat in the inglenook, his head bowed over the cup of warm mead in his hands.

"I thought you had forgotten," he said, glancing at her as she sat beside him. "I waited in the garden as we planned."

"Derwyn, I want to give you your *Calan* gift now."

He took her hands and drew her closer to him, looking into her face, his brow knitted above his eyes in a scowl. "How can you think of gifts, Gwennan?" His grip on her hands tightened. "Do you have a gift for deFreveille as well?"

"Derwyn, I cannot change what has happened."

"What do you give him when he comes to your bed?"

"Nothing."

"You must give enough to keep his hunger satisfied, Gwennan. He takes no one else, though plenty would have him."

"Have you come here to speak to me of deFreveille?" she asked, dismissing the surge of joy in her heart.

"No." Derwyn's hand closed on her wrists, with the other he pulled her toward him. "I have come to claim what you have long promised me and give to him."

"I give nothing to deFreveille."

"You do not have to lie to me. You are no man's wife, Gwennan. You have no man's honor to protect."

"I have my own," she protested, shoving his hand away from her and leaping from the seat in the inglenook. Derwyn rose with her, throwing his arm around her waist, fighting her for a kiss. "They will see."

"Let them," he growled. "Let them all see, Gwennan. Are you ashamed to have *me*, one of your own, when you have been with the *gelyn* for all to know?"

Only deFreveille sons watched them. When Marshal frowned and took a step toward her, Jehan-Batiste held him back. Siriol was in her husband's arms and Aine had taken the four youngest children to their beds. Gwennan dragged her hands free and faced Derwyn.

"You are not eager?" he laughed. "But perhaps you are right. I do not want my friends to see how you are degraded. It is bad enough that they know how willingly you let that pig abuse you. I still have pride enough to seek privacy for my pleasures."

"Derwyn," Gwennan said, as he dragged her through the kitchen. "Don't do this. You do not know the truth. Siriol will tell you, she knows…"

"All women are false," Derwyn hissed as he shoved Gwennan against the ruined garden wall and pressed against her. "All your women are liars. Some, like you, go to the beds of our enemies."

Gwennan's hands were free but they hung at her sides, immobilized.

"You are beautiful," he whispered, dragging his hands over her, pushing her clothing out of his way.

"What are you doing? You told me yourself that whatever there was between us is finished. It was finished long before either of us recognized. I have depended on our friendship, Derwyn—."

"What are you saying?" he laughed. "You were *pennaeth*. I have respected that. How can that be friendship, Gwennan? You led me to believe that we would wed. You gave me reason to believe that."

"I was wrong, mistaken. We are not suited to one another, Derwyn. If we were, you would not expect me to kill myself. If we were, I would not have hesitated to do so when I thought you were dead."

"You did not love Elgan but you slept with him. Does this *gelyn* pig suit you?"

"I do not have to explain myself to you. You want to believe the worst of me," she hissed at him. "How can we be suited if you have no faith? What makes you believe you know what is in my heart?" She pushed his hands away. "You have never asked, never concerned yourself."

"Galar has told me everything," Derwyn hissed in return, slapping her hands away to touch her. "You gave no thought to the *baban* when you took deFreveille to your bed. Did he please you so much?"

"What does Galar tell you?"

"Enough."

"Then I need not speak."

"Even if she kept your shame a secret, deFreveille says plenty."

"He would not tell you," Gwennan replied, astonished by her certainty. Ieuan Emyr would neither lie nor divulge to anyone what happened between them.

"He doesn't have to speak." Derwyn clasped her hands again. "Everything he has done is in his eyes when he looks at you. You have kept what you can offer me a secret. I want what you have always promised me," Derwyn growled.

"I have nothing to give you, Derwyn. If there was ever anything, you would have had my love a long time ago. When have I ever said or promised?"

"I do not want to hurt you," he said from between clenched teeth, "but I will—."

"You will not! I am your *pennaeth*. As much as I care for you as a friend, I cannot, I do not love you. I will never love you."

"You love him, don't you? The man who has killed your friends, your child. You love deFreveille..." Derwyn let go of her hands and stepped back. "You betray your own father for a man like that?"

"You do not know," she replied. "You cannot understand what has happened, Derwyn. I regret that I have misled you for so long..."

"You would take deFreveille in the stockade for all to see," he hissed. "Are you such a whore now?"

Gwennan struck him with as much force as she had ever struck the *gelyn* commander. "That is how I have replied to him. You have no right to speak to me in that way."

"You will regret your choice," Derwyn hissed, grabbing her arm.

"Gwennan!"

"Ieuan!" She ripped out of Derwyn's grasp and hurled herself in the direction of the *gelyn* commander's voice. He was not hard to find even in the heavy mist and darkness of the garden. The mass of his body filled the crumbling archway from the house and the glint of his drawn dagger flashed in the light pouring from the hall.

Seeing her running toward him from the farthest corner of the garden, deFreveille took two steps forward, only the white bodice and sleeves of her frock visible to him, until she flung herself into his arms. He caught her with his left arm and held his long dagger ready against the Welsh warrior.

"Ieuan," Gwennan whispered, her voice catching on a sob of relief.

"Hisht." He listened for the step that would bring the Welshman closer and into combat with him but could hear nothing over her rasping breaths. Backing toward the doorway to the house, he strained his eyes to peer into the darkness, tensing at the sound of rockfall. Pressing his back against the damp wall of the house, Gwennan sank against his chest and Jehan-Emíl laid his arm across the small of her back. "Are you hurt?" She shook her head on his shoulder, her arms limp at her sides and her gasps for breath slowing. "Who?" he asked. "Did he hurt you?"

Gwennan shook her head again and raised her hand to sweep her hair from her face. DeFreveille watched her in the warm light from the hall behind them. When she attempted to pull away from him, his arm convulsed around her and she cried out.

"Be still, *menyw*," he warned. In the distance, someone leapt from the wall and fell onto the slope of the hill, sliding and rolling down the steep incline toward the ravine. DeFreveille lunged forward, pushing Gwennan away from him, to catch sight of the warrior before he disappeared and his guilt was without witness. Gwennan held him back, turning his face away from the ruined wall, her hand draped over his fist.

Jehan-Emíl stared at her loosened hair, the length of her fingers across his hand, the curve of her breast beneath her gown. He had heard the anger in their voices from the bridge. Still he had climbed, in silence, unable to distinguish their words but recognizing who spoke and the tone—the rage in the warrior's voice, Gwennan's plaintive response, the twist in whatever they said that had made her angry with him.

"You want his life?" he asked. He bent his arm, bringing the dagger close to his face. Unless he witnessed, unless she told him who was with her, he could not accuse or punish. Without testimony, the warrior would stay free—alive. "Derwyn Blaenant," he murmured, "do you want him?"

"I do not want you to kill anyone," Gwennan said. "I do not want anyone else to die."

Jehan-Emíl flicked the dagger over in his hand and slid the blade under his wide leather belt, catching her hand before she could withdraw from him. She shivered, the heat of fear and anger subsiding. Holding her fast, her arms pinned to her sides, he released her hand and dragged his fingers over her arm to her throat. His hands were cold. Only the sudden intake of her breath protested as his fingers traced over the curve of her shoulder and fell sharply, sweeping away her clothing, to capture her breast, his thumb exciting and encircling her, pressing deep into her soft flesh. "Do you want him?" he demanded.

Though she granted him this liberty to give Derwyn more time to escape, Jehan-Emíl was surprised by the warmth of her response. She leaned toward him, arched her back and raised her hand to his face. He forgot that she had left him to meet her lover. He forgot that the Welshman had touched her as he was. He forgot she offered her body, her mouth, and her heart to another man only moments before she laid her head on his shoulder. Her lips were hot, soft at the corner of his mouth. He turned his head, closed his eyes, and took them as though she had offered him strong wine and its intoxication flowed through his veins the moment the cup touched his lips. Her mouth opened with only the slightest pressure when his tongue urged her lips to part for him. He thrust inside her body, pushing into her warmth, losing himself in her pliant flesh, helpless in the tangle of her arms around his neck, her fingers locked in his hair.

Gwennan's soft, moaning cries and the plaintive whimpers of her pleasure answered his own harsh and rasping breaths. He leaned his back against the damp, cold wall and lifted her, settled her thighs against him. She dragged her head away, still holding him by the curls of thick brown hair at the back of his neck. For a moment she stared wide-eyed at the stubble-shadowed face tilted up to her, his eyelids veiling his warm gaze, a slow smile edging away the taut and watchful lines along his jaw.

When he lifted her, she was as safe as a child in his arms, his arm clamped hard around her, locking her in the vice of his body. She bowed her head to look down their bodies, pressed hard together from breast to knee. A shy smile broke through her fear. The granite-hard ridge pressed against her body was not the hilt of his dagger. She closed her eyes slowly when his mouth sought hers and his strong fingers dug into the flesh of her thighs. His breathing was deep, mingling with the same hunger she had felt in his first kiss. He murmured her name against her lips and she surrendered herself to him, seduced by the question in his husky sighs.

FiFteen

Gwennan entered the house through the kitchen, stopping by the hearth to wipe a damp cloth over her tear-stained face. From the stores in the pantry she found one of the old *carthen* and wrapped it around her shoulders, tying the front of her gown together. "Ieuan will pay for this," she vowed as she surveyed the damage to her plain clothing. She touched her hot cheek. "And for that." She loosened the linen from her plait and shook her hair free, bringing it over her shoulders and around her face to hide her blush. When she entered the family hall, the room was dark except for the glowing embers. Siriol and Pendryw were still there, finding privacy in the inglenook. Gwennan glanced in their direction. They were absorbed in one another and did not see her until she had reached the landing outside her bedchamber. They made hasty attempts to straighten their clothing and laughed as they disentangled their bodies.

"Where have you been?" Siriol whispered.

"In the garden," Gwennan whispered in return.

"Did you see Derwyn? He was waiting to speak to you."

"Yes. I spoke to him before he left. Did you know that my father has come?"

"No. When?"

"He arrived yesterday," Pendryw told them, stretching out on the bench, wrapping his arm around his wife's waist to encourage her to lie down again. "He's been in the camp with deFreveille. We have all been hunting marauders today, from sunrise. I am not the only man who wants to rest, Siriol."

"Is that what you call what you have been doing to me?" his wife sighed, leaning toward him as his hand found the hem of her skirt.

Gwennan laid her hand on the latch. "Who is with my father from Pendyffryn?"

"One or two of his stewards," Pendryw yawned, teasing Siriol to lift her skirt.

"Siriol, are all the children asleep?"

"Yes, Gwennan, but the little girl would not go to her own bed, I'm sorry. Charlotte was in a rage because there were so many of us in the house and no sign of deFreveille."

"DeFreveille was with me," Gwennan said, slipping into the bedchamber and closing the door. *Ieuan is with me*, she repeated to herself, letting the old *carthen* and her ruined clothing fall to the floor around her feet before she walked to the bed and peered at the sleeping Cecilé. *His daughter is with me. And his sons.* After she had bathed and put on a flannel chemise, she lit the oil lamps on the table. For several hours she worked on the gold tunic, finishing the black embroidery over the wearer's heart and smiling to herself when Siriol giggled. As soon as her work was complete and she had wrapped it, she put the tunic in the chest by the bed.

Crawling under the *carthen*, she gathered Cecilé in her arms. "Tomorrow, everything I have worked so hard to achieve will be mine, *blodyn*." She yawned and snuggled into the bed. "You will like Daran Pendyffryn, Cecilé, and he will adore you."

When Jehan-Emíl entered beneath the flap of the campaign tent, Pendyffryn was in heated debate with Maides. Though, in the stockade, deFreveille's army sang and joked around the bonfires, the two warriors were discussing a battle plan that would be implemented in a matter of days. The coals in the brazier glowed, giving the illusion of warmth. Beyond its reach, in the corners of the tent, lurked the stench of damp and rot.

Artur added more charcoals to the brazier and poured his employer a cupful of cognac.

"You may go to your bed," he told the groom as he seated himself in a chair facing the *pendefig* and listened while the two plotted the campaign. Artur wrinkled his nose at the cold drizzle in the camp, ducking beneath the tent flap to join the other young soldiers in the stockade. On the table, Maides and Pendyffryn considered the map that deFreveille's scouts had drawn of the *ystad*. "I do not want to discuss war," he murmured.

"Your maps are poor, Commander," Pendyffryn commented.

"We only had half the reconnaissance we expected," Jehan-Emíl replied. "Your daughter was not helpful."

"I would have been surprised if she was," Pendyffryn laughed.

Rocaille knocked and entered. "I have just seen my patient."

"What?" deFreveille demanded, already on his feet.

"The other one," Rocaille murmured.

"What other one?"

"The Celt, Jehan. What is the good of my efforts if you are intent on damaging him?"

"What has happened?"

"Paul," Maides commented, "I wounded him, this morning."

"As well as the cuts on his face? I have not treated any wound, Maides. He came to the infirmary demanding ointment for scratches."

"When was this?" Jehan-Emíl asked, relaxing into his chair again.

"Less than an hour ago. He claims he fell."

"Perhaps he did, *meddyg*," the commander replied.

Daran Pendyffryn glanced at the man half his age and smiled.

"They look like the work of a woman to me," Rocaille persisted.

"Perhaps they are, *meddyg*. Will he live?"

"Yes, but my concern, Commander, is for the woman." The physician met Jehan-Emíl's gaze for a moment. "On reflection, Commander, considering the circumstances, I think our young friend was the loser in this encounter."

"Yes, Paul," Jehan-Emíl agreed. "Bring a chair. There is cognac in the jug." Rocaille joined the trio. "*Pendefig*, this is my good friend, Paul Rocaille. He is the man most responsible for your daughter's good health. Gwennan is fond of him." Rocaille greeted the warrior-prince with a bow.

"DeFreveille has told me much about you, Rocaille. I am grateful."

"I am honored to serve the *boneddiges*," Rocaille replied with a glance and puzzled frown for deFreveille.

"The *pendefig* is here to attend my wedding," deFreveille replied to the frown.

"If there is one," Pendyffryn laughed.

Rocaille grinned into his cup. "You do not know deFreveille, *pendefig*."

"DeFreveille does not know my daughter," Daran Pendyffryn laughed. "If he did—if he could—."

"We are mere men," deFreveille replied. "There is not a man at this table who does not realize that Gwennan Pendyffryn is a formidable opponent."

"But you are still confident?" Daran queried.

Jehan-Emíl endured the laughter and the scrutiny, drinking from the cup of cognac, swirling its contents and inhaling the fragrance. Even its hot intensity could not diminish the pleasure of Gwennan Pendyffryn's kisses. Its rush of intoxication could not overpower the headiness of her embrace. Jehan-Emíl deFreveille did not want to talk about war. This man, Ieuan, as he was known to his intended wife, wanted to close his eyes and feel this confidence in his life's blood. Although he had no evidence that would withstand Pendyffryn's interrogation, he said, "Yes."

He blocked doubt and fixed his mind on war until the men at his council were satisfied with the tactics they considered and Rocaille was content with the provision for his infirmary. Only moments before dawn, when he was alone once more with Pendyffryn, did the old man speak again of his daughter.

"I can see that my daughter's only protection from you is the son of my friend, Blaenant," Pendyffryn said, leaning back in the chair. "Do not think I will allow you to steal her from me. I have come to see you fail, deFreveille."

"Your daughter's only protection here is me," Jehan-Emíl said, slapping his hand flat on the table and lunging at the older man. "I stand between her and ruin…death. The son of your friend is not a friend to Gwennan. And, *pendefig, you* are here to secure her to me."

"You have already taken her. Why do you need me to give my blessing? In our country, there is nothing you can do to remove the stain on your honor, deFreveille. What you have done to my daughter does not discredit her, only yourself. Do not think that, by any act of reparation, you will remove that stain from *your* honor."

"I know your laws, Pendyffryn," deFreveille replied, relaxing in his chair again. "As far as anyone else is concerned, I have taken Gwennan as my wife, by your own law of *llathlud golau*. The only significance of this wedding is a public declaration that we have and will continue to live together, in the eyes of God, as husband and wife."

"You have chosen unwisely, deFreveille. My daughter is of no use to you. Gwennan cannot give you a child to secure any claim you make on my land and I have already chosen my heir."

"I do not need more children. My sons will inherit all that I have gained for them."

"And that is nothing. Gwennan will govern as *pendefig* after my death but when she dies, her cousin will be *pendefig*. My only concern is for my daughter."

"Your concern is late, Pendyffryn," deFreveille said. "When did you last see your daughter?"

"I was kept informed of her welfare."

"By whom?"

"Friends, her own and mine."

"Friends? Why did you not come to see her yourself, if you were so concerned? Why did you not insist she came to you?"

"Gwennan is independent. If she had wanted, she would have come." Pendyffryn's eyes reddened as he leaned forward. "I do not want to see my daughter dead before me, deFreveille, nor do I want to see her unhappy. If, *if* I agree, there will be conditions, Commander. We have laws to deal with men like you. Under our laws, Gwennan may inherit my property, and I have the power to keep it out of your grasp as long as she lives. If she dies, you will not escape my revenge. My friends have already told me of your part in her loss of my grandchild."

"If there was any truth in that accusation, do you think your daughter would be silent against me? She has been free to send her messenger to you, Pendyffryn. Did Bedwyn make this allegation on her part?"

"No," Pendyffryn replied, leaning back in the large chair to study the foreigner. "The matter was not raised when her messenger came to me. I will know the truth, deFreveille, and once I know it, you will not live long."

"Gwennan is the only one who can tell you the truth of this miscarriage. I believe there are several who know the truth. I suspect she has told Rocaille, but no one else. I do not know what caused her illness but, I swear to you, I have never raised my hand against her. Word the document as you wish, Daran Pendyffryn, I will sign it." Jehan-Emíl took vellum and ink from a leather-hinged chest, laying them on the table before the *pendefig*. "Tomorrow, we will have more time to become acquainted, but now I have a matter that requires my attention."

"You know you will gain nothing in this," the *pendefig* told him. "Whatever my daughter brings to this union, she will retain. Your children will remain homeless and Gwennan will not give you a child to inherit this *ystad*. You will remain a hired man, deFreveille."

"That is the beauty of life as a mercenary, Pendyffryn. As long as I am paid and my employer is a man—or woman—I can respect, I am content to serve."

The embers burned low in the grate when Gwennan lifted her head from the pillow on the holy day. Her bedchamber was filled with an ice-sharp wind that whistled through the hangings surrounding her like jackdaws swooping from the branches to peck and steal. She let her head fall back onto the cushion with a groan. Cecilé popped her head up from somewhere deep in the pile of *carthen*.

"*Bore da, boneddiges.*"

"*Bore da,* Cecilé."

"I am very hungry," the curly-headed fairy-child announced.

"So am I. Let's see what we can find in the pantry before we have to be good girls." Together they snuck down the staircase and ran across the family hall on tiptoe to avoid waking Siriol and Pendryw. Gwennan filled a small basket with bread, walnuts and cheese as well as a flagon of ale before they retraced their route and picnicked in the warmth of the bed. "We will be very busy today, Cecilé. What will you wear? All of your clothes are with Charlotte."

"I can wear this," the little girl said, wrapping herself in one of Gwennan's shawls.

"You look too old in that," Gwennan laughed. "And you will meet my father, the *pendefig*, today." For a moment, she studied the embers. *My father would not be here with so few to support him, without good reason.* "Your father is very clever, Cecilé, but we will see who wins this game. We women are not without our surprises. We will see which of us is the fox—or who we will allow to believe he is. Although it will be difficult to keep your father oblivious to my—. Well, he can be surprising also." The little girl's face was a reflection of her father and her perplexed pout assured Gwennan that she spoke in riddles, unsure herself what the day's events might bring. "I have something better for you to wear. First you must have a bath. Finish your breakfast while I warm some water for us."

After Gwennan had put logs on the fire, Cecilé pulled off her chemise and stepped into the small tub, sitting in the warm water while her hair was washed and her small body scrubbed.

When she was clean and wrapped from head to toe in flannel, Gwennan filled a larger tub for herself and bathed quickly in the tepid water. Keeping warm by the fire, she brought Cecilé to stand between her knees and rubbed her hair dry. She combed through the tangles with her fingers but when she put the circle of gold cord around Cecilé's brow, the girl shook her head. "Make it like yours, *boneddiges*." Turning her around, Gwennan plaited her wild curls into a braid to the middle of her shoulders, working in a bright gold scarf.

"Let me see if there is anything here to fit you, *boneddiges*," Gwennan said, opening her chest of clothes. "I brought some of my favorite dresses with me, in case I had a daughter," she told Cecilé but the child was intent on admiring her new hairstyle. Gwennan held a few garments up to the girl. "I was always tall for my age," she laughed. "I wore these when I was three and you are only just big enough for them." She held out two dresses. "The green or the blue, *boneddiges*?"

"What color is your dress, *boneddiges*?"

"Green and gold."

"I will also wear green."

"This will not please Charlotte, Cecilé. Are you sure?"

"It will make Father happy," Cecilé replied, looking so stern, so like her fierce father, that Gwennan laughed aloud and continued to laugh in spurts until Cecilé was fully dressed and passed inspection.

"Well, little *boneddiges*, there will not be even one boy who does not fall in love with you today."

"And you—." At the sound of a fist on the door, Gwennan whisked Cecilé behind her and turned as the door flew open.

"*Nadolig Llawen*, Gwennan," Ieuan Emyr bellowed as he burst into the room and stopped as she backed toward the bed. "What are you hiding?"

"What are you doing here?"

"What are you doing awake so early?" he asked in return, lunging to the side just as something green wrapped itself in the bed hangings. "What is that? Who are you hiding?"

"Go away," Gwennan ordered, keeping herself between the commander and his daughter. "I am not dressed."

"You are dressed enough for my needs, *menyw*," he said, maneuvering around her. When he darted left, she followed and he lunged to the right at the curtains. Gwennan grabbed his sleeve and pulled him toward her. Ieuan Emyr whirled around and caught her with one arm while he stomped to the platform. "Come out, whoever you are!"

"It is me, Father," Cecilé squealed, whipping the heavy curtain away to reveal herself. "You see, it is me."

"No," Jehan-Emíl said, setting Gwennan on her feet and facing Cecilé. "This is not my daughter. What have you done with Cecilé, *menyw*?" he demanded, turning on Gwennan and pulling her into his arms. "Who is this *Celtes*?" He stroked Gwennan's hair, studying her face. "Who is this *Celtes*? This most beautiful *Celtes*," he murmured against her cheek.

"Father, I am Cecilé. *I* am Cecilé."

"Can it be true?" he laughed, "my darling child is now transformed. I am pleased to meet you, *boneddiges*." He bowed from the waist.

"I am also pleased to meet you, *bonheddig* Father," Cecilé offered her hand but did not curtsy. "I am to meet the father of the *boneddiges* today."

"Are you?" he asked, turning to study Gwennan. "Perhaps the *boneddiges* will be there to present you," he said, "and perhaps not."

"Go away," Gwennan said again, "you are spoiling everything."

Retracing his strides to the door, he shouted again. The room was invaded by several women and men. Gwennan wrapped herself in a shawl and watched in horror as the women stripped the bed, folding the bedding before stacking it on Gwennan's linen chest. When they had finished, the men lifted the straw mattress, hesitating at the door.

"Burn it," deFreveille commanded. The mattress was dumped into the lower hall and the men helped the women strip the hangings from the bed frame. As soon as these were folded and taken down to the hall, the bed frame was dismantled and removed. The women took the linen bedding away. Gwennan glared at the commander. "That bed is not fit for me," he said, yanking open the door to the women's chamber and grinning at the confusion he caused. "*Boneddiges* Aine, *Nadolig Llawen*. Please tell Artur I want a bath. And Menna, come here to help Gwennan. I want a big fire and the floor swept." He ignored Charlotte and greeted Siriol with a nod.

Cecilé slipped her hand into his and danced, swinging from his arm.

When Menna followed him, the commander closed and bolted the door behind her and returned to Gwennan. "You know how to add logs to the fire, *menyw*, do so. I do not want to die of chill while you bathe me."

Gwennan straightened her back and swung away from him, dropping to her knees before the hearth, her jaw tightening against the curses forming in her head to fling at him. With the whisk, she brushed the ashes into the grate and laid more logs on the embers. Behind her, the foreigner sat in the chair, his legs outstretched, with his daughter on his lap. They murmured to one another and laughed while the two women worked.

Menna swept the cleared platform upon which the bed had stood, collecting the dust in the ash pan, dampened a cloth in the bucket and washed the platform. DeFreveille thanked her and sent her to the hall.

Rising to her knees, Gwennan waited for the bark to catch. Even the small flames seemed to defeat the wing beats of the wind, warming her hands and face as the flame caught. The applewood and fir were fragrant and chased the morning chill up the chimney. Adjusting her shawl more securely around her, Gwennan sat back on her heels, determined not to give him the satisfaction of provoking her defiance or into revealing her plans.

"You father slept well," Jehan-Emíl said, nuzzling the back of his little girl's head. "I think you did not."

"I slept very well," Gwennan replied.

"I slept very well myself," he laughed, "considering what I must do today."

"If it troubles you so much, why do it?"

"I did not say I was troubled, Gwennan," he said, grinning at her back. "I have a duty. It does not have to be unpleasant for a man to wonder why he has lost no sleep over a thing." He set Cecilé on her feet beside him and admired her braid. "Have you learned anything of your duties from the *boneddiges's* tutoring?"

"I have, Father."

"Then you will not need to be told what to do when Artur comes." Jehan-Emíl rose to his feet, towering over Gwennan. "Help me to undress, *menyw*, and find linen for me. You will shave me now, to save time."

Gwennan pushed herself to her feet and moved toward the chest but the commander stopped her. "Undress me now, Gwennan," he murmured, "there will be time enough to find linen before Artur comes." Standing motionless while she unlaced his tunic at the neck and sides, he studied her face.

Gwennan shrugged off the shawl and threw it over the back of the chair to free her hands. Her hands trembled and the cords refused to unfasten. She clenched her jaw and was close to tears when she lifted the tunic over his head. The heat of his body through his shirt warmed her fingers. His chest rose and fell with the deep breaths he took. The cords laced around his arms were as stubborn, knotting themselves at will and tangling with her fingers. The pulse of blood in his neck beat as fast as her heart. Gwennan bit her lips together. A drop of sweat trickled from his temple, following the contours of his neck, coursing into the opening of his shirt, becoming lost in the curls of hair on his chest. The scent rising from his body was so familiar to her that she nearly wept with relief to feel it entering her body and filling her lungs again. His strength shot through her fingertips and her hands shook. *He does surprise me.*

Jehan-Emíl glanced at his daughter, whispering, "I am glad I took the precaution of keeping Cecilé with us, *menyw*. Otherwise, I could not be held responsible. But, today, of all

240

days, I must be good." He gestured to the little girl and she tripped over to him, holding up the linen sheet she had found. As Gwennan freed him from his shirt, Ieuan clasped the sheet in his hand and held it at his groin when she eventually removed his belt and *trwsus*.

The sultry scent of his desire could not be concealed as easily from Gwennan as his hardened manhood was hidden from Cecilé. *This does not surprise me.* Gwennan met his grin as he wrapped the linen around his waist but her expression remained unchanged.

He sat on a stool in front of the fire. "*Boneddiges* Cecilé, do not spoil your gown. Sit until I call you."

"Yes, Father."

Gwennan had lathered his face with a fragrant soap when Artur knocked. He led the brothers into the chamber with the wooden tub from the bath house and buckets of steaming water. The boy organized the bath on the bed platform with Marshal and Jehan-Batiste close by to do his bidding. Gwennan scraped deFreveille's face clean of dark growth, drawing the blade over the tender skin of his neck and swishing the stubble and soap away from the blade in the cold water standing by the hearth.

She took deep breaths each time she bent her head to the task, but just as she was finishing a stroke along the cord of muscle to the edge of his jaw, her hand trembled. He sucked his breath and his muscles rippled in response to the sting. Dropping the knife to the floor, Gwennan backed away. Ieuan caught the hem of her chemise and yanked her to him, thrusting the knife in her hand.

"Finish," he snapped and offered her his throat.

Tears stung her eyes but she rubbed them away on her wrists. He used his discarded shirt to wipe the residue of lather from his face before he rose and went to the tub. Waving Artur and his sons out of the chamber, he lowered his body into the bath and dropped the linen over another stool. The tub was not big enough for him to stretch back and his knees were bent but he leaned his shoulders against the edge and gestured for Gwennan to come to him.

After she had dipped her hands in the water and lathered them, Gwennan raised his arm from the edge of the tub and smoothed the fir-scented lather over his wrist and forearm, around his elbow, stroking his bicep to the shoulder. The scar she had inflicted on him was still raw. He lifted his arm higher to allow her to wash across his chest, closing his eyes with pleasure at the caress of her hands on his body. Gwennan rinsed her hands but, before she could leave him, Jehan-Emíl caught her fingers and lifted the palm of her hand to his lips, nipping the skin between her forefinger and thumb, kissing her fingertips. Allowing her to drag her hand from his grip, he relaxed again, breathing deep of the fragrant lather and her unmistakable scent.

He watched her hair fall over her shoulder and the impatient toss of her head that sent its waywardness back into order. He raised his hand to her brow to feel her hair caressing his skin. He watched her take the soap again and scrub his leg and foot, stroking his thighs. He watched her breasts beneath the thin cloth of her dampened chemise.

When she finished washing the sweat and grime from his body, Gwennan stood and held the linen open for him to step into it. Cecilé was busy with her simple duties and her father rose from the tub, water cascading from his body, coursing in rivulets over his muscles and through the dark hair covering his loins. Gwennan draped the sheet around his waist, securing it and keeping her eyes averted from his face.

He made no attempt to dry himself and, with a deep sense of the inevitability of humiliation, she dropped to her knees to dry his legs. When he ran his hands through her hair, she dropped her arms to her sides, keeping her head bowed. Clenching her fists, she allowed the caress but fought to keep from reacting in anger. Placing his hands on either side of her face, he tilted her head back but she kept her eyes lowered.

"You are free to refuse me for now, Gwennan," he whispered as his lips brushed hers, "but not forever."

Gwennan lifted her eyes, controlled her seething fury, and stared into the brown eyes above her. "I will always be free to refuse you or any man. What you take from me by force will never be enough to make you content."

Ieuan Emyr's smile was unperturbed as he bent to kiss her again and let her go. While she found him a shirt, he rubbed the linen roughly over his chest, dragged on his clean *trwsus* and stamped into his boots. Gwennan smoothed the shirt over his chest and arms, straightened the hem of his black, gold-crested tunic. *I have given him better—why does he not wear it?*

"Remember we celebrate a feast today, Gwennan. The birth of our Lord," he said as he crossed the room to the door. "See that you also wear something special. No brown sacking," he laughed. "Something to please Daran Pendyffryn."

"You are not, why should I?" she demanded.

Speaking so that only his daughter could understand, he laughed, "I will not disappoint you." Ducking through the door before she had picked up the iron padlock she threw at his head, Ieuan shouted his orders to the rest of the household all the way down the staircase.

"Why does he speak so I cannot understand?" Cecilé understood her question no better than Gwennan understood the *gelyn* commander. After she had growled long enough to vent her anger and frustration, she slumped into the chair by the fire and rested her cheek on her fist. Cecilé leaned against the arm and sighed so that her companion was forced out of her own reverie. As soon as Gwennan looked at her, the fair-haired child's smile beamed from her face. She was so like her father that Gwennan laughed.

"Come, Cecilé," she said jumping to her feet and dressing quickly in an old brown sack, "we have work to do before the feast." From her chest, she unpacked parcel after parcel wrapped in remnants of colored cloth and piled them onto her desk. Each parcel had a square of cloth upon which she had embroidered the name of the friend who was to receive it. Cecilé peered at the small gifts. "Yes," Gwennan said, "there's one for you but you'll have to wait like everyone else."

"And my brothers?"

"Yes."

"Eira and Gareth?"

"Yes, of course."

"Father?"

Gwennan hesitated before she answered. "Yes," she said, sweeping out of the chamber and trotting down the stairs with Cecilé close behind her. She asked the cook to select a cheese and dried fruit to be included in the household feast.

Charlotte, entering the hall from the wooden stairwell, looked on with disdain at Gwennan's activity and bluster. "Why have you allowed this woman to make you so ugly?" she gasped when deFreveille's daughter appeared. "Go at once to change into your own clothes—something blue to suit your complexion." When Cecilé slid her hand into Gwennan's, Charlotte strode to the inglenook and arranged the skirt of her sapphire gown around her, waiting for deFreveille to return to escort her to the church. "Your father will be angry, Cecilé."

"Father has already said I am beautiful—a beautiful *Celtes*."

"Darling child, he was only mocking this Welsh creature. Go and change before it is too late."

The little girl looked up and, when Gwennan smiled at her, Cecilé turned to her former nurse. "I think my father believes that the *boneddiges* is even more beautiful."

"You will see, when your father comes, that he does not, Cecilé. He is only laughing at her and when he has laughed enough, he will send her to the soldiers."

"'*Moiselle* Charlotte," Jehan-Batiste said, standing in the door of the room he shared with his brother, "I do not think it is right for you to say such things to my sister. My father does not laugh at anyone and he would not send any woman to the soldiers."

"Oh, you are so knowledgeable about your dear father, Jehan-Batiste. I am corrected."

"You had better dress, Gwennan," Siriol said, "or you will not be ready in time to walk with us."

"It does not matter what I wear," she said, glancing at the resplendent nurse. "There is still much to do."

"Nothing that cannot wait for your return," Siriol insisted. "The whole of the Gaer is full of excitement. More than I have ever seen them—perhaps it is that the *pendefig* is here—but there is tension, expectation everywhere."

Gwennan shrugged. "Everyone waits for the festival." Siriol shook her head. "I will dress now, to please you," Gwennan relented and took the little girl back to the bedchamber, glad to be away from Charlotte's venom and whatever she was saying to deFreveille's children. While she dressed with Cecilé's help, Ieuan Emyr entered the house with a laughing shout for his children. When he called again for Cecilé, Gwennan heard the nurse reply.

"Good. Good," the *gelyn* commander answered with his happy laughter. "Marshal, tell your sister to come to the church with Gwennan."

"I will, Father," Cecilé called down from the door of Gwennan's room.

"And make sure that *she* is as beautiful as you are, *Celtes*."

"That is easy, Father. She has a beautiful gown and so many—. I am not allowed to tell you, Father. You will have to wait," she whispered as she pushed the door closed.

When the *Celtes* and Gwennan emerged again, only Maides remained in the hall, leaning against the edge of the table, his arms folded across his chest. Cecilé skipped over to him and raised her arms. The mercenary reached down and held her in front of him at arms' length, nodded his approval and set the child on her feet. He turned his gaze on Gwennan as she crossed the hall toward him but revealed nothing of what might have been in his mind.

She had chosen to wear another gown which had belonged to her mother, in her father's honor. The fitted tunic was deep gold over a dark green frock with tight sleeves that covered the backs of her hands, held in place by braided loops around her middle fingers and gold bracelets around her wrists. The tunic was embroidered with plants and trees in the style of her country down the front, around the hem below her knees and the edges of the wide sleeves below her elbows. To bind her hair, she wore three twisted cords of gold and green braided through and tied at the end of her ashen plait. She attempted to smile at the raven-haired captain but his unfeeling appraisal did nothing to alleviate her sense of bewilderment.

"I have the honor of escorting you, *boneddiges*," he said with a courteous bow. "We are already late."

"You need not have waited," she said in return. "I know the way."

"You will not be allowed anywhere alone, *menyw*. Not today." He offered his arm and insisted that she take it. "Tempers are agitated and many are apprehensive of the day's events. You will not have the luxury of solitude until it is finished."

"Didn't you sleep well, Maides? Is that why you are so surly?"

"I slept very little, *boneddiges*, though more than deFreveille. At least, I did not pace through all of what remained of the night," he said with a slight smile.

"DeFreveille told *me* he slept very well and untroubled."

"A man need not be troubled to think twice about losing his freedom though his bride is one he has courted at great length and with difficulty."

"Bride," she said under her breath, dropping her hand from the foreigner's arm and standing motionless on the planks of the bridge. *Why am I surprised?* In the distance, the small, light sound of the church bell began to fill the air. "Take Cecilé." She urged the little girl forward.

Maides clasped the child's hand and continued to the opposite end of the bridge, waiting for Gwennan to join them. When she did not move from the spot, he watched her for a few moments before retracing his steps. He was within a few feet when Gwennan noticed and spun away. Catching her around the waist, he held her secure until she abandoned the idea of escaping him.

"I am ordered to bring you. I will do as Jehan-Emíl commands if it means carrying you over my shoulder like a sack of grain, *boneddiges*." He turned her to face him and bent his shoulder to hoist her across his back.

"I have changed my mind," Gwennan declared. "I will not go." Across the bridge, Cecilé was dancing in circles, clapping her hands together and trying to see her plait as she whirled around.

"What is planned will take place. Either you attend, on your feet, or I will dump you there at his."

"Why?"

"I did not ask." Maides took her arm and dragged her after him to the *buarth*. "Will you walk or do I have to put a rope around your wrists?"

Gwennan wrenched her arm free, smoothed her clothing and adjusted the drape of the cloak over her head and shoulders. With her back straight, she preceded the mercenary and Cecilé toward the track leading to the church in the woods between the Gaer and the river. Cecilé swung on Maides's hand, dancing every step.

The day had broken clear and only a light fall of snow dusted the ground but the night had frozen the trampled mud. Gwennan's woolen cloak swept a path for the two who followed her. She kept her eyes fixed on her destination and did not look to see any of the faces of the people gathering at the edges of the track. She filled her mind with Derwyn because raging against him steeled her against uncertainty.

Bride. Why do I care?

sixTEEN

The wooded pathway was quiet. The track to the church was heavily guarded by soldiers but the farmers and craftsmen crowded forward as she passed. From all sides, Gwennan heard their murmurs and felt their stares. *Why am I humiliated in this way? After all he has let them believe, he could have the decency to have told me his plan to wed.*

Before they had gone far, two young men threw a thick rope decorated with bright strips of cloth in front of her, drawing it taut. Maides, uttering a growl deep in his throat, grabbed the rope and was about to cut it with his knife when Gwennan stilled his hand.

"It is a custom," she sighed. "They will not let us pass until we have given them a coin."

"Why?" he demanded, threatening the young men.

"For the bride. All the guests who attend are expected to pay."

The mercenary dug into a pocket in his shirt and flicked a coin over his shoulder. The rope fell from their path while the young men dove to retrieve the coin. A scurrying behind them and to the sides brought the same rope to bar Gwennan's way as soon as she turned a bend in the footpath. Her escort clasped her arm.

"If I do not pay?"

"They will not let us pass."

"What is the purpose of this?" he demanded. "DeFreveille's bride has no need of coins."

"If the bride does not want the small amount her guests give, these men will use it to buy food for their families. Keep an account of what you give them and I will repay you," Gwennan said.

"It is more likely that deFreveille will repay me," Maides laughed.

"I am not poor," Gwennan said. "I am no beggar."

"I would not deprive you of what is yours, *boneddiges*," he replied, digging into his shirt again and tossing a handful of coins behind him.

At the lichgate, Gwennan stopped, and laid her hand on the post to steady herself. Maides stood beside her, his arm around her waist to support her. Lifting her eyes to his face, she said, "I do not want to do this."

"You have no choice. Take my arm."

The coldness of his command restored her sense of outrage. "I am always free. I will *not* do this."

Maides sent Cecilé ahead into the church to join her family. "A sack, *menyw*, or under your own power. I do not care, but I am commanded to bring you and I will do that. If you choose to be delivered like so much grain, that is your decision, but you *will* be delivered."

"If you think I can be forced, you are mistaken." Gwennan turned on her heel and walked forward along the path toward the church door. The door stood open and the church was crowded with the *gelyn's* captains. Outside, the warriors and women of the Gaer stood on either side of the path. She could feel Derwyn's eyes on her but she did not meet anyone's gaze until she caught a glimpse of a familiar head, taller than all the others, inside the church.

"Tada," she sighed, rushing forward, throwing herself into Daran Pendyffryn's arms.

"Maides," deFreveille bellowed.

The mercenary put his hand on the old warrior's chest, holding Gwennan away from him and pushing her forward to the front of the church. Charlotte stood with deFreveille to the side of the altar. His head was bowed to listen to her laughing chatter. Gwennan straightened her back. Cecilé had grasped her elder brothers' hands and was chirping at them, jumping up and down when Gwennan entered.

"She is here, Father."

The brothers looked from their father to the Welsh woman, their eyes wide. DeFreveille made a sharp gesture. Siriol stepped forward and unfastened Gwennan's cloak. The golden-haired woman's smile did not correspond to her friend's questioning stare. Gwennan raised her chin and glared with all the defiance and rage she could command at Jehan-Emíl deFreveille, *gelyn* commander of her—. Only a flicker of her glance revealed her surprise that he wore the wedding tunic she had made, in every way perfect for him.

For a moment, deFreveille hesitated. He drew himself up with a deep breath and strode across the stone flags. Inches from her, he nodded to Maides, turned to face the altar, swept his arm around Gwennan, clasping both her hands in a grip of iron and pulled her down to kneel with him at the railing. Behind her, Gwennan heard his captains' voices raised in confusion and Charlotte's sudden, stifled scream. Maides urged Siriol forward to stand beside Gwennan and raised his hand to keep the others at bay.

"No," Derwyn shouted from the doorway, shoving through the crowd. "Gwennan."

DeFreveille's hand closed on her fingers and the priest began the ceremony when the *gelyn* commander gave him an impatient signal. Though Derwyn's protests were strengthened by others, the priest went on, his voice a drone in a rush of breath. Gwennan felt Siriol move closer and tried to lift her eyes but the priest had laid his hand on her head and held it bowed. She could only hear the muttering and feel the strength of deFreveille's arm around her waist.

"Do you accept this man as your husband?" were the only words she understood. Gwennan whispered her reply.

"Speak louder, Gwennan," deFreveille commanded.

"Yes."

Her husband's voice was drowned by the shouting from the crowd.

"Whore!" Derwyn bolted from the doorway before Maides could reach him.

DeFreveille slid a gold band on her finger but he did not look at her. As soon as the priest had made his pronouncement of their marriage, Ieuan Emyr rose to his feet, shouting his orders at his captains to quell the riot beyond the church doors. Gwennan heard her father's name called, his guidance sought, but the *pendefig* remained silent. The priest began to chant the communion and the small sanctuary was still once again. Gwennan stood beside her husband. Her father stepped forward, the patriarch of the Gaer, as people crowded into the church, standing shoulder to shoulder with deFreveille's captains and family. Ieuan held Gwennan's hand throughout the remainder of the Nativity service. Cecilé clasped her free hand. Only Marshal deFreveille ventured to glance at her. Jehan-Batiste was absorbed in the service, singing the chant with the priest in a sweet, quiet voice.

When, after the service, Gwennan raised her eyes to look at her husband, his head was bowed and he did not lift his eyes until most of the others had left the church.

"Find your father, Gwennan," deFreveille told her, "he will want to be assured you are content to be my wife."

"How can you—?" she began, but thought better of exposing his deceit to those still present who would delight to think she had been coerced and humiliated. "How could you allow my father to stand so long in this cold place?" Gwennan demanded. "You who have reminded me so often he is old."

Ieuan followed Gwennan as she backed toward the wall of the church, amused by her understanding of his tactics. He was unmoved by her protest. In his tunic, he carried the contract that formalized his claim of marriage by *llathlud*, signed by the willing hand of her father, only moments before the two men had walked to the church together but he was no wiser as to the old warrior's change of heart.

"I do not care what you think of my methods, Gwennan. I will see for myself if you are happy," he said, grinning as he caught her wrist and pulled her into his arms. When she resisted, deFreveille leaned his back against the wall beside her and gazed at the beams in the painted ceiling. "You will be happy with me," he said. "You will want me and you will forget your black-bearded lover." When she did not deny it, he smiled. "You have consented and when I come to you, we will make love, as I promised. Already, I can feel you tremble, Gwennan. I will make you happy."

"You cannot make me happy."

"Gwennan," he sighed, taking her hands, "it is pointless to deny what you feel for me."

"How simple you think it is. Do you truly believe that you have forced me to accept you as my husband and that I will be complacent?"

"Do you love me?"

"How would that be possible?"

"Do you?"

"We could ask these questions for the rest of the day, for the rest of our lives, Ieuan, but neither of us would satisfy the other with whatever answers we are willing to give."

"What do you propose, Gwennan, *cariad*?"

"We have a contract by whatever means it has come about."

"True. And I cannot be dissatisfied with the contract I have made with your father."

"Perhaps we will both be surprised—either way—by what transpires from it."

"I understand, *boneddiges*," he replied with a smile. "It will please me to make the most of the terms that govern our new circumstances."

"Please yourself, *bonheddig*," Gwennan said. "There are benefits to exploration."

"I could not agree more, *boneddiges*," he answered, clasping her hand as they left the church and followed the others to the Gaer. "I will take you to your father. How long has it been since you last saw the old warrior?" He nodded for the half-

Cymro, Gethin Wode, to follow with his command of eight guards.

"Months. Eight, at least."

"I will not be so jealous of you that you cannot visit your father for a short time in the spring. And perhaps the summer as well. I have not seen much of the place but Maides tells me that Castell Pendyffryn is beautiful, magnificent. I am not surprised since it spawned such a woman as you. I will come with you and you can show me all the secret places you committed your heinous crimes as a girl."

"They were not heinous, only naughty," Gwennan murmured. When he laughed again, throwing his head back and closing his eyes, she glanced at him. "My father bargained well?" she asked, re-exerting her own power.

"Very well, *blodyn*" deFreveille replied, amused. "He will tell you how he has bested me at every game we have played together, but one."

"He does not like to lose. He will not have considered that he lost."

"I would like to think he did not mind losing this once."

"Do you think that either of you knew the rules?" she asked as they approached the common hall.

"I believe we both thought we controlled the board," Ieuan laughed, "but perhaps we were under the impression that we played our own game." At the door, he bowed to his wife and sent her into the warmth of the fragrant, decorated hall ahead of him. His captains rose to their feet.

The *pendefig* was already at the table, seated in the chair at the center that, by then, even Gwennan had accepted as Ieuan Emyr's rightful place. Pendyffryn was surrounded on all sides by warriors who had resisted allegiance to the foreigner and some who had carried his black and gold crest in recent weeks. When Daran Pendyffryn rose and, smiling, extended his hands to his daughter, the Welsh warriors and their wives also stood. Gwennan stopped herself from running into her father's arms and allowed her husband to present her. As soon as Ieuan nodded and gave her hand to her father, she gripped her father's fingers and left her husband to his well-wishers.

"Tada," she whispered, laying her head on the broad shoulder and sinking into the protective embrace as though she were still a child. Her love for him and her gratitude for his presence was so intense that she threw her arms around his neck. The warrior-prince took the weight of his grown girl as though she was no bigger than Cecilé and led her to a secluded corner while her husband lifted an overflowing goblet and accepted the acknowledgement of his good fortune from his friends.

"Are these happy tears, Gwennan?"

"I am glad to see you, Tada," she answered. "Are you well?"

"A little stiff from sleeping in that tent," he said, laying his hand on the back of her head. "Your husband will be glad to sleep in a bed again." The laughter and merriment in the hall reached them in waves, floating on the drafts of warmth from the pit where joints of mutton were roasting. Wine flowed from the jugs into Ieuan's goblet the moment it was emptied. "You approve of him? He did not force you to accept his plans or threaten you?" He studied his daughter's face. "No doubt he has assumed he coerced you," Pendyffryn laughed. "I will keep your secret, Gwennan, but I knew, this morning, the moment I saw him in that wedding tunic, you had chosen him."

"What do *you* think of him? Does he have *any* redeeming qualities, Tada?"

"What choice did you give me? You had set your heart on him. Does he know the hours of hope that are worked into every stitch of that garment?"

"He knows though I am surprised that he does."

"Surprise is a good thing, between equals. Extraordinary man, this Flemish."

"You think he is my equal, Tada, worthy of my esteem? Or would you have kicked him down the stairs like all the others?"

"He did not ask. You should know, though I had opportunity, I did not threaten to kick him down the stairs when he declared he would keep you as his wife."

"He would not have gone."

"Any more than I, had your mother's father threatened me," Pendyffryn said. "Go to your husband with my blessing."

"I will stay with you, Tada. My husband will call me when he wants me and I will decide if I choose to attend him," she laughed. She shrugged off her cloak, scanned the room briefly, catching Artur's eye. At her bidding, he brought a brazier and wine for them to drink. "How long will you stay?"

"Until I am unwelcome," he laughed, greeting Artur with a broad smile. "But I will leave in a week. I have urgent matters…"

"When you go, will you take Galar and Derwyn with you?"

"Do you ask or bid?"

"I bid." Gwennan smoothed the fabric of the gold tunic over her knees and prepared to lie to her father.

"You have reason?"

"Galar can take better care of you than any with you now and I do not need her."

"And Derwyn?"

"Tada…" she sighed, unable to find any lie that would satisfy him. "I thought you had sent him—as you promised, that he was the man worthy to be my husband. I allowed him to believe I would be his wife—."

"You do not have to say more. I saw for myself. I was foolish to send him. I should have known he would begin to love you…" Gwennan's sharp glance stopped him. "If your husband will release him from his duties in the Gaer, I will send Derwyn tomorrow."

"I never discovered any quality that made Elgan Maergwn worthy either, Tada."

"You discovered what made him and many others unworthy. Why didn't you return sooner? There was no reason for you to be alone here."

"I was not alone—anymore than you are."

"So you have learned that truth," Daran said, clasping her hand.

"That was a problem of my own creation. I did not want to admit how foolish I had been."

"Did you think I would not understand or support you because you took command here without my blessing?"

"No, Tada. Do not concern yourself. I did not fail and I am not alone now," Gwennan said as she turned a smile in Cecilé's direction. "There is someone here I would like you to meet, Tada. Someone very special, who has been waiting to meet you."

When she beckoned the little girl forward, Pendyffryn studied the child. "Did you accept the father to have the child, Gwennan?" he asked, turning a frown on her.

"Tada," she laughed again, "I accepted him before he spoke a word to me."

"How is that?"

"He laughed," she replied, gazing at her bridegroom with an indulgent smile. "How could I refuse a man who allowed me to browbeat him and laughed when I did?"

Cecilé had crept up beside her and half hid behind Gwennan, peering at the powerful father whom even her own father respected. Gwennan set Cecilé in front of the *pendefig*. "*Boneddiges* Cecilé Ieuan, this is my father, Daran, *pendefig* of Pendyffryn."

Cecilé stepped forward and extended her right hand. "I am happy to meet with you, *Pendefig*."

Daran folded his arms and rested his elbows on his knees, examining the child for a moment. "The pleasure, *boneddiges*, is mine," he said, taking her hand and opening his arms to her. Cecilé allowed herself to be lifted onto his knee.

"My husband also has two fine sons," Gwennan informed her father. "They are not as fond of me as their sister." She drew his attention to the two boys standing among deFreveille's senior captains. Although she was pleased to see Pendryw raising his flagon in the crowd, Derwyn's malignant festering in the far corner troubled her.

"What are you thinking, Gwennan Ieuan?" her father asked, allowing Cecilé the liberty of examining the scar on his face.

"As you, Tada," Gwennan replied. "I will make him one of us."

"I believe you already have," the warrior-prince laughed, setting the enchanting *Celtes* on her feet in front of him. "Bring your brothers, *boneddiges*."

"I will, *pendefig*." Cecilé trotted into the crowd of guests.

Her brothers bowed from a distance but required their father's firm encouragement to come forward. Jehan-Batiste stood in front of his brother and spoke in his native language.

"I am also pleased to meet you, Jehan-Batiste deFreveille," the *pendefig* replied to the boy, "and your brother, though I think you are not as pleased to meet me as you say."

Marshal leapt forward from behind his brother. "How do you know our language?"

"I have travelled, my boy, like your father—though not for the same reasons."

Marshal's relief was equaled by his older brother's consternation. The ten-year-old stood squarely before the *pendefig* with his arms straight at his sides. "Sir, my father has told us that you are very powerful."

"I am pleased to hear it," Pendyffryn laughed.

"He has also said that we will now live here with Gwennan Pendyffryn who will be our stepmother." He shook off his older brother's restraining hand. "I would like to say that this proposal is acceptable to me, sir."

"And to me," Cecilé added, insinuating herself between Marshal and the *pendefig*. "I am very happy to have a stepmother."

"I'm sure your stepmother will be very happy to have stepchildren, *boneddiges*." Daran Pendyffryn turned his hawk-like gaze on his daughter. "Did you know he had so many children?"

"We will have more, Tada. Who better to father my children than a man who has proved his ability?"

"Gwennan," he sighed. "This is not good. DeFreveille already has enough children. He does not want more. Galar claims he has already destroyed my grandchild."

"Find your father, Cecilé. Take your brothers with you." When she was once more alone with her father she asked, "Do you think I would wed him if he had?"

"You miscarried?" When she gave no answer, he clasped her hand. "Derwyn or Elgan? Gwennan, which?"

"Derwyn did not dare. And Elgan had more interest in his brewery."

"So you did discover Elgan's one redeeming quality," Daran laughed. When Gwennan turned a cold stare on him, he said, "I did not want you to wed. You defied me. I cannot reveal the private sorrows of my warriors, Gwennan."

Gwennan turned to find her new husband and smiled as his adoring children, his close friends and so many of her most loyal warriors surrounded him. *He has won them fairly.*

"The *baban* was deFreveille's?"

"Tada, do not concern yourself."

"Galar swears he is a murderer, Gwennan, and your husband believes you have lost a child. He feels the weight of his responsibility. He will want to know—he has a right to know—who among your warriors was your lover."

"He will know the truth, Tada. You need not."

"He claims you have lived as husband and wife by *llathlud golau.*"

"Does he?" Gwennan laughed. "It certainly was not *llathlud twyll*, Tada. Ieuan does not understand secrecy."

"Do you carry a child for him, Gwennan?"

"No, Tada, but I will."

"Gwennan, I do not wish it. There is no need. You will be *pendefig* and Heilyn ap Alun will follow. DeFreveille knows this. He does not require a child. You know what it cost your mother...what it will do to you."

"Tada, I require a child. As much as I respect my Gernant cousins, *I* do not want them to live in Pendyffryn and call it home."

"Your mother was Gernant."

"And I am Pendyffryn. My children will be Pendyffryn and," she smiled again at her husband, "something else."

"This *gelyn* commander is content to be your hireling. Keep him as that, in his place."

"Is there anything else I should know about *my* husband that you have not told me?"

"Nothing, unless you count that he has signed a contract that will deny him and these children any part of my *ystad*."

"That was foolish."

"He understood the terms, Gwennan."

"I told Siriol she would be surprised what a man will do if given good reason."

Daran Pendyffryn's booming laugh turned the heads of every man, woman and child in the common hall. When deFreveille glanced at his wife, she was smiling at him. He returned the smile though he had a strong feeling that Pendyffryn's laugh was at his expense.

"All the more reason for me to demand he provides me with a child to hold *my ystad*, Tada," she declared, brushing her skirts as she rose from the chair. The moment she did, Ieuan Emyr broke away from his friends.

"You see, Tada," Gwennan said. "I have not been so foolish with this man. What he thinks and feels is there to see. It is a good thing that I did not succeed in killing him."

"When was that?"

"I have made many attempts to kill him. If not for this," Gwennan said, pushing her hair away from her cheek, "he would be dead, but—."

Daran Pendyffryn studied the last tinges of the bruise for less than a moment before his dagger sailed across the common hall to shiver in the post above deFreveille's shoulder. The warrior-prince's hand was on the hilt of the weapon before either the bridegroom or his closest friend had seen him lunge.

seventeen

"Tada."

Pendyffryn eased the weapon free as though the blade had flown into nothing more resistant than tallow, his fist clamped around his son-in-law's throat, breathing hatred like red iron into the foreigner's face. "Give thanks to God, deFreveille, before you die."

"Tada. Let him go," Gwennan ordered, stepping between the two men and holding her father's wrist. She met her husband's eyes for a moment as the common hall screamed with the hiss of weapons drawn and divided hearts declared loyalties. "I am *pennaeth* here. If there is any killing to be done, it will be on my order. When you next threaten my husband, *pendefig*, you will first seek my permission. I may grant it but you will not kill him today."

"I demand an explanation for this," Pendyffryn said, raising his hand to her cheek.

"Ieuan cannot explain this, Tada. He knows nothing of it."

"Then who did this?"

"We were at war. If you force me to explain, I will. Let him go, Tada." Pendyffryn loosened his grip, one knuckle at a time until Ieuan was free and able to breathe, but the *pendefig* kept an eye fixed on the *gelyn* commander.

"Explain."

Gwennan lifted her chin, glanced over her shoulder at her husband and said, slowly enough for Ieuan to understand, "Had I been a better archer, Tada, my arrow would have struck its mark and I would have no mark as evidence of my poor skill."

"What was its mark, Gwennan?"

"I aimed for his heart, to kill him, but my method was undisciplined. He bears one scar and I this other."

Ieuan deFreveille covered the wound on his upper arm with his hand, a smile overtaking his features as his wife's confession became clear to him. "I am happy you did not kill me that day, Gwennan," he said as he turned her to face him, "or any other, but if you had not wounded me, I think we would not be here together today."

"Why is that, Ieuan?"

He pressed his lips to her cheek and whispered, "I was too weary to make the most of my opportunity that night. For your sake, I am happy to have been weakened but, had I been dead, as you wished, another would have been in my place."

"You well know that was not possible."

"That is true, Gwennan, *Pennaeth* Gaer, Commander and Tactician. Only one who would be a friend to you could have succeeded against your skill."

"Friendship is a good thing, Ieuan, between equals."

"And honesty, Gwennan Ieuan." When she lifted her eyes to his ordinary, pleasant face, the *gelyn* commander met her scrutiny with one of his broad, candid smiles and his laughter filled the common hall for a moment before he silenced it with a kiss—as warm and eager as the kiss he had stolen from her on the night he had survived her first attempt to kill him and found as little welcome. He pulled his head back to search her eyes but still found no answer to his question in the chapel. "If I give you cause to grant your father permission to kill me, Gwennan, I will hone the blade for him."

"If you give me cause, Ieuan Gwennan, to wish you dead, I will dull the blade to make your death more pleasant."

"Will we come to an understanding?"

"We will, on that point." Gwennan glanced into the faces of the men gathered around them, their weapons not far from their reach, anticipating violence. She slid her arm through his and turned to face their guests.

"Are you tired of my neglect," Ieuan asked, "or my children?"

"Neither, it is time we go to the house. Our meal will be served soon."

"My daughter is tired of me," the *pendefig* told his son-in-law. "Another reason we have come to avoid each other in recent months."

DeFreveille glanced from one to the other. "I regret if I am the cause of ill-feeling."

"You aren't," Gwennan replied. She took his arm. "My father is opinionated. Our opinions differ—on one subject in particular."

"Am I to know what this subject is so that I may avoid it and escape becoming embroiled in your argument?"

"Your opinion on this is irrelevant," she said, "express as you see fit." Gwennan extended her hand to Cecilé. "But, I should warn you, Ieuan, my father's feeling on this subject was the cause of our estrangement and I will not tolerate any like opinion from you."

Jehan-Emíl studied her expression but saw only amusement in her eyes. "I am not like him. Or any other man you have known."

"In some important ways, you are not—in others, I do not yet know. Time and exploration will tell."

"Explore as you see fit, Gwennan Ieuan," he said. "I am as you see me—I have nothing to hide from you."

Only Gwennan's friends, members of the household, their families, Christophe Maides, Bedwyn, Gethin Wode and Bown accompanied the bride and groom to the house when the morning's celebrations became rowdy and spread throughout the Gaer. Several bonfires had already been lit though the sun had only begun its afternoon journey westward. DeFreveille carried his daughter on one arm and gave his wife the other but as soon as they entered through the doorway, he sent them both away from him and led Maides, Daran Pendyffryn and the others to the table. Ieuan deFreveille deferred his place to his father-in-law and they sat sprawled and comfortable with each other for the first time, content to drink more until another meal was provided.

The hall was more fragrant than the night before. The aroma of roasting nuts and mead mixed with the fir and lavender. Mistletoe had been hung from the beams. Gwennan removed Cecilé's cloak and her own, accepting a cup of mead from one of the girls who took the cloaks to the bedchamber. Aware that her husband had not taken his eyes off her since he sat at the table, she took the little girl with her to the hearth, returning his gaze—when she chose—with the same intensity. Cecilé stood beside her, staring at every movement and expression she made.

"Don't you want to play with the others?" Gwennan asked finally, putting her cup aside.

"No, *boneddiges*, I want to stay with you."

Gwennan offered to play a game with her but Cecilé was not interested. When Charlotte joined the wedding party, her fine red-golden hair floating about her shoulders and the bodice of her gown loosened to reveal more of her pale breasts, she sat opposite Gwennan and smiled. Cecile leaned against Gwennan's knees and kept her eyes on her stepmother's face.

"That pathetic child thinks you are her mother," the nurse confided, in a low voice, using a combination of Welsh and that of the *Sais* tongue she suspected Gwennan understood. She draped her hands over the arms of the chair, several fingers of each hand bearing a jeweled ring. "But *you* are pathetic to believe a man like deFreveille wanted you for anything more than suits his ambitions. See how your friends melt to him, Gwennan? He will have them all, devour and discard those who are not useful. He has already won your poor father. He will have you next. And then he will return to me, probably with a gift more precious than any he has given me in the past," she said, wriggling her fingers so that her jewels glinted in the torchlight, "begging me to forgive him. I sent him to you, did you know that? I could see he was besotted, only because you resisted, of course. He is curious, when he has had his fill, he will return to me. You do not have much to offer a man with appetites." She leaned back in the chair for a moment and laughed, filling the room with the happy sound. "Such appetites," she whispered again. "You will not know even how to begin."

"I hardly understand what you are saying and it is better, I think, that I do not."

"Whatever you have to say is unimportant. But I will tell you this, Gwennan, your days as wife will be few. Save your dignity and let him go when your husband seeks me for his bed. I know what gives him pleasure. You will only make him laugh with your clumsy innocence. Bear his lust and keep your pride. He will soon be done with you." Charlotte rose gracefully from the chair, swept the wide skirt of her gown around her and let it float around her legs as she crossed the room to join the men at the table.

Gwennan looked on as the nurse took a place near deFreveille and Pendyffryn, attracting the attention of both men with her happy laughter and flattery. The smile Gwennan turned on Cecilé was warm. "Do you remember all the work we did this morning?"

"Yes, *boneddiges*."

"You may call me Gwennan if you like or any other name, *Celtes*. I know it will be hard for you to think of me as your mother."

"I have never had a mother."

"Neither have I," Gwennan confided, touching Cecilé's cheek.

"If you did have a mother, what would you call her, *boneddiges*?"

"I would have called her 'Mam', *Celtes*."

"I like that name," Cecilé said, leaning her head on Gwennan's shoulder. "Mam?"

"Yes, Cecilé?"

"When can we have our gifts?"

Gwennan laughed aloud and hugged the little girl. "It is our tradition to give one gift today, to play games, tell stories and have a feast. Tomorrow, all the children have gifts and more stories. Near the *Calan*, we give more gifts and all the children have to sing verses to have sweet treats."

"That is a lot of work."

"And a lot of gifts, *Celtes*."

"I can work," Cecilé replied.

"Good, because there is a lot of work to do on a farm, even in winter."

"I am good with horses," Marshal said, standing in front of Gwennan as he had the *pendefig*.

"That is excellent, Marshal, I know very little about them."

"They are magnificent," he told her, moving closer. Gwennan rested her chin on her upturned palm, gazing at the earnest ten-year-old. "They are also stupid."

"Mam?" Cecilé murmured, leaning against her knee and distracting her from her attention to Marshal. "Mam, I do not know what I can do on the farm."

"You are very good at helping me with accounts."

"I can do that," the girl replied and smiled at her brother.

"Anyone can do that," Marshal complained.

"Can they?" Gwennan asked. "It is not the same as working with horses but it is just as important." She glanced at Ieuan Emyr. He was no longer talking to Pendyffryn or Charlotte de Guidry. His attention was absorbed by the group near the hearth and the lone figure of his eldest son. After a moment, he spoke briefly to the *pendefig* and left the hall, gesturing for Jehan-Batiste to follow him.

While her husband was out of the hall, Gwennan called one of the girls to her. "There are parcels in my chamber," she said. "On the table. Will you bring them all, please?" When the girl returned, Gwennan directed the parcels be left by the hearth until after the meal that the cooks had begun to bring to the table.

DeFreveille laid his arm across his son's shoulders as they reached the archway into the garden. The boy shrugged his father's embrace away and walked ahead. When he could go no further in the walled space, he concentrated his attention on the residue of dirt between the stones in the wall and the tiny plants that had begun to grow there.

"I should have told you sooner."

"Yes," Jehan-Batiste agreed, "but I knew—I just didn't want to believe you could do this to us."

"Jehan," deFreveille said, laying his hand on his son's shoulder. "It is hard to explain but I have done this *for* you."

"You need not bother, Father. Charlotte has explained."

"What did she tell you, Jehan?"

"That you want to live here and have other children."

"I do want to live here—it is a good place for *us*, for our family. I have children, Jehan, for whom I have done all I can to ensure that they are safe. I do not need more. But," he said, turning his son to face him, "if we, as a family, are blessed with others, I will do as much as I can for them as I will *always* do for you, your brother and your sister."

"I do not mind that I am to go to a monastery, Father."

"I will never send you away, Jehan-Batiste," deFreveille declared, ready to throttle the meddling nurse. "When you are old enough to make your own choice, we will see."

"What about this woman, Father? Why—?"

"Gwennan is my wife, Jehan. In time, you will understand that I—she is important to me, my son."

"And my mother?"

"She was important to me as well. She has been dead a long time, Jehan. This woman fills me with joy, as your mother once did."

"Do you think about my mother, Father?"

"Yes, often," deFreveille replied, "and I am always grateful that you are so much like her, but now, I have another wife. Gwennan is part of my life, Jehan. I was very young when you were born, but from the moment that I held you in my arms, I knew that my life had changed forever. From that day, you, my children, have been my sole concern." He glanced up at his banner now flying below that of Daran Pendyffryn. "I am not ambitious in the way of many men, Jehan. I know what I am doing and why. Gwennan, if you allow her, will be the influence you have missed since your mother died. I do not expect you to love her as your mother but I do expect you to consider what is best for your family."

"What does that mean, Father?"

"Marshal and Cecilé are younger. They need a mother in a way that you do not. Accept Gwennan as a friend, Jehan. She will be that to you, gladly, and allow Marshal and Cecilé to have what she can give them. I know she will love you all. It is up to you to accept."

Jehan-Batiste pursed his lips. "You do not want to be powerful, Father?"

"I believe I am among the most powerful men of my acquaintance, Jehan-Batiste," deFreveille said, beaming at his dark-haired son. "I rule myself. But I have left you too long among men who do not."

"Haelsted is powerful."

"He is one who believes if he can do a thing, it is right for him to do so. He commands by fear and governs by terror."

"But you were with him, Father."

"I was wrong to do so, Jehan. I thought then it was for the best. If I am fortunate, I will not live to regret it. Come, we will join our family to celebrate our first Christmas together in our new home."

Cecilé greeted her eldest brother with her arms flung wide and a tapping dance that brought tears to her father's eyes. "There is one for you, Father." Cecilé exclaimed as her father lifted her into his arms and kissed her reddened cheeks. "And me."

"Then I am a fortunate man, little one, I have already had the gift I most wanted today and you say I am to have another. You are very fortunate indeed to receive two gifts from *Boneddiges* Gwennan."

"Two? I saw only one with my name." She turned in his arms to look at the pile of gifts. "Which is my other gift?"

"I will tell you later," he replied, setting her on her feet again before him. "Go now. Sit with your brothers and your friends." He held his hand out to Gwennan. "Wife, will you share this happy feast with me?"

"Of course, husband," Gwennan replied, holding her hand up to him. DeFreveille slid his arm around her waist.

"Will you let me kiss you, Gwennan?" His wife laid her hands on his arms and, though he was prepared, did not push him away as she had earlier.

"I will, Ieuan."

The questions that could not be satisfied by words began to find their answers in the first kiss that Gwennan shared with her husband, Ieuan Emyr, before witnesses. Daran Pendyffryn started the drumming when he brought his cup down on the table. His warriors took up the beat and where joined by deFreveille's captains. Gwennan began to sway to the rhythmic clamor and Ieuan followed her lead for a turn in the center of the hall. When the other women joined the dance and Gwennan invited his children to come to them, Ieuan deFreveille threw his arms around her waist and spun. Gwennan opened her arms and laughed as she flew in a circle. He stopped suddenly and kissed her again.

"Dance, Gwennan, I will watch," he murmured against her cheek. "After this feast there will be music *and* dance, Gwennan. A friend has told me that you enjoy these things."

"Who?"

"Someone," he laughed at her suspicion. Though she pouted at his desertion, she kissed his cheek before taking Marshal and Cecilé's hands. Jehan-Batiste bowed to her and left his younger siblings to dance while he retreated with his father.

The meal seemed interminable to the children who ate, gazing and wondering at the gifts by the fire. Marshal ventured more often than the others to see which of them belonged to him and brought news back to Jehan-Batiste and Gareth that *very* small parcels bore their names. Jehan-Batiste watched his father with his new wife, ate his mutton and drank the wine poured for him.

"There is a gift for Artur," Marshal announced, clamoring back onto the bench and grabbing a fistful of the little hazelnut and honey cakes.

"Did you see Father's? Is it the biggest one?" Cecilé asked, clapping her hands.

"His name is not on any that I could read," Marshal replied, "but the biggest one is covered by all the others."

DeFreveille kept their cups filled and encouraged his wife and her father to drink more than he did himself. Gwennan saved her attention for her husband as he offered her slices of dried fruit and cheese. He fed her and stole food from her fingers but did not put his hand on her throat, contenting himself with looking. He was as glad to see the honey cakes as his sons. Taking one between his thumb and forefinger he demanded Gwennan's undivided attention while he held it up to her lips, teasing her and urging her to take it from him. When she opened her mouth to accept it, he tossed it onto the table and gave her his mouth instead, crushing her against him. The laughter and encouraging cheers from deFreveille's captains filled the room.

eighteen

The *pendefig* watched impassively as his son-in-law made the most of his privileges as bridegroom to display his passion openly among his friends. Daran Pendyffryn leaned back in his chair and watched his daughter, beckoning one of the musicians to set his harp on a bench in front of the table. The musician tuned his instrument and began to play a tune while another of the musicians joined him. The harp provided a melodic, rhythmic focus for the singer who cleared his throat and waited for the bride and groom's attention.

DeFreveille cursed the disturbance which forced him to return from the happy depths to which he had sunk with Gwennan in his arms. He opened his eyes to look into hers, hoping that whatever threat came at him, someone among his friends would defend his back. No one came to protect him from ambush and he shifted his gaze, resigned to misfortune. He lifted his head and acknowledged the *bardd*, relinquishing his wife's mouth. With his nod, the *bardd* began to sing. Though the singer's voice, the tune and the song were beautiful, Gwennan could see that Ieuan did not understand the *bardd's* words well enough to enjoy the tale. Urging him to sit back, she pulled her chair closer to him and murmured the story of Tristan and Esyllt as the singer continued.

"Esyllt had been wed to March for many years when her husband's kinsman, Tristan, came to visit. As soon as the two met, they loved one another. Tristan and Esyllt ran away to the forest to be together. March complained to the king, Arthur.

Both Tristan and March were kinsmen to Arthur so he could not make either give up Esyllt or favor one more than the other. March was given the choice of time in the year he would keep Esyllt."

"He chose well?" Ieuan asked, his sympathy with the husband.

"He chose winter," Gwennan replied in a low voice, laying her hand on his arm and sliding her fingers to entwine with his, "because the nights are long and cold."

"Good choice," he said, watching her slender fingers curl into his palm.

"When the world is gray and the trees are bare." The harpist and singer continued their performance as Gwennan rose from her chair and filled her arms with boughs of holly, ivy and yew, spilling them onto the table before her husband. "Arthur proclaimed that Esyllt would live with Tristan while there were leaves on the trees, with March when the trees were bare. Since it was winter, the king told Esyllt to go with her husband but she refused." Gwennan plucked a leaf from the ivy and wove its stem into the fabric of Ieuan's tunic. "When Arthur demanded that she obey, Esyllt said, 'As long as there are leaves on the holly, the ivy and the yew, I shall stay with Tristan.'"

Tracing his finger over the edge of the leaf Gwennan had placed above his heart, Ieuan asked, "What did Arthur do?"

"What could he do?" Gwennan took a sip from her husband's cup. "March himself had chosen. The leaves of the holly, the yew and the ivy are always green. Esyllt was always free to choose."

"Esyllt did not love her husband?" he asked, his hungry, brown eyes searching her face.

Gwennan swept the greenery into her arms and tossed it high above their heads as the singer and harpist came to the end of their story. Many of the Cymry cheered the performance, believing the choice of the tale to be a show of defiance which the commander and his captains could not understand.

"Esyllt did not love her husband as was proper," Gwennan murmured beneath the merriment of her friends. "But she loved Tristan and stayed with him for the rest of their lives."

DeFreveille rose from his chair, his wife locked in his arms. She had not answered his question but his captains roared their approval of his response, encouraging him with their own cheering, vaguely aware that the Cymry in their midst were not as much drunk as rebellious. His kiss was searching—the same uncertainty that Gwennan had sensed in his first kiss—fueled by the fear she had instilled in his heart and the loneliness that, until that moment, he thought had ended.

When he released her to present her gifts to the children, Bown muttered to Wode and Maides, "He lets her insult him and her warriors know it."

"The tale is more than you think, Bown," Maides replied, tilting his cup to his lips. The other captains waited for him to elaborate but the mercenary refilled his cup with his own liquor and watched his friend.

"What does it mean?" Bown demanded, leaning forward.

"I'll tell you," Gethin Wode said. "It means she knows he has tricked her father."

"That is one interpretation but think as you like," Maides commented, forcing the cork stopper into the neck of the clay jug containing his preferred drink. "The Cymry are not the only listeners eager to see as their bias directs them." The mercenary looked at the young warrior. "The woman chose life."

"Speak plain, man. Your dark mysteries mean nothing to us," Bown laughed. "We'll see how deFreveille thinks when he takes the woman to bed now that he owns her. If she found him rough—."

"Keep your ignorance to yourself, Bown," Maides growled.

"Everyone knows what he did to her brat—." Bown left the hall with his hand over his mouth. Gethin Wode watched him go.

"Too much to drink," Maides commented, leaning back in his chair.

DeFreveille followed Gwennan to the hearth and stood behind her as she called the children. He was content that Cecilé's presumption was not disappointed as his had been and his daughter was not the only child to be pleased by her gift. Marshal took time from his game with Gareth to discover the secret of the hidden drawer in the wooden box Gwennan gave him. Jehan-Batiste thanked her formally for his parchment and ink, setting them reverently to the side at his elbow while he continued his game of *Gwyddbwyll* with Artur. Eira demanded that her mother style her hair to accommodate her red and gold scarves and Gareth received a carved whistle, "So you can play the tune without singing the words," Gwennan laughed.

"Artur, I have a gift for you as well," Gwennan said, beckoning him to her. The young groom looked first at her and then at his employer. His was the largest of all the gifts and Cecilé peered at it, cocking her head. "For all your kindness to me," Gwennan murmured as she placed the parcel in his hands.

"Thank you, *boneddiges*," Artur said with a deep bow.

"Open it," she urged him with a smile.

He sat on a stool near her and untied the cord around the cloth-wrapped bundle. "... *Boneddiges*, I did not think...I did not expect this."

"That is what is so wonderful about gifts," Gwennan said, patting his knee and glancing up at her husband. "Do you like them? If they do not fit, I will adjust them as you require."

"Gwennan," Ieuan whispered, bending over the back of the chair and watching her push a gift under it with her foot. "You will dance again?" Many of the women had begun to gather in the middle of the floor. Gwennan realized it was not a question, though the intonation implied one. She rose and smoothed the skirt of her gown, before she took a few reluctant steps toward the other women.

Cecilé caught her hand and tugged her down to whisper in her ear. "Where is the gift for Father?"

"Your dad is grown, *blodyn*. He will not receive his gift with the children."

"When will he have his gift?" the child insisted.

"At the end of the celebrations. There are still days and days before then, *Celtes*. Would you also like to dance again?"

"Yes," Cecilé exclaimed, slipping her small hand into her stepmother's. "If you dance again, Mam, I will dance too."

"Of course." Gwennan scooped the little girl into her arms and carried her to the center of the hall, delighting in the pleasure of the child's innocence and the generosity of her affection. Before they joined the others, Gwennan helped the child pin her brooch to her bodice. Cecilé swept her arms around Gwennan's neck and they whirled together into the circle of women and children.

"You do not dance well, do you, Jehan-Emíl?" Charlotte said, leaning against his arm. "You have many skills in war, with men. But you are not as good with women, or in love." Charlotte watched the line of his jaw harden. "Your new wife always prefers the company of others, does she not?" Her companion shrugged. "Did the Celt warm her enough for you last night. Is that why she was so willing then and so cold this morning?"

"There is," he said softly, laying his hand on hers as she leaned against him, "a place for you among Haelsted's women. Suggest again that my wife is unfaithful and I will flay your back so you are never able to proffer your wares except to sell yourself as the bitch you are."

"That has never displeased you, Jehan," Charlotte replied, breathless, pressing her hip provocatively against his thigh.

"I have had my fill, Charlotte. I told you I had finished with you before I came to this place. You should have stayed with Haelsted as we agreed." He settled himself in the chair, a leg thrown over the arm and held his cup for Artur to fill.

Gwennan's body swayed and whirled before him. Nothing stood between her and his desire. He grew drowsy with lust and was at the edge of his passion, ready to claim his right to explore his wife's secrets when Derwyn Blaenant strode into the hall. There was an imperceptible shift of focus in the commander's eyes.

No one but Maides saw that he was prepared to kill. DeFreveille appeared as lazy and drunk as all the other men in the hall. He had not taken his eyes off the women nor moved a muscle in his finger but he was alert. The Welshman stood at the entrance but he was neither hesitant nor indecisive. Derwyn's entrance was his challenge.

Daran Pendyffryn shifted in his chair at the center of the table, releasing the strap that held his dagger with a flick of his thumb. Though he kept his eyes on Derwyn, he calculated the distance between his daughter and the son of his friend. He also assessed his son-in-law's drunkenness. The two men exchanged an indiscernible signal with the mercenary who had not lifted his eyes from his contemplation of the boughs of poisonous yew strewn over the table.

The women stopped dancing when they felt the tension in the cold wind sweeping through the rushes beneath their feet. As one, they turned to stare at the tall, enraged warrior. Gwennan stiffened momentarily but the musicians continued their tune and Cecilé was impatient to dance. Her stepmother followed, grateful to have the excuse to ignore the intrusion, steering her stepdaughter away from the entrance. A glance at her husband assured her that she was in no danger from the warrior's assumption he could enter with impunity.

"Celt," deFreveille bellowed. "You are late. The wine is finished, gone," he announced, tipping his cup to the floor, spilling what was left into the rushes. The musicians stopped playing at the sound of his drunken voice. DeFreveille swung his leg to the floor and directed them to continue. "My wife," he said, grinning at the scowl on Derwyn's face, "she has a gift for you, Celt."

Gwennan's gasp was lost in the shocked murmurs of the women. She stared at her husband but he waved her back to the dancing. When Madlen whispered, "He will kill her for this," Paul Rocaille stepped forward between the commander and his wife.

Jehan-Emíl dragged the red, cloth-bound parcel from under the chair where Gwennan had concealed it. He stared at the name on the fragment of vellum, weighed the parcel in his hands and extended it to the warrior. His face was a mask but he smiled.

Derwyn stared at the parcel but made no move to accept it. He narrowed his eyes at Gwennan then looked from one to another of his own friends sharing the wedding feast with their enemy. His eyes settled on his *pendefig's* face. Daran met his warrior's glare but made no response.

DeFreveille laid the parcel in Artur's hands and urged him to take it to the warrior. The groom pushed it at Derwyn who could not resist the impulse to accept it, though he flung it away from him immediately. Gwennan followed the flight of the gift until it hit the wall near the staircase and landed, half-open, on the first step.

Ruth murmured from behind her hand, "She will pay for this, but what a clever insult—to give her husband nothing and this to her lover."

"There is dance, Celt," deFreveille told Derwyn. "And there is music for singing. You are welcome," he added, an afterthought thrown over his shoulder as he strode toward his wife, forcing the other women to dart from his path. Gwennan still held Cecilé's hands, bending down to her. DeFreveille clasped her arm and drew her up to him. He bent his head to kiss her cheek, his mouth pressed to her ear. "I want to be alone with you," he said under his breath, kissing the inside of her wrist, his gaze fixed on her face. "Do I ask too soon?" His mouth was hot against her tender skin. She trembled and drew nearer to him. His eyes shifted slightly and in them was a command. "You are tired," deFreveille told her aloud. "Go to bed."

Gwennan stared at his hand on her arm until he released her. She bent down to Cecilé and said, "Your dad and I have matters to discuss, *Celtes*. Siriol will look after you this evening." She straightened her back, catching Siriol's eye and sent the little girl to her friend. After she had given her father a warm smile, she turned to obey her husband's command and began the climb alone, her hand trailing on the cold stone wall.

Neither a struggle among the men nor Charlotte's sarcastic laugh stopped her. Gwennan did not look back, stepping over the discarded gift.

When all was silent in the hall except the footfall of heavy boots on the staircase behind her, the iron hinges creaked as Ieuan Emyr reached around her to shove the door open. She hesitated to enter and he lifted her into his arms. Glancing over his shoulder, Gwennan saw everyone in the hall below watching as her husband carried his wife over the threshold but only one pair of blue eyes bore into Gwennan. The nurse's glare was so fierce that Gwennan felt she had been violated.

Ieuan kicked the door shut and set her on her feet while he bolted it. He loosened the neck of the wedding tunic and dragged his shirt free of his *trwsus*. When he crossed the room to stand before the fire and stared into the flames, she allowed her eyes to take in the changes which had been made in her bedchamber to accommodate him. The floorboards were covered with woven carpets. There were no gaps to let in drafts from the hall or for spying. Tapestries had been hung from top to bottom of the screed leaving no chinks and muffling all sound. A new bed stood on the platform. The mattress was thick, piled with brightly colored cushions. The bed had no curtains and would provide no privacy. The whole of the chamber was a private place for them.

His maps and documents were strewn across the table exactly as Gwennan had last seen them. The clothes that were not in his chest, standing beside hers, were cast carelessly wherever they fell. All of the changes, she realized, could not have been made in haste. The bed had not been carved and built that day nor had the mattress been stuffed and sewn in the few hours they had been wed. She recognized the carpets and tapestries, though she had not seen them for many years. Stepping back until she stood against the wall, she took comfort from the warmth of the room. The bright colors and deep textures pleased her. They were so familiar to her and so closely reflected her preferences that Gwennan covered her lips with her fingers in awe. "I remember these," she said. "I only saw them once, when I was a little girl and had stolen into a room that my father sometimes visited."

"Your father brought them," Ieuan told her. "As a wedding gift. He said he was certain he would be taking them back to Pendyffryn tonight."

"These are too beautiful to be locked away in my mother's room, Ieuan," she murmured, tracing her fingers over the thick stitches. "But it will hurt him to part with them."

"This is his house, Gwennan. He has not parted with them, only moved them."

"This is not my mother's bed," she said, running her hands over the simply carved post at the foot of the bed.

"No," he admitted. "I told you the other was not fit for me."

"I remember that as well," she laughed. Kicking off her shoes, she flexed her toes in the carpet. She rolled her shoulders to relieve the ache in her muscles from the weight of the heavy tunic, stretching her arms and neck.

"Are you tired, Gwennan?" he asked without turning to look at her. When she did not answer, he glanced over his shoulder to find her looking at him. "My name is Jehan-Emíl," he said. "Say it, Gwennan. Say my name to me."

"Ieuan."

"What is that?" he demanded. "You say this word only when you are ill, when you are frightened."

"It is your name," Gwennan replied, pulling herself up with pride in him.

"Say it again."

"Ieuan."

"That is what you will call me?" he demanded, glancing over his shoulder.

"If I may."

"If it pleases you to say this 'Ieuan', I will allow you to call me by that name."

"Ieuan is your name to me and it pleases me to call you by name. Not commander, or governor, or master…"

"Or husband?"

"I will call you husband," she said, "…when you are my husband." She lifted the tunic over her head and folded it.

"Gwennan," he murmured after a pause, taking a step toward her. "If you do not come to me willingly, tell me now. I cannot force you. Leave me now, if you choose not to stay with me. I will only offer this one chance for you to escape me."

"You are repudiating me? After all you have done, you can be so cruel?"

"Gwennan…"

"I will not be shamed in this way. You have dishonored me and now you wish to humiliate me, rejecting me as your wife when all my friends, and even my father, believe you have used me as your whore."

"Gwennan, listen to me—."

"No. I am always free to choose and I choose you shall be my husband. I will not be sent from my own home to satisfy your hatefulness. You cannot punish me that way."

"I do not want to punish you," he sighed, sinking into the chair, laying his head back in despair of finding the words to explain his meaning. "I meant—, I thought—. Good God, *menyw*, I did not want to frighten you. I only meant to give you choice, so you would not be afraid…"

"Liar," she cried, loud enough for the household to hear.

"If you stay, Gwennan, I will never give you another opportunity to leave me."

"*You* will not give? It is *my* choice, deFreveille. *I* decide."

He held out his hand to her. "Come to me, Gwennan. Take my hand."

"I am here," she informed him. "You will come to me."

Ieuan dropped his hand over his eyes. "This is not how I meant it to be," he said. "This is not what I wanted for you…for us."

"It is what you have…and deserve. Come here," she commanded, taking him at his word that she governed. "You shall be my husband and you will take me as your wife," she said. "Come here."

He complied, crossing the distance between them and standing before her. Gwennan raised her hand and pushed him back at arm's length to sit on the bed, her own distress making her blind to the sadness and confusion in his eyes, glaring at the top of his bowed head. "You will look at me," she ordered. Ieuan lifted his eyes slowly, studying her.

After a moment's hesitation, Gwennan unclenched her fists. Her husband kept his eyes on her face until she raised her hands to the lacings from her breasts to her hips down each side of her dark green gown. A sharp tug at each bow released her from the constraint. She dragged the gown free of her shoulders and pulled her arms from the tight sleeves. By degrees, she pushed the garment down her slender body, her expression as cold and blank as she could make it, stealing herself against the fire in his gaze. When she stepped from the fallen dress, Ieuan swept it from the floor and filled his senses with her fragrance before hurling the gown behind him.

When his attention returned to her, Gwennan unbound the tightened bodice of her chemise, one tiny eyelet at a time and did not take her eyes from his face. His reaction as she unveiled her body to him, one treasure after another, gave her courage. Only the force of will kept him from acting on every impulse driving him to take her. She rolled one shoulder and the other, drawing his attention to their supple movement beneath her pale skin. With her slim fingers, she drew the flimsy bodice away from her breasts and let it drop to her waist. Before she freed her hands, she swayed her hips, dancing before him. The chemise fluttered over the curve of her thighs to the floor. His jaw and shoulders clenched as he stared at her, caressing her with his eyes.

She turned, raising her arms above her head. She hid nothing from him. When her back was fully turned, she glanced over her shoulder, lifted her hair for him, arching her back.

"*Duw annwyl,*" he hissed. His hand, trembling with the violence in his body, reached out and fell on her sleek hip. Close to overpowering him, responding to the weight of his hand, Gwennan swayed her hip toward him, inviting him to touch her wherever and however he pleased. "Give me strength," Ieuan murmured. Leaping from the bed, he threw his arms around her waist and held her hard against him, his hands fondling and probing her, eager to feel her breasts tight with desire and her sex moist and hot for him. Gwennan arched her back again, pressing against his thighs, moved her hips and felt the urgency of his lust thrust against her back with a will of its own.

"Show me what sort of husband you will be to me," Gwennan sighed, arching her neck and rubbing her head on his shoulder. She wrapped her arms behind her, stroking the rigid muscles of his thighs. Turning in his arms, Gwennan opened his belt and pushed his *trwsus* out of her way.

"Now," he groaned. "Hold me." He clutched her hips to hold her and thrust upward. His hearing filled with her sighs, his vision with the beads of moisture on her skin, his lungs with the scent of desire, his touch with the feel of her arms clinging to him and her legs locked around his back. He found her mouth, pushing his tongue into her to taste her passion. Lowering himself to his knees, he pressed her back to the bed, forcing her knees as wide as she was able to open herself for him and gradually drove deeper into her until he had nothing more to give her.

The room was filled with the scent of love, mingled with the fragrance of soap and new wood. Somewhere near her, Gwennan caught the aroma of hot wine but preferred to fill her lungs with the scent of his power, by now so familiar to her.

Wresting himself free of her embrace, he supported his weight on his arms and watched her face as he lifted his hips away from her, withdrawing to the brink of quitting her.

"More?" he asked, thrusting to the depths of her body. She sighed, whimpering her acceptance of his possession. Her legs relaxed, fell away from him.

Gwennan lowered her eyes to watch him take her, the turgid arteries beneath his skin filling every fraction of her, the hilt pressing against her tingling flesh. She ground her hips to keep him in contact with her sensitive muscles, the center of her being, raised herself on her elbows to offer her breasts for his kisses, driven by her instinct and her own hunger to satisfy his appetite.

He murmured her name, bowing his head, straining to be deep inside her body when he came to climax. He took her helpless cries as a sign she was satisfied. Using the contractions of her channel for his own pleasure, he breathed her name as he caressed the last of his oblation to her from his body.

"Thank you, *boneddiges*," he said, lowering himself to pin her to the mattress. While he caught his breath, he rested his head on her shoulder and smoothed her hair back from her brow. Gwennan closed her eyes.

He pulled her onto him, studying her eyes. She had withdrawn from the intimacy of love. Scattering the cushions from the bed, he kicked away the *carthen* and twisted to face her. "You are everything I wanted," he whispered, "more than I dared hope." Gwennan's eyelids drifted closed. A tiny sigh of fatigue escaped her lips. "I wonder how Derwyn could have let you go…" he said, unguarded.

"He was never my lover," she admitted.

"If he was, he would have killed me to keep you."

Gwennan dismissed his assertion with a shrug. "I have had only one lover."

"Who?" he inquired, leaning over her.

"I have not asked you, deFreveille, to name *your* lovers," she replied with a yawn.

She had called him 'deFreveille', not this other name, 'Ieuan' as she promised. He rolled onto his back, a perplexed frown on his face as he stared at the beams dancing in the firelight below the thatch. He turned toward her again and stroked her shoulder with his fingertips. "Gwennan, you have made me happy. I have never been happier."

"You do not have to lie to me," she said, "or say pretty words that mean nothing." When he did not reply, she turned onto her side to face him and traced the line of his chin with her finger. *This man will father my children.* Gwennan wove her fingers through her husband's wild curls, caressing his eyelids with her kisses. *This man will father generations of the pendefig.* As he met her gaze, she said, "I said you did not have to say pretty words, Ieuan. I did not say I did not want to hear them."

"You are bad," he declared, wedging his hips between her thighs, claiming his right of possession.

"And what else?"

GLOSSARY

In most instances, the following words are used so their meaning is explained within the context of the story. I have taken a few liberties with the plural, adjective and possessive forms of some words. Welsh follows the Latin & other Romance languages noun/adjective (as in *vin rouge/ vino rosso /gwin coch*) rather than the Teutonic adjective/noun (red wine) but to do that in a book written in English would be a step too far. I wanted to use some Welsh to give some flavor of the language Gwennan and her compatriots speak as well as convey the difficulty for Jehan-Emíl to learn the language of his new home.

Welsh also uses a similar form of expressing ownership: the object is dominant and the owner is subordinate: her cloak is *ei chlogyn hi*. For the purposes of this story, I have used the English possessive construction of adding 'apostrophe s'.

I simplified the mutations that occur in specific juxtapositions of words starting with certain letters, such as in *ei chlogyn hi*: ei designates (in this instance) female when followed by hi. If followed by 'e' then the mutation is male and is *ei glogyn e*. These mutations are the aspirate and soft mutations, respectively. There is also the nasal mutation which replaces the beginning consonant with an 'ng', 'ngh', 'm', 'mh', 'n', or 'nh' when the word is proceeded by 'yn' (and a number of other instances that I won't mention!) as 'c' becomes 'ngh'; 'g' becomes 'ng'; 'b' becomes 'm'; 'p' becomes 'mh'; 't' becomes 'nh'. Gwennan refers to her father as *fy nhad*.

You can hear how these words are pronounced on many internet sites. The emphasis is almost always on the next to last syllable, as in most Romance languages.

Courses in the Welsh Language (Cymraeg) for adult learners are offered by Cymdeithas Madog (madog.org) in the United

States and, in Wales, in Nant Gwrtheyrn as well as Llanbedr Pont Steffan.

Pronunciation and Phonetic
Equivalents

Annwn: underworld (*AH-noon*)
Baban: infant (*BAH-bahn*)
Bardd: poet (*BAHrTH* - *dd* is always pronounced as in wi*th*[*TH*])
Blodyn: flower / term of endearment (*BLOH* - *din*)
Boneddiges/Bonheddig: lady/gentleman (*BOHN-neTHiges*/ *BOHN-eTHig*)
Buarth: farm yard (*BEE-ahrth*)
Calan: New Year (*KAH-lan* - 'c' is always pronounced as 'k')
Calan Gaeaf: beginning of winter, All Hallows' Eve (*KAH-lan GEYE-ahv*)
Carthen: blanket (*KAR-then* - th is always pronounced as in thin)
Cariad: beloved (*KAHR-eeahd*)
Clais: bruise (*Klaheesh*)
Cymry: fellow countrymen (the Welsh) (*KUHM-ree*)
Cynhadledd: conference, gathering (*kuhn-HAD-leTH*)
Diawl: devil (*DEE-ahool*)
Drych: looking glass (*DREEch* - ch is always as in 'loch')
Duw annwyl: dear God (*DEW AH-nooeel*)
Gelyn: enemy (*GEL-in* - 'g' is always hard as in 'gain')
Gwraig: wife (*GOOR-eyeg*)
Gwyddbwyll: a board game, similar to Chess (*GOO-iTH-boo-eell* - 'll' is always aspirated - this is a tricky letter! Tongue at the roof of your mouth, blow an L sound without annunciating.)
Hafod(ydd): small house(s) (*HAH-vod* / *hah-VOD-diTH*)
Llathlud golau: "openly living together as husband and wife" (*LLAHTH-leed GOL-eye*)
Llathlud twyll: "living together in secret as husband and wife" (*LLAHTH-leed TOO-ill*)
Llys: court (*LLEES*)
Mab: son (*MAHB*)

Meddyg: medic (*METH-ig*)
Menyw: woman (*MEH-ñoo*)
Merch: daughter, girl (*MEHRch*)
Pafais: long battle shield (*PAH-vice*)
Pendefig: high ranking landowner (*pen-DEH-vig*)
Pennaeth: chieftain/leader (*PEN-eyeth*)
Plantos/Plant: children (*PLAN-tohs*) Plentyn: child
Porth: entry way to house or castle (*PORth*)
Sais/Saesnes/Saeson: Saxon man/Saxon woman/Saxon people
(*SEYEs/SEYES-nes/SEYE-sohn* - 's' is always 'es' not 'z')
Seiat: council (*SAY-aht*)
Trwsus: trousers/leggings (*TROO-sis*)
Uffern: hell (*EEFF-ehrn*)
Uwd: porridge (*EE-OOD*)
Ysgolor: scholar (*us-GOHL-or*)
Ystad: estate of land (*US-tahd*)

○ ○ ○ ○ ○

You may also enjoy the other novels I have written set in 9th and 10th Century Wales. These include the series, *Pendyffryn: The Conquerors*. The next four books to be published as print editions:

Salvation
The only woman he has ever loved, the one woman he can never have.

Betrayal
The best of men... The most treacherous of lovers.

Revival
A man may have all he has ever wanted, a woman can take his life with a kiss.

Reconciliation
A slave may be a given as reward, but her love must be won.

Or a thief can steal it.

o o o o o

Traitor's Daughter, the first book in *The Tywi* series.
Her honor or her life, her life or her love…his choice.

Readers' Praise for *Traitor's Daughter*:

"I like the premise of the story and the setting a lot. It's not an era that's been done a lot, so that's a good thing. I like how manipulative Alys is…. And now you have left me hanging, you temptress!"—Lizzie W.

"Well researched and written. …I loved your characters."—Judy C.

"I enjoyed reading this awesome book."—Denise P.

"I loved Garmon. I think about Heledd and Garmon all the time."—Celeste A.

"…I thought this book was awesome. The story has depth and I liked being swept back in time. The plot is great. …I find myself thinking about this story days later."—Tifferz Book Reviews, May 2012

For *Invasion*:

"Your writing and craftsmanship are absolutely lovely. This is a wonderful story and I was very engaged in it. …It is wonderful and epic."—Christa D.

ABOUT THE AUTHOR

Lily Dewaruile is an American author who lived in Cymru/Wales for thirty years, an immigrant to this Celtic country who fell in love with the language and the history as well as *un Cymro arbennig* (one special Welshman). While she and her Cymro were raising three fine young men, Lily continued her writing about her adopted country, set in one of her favorite periods in its history, the 9th and 10th Centuries.

Her novels reflect her deep admiration for the people whose strength and commitment to their way of life and culture, endure and overpower those who come to conquer. Though none of her characters, nor the events of these novels, are real, they reflect the spirit and essence of Cymru and the Cymry.

If you would like to share your thoughts about *Pendyffryn: The Conquerors* series or *Traitor's Daughter*, please contact Lily:

http://lilydewaruile.com
http://facebook.com/LilyDewaruile,
http://lilydewaruile.wordpress.com,
Twitter @LilyDewaruile

Diolch yn fawr,

Lily Dewaruile